Enemies No More

Patrick Miller

Enemies No More

Dedication

To Jackie, who never doubted
and always encouraged.

Table of Contents

Prologue

To Pausanias, the son of my advanced years,

The events and people of this history may seem foreign to you, especially since you have been so many years in Greece studying the exploits of Pericles, Demosthenes and other mighty men of Greece. The events of my narrative were not so long ago but the people are already just names to you, whispering ghosts who once lived and loved, wept and fought. Most have gone to glory but this story may cause them to breathe again, for a moment, and allow you to witness their deeds, hear their voices and understand why this journey saw one world obliterated and another brought squalling and bloody to life.

This is not a military history. If you seek such, I recommend Julius Caesar's story of the Gallic wars. There you may see men slain and the author of their deaths proclaim his own greatness. There are no great feats of arms in this history, rather the tale of haunted dreams, vengeful hatred, and two loves – one in this world, the other beyond. And you may learn that while battles may loom great for a moment, a simple word can thunder through eternity. And you will see that a story of danger and rescue is most truly a tale of a warrior and his redemption.

I pray you indulge my commentary on the Roman state and its ways. Many men who write history weave their own visions and understanding into the tapestry of tales. I confess I do so also. There are ages separating us from the adventures and legends we learned at our mothers' knees, but if this poor book should reach beyond you and your children to future generations, I trust my feeble narrative will help them understand the terrible forces that shaped our lives and brought about the volcanic changes here touched upon.

Though weakened in body, I am still blessed with an accurate and powerful memory, and drawing upon my unfinished history of the early empire which I have so long labored to complete, I assure you that the words and deeds recorded herein are accurate. If there is any exaggerated nobility or minimized baseness, be assured it applies to the author alone.

Your father, Tychon

Chapter 1   The Horse

The horse refused to die.

It lay there, eyes barely open, legs stiffened, askew, blocking the road. Its nostrils flared, desperate to fetch air. Skin twitched as blowflies settled, drew blood. It could not rally, shallow following deep breath. Age and brutal war had stoned its insides.

At first it had looked at Quintus, who had been its master for many campaigns and who now sat with it, stroking its neck and whispering softly. Now the beast, black as a moonless night, gazed off into the distance, perhaps sensing an end to struggle.

Lucius sat at the side of the road and waited. Another such officer, who had seen so many men die, who had sent so many to the dark sleep with a sword thrust or a command, would be angry that a horse's death throes would halt his column of men. But Lucius, tribune of the legions and my brother, was not such a man. Quintus was a good soldier, the horse had been faithful, and both counted for much. The horse raised its head slightly and then lay back, barely making a sound. Quintus continued whispering something that sounded like consolation. My master stared away, eyes hooded. If asked, he would say we were waiting for guides from Ephesus.

He turned to look back down the road at his command of one hundred and twenty legionaries and wagons. They were at rest at the side of the road or standing loosely in clumps, blocking the road. A dozen travelers and merchants, with foodstuffs, pottery and other wares, also were stopped. They would wait. Their plans would wait. Their commercial appointments, trading, and getting wealth would wait. The whole engine of empire would wait while this horse died.

The valley we were in reminded me of our home in Campania. The sheltering hills rolled slowly to the horizon, unbroken except for a few trees and low stonewalls marking grazing pastures. The pastures shone green and their cuttings filled me with longing. No humans marred the scene, instead random flowers were erupting into that time when men would spend long hours tending crops and hoping that the god of the harvest would send rain and sun to bless their dreams of full barns and purses. At such a time, a field released a fragrance, and it was hope.

Lucius' farm in Campania, our childhood home might be over the hill before us. It had shaped our view of the world, filled with exhausting work, careless play, festive dinners and, before that deadly summer, laughter. Pains in my sore back recalled the blows of harsh tutors, and I heard their voices declaiming the mighty triumphs of ancestors long dead and the expectations their dead hands placed so roughly on us. Now Lucius' farm and mine waited for us to return to their seasonal music. And Lucius could look forward to the warmth and comfort of his beloved wife's embrace. As soon as we completed the brutal task that awaited us in Ephesus, we would leave behind the butchering of Jewish rebels and return home on leave.

My brother peered at something at the back of the column, where there seemed some commotion. Taking their cue, soldiers near him turned to look. At last, Marcus Strabo, the centurion of our cohort, came forward. He was a weathered veteran, scarred in face and arms, and half a head shorter than Lucius and I. He was an excellent soldier, a rock of devotion to the army.

"Tribune, there is a merchant who insists on seeing you. We seem to be blocking his path." Strabo smirked.

"Bring him forward," Lucius responded. "And send out two riders to see how far this backup reaches."

Lucius motioned to his dog, Boudicca, and began scratching its massive head

A few minutes later the protesting merchant stood before us. He was of medium height, with the mottled cheeks of the man who drinks his wine without much water and eats more meals than a true Roman needs. His hair, thinning and styled to give the illusion of bulk, still held a slight auburn hue. His clothes were foreign made and new, glistening in the sun and ill chosen for a hot day. His manner was assured but ingratiating. At one time, he had been powerful. Now he was merely prosperous.

"Lucius Licinius Lucullus, Tribune of the mighty legions of the renowned Titus Flavius Vespasianus, it is an honor to be in your company. My traveling companions and I rejoice that so illustrious a soldier, and so many of the empire's finest warriors protect us. Although this is a province known for some banditry, we will sleep with perfect security knowing you are here."

Lucius sighed, hearing the echo of other self-important citizens, senators and legates. He smiled slightly.

"We are not here for your protection. We are merely passing through on the way to our destination."

"And where might that be?" The small man smiled more broadly, and tilted his head. Perhaps the answer would yield information that could be turned to commercial profit. This was a man who was servile to the mighty and a tyrant to the weak.

"Ephesus lies ahead, some twenty miles according to the sign post," Lucius replied, nodding to the marker next to the dying horse. "Beyond, that is no business of yours, citizen. Why did you want to speak to me?"

At this, the man paused.

"I know you assuredly are on an assignment of great importance, Tribune, since you do not have your full cohort of six hundred and must move in haste. I was wondering how much longer we will be delayed here. I understand it is a mere horse that is blocking the road." His weak smile carried no mirth.

"A mere horse?" Lucius stood up and Boudicca assessed the traveler, deciding if he was dangerous. "No, citizen, this is no mere horse. This horse is a member of the empire's legion and has carried its rider against painted savages in Britannia, fierce hill tribes in Gaul and the treacherous and violent Judean rebels. His record of bravery is beyond question and he has served the empire faithfully. He now lies before us and we will not move until his time is done." Somehow he was suppressing a smile at his own speech. "This equine member of our cohort may reach his end this afternoon or perhaps this evening. Is that delay more than you can bear?" Lucius loomed large and powerful over the man.

"No, no, I can assure you, we were merely inquisitive." His throat seemed full, his face flushed. He began to back away from us. "I will pay my leave and return to my companions to tell them what I have learned."

As he turned to go, Lucius asked, "Are you a merchant?"

The man turned back and spoke softly, "No, I am a *telones*, a representative of the imperial treasury."

"A *telones*? A *telones*? No," my master corrected, spitting words, "you are a *publicanus*. A tax collector. A shearer of the sheep. A hand placed in the purse of laborers and farmers and shapers of pots. You call yourself a *telones* to confuse the issue. I know enough Greek to know a *telones* is nothing more than a *publicanus* who seeks to cover his thievery in regal garb."

He motioned dismissively. "Go about your business and watch your treasure box carefully. If you are traveling with other *publicani*, you will find their light fingers more a danger to your moneybox than any bandits in this area. Go, tax collector."

The redness of the publican's face deepened and he hurried away, leaving a small trail of dust rising behind his mincing steps. Just before he disappeared among the travelers, he paused and looked back at Lucius for a long moment, a strange look on his face.

"I wonder which sheep he has been shearing?" I asked. "Greek, Judean, Macedonian?"

"I do not care, brother. His kind is a slave trader one day, a moneylender the next and a tax collector yet again. He shears the sheep until they cry out and rebel. Then violence is provoked, leaving honest soldiers like us to clean up the mess. His is a stinking trade as he accumulates wealth through overcharging the poor; let his money stink with our contempt."

"But, brother, our general and friend Vespasian had a father who was a money lender."

He looked at me as if having forgotten. Then his manner grew grudging.

"There are some honest money lenders. A few."

"Ah, even a pile of manure sometimes yields a flower." I smiled at my great wit, smelled the air and deemed it sweet.

My master often spoke such sentiments. Countless times he had given food and money to veterans made homeless by the dreaded *publicani* who went about their collecting taxes with the help of predatory senators. When veterans were taxed into poverty, their small farms swept up into the senators' vast holdings, they appeared at Lucius' farm. And so my brother had added tax collector to the list of those he despised.

And yet, despite his contempt for these vultures and their grinding greed, Lucius would certainly defend them if the need arose. Duty called for it and duty was a fundamental virtue of all Roman patricians and was undiminished in Lucius, son of one of the most ancient and revered of patrician families. Duty was one of the few Roman virtues Lucius had not discarded. .

"Brother, did you notice his hand, the right one?"

"What about it?"

"It was red, the color of blood. Surely an ill omen. Or a judgment of the gods on his greed."

Lucius said nothing, but his eyes grew dark and he did not smile. After a moment, he strode toward the back of the column.

"Let us go see the prisoners and see if they are equally honored to have us as their protectors."

We came to the end of the column where two dozen Jewish rebels sat under the watch of their guards. They huddled together, as if chilled on this most sunny day, their heavy cloaks dirty and blood stained from the skirmishes that delivered them into the empire's hands. Their faces were mud caked and unshaven, giving them the look of beggars, bandits. Many bore wounds, their chained hands hung limply at their sides, and they regarded us with eyes that gleamed with hatred and the promise of a throat slit if our vigilance slackened.

Lucius stopped in front of their leader, a man of narrow face and dark fire eyes named Simon. The young man glared at us without a hint of fear, or defeat. He was a Zealot, one of those who fought to free Judea from the empire, and he was of a particular fanatical branch, the *secarii*, assassins with daggers, night crawlers, feared by legionary sentries and even by their own people.

"I understand it is a dying horse that makes us wait, Roman."

Lucius smiled without humor. "Are you in such a hurry to see Rome, Judean?"

Simon raised his chains for inspection. "Who would not want to see the city that is so generous in freely providing such handsome jewelry to her beloved and protected subjects."

"You will have opportunity to show off your wit when you meet with the emperor and decorate his gardens from your cross, assassin." Lucius started to move when the zealot stood up.

"You are one who may join me there all too soon, Lucius Licinius Lucullus. You and your family."

Lucius turned to him, his hand moving to rest on the hilt of his *gladius*.

"Watch your speech, assassin," he growled. "You will have difficulty eating without teeth. Or hands."

"I merely know what visions I have had." Simon sat motionless, almost smirking.

"Visions!" Lucius spat the word.

Every second holy man in Judea claimed visions. Most predicted victory over the empire and just before the fall of Gamla a few months earlier, before thousands of its defenders were put to the sword, these same visionaries predicted a wind sweeping Roman armies from the plain. No wind arose, the armies of Rome were victorious and another city was sacked on our way to capture Jerusalem. The seers lay in the charred ruins. Visionaries could not withstand a spear thrust.

As Lucius turned to go, the prisoner shook his chains.

"Dismiss these words at your peril, killer of cities," he hissed. "There will be a smile where there is no mouth, lightning where there is no storm, rope where it does not belong. You have been warned, Lucius Licinius Lucullus."

"Madmen, all of them," Lucius muttered as we walked away. "Judea. A land of madmen and insane priests. They spout riddles as wisdom and stupid sheep heed them. We would be well rid of them all. Burn their cities, chain them all and let the desert swallow their memory. We destroyed Carthage and the sand blows over its rubble. It should be the same for that Judean blight."

He stopped and seemed dismayed at his own outburst. He looked at me. I shrugged and said nothing. I could point out that Carthage was rebuilt under Rome but this was not the time to correct his history. When he began to rant, as he was doing more, the best thing was to let him exhaust his impulse. Despite his large and powerful frame, Lucius was no young man and in the campaign in the forlorn deserts of Judea, he had turned to long musings and recitals of rot within the once glorious empire. I had always been his favorite audience and as such, I sought to conserve my strength for the evenings' orations. In the last few weeks however, since we began this journey, there were only dark silences and moaning sleep as some terror prowled his dreams. This was proving to be a very long trip.

As we returned to the head of the column, two horsemen reined up to report the road ahead clear all the way to Ephesus. Locals had reported no bandits in the area. Engineers sent ahead had located the place for our camp and scouts were still seeking a leader of the city. The cavalry remained on their horses at first and then, seeing that we were not moving, they dismounted and took the horses to the stream that paralleled the road.

The sun moved straight over our heads and I began to sweat. Why did that horse choose the daytime to die? He could have done it at night, when no one would have been disturbed. I heard the words in my mind and thought of Lucius' daughter, Lucia, and my son, Aulus, when they were quite small, when they learned that the stars and gods did not arrange things each day for their convenience and ease. They discovered the gods were capricious and unconcerned with anything in our lives except our servile piety. Perhaps I needed to learn again that lesson. If only I believed in the gods.

I found a tree and sat beneath it. Soon I closed my eyes.

In my half sleep, I saw my mother on this road. Devout and serious, she certainly came to Ephesus to purchase statues of Artemis and worship at her temple. My father was less pious, fearing Zeus and his thunderbolts only. Then she faded and reappeared on a battlefield, bathed in blood, lying dead alongside my father. Beside them was a boy who had seen four summers, crying, tugging at his mother's dead hand, soaked in blood. A giant's hand appeared and seized him, swept him up and away into the shadows. I sighed, recalling the feel of that hand. As always in these dreams, I asked why did Lucius' father pluck me out of the carnage? I felt him carry me by the hacked limbs, contorted warriors, and screams of the wounded, to a place where the prostitutes and thieves camped. I felt strange arms take me and I knew, as I did each dream, that rebirth had begun.

Then faces and places began to flash in memory. A summer of suicide. Sweets dispensed from weathered hands. Bloody battles in cold and mud. Horses pinning to the ground and raised swords. A war dog. Sunset walks among olive trees. Burial beneath mounds of dying men. Surgeons hacking limbs amid screams. And finally, a useless arm.

I awoke to the sound of voices and looked down to see that my one arm was still unmoving. I sat for a time, rubbing my leg to relieve its throbbing, soothed by the whispering stream and the slight breeze overhead.

The voices came from two men finishing a conversation with Lucius and Strabo. As I walked over to them, Quintus came up to us.

"My horse is dead now, sir," he said in a low, tired voice.

Lucius looked at him with some gentleness. "Return to your men, Quintus. We move."

Quintus moved slowly to the rear and Lucius mounted his horse. Boudicca stood alongside and looked up at his master. I mounted my horse and pulled even with Lucius. Strabo had the men already in column and shortly we moved out.

As we passed, the dead horse was pushed off the road and lay quietly, its legs relaxed, its eye closed, almost as if asleep. I wondered if I should look so peaceful when I breathed my last. After a time, I turned to Lucius, who informed me the two strangers were an official and his son from Ephesus.

"I wonder if these Ephesians would be so anxious to hand over these Christians to us if they knew they were destined for fire and crucifixion in Rome."

"They would probably be undisturbed by the prospect, Tychon. Their trade in statues and worship merchandise has been most seriously damaged by this new religion and its preachers. They most certainly desire its extermination for more profitable commerce."

"But they are all Greeks. Should they not resist surrendering their own blood to Nero?"

A hard voice came from somewhere deep inside him.

"The one called Timothy and his fellow believers in that Jewish carpenter will surely light up Nero's garden on their burning crosses before the summer harvest arrives. No matter they are Greek. The Ephesians will deliver them to chains. Commerce conquers blood."

I looked at Lucius. His gaze was fixed on the road. A road that would soon shimmer into darkness.

Chapter 2   The Camp

Lucius Licinius Lucullus began his final campaign after four decades of service in the legions. His tall, solid body bore the limp, the scars, and the leashed violence of army veterans accustomed to treachery. His dark eyes and thick hair, worn longer than fashionable yet not so long as to be womanish, spoke of vigor and confidence. His speech was soft in conversation, acid in confrontation and thundering in battle. Those who knew him well, and there were not so many, saw within him rough currents and storms that rose, then dissipated, leaving only torpor.

In the last few years the philosophic bent, which had been instilled in him through his childhood education, took dominance. Like a runner who has outstripped his competitors, he savored his service in the legions, forsook revenge on those who had wronged him, and settled into peaceful retirement at his estate in Campania. Returned to his beloved wife, Julia, he dug into the soil, pruned grapevines, planted trees, and fell asleep at night with his wife on his arm. There were no more trumpets or screams of death, just the breath of breezes and his wife's warm fragrance.

Then one blistering summer day, his old friend, general Vespasian, rode up to the sweating farmer on his great grey charger and asked him to join him in one last campaign. He spoke soberly of Lucius' incomparable record and his great value in this war against the rebels of Judea, as a tribune of cohort.

Julia thought he would go, duty and friendship and loyalty calling to him, while I doubted he would leave. She knew him better. He put aside the plow and took up the sword and persuaded me to join him. And we went to Judea and we killed rebels and burned cities and except for the burning heat and desolate vistas, we might have been back in Gaul fighting Germans. Each day we pursued and crushed rebellion, relentlessly and without mercy. And each night we spoke of fruit trees and wool prices, we argued Plato's perfect society and we grew silent thinking of the beautiful hills of Campania.

In our dream, we returned and the land and family embraced us as if we had never gone.

That dream filled the night and whispered to him as he fell asleep.

It was a nice dream.

"A magnificent city," Lucius sighed. We sat on our horses, looking down on the beauty that was Ephesus.

Ephesus is a very large city, easily able to provide for its 250,000 citizens. It sat on a level plain, just below our hill camp, with distant hills to our right, and beneath us the main road snaked into the city center, suburbs spreading out to the mountains surrounding it. On our left was the sea, waves roiling against the rocks far up the coast, peaceful at the docks, rising and falling, playing that gentle, calming music that whispers sleep and the lure of far-off adventure. White marble buildings and streets, well laid out, orderly and bustling with commerce, shone in the sun and boasted of the wealth and fame of the city.

The Temple of Artemis was the city's most prominent feature, at the far end of the city from us, large and dominating, gleaming red, blinding white and quiet blue. It was magical and promised secret treasures, hidden delights. It captured the eye and held it, as it did the visiting worshippers and their gold.

Behind us, soldiers shed their armor and began the ritual of creating a Roman legion's camp. Every Roman camp in every part of the empire was laid out in the same precise manner and had been for two hundred years. There was a wooden wall, to the height of two men, stoutly and quickly built, and in front of the wall, a deep ditch, facing any enemy who meant us harm. Into each wall were put gates, each smaller than the double wide, heavy gate at the entrance, facing Ephesus. Lanes were drawn within, in geometric squares, with tents neatly arrayed along each lane, with established areas for armorer, cooks, medical care, storage and supplies. And in the center was Lucius' tent, the *pretorium*.

The camp of the Roman army was predictable and secure for all who dwelt within it and any legionary, plucked up and moved to a camp a thousand miles away, could find his way through it in the dark with complete certainty. He could find the place where the water clock told the hours, where mail and the weekly newspaper would be delivered, where the blacksmith could shod his horse, the armorer repair his shield or the physician treat his boils. The camp's regular streets and consistent order provided a constant reminder that the empire brought order wherever it reigned. Its strong walls, deep ditches and vigilant watches gave comfort that a soldier could lay down at night and sleep without terror. And on more than one occasion, past wars had seen battles turned to Roman advantage when enemies' successes floundered at the formidable walls of a Roman camp.

The camp was wonderfully placed and the soldiers and centurions knew their work. Nonetheless, Lucius went about his inspection as he had a hundred times before. I watched as he paced off the width of the front gate, assuring its width was that of ten legionaries side by side. He mounted the wall to be sure it was 12 feet high and had a clear view and solid construction. He patrolled the tents to ensure they were aligned and placed rightly. He inspected the food, the armory, the horses, and their feed, tasting both men's food and horses' meal to ensure it was fresh. He doubled the number of sentries since our numbers were reduced and greater caution was called for. He finished by checking the prisoners, reminding the guards that these were dangerous and treacherous men.

As the soldiers settled in for their short stay at Ephesus, Lucius returned to our tent. I stayed for a while at the edge of the hill, outside the gate, overlooking the town and then joined him for the evening meal.

"Tychon, you have waited nearly too long. The meal is excellent. The local cattle are quite delicious and the wine almost adequate. What has kept you?"

"I was viewing the town. The streets glow with life and the sea breezes promise return to home. The streets are clean and full of life. Everyone hurries about but seems content. If we can stay for a few days, I would like to visit the Temple of Artemis. Perhaps there may be a lady or two hungry for manly warriors." I tried to eye him carefully while filling my plate with the steaming stew.

"You will certainly have no time for educating young ladies. And as for temples, we are not here to visit them but reduce their population. We shall do what we have been charged to do and leave. We are soldiers, not visitors of antiquities." I heard the stern tone of our father.

I held up a particularly large chunk of meat and waited for it to cool. "What a waste of opportunity. Ephesus is unique in its beauty and its temple. Our old Greek tutor would not have us bypass such wonders of our world." I paused to bite into the meat. It was delicious. I paused for a moment before posing the question.

"Why have we been sent on such a task, brother? I know I have asked you several times but you have never given a satisfactory answer."

He sighed, dropped his knife and glared at me. I stared back.

"You are a veteran of the empire's armies," I continued. "You have served in three different legions. You have fought in Gaul, Britain, and now Judea. You are esteemed and regarded as one of the two or three finest military tribunes in the Roman military. You were specifically requested by general Vespasian to serve as the tribune of his best cohort in the Judean war. And now you have become a jailer and transporter of rebels to Rome. A centurion could do as much. A seasoned senior officer is not required."

Lucius looked down at his food and continued eating. As he spoke the light seemed dimmer in the tent. His voice was low.

"A soldier follows orders, Tychon. The general wants me to go and do this or that thing, I go and I do." He dished up more stew, refilled his wine cup and did not look at me. He certainly expected further hectoring. His digestion might be disrupted if I were compliant and offered no counter. So I proceeded.

"Ah, 'Orders…the last strained gasp of a weak and uninspired soldier,' I recall a great officer once saying. 'If one is going to die, it seems only right he know why he is dying and if he is to complete an assignment well, he needs to know the reason for the thing that is to be done.'"

"That officer was younger then and had few scars." He was moving a piece of meat around his plate with his knife as if arranging troops for a battle. "Enough battles and a soldier learns to adapt to the political sea in which he swims."

I knew my master would never swim in a school or bite at the first bait. There was a whisper.

"After all," he continued, his tone seeking to reassure, though I could not tell whom, "the siege of Jerusalem will soon be underway and will not require us. If battle were imminent, I do not think Vespasian would have given us this assignment. The siege may take a half-year or more to be completed before walls are breached and the occupants put to the sword. He can certainly spare us for a month or two, especially since he has so many able officers there, as well as his son, Titus."

"To be a jailer." I smiled between bites of what was proving to be one of the best meals we had shared on our journey. But he was right; the wine was just adequate.

"Orders, Tychon, orders."

"There are orders and then there are orders. Someone of a more conspiratorial bent might think you were given secret orders of some consequence that could be completed only by a seasoned and wily officer. Scouting? Theft? Provocation?"

His voice brightened for a moment.

"Your literary spirit is gaining the best of you, Tychon. We have too few cavalry for scouting, too little need for theft and with only 300 men, too few to undertake a serious provocation while guarding prisoners. Rest your mind, friend, and think more of the destination, our beloved Campania and our families." A look passed over his face. It was not excitement. I lost my taste and stood up.

"Let us go look at this great city and see its wonders before we sleep." I moved to the tent flap and held it back for him. He sat for a moment, looking at his plate, its meat neatly arranged, unfinished. Then he put the plate on the ground for Boudicca, motioned for his servant to clear the table and rose and followed me outside. We walked to the edge of the camp and looked down over Ephesus.

"A wonderful city, Tychon. It is a commercial hive, with much money to be made here. It was well the general Sulla drove Mithridates from these regions. This makes a magnificent addition to our empire."

I was not inclined this beautiful evening to relive the wars of the infamous Sulla, and Lucius' great grandfather's special loyalty to him. I reveled in history in its sweep across the years and empires but that part in which our family had played its role was a distressing intruder in this beautiful night. As we watched the flicker of torches as men went about concluding their business for the day, I changed direction.

"How will we know these men we seek, Lucius? Will we use spies to identify them for us?"

"No, that will not be necessary, brother. These men have come into this city of Artemis before. Or their comrades have. One of their ringleaders, a troublemaker named Paul, sought to convert these Ephesians. Trouble broke out. Ephesian merchants and leaders wanted him dead. Others have come behind him and are surely no different. They are his students and disturbers of order. He is dead but his enchantment is carried on. We shall not need spies to capture the Christians. We have their enemies, better than spies."

"And we can rely upon them?"

"Tychon, you know this city is shot through with religion, as much as Rome has always been. It contains soothsayers, fortunetellers, mediums, witches, and diviners of bird entrails. Throw a rock in any direction and you will hit someone who earns gold from these beliefs. Religion is business to them and for money, the merchant will sell whatever smoke-muddled vision the gullible believer wishes. These Christians are hated. Our problem will not be finding the troublemakers. The merchants will hand them over gleefully, without pay, and we shall be on our way. The town clerk says they gather quite early and should be easy enough to round up."

"How many men are we looking to take? Surely we do not have enough troops for many prisoners."

"Only a handful, no more than 50." He paused for a moment. "And there may not just be men."

"Women?"

"It is said. Not only that. Slaves also follow these enchanters. And the poor and outcast are said to fill its ranks. What madness. A religion filled with women, slaves, outcasts, and the poor? How can it be taken seriously? Only magic, Tychon, bewitching, can account for its growth."

"Women, my brother? Do we know if they are free women? Greeks?"

He looked at me in the vanishing light with a small smile.

"Do not get your hopes up. The women are said to be old and wrinkled and soft in the leg, waiting to enter the afterlife and desperate to believe they will find their warrior lover there. You have slender hopes," then adding, "of a slender waist." He chuckled at his cleverness.

"At one time, Lucius, we escorted defeated warriors and their kings to Rome for display and executions. Now we take religious dreamers to Rome? Is the world not turned crooked by these changes?"

Once again, my words sobered him. He looked down at the ground, like a man searching for something dropped. Not finding it, he looked at me in the gathering shadows.

"No, my friend, the world is as it always has been. Some men seek power through politics, some through the sword, some through religion. Different paths toward the same summit."

"And how would your beloved Seneca and his stoic philosophy interpret this?"

Lucius was silent for a time, perhaps remembering his beloved teacher Seneca, who was dead just a few years before, at Nero's command. At last he bent over and picked up a handful of grass and began stroking its softness.

"Seneca would point to our Jewish prisoners to demonstrate his truth. Look at those Zealots. Murderers, assassins. Their hearts are filled with destruction and they have no check on those instincts. So they move in the darkness and kill without mercy or virtue. They are most in need of Seneca and his teachings on control of emotions but they would never accept it. While Seneca lived, I thought perhaps…"

He stopped and, dropping the grass, looked at me in the shadow. His voice grew lower and began to merge with the night breeze.

"Now he is dead and we do not have his wisdom to guide us. There is no help from him for… any of us."

As we watched, the figures in the forum began to disappear and more lights of the city began to wink out. What was left was darkness spotted with lights now still. I thought of Rome, so different from this lovely place. With its winding and confused streets, its overcrowded buildings and sewage in the narrow ways, its terrifying darkness at night that promised the foolish traveler death or injury or, if he was lucky, only robbery, Rome was a stinking maze. And on a moonless night like tonight, Rome was a coiled animal, waiting to snare the unwary.

As we turned back to Lucius' tent and our sleep, I looked around, to see what beast was in the dark here, watching us, hungry and irresistible. Perhaps it was the Shadow Wolf, who had appeared that night at Vespasian's tent and had dogged our journey. It was a dark thing and it was in Lucius. It hinted at its presence after the sun went down and showed itself in Lucius' long brooding silences and sharp, murderous words. It hung beyond the light, only showing itself in a motion, a color in the eyes, a deadness of word

All should have been peaceful in this most serene of places. My sleep was fitful.

Chapter 3   The City

Ephesus is one of the largest cities in the Empire and a crossroads between Asia to the East and Greece, and Rome to the West. Its port was a channel of commerce, and merchants and moneylenders skimmed uncounted riches from the flow of gold passing through the city. Fleets of cargo as well as tourists drawn to worship at the Temple ensured a steady stream of wealth.

The Temple drew religious adherents from across the empire, its splendor and size unmatched, its security so complete that untold fortunes of gold were stored there in perfect safety, its temple prostitutes famous throughout the empire. One could travel anywhere in the Empire and find the silver statues of Artemis purchased here adorning the alcoves of wealthy homes. And wherever those statues were seen, from the marbled homes of Egypt to the wooden huts of Britannia, men dreamed of making the pilgrimage to Ephesus. And Ephesus was as impressive as the temple that was its heart.

For most, Ephesus is a destination, a place to worship, trade, and rest. For us, it was a city on our way to Rome. It was a place where we would take prisoners, not statues.

After our breakfast of olives, cheese and bread, Lucius called for Strabo. The centurion did not seem very alert, but listened carefully to his instructions. He was a second-generation legionary whose father had served in Judea for many years. In his second twenty-year enlistment, he proved to be the kind of leader Lucius preferred, brave, tough, strict, and above all, fair. Lucius believed him to be one of the best we had ever served with, and I agreed.

At last, we went outside. Strabo went off to prepare his men and Lucius seemed glad to be in action.

"A fine day for us, Tychon. No clouds threaten and our transport ships should have clear passage to arrive soon. Our business should be well finished before they dock."

"You sound almost eager to begin the voyage." I was well aware of his aversion to sea voyages, birthed when we traveled to Greece as young men and made greatly worse in our travels through the treacherous and stormy North Sea when we invaded Britannia. He always grew sick in storms and even in mild weather, the slightest turbulence sapped his appetite and soured his disposition. If Lucius had his way, only streams and lakes would require crossing.

He ignored my jest and began walking toward the edge of the camp. He was not carrying his helmet, nor did he wear breastplate or greaves under his cloak, which itself was that of a farmer, not a soldier. And his sandals were not military but the sandals he wore when on the farm. He was not dressed for battle.

"Are we not a legionary today, my friend."

"I do not expect to need anything more than this." He patted the *gladius* under his robe.

Strabo joined us a few minutes later. He wore a long plebeian cloak over his legionary armor. His military cut of hair betrayed him but I said nothing.

Together we walked down the hill to the town as, to our right, soldiers moved to their positions to ring the town and cut off both visitors from the outside and escape from the inside. Lucius looked at them for a moment, quickly counting to ensure that the numbers were what he had instructed, and then moved forward at a brisk pace. He motioned to the city clerk who met us at the crest of the hill.

"Where will they be?

"Most likely at the theater, where that wretched Jew started all this trouble, or at the commercial agora, harassing our merchants and tradesmen. Sometimes they meet in one of the homes over there, where some of their followers live. That is where they practice their blood rituals and eat their flesh. But usually they meet there before dawn. At this time of day, they are likely to be at the theater. They will not be hard to find."

We entered the main street at the bottom of the hill, passing by the civic agora, which contained the town hall, the council house and the Temple of Vesta, where a perpetual hearth was burning to gain the blessing of the goddess. It was beginning to throb with business at stalls, law trials in the corners and worship at several temples. At this hour tourists were scarce, sleeping off their nightly debauches and not ready to begin anew.

We continued on the Via Curetes, but at a slower pace. As we neared the corner of Marble Street, the main street of the town, Lucius stopped and raised his hand.

At first, I wondered why we had stopped but then I heard it. Singing. Not loud, not strident. A kind of chant but rhythmic and simple. At first, I heard only male voices, then they subsided and women's voices rose. Then both joined and their union produced a quiet kind of harmony. I felt a shudder and found myself holding my breath. The sound did not stop but gradually faded and was overcome by voices, repeating something again and again.

Lucius moved forward and we came to the sounds' source, a building set back slightly from the main street. It was made of simple stone and pillared on each side with ornate columns and an inscription over the entrance said simply "Tyrannus." It was open at the front, but deeper than the narrow entrance would suggest. The roof rested upon the sidewalls by columns, providing light and air to enter, suggesting Grecian creativity in its design more than Roman practicality. The interior had a warm and welcoming feeling with sky and sun and breeze mixed. My Greek ancestors would be proud.

Lucius gestured for the soldiers to halt outside, beyond view from those inside, and motioned for Strabo, the town clerk, and me to accompany him inside. When the clerk thought to say something, Lucius motioned silence. He nodded and the four of us moved into the lecture hall of Tyrannus.

As we moved inside, the sun disappeared behind us and we saw more clearly the occupants. We stayed in the back, in the corner, and I began to make out those who were gathered. A hundred or so in number, they included an equal number of men and women, some well dressed, others workmen or farmers. None appeared to be merchants. In the front, in the shifting shadows, a handful had the look of slaves.

A man stood to speak. He was Greek, fully bearded and dressed in simple peasant tunic, looking like a Greek olive farmer. Stocky and short, eyes deep set and hair unkempt, his arms, even in this light, were massive and muscled. He moved to the center of the front. When he spoke, his deep, powerful voice carried easily to our corner. Lucius and I were fluent in Greek and his words were clear and surprisingly educated. Too bad Strabo did not speak Greek well.

"Beloved saints, grace and peace to you from our Lord Jesus, the Word of all eternity, and His Father, our God of all creation. Before we hear the precious words of our late brother Paul, I want to speak to you of the spread of our God's saving truth across the Empire. As the Empire extends its borders, so our Lord and God is extending his Kingdom among all men, Jew and Greek, and His hand cannot be forestalled."

Next to me, I felt Lucius tense. What had the man said?

"In this world, in this city, there are those who oppose us."

The speaker paused for a moment and I waited to see if anyone would turn to stare at us. No one did.

"They seek to silence the preaching of the gospel. They prefer darkness to light, death to life, injustice to justice, violence to peace. As we stand here, our fellow saints are imprisoned, their bodies torn and burned, their families slaughtered, their property stolen, their names erased from the memories of men. But, beloved, our names cannot be torn from the pages of the book of life, which our Lord and Savior has recorded. Our true properties do not reside in this world and cannot be confiscated. Those whom we love who die in our Lord's name have passed to a place of unending beauty and peace and await our joining them if we are faithful."

Lucius stirred on the bench he sat on. Perhaps one of his wounds was hurting.

The speaker paused and looked at the faces before him. His eyes lit on our party and then he continued.

"It is said there are animals in far off lands who live their lives in perpetual darkness. They are born in darkness, they grow in darkness, they are joined to others of their kind in the darkness, they give birth in darkness, and they die in darkness. Take them out of their holes and into the light and they are said to be terrified. They scuttle back into the darkness and prefer a life without the sun, without the fresh breeze, without the sound of life."

"There are those among us, who are not yet in the family of faith, who dwell like those animals in the darkness. Their god is the belly, the purse, drink, the woman who lures to destruction, or the statue that cannot move or speak but is worshipped and bought and sold."

The town clerk hissed and started to say something but a stern look from Lucius silenced him. He closed his gaping mouth and said no more.

"But we are messengers of the light that has come into the world. As the word tells us, 'The light has come into the world and the people loved the darkness rather than the light because their works are evil' and our Lord himself said 'I am the light of the world. Whoever follows me will not walk in darkness but will have the light of life.'

"These live in the darkness of the world, subject to the prince of the power of the air, and are taxed with their lives. Believing themselves free, they are slaves. Believing themselves rich, they are poor. Believing themselves powerful, their very breath is the work of our Father. We are most blessed to be the ones to bring them the light that lights all men of faith. We carry the good news of light and life, eternal and blessed. It is not our hand that will rip them from their holes and into the light. That is the almighty hand of the Spirit of God. God brought Moses and His people out of Egypt by a fire ..."

As he spoke, he picked up a scroll and began to read from it. I found myself staring at a single shaft of light that came through the roof and touched the wall in front of which he had stood. Among superstitious Romans, which is to say all Romans, that shaft of light would be interpreted as a sign, an augury, a message of blessing from the gods. Among the Greeks, it would have similar meaning. I did not know if it was anything more than just the sun shining through a gap in the roof. Perhaps that was all it was. But then I remembered what he said about the animals in their holes. I wondered what name those animals bore.

Lucius touched my arm and motioned us to leave. Outside he spoke to Strabo.

"Bring them out so we can sort out the leaders. Keep it orderly and no force unless they resist."

We stepped back, Strabo shed his cloak and he and the legionaries moved in. Voices were raised, one single female voice began to cry and then the entire group was outside. As they emerged into the light, Lucius stood apart, looking off to the western horizon, where clouds scuttled in the morning breeze. Then he turned to them, looking slowly at each one in turn. Once we were compelled to attend a festival at Rome where a new animal was shown to us, a large, fat animal with a single huge horn on its forehead that was captured in some land south of Egypt. Lucius had studied that animal for a very long time, not speaking, just moving about it, considering its size, its power and its threat. Now here was a new beast worthy of scrutiny.

They were lined up in two rows, stretching well past the entrance and reaching back to the turn of Marble Street. Legionaries moved behind them, to their side, swords and spears at the ready. Strabo walked back and forth, holding the list of names we had been given.

As we stood there, I surveyed the assembled Christians, for so they had been named recently. In their group, there were more slaves than I had first noted, some of them branded as former runaways. I wondered where their masters believed them to be if not at work at home or in the fields. There were several men dressed in the togas and dress of Greeks and a few who had the rough and poor clothing of the Judeans we had so recently come to know. And most remarkably to our Roman eyes, there were many women, mostly dressed simply but a half dozen dressed in rich robes. One particularly was notable, a tall, older woman with grey hair and a stunningly beautiful face, hair worn loose and jeweled broaches adorning a dress of purple.

In the front line was the man who had spoken inside, his rough bearded face and deep-set eyes more forceful in the light than they had been inside. His face resembled nothing so much as a bull and his powerful build suggested a brawler, not a philosopher or teacher. He shifted his weight from side to side and it was the man beside him that finally spoke. He was very thin and youthful, and his light colored hair and clear eyes made him seem almost too young to be the front rank of these troublemakers.

"What do you want of us?" he asked, directing his question at Lucius.

"You are under arrest. Be silent until you are spoken to." Lucius replied, motioning to Strabo.

Strabo held the scroll up to read.

"Timothy, identify yourself." As the first name, this would be the most senior and chief of the rebels.

I looked at the bearded speaker and was surprised when he did not move or speak. Instead, the slender, young man next to him identified himself as Timothy. Strabo paused and looked to Lucius. Lucius turned and looked at the town clerk. The clerk nodded. "That is the one called Timothy. Don't let his appearance deceive you. He is not so young as he appears and is their leader. A most dangerous man."

Lucius turned to the bearded man. "And who are you?"

"Apollos," he replied.

Lucius looked inquiringly at Strabo, who shook his head. The town clerk spoke quickly. "He is an itinerant trouble maker, tribune. He comes here, fomenting treachery, then moves to other towns to do the same. He deserves death. Take him."

Lucius nodded and Strabo pulled Apollos from the front line. As other names were read and men and women stepped forward, I looked more intently at Timothy, the ringleader of these rebels. As the clerk had indicated he was not so young as he first appeared. There were the signs of age around his eyes and mouth and not noticed at first, there were scars on his hands and arms and the rough red mark on his neck where a rope had once had its way. But his eyes were not old and his manner, even in repose, suggested a frail nervousness. He seemed distracted as chains were put on his wrists and a prisoner's rope tied about his middle, as if they were familiar dress. Apollos was more defiant, thrusting weathered hands to the manacles and glaring at Strabo, showing neither fear nor anger.

As names continued to be read, men and women were pulled or pushed forward into chains, I heard the voice of the town clerk speaking to Lucius, suggesting others be added and tallying the woes these traitors to the Empire had brought upon his city.

"Those two, Tribune," he said, gesturing to two quite ordinary looking men, "were the ones who confronted pilgrims at our sacred temple and urged them to abandon worship of our great goddess and listen to their fanciful tales. A whole week's worth of commerce ceased when they were preaching and a riot nearly occurred. Take them and give us peace. Or kill them and rid us all of this misery….and that one," he said, motioning to an undistinguished man dressed like a farmer with a shock of wheat-colored hair, "stood for two whole days in the forum, reading from a scroll of the fables of the Christians, singing and praying and calling out to visitors to come listen. We arrested him, flogged him and threw him into the street and told him never to visit the forum again. We thought perhaps he would die from the flogging. But a few days later, even before his back healed, he was at it again, this time in the amphitheater and we had to arrest him again…."

Lucius listened to some of what the town clerk said and gestured for Strabo to add these men to the prisoners. The town clerk seemed pleased and continued.

"We do not require them to abandon their beliefs, Tribune. We pleaded with them merely to keep to themselves, to not proclaim their beliefs in public or seek to convert others. We are tolerant of any beliefs but we cannot allow these fanatics to undermine the faith in our beloved Artemis. But they would not listen. They insist on bringing their teachings into the marketplace. Our citizens and visitors cannot find a safe space where they do not have to hear these disturbing troublemakers. And when one is thrown into prison or taken away for execution, two spring up. It cannot be tolerated. Our visitors to the great temple will not continue if these vermin are not removed."

The last name was read and the lovely older woman stepped forward. She moved with the grace of her apparent rank and looked at her manacles as if they were an unfamiliar trinket. I had not heard the name and asked the town clerk.

"She is called Lydia. Wealthy. How she came to be mixed up with this scum I do not know."

Alongside Lydia stood another woman, somewhat older and more agitated. While her dress was not wealthy, she seemed on close terms with Lydia and they looked at each other, some unspoken communication passing between them. She looked strangely familiar to me.

At last the separating of the sheep and the goats was complete. Over half the assemblage from inside was now in chains and Lucius spoke to them.

"You are now the prisoners of the empire and the emperor. You will be taken to Rome and dealt with as any other seditious and treasonous rebels. Your lives are forfeit because of your actions and you should not expect any mercy from our emperor. Your comrades tried to burn Rome to the ground not so long ago, your people encouraged the kind of anti-Roman feeling which the Jewish zealots used in taking up the sword against the order of Rome…"

"We do not lift sword or teach revolution," the one called Apollos spoke.

"Silence," Strabo commanded.

"Nor do we set cities afire, tribune. Burning cities is the Roman way."

Lucius stepped forward and backhanded Apollos. The force of the blow dropped him to the ground. Timothy stooped and helped him to his feet.

"When we give a command, you would do well to obey it, quickly and without question," Lucius said as he stepped back beside me. "We will feed you and provide you with safe passage on ships to Rome. Beyond that, how you travel is up to you. Continue making trouble and you will be flogged. Disobedience brings a flogging. Refusing to eat brings a flogging. Speaking sedition about the empire or the emperor will cost you your tongues. Violence will bring you more violence. It is your decision whether to make your last few weeks of life quiet or troubled. As long as I deliver you to justice in Rome, it does not matter to me what condition you are in when judgment is passed upon you there."

There was a pause and silence as the words hung in the air. Finally it was broken by the sound of chains as Apollos lifted his hand to his face to brush away the blood from the gash on his temple opened up by the ring on Lucius' hand. Someone in the back row was crying.

We turned to move away when one of the slaves, none of whom had been taken, stepped forward.

"Tribune," he said, in a low and frightened tone. Lucius turned to him. "Yes?"

"We would like to be taken too," he turned, indicating several of the other slaves.

Lucius frowned in puzzlement. "What do you mean? Whom do you speak for?"

"We are both slaves and freedmen. We want to go with the brothers and sisters you have taken." His voice was barely audible.

"You are not on our list. You are not one of the leaders. Go home to your owners."

"These are our masters, and our brothers. We want to accompany them."

In the growing heat, with the hum of a city pulsing to life, Lucius hesitated.

"As traitors, they have no authority over you, or your friends. You are not on our lists and the empire is not interested in you. You should return home and count yourself lucky you are not in chains."

"We are not compelled by the empire to go with them, Tribune. We know what awaits. We are compelled by the spirit to go with them."

The town clerk spoke, impatience in his tone. "Take them, Tribune, and let us be rid of them. They have long since lost their value in our world and we do not wish to have to deal with them. They are infected with treachery. Take all the vermin."

Lucius sighed and looked at the slaves. He said nothing for a time and I knew my old friend was wondering what was happening here. We had fought many battles and in the aftermath, as slaves and freedmen alike were scooped up by the slavers who followed our army, we had never seen slaves who volunteered for chains or death. This was most strange.

Finally Lucius motioned to Strabo to take the slaves and move the prisoners out. As we moved back down the Marble street to the hills of the camp, the town clerk prattled on, suggesting other ways his life might be made easier. We should gather up anyone even loosely associated with these Christians. We should turn them out of their homes, or burn their homes. Lucius listened to this litany of requests without responding and, having sent a messenger on to the camp, seemed relieved when the town clerk's son was brought out and reunited with his father. Lucius bade them farewell, managed a half-smile and turned back to me as they walked back into the city.

"Jupiter protect us from provincial merchants and their leaders."

The prisoners disappeared into the camp, and legionaries followed, except for two cavalry who stood off a little distance from us, maintaining watch over us. Lucius slowed as we approached the main gate, stopping at last to stare at me.

"Tychon, why do you think the slaves chose to go with us?"

His tone was that of a child asking for an explanation the first time he encounters a madman running through the streets.

"I don't know why they stepped forward. Or why you agreed to take them."

"They add to the numbers, Tychon. And the emperor loves a larger group of victims than a smaller one. He might even choose to kill the slaves more quickly than the others. One never knows with that…"

"I don't know," I repeated. "Perhaps they did not want to stay in Ephesus as hated slaves when their masters were not there to protect them. Or perhaps following their masters was a habit they could not relinquish."

"They did not seem either frightened or dulled by habit, Tychon. They were making a choice. And it was a choice I do not understand. And what I do not understand, at least a little, makes me uneasy. What are we dealing with here, Tychon?" He stopped just inside the camp and looked at me for an answer.

"We are just taking prisoners to Rome, Lucius." I shrugged. "Nothing more." It is often best to defend by using the words spoken by the other. His look said he did not believe my words. Nor did I.

Chapter 4   The Dog

Our warden's task began weeks earlier before the walls of Jerusalem. For months we had leveled towns, burned crops, slaughtered livestock, and killed rebels. At last, the remaining rebels and their bickering leaders retreated to the walled city of Jerusalem, a city more sacred to these people than our native Rome, or my ancestors' Athens. Their god was said to have designated this city as their heart and for centuries, it was the wellspring for all Jewish worship, commerce and politics.

General Vespasian, having driven the traitors into their nest, proposed to surround, besiege and destroy them. We set up our legions about the city, brought our siege works against the walls, and prepared to starve them before assaulting their stout defenses.

Then one night, a month ago, the general called Lucius to his command tent. It was not uncommon for Vespasian to meet with Lucius. They were old friends, going back decades to their time together in Rome, working their separate ways up the cursus honorum, which every youth of nobility undertook if he fancied any career in politics or the army. And Vespasian, in asking Lucius to join him in this latest campaign, counted on his friendship and loyalty.

When we arrived at the general's tent that night, I was turned away. The general met with Lucius alone. The night was quiet, or at least as quiet as normal in a camp housing tens of thousands of legionaries settling in to sleep. Finally, clouds moved away, moonlight bathed the scene, and Lucius emerged. His face looked ghastly in the light. He walked by me and when I asked him what had been discussed, said nothing. As he prepared to mount, he lost his balance and fell back against me. This had never happened before.

On our long ride back to his tent, he did not speak. When we arrived, he dismounted, gave his horse to a slave, and asked me to sleep elsewhere for the night so that he could be alone in his tent, with only his faithful Boudicca. I asked him what was wrong but there was no answer.

The next morning, we broke camp and despite my questions, he would say only that we were to take prisoners to Rome and would be gone for some time. We gathered three centuries from his cohort, some 250 men, 50 cavalry and three centurions, including Strabo, and began our journey. Pack animals and wagons were loaded with supplies, arrangements made for messages to be sent ahead to arrange transport ships and couriers sent to Rome to inform Nero's court that prisoners were being brought to him. We departed from Caesarea and proceeded up the coast to Antioch and Damascus, dropping off two centuries of troops on the way, proceeding with our one century to Ephesus.

On the way, I saw Lucius often take from his cloak and study one of several documents, which he bore from the tent of Vespasian and which never left his person. I assumed these were orders and perhaps a message from the general to any reader that the bearer, one Lucius Licinius Lucullus, had the full authority of the general and the empire to complete his assignment. He had a task to complete and I believed he was about doing it with his usual skill and confidence. It was well I did not know their contents.

After the prisoners were put under guard, Lucius and I settled in to our midday meal, cheese, wine and locally prepared bread, with figs, and a streaming bowl of some kind of meat. Several locals had learned what we were doing for them, removing a source of great harm to their commerce, and brought us food in appreciation. Strabo had the food tasted to assure its safety and now the cook was sharing it with the troops and us.

"Who had the pleasure of testing it for poison?" I asked, as I bit into a particularly delicious fig and scooped a large portion of the meat onto my plate.

"The Jewish prisoners," the cook answered. "And they proclaimed it most delicious."

"Perhaps we should have given some to the tax collectors," Lucius added.

"No, Tribune, they have gone on ahead of us and are now in the city. Shortly, I believe, they will be going on by themselves."

"Good," Lucius grunted.

We settled in, finished our lunch and went outside. As we watched, the docks were filling up with ships, big commercial ships, heavily rigged and bursting with grain, smaller ships whose decks were filled with traders and visitors to the temple, and two warships, oared and menacing. Cargo was being loaded and unloaded, docks crowded and bustling. Occasionally the wind bore us the shouted commands and curses of longshoremen sweating in the sun to hurry their work.

The breeze from the sea made tolerable the blazing sun. The rolling waves, the sun reflecting a glittering rainbow, the white caps in their rhythm all harmonized. I was getting sleepy.

"Remember our camps in Britannia, Tychon?"

"I am not likely to forget them, Lucius."

"On a beautiful day like today, I recall the terrible weather there, Tychon. Fog and rain and dark days. Windy coast. Cold, cold, cold." He sighed at the memory. It seemed so long ago.

"Only a man of peculiar cast of mind would think of foul weather on such a sunny day."

"Britannia was more than a legionary should have to deal with. We faced sword and javelin. We endured long marches and long watches in the night. We dealt with treacherous allies and rebels who would put your head on a pike if you drop your guard for a moment. We served under poor commanders who sent us off to die for their vanity, ambition or stupidity. We should not have had to endure the cold of Britannia also."

I had heard this litany of complaints before. A soldier, along with his sword and armor carries with him the right of complaint. Too much heat. Too much cold. Too long marches. Bad food. Reckless leaders. Treacherous natives. The list was endless and the same words echoed in camps across the empire. The right of a legionary to complain was almost as precious as his morning bread allotment. I seldom listened very closely, especially as I knew the high regard Lucius held for our commanders in Britannia.

"No indeed," he continued. "That was a miserable place. But here we are in sun, with a wind to cool us and fresh water and grass for the horses and a simple assignment. The food is good, the wine is not remarkable but adequate and we have the zealots in chains, not prowling about the dark, seeking to cut our throats while we sleep. So we have respite from Jupiter here, in this place."

The joy of his words was not matched by his expression, which was still clouded. I was not the audience for his speech. He turned quickly to me, as if just noticing me.

"We should enjoy it, Tychon, for as long as you can." He paused. "One good thing came from Britannia, though."

"Other than your life?"

Lucius let slip a thin smile.

"My life, certainly. Twice over I almost lost it, Tychon. And in both cases, due to a horse." His eyes turned to search for the scene.

"Remember that first time, the horse took a javelin and brought me down, pinning me. I owe you my life for the way you defended me from those savages who rushed me when I tried to get free. How many were there, three?"

"No, my friend, I recall there were at least a dozen."

Lucius laughed at my familiar retelling.

"Well armed, skilled and savage. Nothing could have protected you from their murderous blows but a mighty warrior and his sword and shield. Or perhaps there were a dozen and a half."

"Three, Tychon, and I recall they were quite old, at least one dragged his leg and another had only one arm."

"Brother, your advancing age has robbed your memory of the details. I recall the heroism I displayed and if we should ever have a triumphal march to herald your accomplishments, I trust I will be prominently honored."

"Don't rest your hopes on that, Tychon. I will never have a triumphal parade. Nor do I want one." He bent over and plucked a blade of grass and turned it over in his rough hands. "It is enough for me to see my soldiers retire alive from battles and return to fair treatment and just reward for their faithfulness. That is worth more than a triumph."

"And to return to a family such as yours in peace and happiness, as is their right."

He dropped the blade of grass and after a pause, looked down at Boudicca.

"And the second time that accursed island sought to kill me, with its painted and barbaric warriors, where were you then, Tychon, mighty Achilles?"

" You recall I was engaged trying to save my own life? At least two dozen Britons hacking at me, trying to separate my head from my body?"

"Two, I recall, not two dozen," he answered. "And they may have even been women."

"A slander most foul, Lucius. They were giants, a good head taller than any of our troops, and armed with most fearsome weapons. And as their queen attested, even their women fought like amazons. And you again had a problem with a horse."

"Yes, another horse, Tychon. That animal shied when rushed, against every bit of training it had received. I was foolish to choose that black beast to replace my dead horse."

"Did it truly bolt or did your forget how to ride a young stallion? Was forgetfulness already stealing up on you?"

He ignored my taunt and bent to stroke the head of Boudicca. "And then you appeared, my faithful friend, the one good thing to come from that campaign. I will go to my grave not knowing where you came from. But I am glad you did."

He was silent, no doubt recalling that day. Thrown from his horse, temporarily stunned, he was a target for several Britons who rushed him. All but one were cut down by javelin and arrow from our troops but one made it to stand over Lucius, prepared to deliver a killing blow. Then from somewhere a dark form appeared. Large, weighing more than most men. Massive head and broad muscular chest. Large and bristling teeth set in a powerful jaw. Britannia is renowned for its hunting dogs and never was there one more fearsome or overpowering. His leap knocked the Briton off his feet and no sooner had he landed than the dog set about tearing at him, first his sword hand shredded by those teeth, then his massive claws tore at his face and neck before finally his teeth ripped at his throat. When he lay dead, the dog turned and looked at Lucius, who was now sitting up. Lucius held out his hand to it; it padded over to him and licked his hand, turning it red.

And ever since, they have been together. Boudicca, Lucius named him, after the Briton queen who had led the revolt. In the years since, seeming not to age, the dog guarded him in battle, on march, and at repose, and every night he slept by his side. His unfailing instincts were a guarantee that anyone meaning harm to Lucius would be caught by his unfailing instinct. A low growl signaled threat. Raised hackles promised defense. Bared teeth guaranteed attack. Lucius had no need of a guard or slave to protect him at night. He had Boudicca.

"Yes, old friend, you and I have seen troubles and know the smell of battle. But unlike other legionaries, you never complain about food or cold or long marches. And that is truly remarkable."

He crouched down and rubbed his ears. The dog wagged its short, scarred tail.

I reached to scratch its head and it looked at me. His expression was indifferent. He never worried about me but I often thought that if I changed sides and sought to harm Lucius, that animal would know it in an instant and its growl would alert Lucius to new danger before it ripped my throat out. Perhaps he was indeed a gift from Jupiter.

"Horses and dogs, Lucius. Your undoing and your salvation."

"My undoing and my salvation. Well put, Tychon, and almost a portent."

He stood up and looked out over the city.

"I dreamt last night, Tychon." He paused. "I seldom dream. But last night I did dream."

"And?"

"I dreamt of that horse."

"Which horse, the first one who tried to kill you or the second?"

"Neither. The one who died on the road yesterday.

"It was the third, Tychon. I felt it. It wanted me dead. It was looking at me, its eyes large, like those it had as it lay on the road, but glowing red in its great black head. It was standing, fully alive, looking at me. It meant death for me."

"How do you know?"

"There were two dead next to it. A man in a toga, slumped on the ground, handsome face disfigured and arms and legs shattered. A woman crumpled on the ground, wearing a peasant dress. The horse had struck them down and I was next."

"How can you be sure it trampled them?"

"I just knew," he said and then he sighed, slowly letting out his breath. "As you know in a dream. The woman's face was turned away and I could not see it. But as I watched the man, his face changed. His face became…"

"Who was it?"

"Our father."

I said nothing. Years unfolded their sights and smells. His father had once held the infant Lucius in his arms along with a terrified and bloody orphan. But such kindness purchased no protection against a death sentence from the emperor. More than just a father's wrists were severed that day.

Before we could talk further, Strabo approached and Lucius stepped away.

I considered what he had said. I had cast off a great number of the superstitions and almost all the beliefs of the world I grew up in. I had not cast off a fascination with dreams, however, and this dream seemed both puzzling and disturbing.

After a few moments, he returned to me.

"The prisoners want to speak with me. Go on back to the tent. I know you will want to rest after a good meal."

I entered the tent as he and Strabo went to join the prisoners. I drank some wine and lay down to rest, a habit I had picked up during our time in the decadent East.

My last thoughts before sleep were of home, of Campania, of my dead wife and our children. I saw my son, Aulus, as he had been as a boy, not as he now was, a young man. And his dead sister, she who had no name or face, just a marker in my life. But my wife's face, laughing and marked by the stain of grapes I had thrown at her, was the same face I had seen when we first met in Campania all those years ago. She spoke to me and while I could not hear her words, I knew their meaning. Longing.

I awoke to the sounds of chains. At first, coming out of a deep sleep, I was confused where I was but my head cleared and I sat up. Outside the tent, the movement of men in chains grew louder. Then they stopped and the tent flap opened. Holding the flap open, Orestes, Lucius' personal slave and attendant, stepped inside. Entering, Lucius moved to his accustomed chair behind the table, which held maps, correspondence, goblets and plates from our lunch meal, and was seated. Then entered two people, the older woman called Lydia and the chief rebel, Timothy, and behind them, two legionaries, swords drawn and at the ready.

They stopped just inside the tent and waited until Lucius gestured for them to come closer. After a moment, he turned to me.

"Tychon, this is Lydia and Timothy, two of the leaders we have placed under arrest. They have a most unusual request, which they have put before me. I would like to hear your opinion whether I should grant it or not."

The two looked at me, with no hint of malice or fear. I said nothing, seeking to clear my mind.

"They have asked that we free their slaves from chains."

"Remove their chains?" I stood, steadily I hoped, and stretched.

"Yes, Tychon, clear your mind. They want us to remove them and give them freedom to move about."

"Prisoners are never unchained," I laughed. "Never."

"That is why I would like your judgment in this matter. It is most unusual."

"Why?" I asked.

"Tell him," Lucius prompted.

Timothy turned to me. Closer than we had been before, I saw the face of a man who would always look younger than his years, whose death would prompt onlookers to remark that it was unseemly for so young a man to die. In this close place, his voice possessed the softness and tone of a man just entering manhood. But the rope scar on his neck, the almost invisible scars on his hands and face and the firm and relaxed stance of his body spoke of a man, not a boy. His eyes, blue and direct and almost challenging, were those of a man who had seen much, understood more than he acknowledged and was unafraid. When he spoke, in a soft and firm way, he looked at me as if I were the only person in the room.

"The slaves in our company come from many parts of this country, as far away as Galatia, Pontus and the border with the Parthians, noble Tychon. They have served their masters loyally for many years and have seen their families grow up in the farms and estates of their masters. But before they and their masters became followers of our Lord and Messiah, they spent unnumbered years in chains, either sold or worked as mere cattle. Now they have lost their chains and have chosen to stay in their masters' employ. Chains are a rude and painful reminder of their former state and our concern is to lighten this burden. The days ahead are uncertain and none of us may live, as our Lord wills, but if we can make this journey a little easier for them, we cannot forego this small kindness."

"'Small kindness?'" I asked. "Set loose prisoners so they can cut our throats in the night and free you and your superstitious band. What nonsense!"

"They are no threat," Lydia spoke up, her tone direct. "They are neither violent nor hateful. They wish to come with us and serve us, as they are accustomed. They certainly mean no harm to you."

"Of course not. They must harbor great feelings of kindness to those of us who put them in chains and are taking them to Nero's court for judgment. Of course they mean us no harm."

My tone was sharp and I caught myself leaning toward them as a lawyer might confront a dangerous and duplicitous witness. Yet Lydia only smiled a strange smile, as if I were a child having an outburst.

"Sir, please recall that they volunteered to accompany us. Surely assassins would do no such thing," Lydia gently corrected.

"And if they are so fond of you, and if you hold them in such high regard, why have you not already freed them? If they are so tame, then you should not have to…"

I could feel a headache coming on and was not much inclined toward patience, and I realized she had already said most of them were already free. My mind was not working well.

"They have been freed," Timothy responded, "but they choose to stay in their masters' employ."

"So they are freedmen," Lucius interjected.

"Every one of them," Lydia noted "and they have chosen not to leave our employ. They are without guile or treachery and can be trusted, as we have trusted them for years."

I could not shake the wisp of a memory that troubled my concentration.

"Well, Tychon, what do you think?" Lucius' usually dour expression hinted at a smile as he waited for my reply and I realized he had long since made his decision and was playing an old game that had been repeated many times in our lives. It began when our childhood tutor would pose ethical questions to us to test our reason and judgment. Even if our answers were correct, our tutor would beat us when our reasoning was faulty. Now, as before, Lucius was poised to cluck and chide me for my errors of logic.

"Well, Tribune, it does not seem that these slaves, or freedmen, from what I have seen of them, represent much of a threat or danger. They are not warriors. And this man is not Spartacus. But on the other hand, they are prisoners and as such, should be chained and guarded." I belched the luncheon figs. "Regulations."

Lucius looked at me without smiling.

"The regulations are meant for prisoners of war, Tychon. Are these such?"

"Yes." I did not want to spar over the point. The figs were disturbing my stomach and I did not much care if the handful of servants were chained or not. This whole lot was sheep, not lions. My stomach churned.

Lucius nodded. It was clear he had decided before bringing these two into the tent. Why had he disturbed my rest?

Then, as we stood waiting for his answer, it happened, something most remarkable, something that had never occurred before and which I thought impossible.

From his place beside the table where he had been watching, Boudicca rose to all fours. A few steps brought him to stand in front of Timothy. He looked up at Timothy, then Lydia. Then, without warning, he began licking Timothy's hands, manacled and resting in front of him. He stopped, looked again at Timothy and then resumed licking, much as he would the hand of Lucius when there was the taste of sauce left upon it.

No one moved. The very air seemed frozen. No one spoke. There was no sound save the sound of the dog licking the hands of the prisoner.

Lucius stared at the dog.

Then Lydia reached forward, for the dog's head was even with her waist, and stroked his head. He turned his head and began licking her outstretched hand also.

The dog, which had killed at least two dozen men and crippled twice that many, was licking the hands of these two rebels. Lucius was transfixed, frowning. I wondered if there was some magic being cast upon us, some incantation that suspended time and place and would turn us into some strange, fanciful creatures. After all, what did we really know about these rebels and their strange beliefs? Perhaps they had whispered words that controlled the wills of dumb animals or gullible men.

But no, I concluded. There was nothing magical. But I was not sure what was taking place here. I recalled that never, even when I offered my hand, had Boudicca licked me.

At last, it grew bored and went back to lie down beside Lucius.

Lucius sat down and stared at the two of them. Nothing was said for several moments. Then Lucius looked down at Boudicca, who looked full in his face and yawned. Lucius stood and faced the prisoners.

"They will be unchained during the day and your lives will be forfeit if there is any trouble. Understood?"

"Understood," Lydia and Timothy said in unison.

"Thank you," Timothy said. "May the Lord bless you," Lydia echoed.

The two guards started to lead them out but Lucius stopped them.

"I have one question." They turned back to him.

"Why did you not request your own chains be removed?"

"You would not be so trusting of us, Tribune," Timothy answered. "You have been told many lies about us and believe us to be dangerous and violent traitors. Until you learn differently, you cannot betray your obligations as a Roman officer and unchain us."

"So you admit that believing in your god would cause me to betray my obligations as an officer of the empire?"

"No," Timothy replied in mild tone, "there is no conflict between being a good soldier and believing in our Savior and Lord. It only appears to be a conflict to those who do not believe."

"So once under the sway of your illusions, then mysterious understanding is revealed." Lucius was becoming more agitated. What words of Timothy agitated him?

"Belief begins in the heart of a man, as the Spirit leads. Then the mind is illumined."

"A confusion of words," Lucius said as he moved from behind the desk, his tone sharper. His hand touched his armor, as if seeking to assure it was still there.

"The flint of belief is struck in the heart and the flame of knowledge, however small, grows to light a man's mind and his path. Our belief does not require initiation into secret rites but it does require...."

Timothy paused as Lucius moved to stand in front of him, his face a few inches from the prisoner.

"...*humilitas,*" Timothy completed the thought by turning and translating the same to me, "or *tapeinos*, as you might say in Greece, Tychon."

"The Roman word *humilitas* or the Greek word *tapeinos* are equally foolish, Christian," Lucius spit the words back at Timothy. "These words speak of being crushed, brought low and made nothing. This world does not put its stock in such words, Christian. *Philotimia*, love of honor, drives this world. We treasure our reputations and revere those who have drawn acclaim. You cannot believe men will seek *humilitas* when the cheers of thousands beckon."

Lucius turned and went back to his desk. He whispered the word in disgust.

"You are a very clever man, Timothy, skilled at convincing the weak of mind, the uneducated and the slave of your religion. But do not think you can entrap me, or any man of education or position."

No one moved. The air was full of dust particles floating in the slight sun, glittering occasionally like the spark of swords clashing.

"We do not seek to entrap anyone, Tribune. We speak the truth and tell the story of our Savior and men find light or choose to stay in darkness."

"Enough. For now, take the empire's generosity and tell your slaves the empire's decision."

"It is not the empire who is most kind, Tribune, it is you." Lydia said.

"In this time, rebel, I am the empire to you and all about."

"Then the empire has a surprisingly kind face to show us here."

After a further moment, Lucius spoke, his eyes studying Lydia.

"Enough. Go now. I will give orders to have your freedmen unchained." His voice had grown weaker. He turned back to the table and did not look at them as they left.

Lucius sat, Boudicca looked at him in silence, and I pondered what had set Lucius on edge.

The afternoon was spent with Lucius writing correspondence to Vespasian and reviewing messages from our two cohorts who were on their way to join us. I retrieved my history and tried to continue writing but made little headway.

When it was time for dinner, the cook brought us our dinner and Lucius called for Strabo. Upon his entrance, Lucius gave orders. The freedmen were to be watched for any treachery until our transports were loaded and we were underway. Then surprisingly, he ordered Strabo to also free Timothy and Lydia from their chains.

As we began to eat, Lucius watched me, waiting for me to ask why he had released them but I said nothing, enjoying particularly the bread and cheese we were served. When we finished, I refilled my cup and leaned back in my camp chair.

"Did the prisoner Lydia remind you of anyone, Lucius?"

"Yes she did," he replied.

"Who? She reminded me of someone, in her voice and manner, but I could not place who or when."

"Our mother."

Lucius said nothing, his mouth pursed.

"Yes, I see that."

"And her friend, the older woman, the one named Claudia, I believe?"

He shook his head.

"Do you remember our aunt, Alexia?"

A quick exhalation of recognition. Aunt Alexia. Our father's sister. Widowed when we were infants, she had foregone convention and never married again. Like this Claudia, she was plump, her cheeks always flush. She laughed loudly, like a laborer, and ate and sang like a farm hand. She managed her family farm, and its produce and crops improved even more under her tireless hand than it had when her husband, more hedonist than farmer, had lived.

Her small farm abutted our estate and she was a frequent visitor, at meals and celebrations and harvest times. When a particularly good vintage of wine was grown, she would attend the harvest celebrations, her small stout figure a fountain of stories and songs. When slaves were freed, she would attend the ceremonies and toast the freedman, always bringing the gift of a fine horse, toasting a life free to ride the roads and visit foreign cities. On festival days, she was there to sing, enjoy the wine and tell stories of gods appearing to men and tricking them. In sickness, she was there to act as physician. Her knowledge of songs and herbal medicines seemed magical to our childish minds.

In all of these times together she was kind and gentle. Childless herself, she was our advocate and protector. She had counseled her brother and our mother not to let our tutor treat us too roughly. She would hide treats in her voluminous clothing for us and could sense when a sweet treat or dried fruit would lift our spirits or distract from the pain from injury or beating. When a horse or cow was sick, she would sit up with us as we stood vigil over the sick animal. Her smile was luminous, her voice unusually deep for a woman and her hands rough and dry from years of threshing and plowing. And her spirit was unfailing, at least until that dread year when our father died.

After his death, we saw more of her but less also. She visited more frequently, spending time with our mother alone as well as with Lucius and me. But something inside her died with our father and like a tree whose roots are no longer watered, she seemed to dry out and surrender life. She aged and grew fragile. She grew more fatigued at the festivals, her stories ceased and she drank rather more wine than before, but with less gaiety. Then two years after his death, she fell from a horse and her leg was broken in several places. She took to her bed and never rose again. Her last days, Lucius and I stayed with her and slept on the floor of her room. She was weak and pale and slept so soundly, her breath so wispy, that several times we thought her dead. At the last, she called for us and reached out for us as we came near. She opened our hands and placed in each of them a sweet she had produced from beneath the covers. She tried to say something but had no strength for words but only for a weak smile. Then she was gone. We mourned her a very long time.

Now as the shadows lengthened in our tent and lamps were lit, we sat there in silence, eating our dinner and then retiring for the night. No doubt Lucius was remembering those distant days as did I, images and voices come to life. And perhaps ghosts were come to care for us again.

Chapter 5   The Letter

It was in the sixth year of the reign of Claudius that our father came home to die. He had fallen afoul of the plots of the imperial court and was commanded to commit suicide. Lucius and I were on leave from the army and we were at our farm, awaiting his return. Both of us had been wounded, and we had much to relate and celebrate.

Lucius and I, our mother, aunt Alexia, Antonius, our farm manager, and several of the servants stood outside our home, watching the road that led to Rome. Then, a swirl of dust thrown up by several horses signaled his arrival. What we saw filled us with dread.

He was not alone. He was accompanied by three members of the Praetorian Guard, agents of protection for the emperor and vengeance against his enemies.

We moved from the sunny courtyard to the shadowed, cool atrium of the house. We embraced him, and stood silently, waiting. After a moment, he informed us quietly of the judgment passed upon him. The emperor had deemed him a traitor and pronounced a death sentence upon him, requiring him to return home and commit suicide. A quick intake of breath from my mother and the muttered curse of my aunt were the only sounds, apart from the burbling water in the atrium's pond.

Such a sentence was not uncommon for Senators who fell afoul of the emperor or his scheming wife, and now that dark shadow had come to our home. We understood the soldiers were there to ensure the sentence was carried out.

After a while, Lucius spoke, his voice growing louder, eyes filling with rage. He cursed Emperor Claudius, his degenerate wife, the evil courtiers and cowards that infested the court and the rank injustice condemning a loyal and honorable citizen such as our father. And in a hissing whisper, he said he would kill these Praetorians, these soldiers grown soft and corrupt, like their weakling emperor.

At these last words, father cut him off. He raised his hand and said "No." He smiled at his son's instincts and putting his arm around Lucius' shoulder, he pulled him close. "Your life and the life of your mother and these of my family here have been spared. Only my life is forfeit. There is no choice."

He turned Lucius to face him and embraced him. He whispered to him "You are now the protector of this family. Be wise and prudent and not rash. You are a Roman. You are Lucius Licinius Lucullus, heir of greatness and honor."

I watched as Lucius broke down in tears and when our father came to me, I could scarcely make out his face. How could I say farewell to the man who had plucked me from death and given me life? I could do nothing to protect him. The strong arms that lifted me from blood and death enclosed, then released me, for the last time

After a farewell whisper to Aunt Alexia, he took his wife in his arms and led her to an inner room. After a time, he called Lucius and me to his room and bade goodbye, wishing us a long and peaceful life.

Then we left the room and he fell upon his sword.

The praetorians came into the room to assure that he was dead. Only my mother's presence kept Lucius from killing them there. A day later, his body was buried on the estate. Thereafter we never spoke his Roman name but only spoke of him as our father.

A long summer passed, almost as in a dream. Our mother sat in the sun during the day, or walked in our father's beloved olive orchards. At night she retired to her room and we heard her soft weeping. Aunt Alexia stayed with us for a while and then overburdened by the pain, left for her own home. Antonius maintained the affairs of the estate, his usually cheerful manner become mechanical and sluggish. I wept alone and drank much wine.

And Lucius began to die. For days at a time, he slept outside, on the bare ground in the orchards, in the vineyard, even among the cattle in the fields, as if he could find his father's face or voice in those beloved places. Then he would return, dirty and looking like nothing so much as a madman, and would drink long into the night. Then his face would redden, his voice would rise and he would begin to cry out to the gods, finally shouting that he would kill all of them, emperor, his demonic wife and all the court. He would take on the whole empire and kill anyone who had a part in this death. He muttered that the treachery that blighted the honor of our ancestor, the General Lucullus, was now at work again to destroy the family. Then he would take up his sword and call for a horse to be brought. Often it fell to me to wrestle him into submission, aided by his mother and Antonius. On one occasion I faced his rage alone and when his overpowering strength threw me off, I fell against the pedestal, which held the bust of his long dead great grandfather, sending the bust to the floor, shattering it and leaving his mother's tender arms to quiet his rage.

Some time later he took to bed and waited to die. We tried to force him to eat but he was implacable and would throw the food to the ground or would take it and then, when we had gone, put a feather in his throat and throw up the food. We did not know how to save him from his plan to join his father. Days became weeks and he grew more gaunt and pale, a bleached skeleton from an ancient battlefield. The contagion of dread infected the servants and *slaves of the estate, who began to speak of ill omens and an uncertain fate when their new master would die.*

After a time, my drinking subsided, but our mother grew weaker. Without our Lucius, we were still a family drifting toward the rocks. It seemed death would visit us again.

Then, Julia arrived. Only daughter of Antonius, she had been sent to Greece to obtain education and view the wonders of a Greek civilization that had radiated fame and beauty when Rome was still a dirty village filled with grunting savages. Now she was back, having been summoned by Antonius.

Julia was five years younger than Lucius. In our early years she worked with us, played games with us and was tutored with us. Her natural fluency in Greek had aided us in our lessons, especially when we had spent our time racing horses instead of memorizing verb declensions, and spared us many beatings from our tutor. At last we donned the <u>toga virilis</u>, signifying our entry into adulthood, and prepared to enter the larger world of politics and the army. When we entered the army, she became a warm memory of our youth and nothing more.

Now, this summer of despair, she returned. A full head shorter than either of us, she was slender and graceful. She wore her luxuriant brown hair long, cascading over her shoulders, contrary to the short curled ringlets which adorned women of the upper class. Her eyes were dark brown, wide and seemed to glow when she laughed, which was often. Her mouth was wide and full-lipped and her nose was small, with nostrils that flared with emotion. But her hands were most striking. Long, slender and unmarked despite her countless labors in the fields, they were graceful, almost magical, in their movements. And she was certainly aware of them, as she would shape a word with a gesture. She was beautifully unlike the shallow and vapid Senators' wives who infested the capitol. She was the stuff of legend, with her virtue, endurance and quiet determination.

That determination took hold of Lucius. Each day she sat with him, first speaking a few words while she moistened his lips, then recalling for him the games and sports we had played together so many years before. As he rallied, she fed him bread, cheese and olives. When he sat up, they would have long conversations, out of my hearing. One day, as I sat with our mother in the arbor just outside our home, we heard something we had thought vanished. Laughter.

I saw much less of Lucius after that, as he and Julia walked the estate, rode horses, took food and sat by the stream which crossed the property just below the grape arbors. Nights saw them sitting outside until the moon dropped low in the sky. Our mother and I talked about crops, cattle, servants, slaves, weather. But we did not speak of Lucius and Julia, lest our words rip that thin thread that was hope.

One day, after Lucius and Julia returned from one of their walks, Lucius summoned all of us, Antonius included. Standing next to me, Lucius spoke to Antonius and quietly asked that he agree that Julia and he would wed. Antonius smiled and quickly agreed. In Rome, then and now, marriages in the great families are arranged for political alliance, alignment of interests, financial gain or advancement in social standing. This one was not. Instead it occurred for that most rare reason, one scorned by proper Roman society, love. Years before, Pompey, the great general and politician, who had contributed so much to our great grandfather's troubles, had come to love the wife he had married for political advantage and gained the sniggering contempt of the noblest of Roman families for his affection. Now Lucius, contemptuous of such estimations, loved Julia and would marry her. And since she was not even an aristocrat, his wife would be shunned by the very people whom Lucius held in contempt.

They married some weeks later, and after Lucius told his mother that he would not be pursuing a political career in Rome but would make his life as a soldier, we left for military service. On that day, it was the embrace of Julia as well as his mother, which brought Lucius close to weeping. It was the beginning of a marriage as untroubled and joyous as any man would know. And all of us wanted to believe that it would be so forever.

I awoke alone. The sun was higher than usual and no one was in the tent. I sat up, rubbing the sleep from my eyes and looked about. Everything was as it had been the night before except strangely, Lucius' armor, helmet and weapons were still there. It was not like him to leave the tent without them and I went outside to see what was going on. Orestes, Lucius' attendant, was standing there and turned to me.

"Where is Tribune Lucius?" I asked.

"Gone to visit the prisoners," he replied, gesturing down the main lane of the camp.

I started to walk in the direction Orestes had gestured. I had taken only a few steps when I saw Lucius returning.

"Good morning, Tychon."

"Not so good; I have not eaten."

"Food can wait," he said.

I followed him in and stood as he began to don his armor.

"Are we going someplace?" I asked.

"You said you were interested in seeing the Temple of Artemis, Tychon. Let us go see it this morning, before other business. You can have a late meal when we return, or we can eat in the city."

"Can I not eat first? I always eat before undertaking travel."

"You are growing soft. Perhaps we need a little battle to sharpen your edge."

"I don't need an edge. I need bread."

Lucius frowned at my decadence and, securing his breastplate, proceeded outside. I quickly dressed and followed, my stomach complaining. Orestes handed me a large piece of bread to quiet my hunger and my complaints.

We walked to the edge of the camp and looked down over the city. It was quite busy now and the position of the sun told me I had slept quite late. Quickly we descended the hill, followed by three cavalry riders who kept their distance. We passed the civic agora, with its politicians, merchants and religious pilgrims busying themselves with their pursuits of renown, gold or divine favor. We passed through the sun-drenched marble streets, past sellers of chickens, pottery or grain, past restaurants with their smell of onions and fish mingling with the fragrances of frankincense, cinnamon and savories from spice shops, past customers laden with silver statues of Artemis, past endless barbers, cobblers, and sellers of slaves. All was bustling and noisy and quite normal. At last we passed to the Shrine of Artemis.

The Temple was in the north part of the city and could be seen far away. The streets widened as they approached the magnificent temple and bright light pulsed to us as marble replaced stone and wood. Crowds grew in size and traffic slowed. Everyone, it seemed, was pushing toward the temple and a babble of different languages added to the confusion and excitement of the roiling movement.

The temple itself sat at the rear of an enormous square court, dwarfing in size anything in the empire and rivaling the Circus Maximus in Rome for sheer pomp. Alongside the court on either side were thin Cypress trees, fronting marble and gold porticos and blazing hearths. The air was filled with the fragrances of burning meat, Asian fragrances, and the music of coins and commerce. The entire court was marble, white, polished and glistening. And the temple itself was gargantuan, twice as large as the Parthenon in Athens. Square in shape, it stood raised some fifteen steps above the level of the court and was ornamented by over 120 marble columns on all its sides, each column the height of a dozen men. The columns were marble also and supported a massive arch beneath the roof so large it was said only the goddess herself managed to put it in place.

Inside, among the eunuchs, slaves, young virgins, priests and priestesses who served her each day, along with the prostitutes who were part of the goddess rituals, was Artemis herself. Towering above all who entered, only somewhat smaller than the mighty columns, she overpowered all her worshippers. Her eyes were fixed straight ahead, a royal sun shone behind her head; dozens of seed pods, betokening fertility, hung from her chest and lions clung to her arms. Her lower body was enclosed in tight wrapping, with only her feet showing, and her customary bow and arrows were missing. She had brought her power and fertility to the city and now was imprisoned in the wrappings to prevent her leaving. She must hunt no more; she must stay, protect Ephesus and ensure no interruption in the flow of gold.

And great wealth she did bring. Inside her inner chambers were vast fortunes, deposited for safe keeping from wealthy men across the empire. And outside, men clamored to add to her wealth and find riches multiplied by their adoration of her.

The courtyard was full of these pilgrims and visitors, bringing gold, ivory, precious jewels and rich treasures to honor her. Pilgrims from Egypt, Britannia, Illyricum, Pontus, Syria, Mesopotamia, Hispania, and the far off lands of India worshipped here at this wonder of the world.

As I moved toward the temple, Lucius caught my arm and directed me aside to a seller of bread. Following him and urged on by hunger, I quickly bought bread, some cheese and wine. Nearby we sat and ate, in a shady arbor set apart, some way from the crowd of devotees and merchants. Glancing about, Lucius had nothing to eat or drink and sat still as a statue and unsmiling while I ate. We were not here to see the temple.

"What do you think of this place?" He inquired, knowing my answer.

"I like Ephesus. I have always liked it."

"No, not the city, the temple." He turned to look at the temple.

"It is beautiful. Glistening and elegant and beautiful. Truly Greek."

I bit into the cheese. It was wonderful. "Sometimes, when I see the wealth flowing through this city, I think the marble roads should be repaved with gold."

He paused and looked at me. Then he turned back to the temple.

"It was not always so beautiful." He said softly, his eyes unfocused. "It was not so beautiful on the Night of the Asiatic Vespers."

I stopped eating for a moment. I sensed that the Shadow Wolf was returned.

Lucius was referring to that awful night eighty years before, when the Parthian king, Mithridates, bold and unrelenting enemy of Rome for decades, decided he would kill every Roman who lived in the cities along the coast of Asia Minor and reconquer the lands he felt were his. Ephesus, Pergamum, and a hundred other cities that held Romans, were targeted for death. Secretly the plan was drawn, and on a single day, his agents and soldiers went to all those cities and dragging Romans out of home, square, field and temple, and killed them, men, women and children.

In Ephesus thousands of Romans fled to the Temple of Artemis, this very place, for sanctuary. In panic, they believed no one would violate the temple of Artemis and risk the goddess' wrath. They were wrong. Mithridates' men pursued them, and even as they clung to the very statue of the goddess herself, they were cut down. The hours passed, the killing continued and no one was spared. The bodies and severed heads, arms and legs, many of them children, lay in rough piles all about in the courtyard and temple. The walls, statues and floors ran with blood.

80,000 Romans died that day. Where we were sitting, at the edge of the courtyard, our legs would have been deep in that blood. As I thought of it, I heard the screams, the pleas for mercy and the blunt sucking sound of swords cutting through necks and arms. I looked at my foot and was surprised it was clean.

When I was a young child visiting this temple, I could not imagine such bloody butchery in such a beautiful place. Now after years on battlefields filled with hacked limbs, rivers of blood and screams and moans of the eviscerated and dying, it was not difficult at all to see. I resolved not to think of it again but to concentrate only on the beauty and peace of this city when I returned here. Now Lucius had awakened that memory.

"I know, my brother, you have questioned this journey and our role as jailers."

I leaned forward, trying to make out his quiet words against the sounds of chattering pilgrims and chanting priests.

"And you have wondered at my change in manner. I am sure I am not the brother and companion I once was."

He looked at me with a question and I said nothing.

"It is as you suspect, Tychon. There is more to this trip than appears. And we have been chosen to complete this assignment for one very good reason: our general is my friend as well as my general."

"'Friend'? Does a friend give an assignment far below your rank? You have served in the legions for four decades. This is a job for a centurion."

He sighed and his eyes clouded over. His lips seemed not to move as he spoke. He sipped wine.

"It is not beneath me, or what I hold most dear."

I put my food down and stared at him. For a very long time, he said nothing. Once or twice his lips moved as about to speak, but no words came. The crowds milled, the noise grew louder, the sky clouded over, then cleared again before he spoke. He turned to look at me, and his eyes were those of that summer of despair so many years before.

"It is not beneath me, Tychon, to try to save my Julia's life."

He stared at me for a moment and then off to the milling crowd. I said nothing. Then he produced two letters from beneath his cloak. He handed me one, the well-creased one he had been reading.

I opened and read.

"Dearest Lucius,

Long have we been married and long have we shared our days of joy and sorrow. Alone among men of my acquaintance and knowledge, your honor and fidelity to me and to your family have been constant and true. Your bravery, strength and valor in defense of the empire have raised you to the highest rank and no one can gainsay your loyalty. Know then that it is with an admixture of joy and concern that I bring you news of a great and wonderful thing I have experienced.

You may remember that young servant girl you brought home from Britannia many years ago, the one we named Beatrice, the dark-eyed one you said so closely resembled me that she could be my sister, except for the broad streak of white in her hair. Through the years, she has served me faithfully and well, and especially so in the long months since you left for the campaign in Judea. Some months ago she spent time in Rome, at my direction, assisting my father in business. There was nothing extraordinary about the work but I was somewhat surprised to receive a request from her that she would be allowed to stay on for a few days after my father returned. I agreed and after three days she returned and I learned why she had stayed.

In Rome she heard a speaker, whose name I do not know, talking in one of the precincts, near the temple of Jupiter. He spoke of a king, a man who had performed miracles and even raised the dead. He taught the most wonderful things, about a kingdom that is in this world, but not a kingdom of sword and rulers but a kingdom of love and truth and forgiveness. Those who did not want this kind of kingdom but preferred this world, with its petty scheming, deceit, and cruelty, persecuted that king. They killed him, persuading the Roman governor of Judea to crucify him. Then, to the amazement of all, he rose from the dead. After a time, he rose to the skies and left his followers to proclaim his truth. It was one of those followers whom Beatrice heard.

Excited and unable to restrain herself, she went back each day, and listened and came to believe. When she returned from Rome the next week, she could not restrain herself but poured out her story to me. I was dismayed at what she told me. These were Christians she had been listening to and she was risking her life and the lives of those around her. The Emperor has been executing followers of this Judean prophet for a long time, as you certainly know. And his persecution has been increasing since your departure, especially as his counselor, Tigellinus, urges him on. I forbade her to speak of her actions to anyone, neither slave nor servant. I determined she would not go to Rome again.

Strangely she did not object. She smiled and asked if she could speak with me about it, so long as we were alone. I agreed, thinking I could cool her fevered mind. As the days and weeks passed, she sought every opportunity to share her beliefs. I sought to argue the foolishness of believing in a person returning from the dead and being the son of god. I argued for our Roman pantheon of divine persons but she seemed immune. After a time, I realized she was not bending to me but seemed to gain strength. At night I found her on her knees in her room next to ours, praying quietly.

One night I entered her room and stood unobserved in the shadows. I listened to her prayers, thinking there might be something in her words that would open a place for me to help her. Much to my astonishment, that part of her prayer I heard concerned you. It was something like this 'Gracious Father, hear my plea. Watch over our beloved master Lucius, whom you know and whom you have loved from before the stars were in the sky. Keep him safe from harm, aid him in doing his duty with honor and mercy and bring him home straightaway to us. He is a good man but he needs you. You are gracious and merciful and faithful. In the name of the Christ I pray.'" As I had been thinking her prayer would be for my conversion, I was most astonished she was praying for your safe return.

Later, after much thought and thinking myself quite clever, I determined to learn more about this traitorous sect. Accordingly I set out with Beatrice for Rome. We found the place she had gone before but there was no Christian there speaking. Later we found where he had moved, to a home near the emperor's palace, a most luxurious home of a highly respected aristocrat. We went there and entered, admitted by a slave and the mistress of the house, an older woman richly dressed and exceedingly gracious. As women we were not suspected of being spies and for several hours that night we heard what the older man had to say. We were two of about twenty in the room. Among them were slaves, women, two legionaries, several young men and three older men, one of whom was the Senator whose home it was. I confess I cannot recall all of the old man's words as he talked about this Judean carpenter but something stirred within me, not unlike a breeze, which I could not understand or dismiss. A second night we returned, then a third.

Finally we returned to Campania. The fields seemed the same, and the food tasted the same. All seemed the same. But at night I felt restlessness I had never felt before, not unlike that expectancy which I felt when Lucia was in my womb or when you are about to return from war. I began to sleep fitfully. I took to wandering the house, then the farm, late at night. I thought of the many times you and I had walked among the orchards when you were ill, but thinking of those times, I was even more restless. It grew worse and worse, until Antonius inquired why I was not eating. I did not tell him that the words spoken by a man I did not know were haunting my nights and days, whispering unbidden when I ate, or lay down or walked in the fields.

Then one night when I knew Beatrice would be about to retire, I crept into her room. She was praying, as usual. I paused in the moonlight for just a moment and then as if bidden, I was on my knees beside her, repeating her prayers. She put her arm about me and her prayer become one for me. I found myself weeping, being drained, melting. At last I spoke a prayer, just a few words. One word was 'mercy' and another was 'forgiveness' and a third was 'believe.'

So it was, my beloved, that I came to number myself among those who are called Christian. I have gone back many times to Rome to hear, to learn, to worship. I cannot tell you what joy fills my heart and how I yearn to be with you and tell of the wondrous things that have happened. Do not think me foolish or mad. I have a wonderful gift I want you to share.

My love and prayers are with you. I yearn to see you face and feel your arms around me.

Julia."

I sat, overwhelmed, the ground no longer solid. For many minutes, I held the letter in my hand, unmoving, unseeing. No thought except death, no sound except a silent scream.

It was simple. It was clear. It was certain. Julia had condemned our entire family to a death sentence. Our family was now judged traitor. Julia, Lucius, their daughter Lucia, Antonius, the servants, my son Aulus, all of us. Executed. There could be no defense, the act was done and we were dead men.

The burning crosses which lit Nero's garden awaited us. He would not be content to kill Julia. Our large estate and Lucius' wealth would prove ample reason to condemn us all. No one could save us. Rough hands would cover us in pitch, nail us to our crosses and set us afire in Nero's garden, alongside our prisoners in chains. Doom.

Chapter 6   The Plan

I could not speak or move. Pilgrims and merchants passed all around us and we sat, like misplaced statuary

I finally passed the letter back to Lucius and looked at the crowd entering and leaving the temple, eating bread and olives, talking and laughing. In a few weeks, they would still be breathing, moving about, eating, drinking, talking and planning, blood coursing through their veins. And we would be charred carcasses being dumped into the Tiber.

Lucius read my face and spoke.

"There is a way out, my brother."

"Oh?"

"A way out. And we are going to take it."

I looked at the scarred wood of the table and its dark wine stains.

He put Julia's letter back under his cloak and held up the second parchment, bearing the imperial seal.

"This is a message from Nero's court, commanding that our general send back to Rome any Christians he finds, along with the Jewish rebels he captures." He held the scroll tenderly, like a sacred text. "Nero is bent upon destroying both Christians and rebel Jews. He wants blood, and a lot of it. He enjoys watching them be tortured and die, and his blood lust is raised." He paused and looked about him, as if ashamed. "And we are the ones to bring him those sacrifices.

"Vespasian opened Julia's letter by mistake, as it was mixed in with the official dispatches. He read the first part, thinking to pass it along to me but when he saw what she had written, he put it aside and gave it to me that night he called us to his tent. He had kept it for several days and was not sure how to proceed. Then after he received this order from the emperor he determined to send me as the jailer."

"Why, to talk Julia out of this madness?"

"Yes, but more than that, also to protect her. Pay heed, Tychon, our lives depend upon this. If I am the one who brings these Christians to die, if I, after a lifetime of loyal service to the empire, am the one who delivers these prisoners to their death, no one could possibly suspect me of being a Christian or harboring one in my family. No man would bring his fellow rebels to be tortured and killed if he were one of them. These prisoners are protection for my family. For you. They are the demonstration of loyalty to the state, our *bona fides*. We will build a wall of protection before she can be found to be one of them. "

He paused and tried to look confident.

"They will be sacrificed to save us."

I looked at him, wishing to believe. I had never been wrong in trusting his judgment. But hope often conceals desperation.

"But what if she is found out? What if Julia speaks of this to others? Or Beatrice?"

"I have written to Julia, forbidding her to speak of what she wrote to me and instructing Beatrice likewise. Silence is her best protection while we complete our mission." The last word hung there, a small child trying on linen armor.

"There are so many ways this plan of yours can fail, Lucius." I shivered in the noon sun. My words were lost in sounds. "We are doomed."

He stood and looked down at me. His voice echoed victory.

"Take heart, Tychon. I will not permit this Nero to do what Claudius did to my father." His eyes peered into the tomb of Claudius. "I will sacrifice ten thousand of these Christians if need be, however innocent they may be, to save my Julia. Take heart, Tychon. We will fortify our defenses and defeat the attacker. We cannot lose heart now."

Such were the words I had heard before the battle where I lost my arm.

He sat down again and we stayed there a long time, neither speaking nor looking at each other. My thoughts were clouded, my spirit flat. As every man does, I had thought tomorrow would be much like today. As every soldier does, I had thought our service in this campaign would lead to home and peace. Now the solid ground was behind us and ahead, the river was wide, the tide rushing and I could not see the stepping-stones Lucius visualized. And on the far side, the woods were dark.

At last, as the sunlight began to fade, we rose slowly and left the Temple, silent, all words spent. At last we fell away from one another. He returned to the camp with his thoughts. I stayed in Ephesus.

I found a tavern and sat in its arbor, in the corner, and ordered the local wine. I was unable to turn from the dread. I imagined Vespasian's worry for his old friend. I saw a garden filled with flaming crosses, my face and my son's through the flames.

Countless times we had faced death in battle. Our troops were often outnumbered, our leaders weak, the enemy fearsome, the weather foul, the footing treacherous. Death was always about to call our name.

But in those battles, we depended upon the person near us to protect us. Our own strength and valor would save us. The battlefield was a circumscribed world far from Rome and if we fell, no one in our families would be deprived of life, only us. Now the battlefield was a stone's throw from our homes and if we fell, our families went down also.

And I thought of Boudicca, the brave queen of Britannia, whose armies we fought. She had not sought war but when Rome refused to recognize a woman as queen of her tribe and Roman officials stripped her, flogged her and raped her daughters, she rose in revolt and for a time, her warriors beat the best of our legions. But our army, my sword, Lucius' sword, beat them down and the empire triumphed. Now a very different woman put us in peril and that power of the empire was turned on us and would kill us.

I remembered how Julia had once saved Lucius and how he now sought to save her. I thought how Julia had once saved him and now was about to destroy him.

As I drank the wine, I grew more certain this battle would be one we should not expect to survive. We were in a land with no signposts, no scouts to tell us the way ahead. We were alone. All was unseen, as dark as the wine I drank, undiluted and overwhelming my senses.

Then, as the light faded and evening came on, I looked out at the street and saw a dark black horse being lead down the street, by the arbor. For a moment, I thought the horse that died on the road was alive. It stopped and turned and looked at me briefly. Its eyes seemed to glow ruby in the twilight. Its nostrils flared as it took in my smell and calculated my demise.

Its handler was familiar. In the shadows, he turned to see what the horse was regarding. It was the *publicanus* from the road. He looked at me and perhaps smiled, a small gesture that seemed serpentine in the gathering shadows. The horse looked fixedly, unmoving, assessing. It stared and then its lips moved back from its teeth. They shone in the twilight and seemed a smile. Finally, the horse or the man snorted and they moved on, the man's blood red hand holding the bridle. In the cold, I shuddered.

I drank more deeply, draining another tankard quickly. My thoughts turned back to Nero's garden and in gathering shadows, as the tavern owner went about lighting torches, I thought I saw faces in the fires, as the torches became crosses and the victims were faces I knew all too well. Their mouths moved, perhaps speaking, perhaps crying out.

And I heard the terrified screams of ten thousand people clinging helplessly to marble statues.

Chapter 7   The Assembling

I awoke in a painful haze. I had stayed in the city until quite late, drinking heavily, and it was only with the help of the cavalry rider whom Lucius had assigned to watch over me that I returned to the camp when the moon was low in the sky. When I stirred, it was only to the sound of horses and men moving about the camp. Then trying to sleep again, I burrowed into the covers like Apollos' animal afraid of the light.

Then my stomach revolted, making strangled noises, cramping, relaxing, spewing bitter into my mouth. I sat up, staggered outside and expelled a most noxious liquid. Excess had claimed its due.

I returned to my bed. A little while later, Lucius came in.

"Well, my friend, I am heartened to see you are alive. I was given odds you would not wake until evening."

He sat beside me and seemed totally unaffected by the conversation we had the day before. Even as my head throbbed and my body lay lifeless, I thought of the terrible secret and the deadly prospect that awaited us. Perhaps it had been a dream.

He helped me up and only drew back when he smelled my breath. I looked about for something to drink but found nothing but a cup filled with a strange looking liquid, neither wine nor water.

"What is this?" I asked.

"Something for your stomach." He handed it to me. I tasted it. It had a strange odor, not unpleasant, which hinted at some plant or other. I swallowed it and lay down again.

"What is it?"

"Medicine."

"I have never tasted it before. Where does it come from?"

"A prisoner provided it." He smiled. How he could smile I did not know.

"A prisoner?" I struggled to sit up, and failed.

"One of the Christians. The older woman who reminds us of aunt Alexia. She heard you were sick and brought it to you."

I let out a groan, pain mixed with dismay. "Am I poisoned? Are you mad letting one of them give me drink?"

"Don't be afraid. It is an herb that settles the stomach, she says. And I forced her to take some of it before leaving it to you. As far as I know, she still lives." He was not smiling now but his dark eyes seemed to enjoying my distress.

"As far as you know?"

"Up, Tychon," he said, slipping his arm under mine and pulling me to my feet while keeping his face turned away. "You need to walk this off."

We went out of the tent and proceeded down the main street of the camp. The noise of the legionaries was louder than usual and tents stretched farther to our front than before I sojourned in the land of Bacchus. I looked at Lucius.

"Our two other companies have arrived. While you slept. One century arrived late last night with 60 or so prisoners and a second century this morning with another 100."

"So we are complete now. Unless we are we expecting other troops?"

"No, this is our little army for this journey. 300 soldiers and 200 prisoners. It is sufficient for our purpose."

"And our purpose is?" I tried to spit but my mouth was dry and tasted of rotted parchment. I wanted him to lie and he did so.

"We are to provide prisoners, both Jewish and Christian, for the Emperor to deal with, according to imperial justice."

It was obvious our conversation had not been a dream and he would not discuss his personal mission in so open an area, where eager ears and wagging tongues might bring catastrophe. So we proceeded in silence toward the far end of the camp. My stomach had quieted and strength was slowly returning to my legs as I sought to walk in a straight line and without aid.

As we reached the end of the main street and turned back, the centurion in charge of guarding the prisoners, Gaius Metellus, approached Lucius.

He saluted and leaned into Lucius and spoke in a low voice.

"Tribune, you instructed that our prisoners should be kept together and allowed only limited freedom of movement. A situation arose this morning which I need to bring to you." Lucius nodded.

"Some of the Christian prisoners have been speaking with their guards. They were not threatening, nor did they appear to be planning some sort of violence. But the guards were most uneasy and unsure whether to engage in conversation with them. I told them not to speak with them."

Lucius continued walking, without replying. Then he turned on his heel, and moved to the prisoners compound. They were loosely bunched together, some sitting on the ground, some sleeping, some staring off into the distance. But a few, no more than perhaps a dozen, were standing closer to the guards. One, a particularly lovely young girl, was standing near a young legionary as if inviting conversation.

I sensed a tightening in Lucius, a small intake of breath. He turned toward the centurion.

"Bring that soldier to me," he said, gesturing to the young guard.

The soldier, when approached, seemed to grow pale. He brought his arm across his breastplate in formal salute and came to us.

"Yes, Tribune."

"Soldier, have you been speaking with that young girl?"

"Yes, sir." He swallowed. "Briefly."

Lucius put his hand on the young man's shoulder. "What is your name?"

"Marcus Valerius"

"Marcus Valerius, you are young. Guarding prisoners is a serious business and except for giving orders or correction, a guard should not speak with the prisoners. A lesson learned now will help you avoid serious problems in the future. Return to your post and tell the other guards what I said."

The legionary started to leave. Lucius stopped him.

"Marcus Valerius, what was the girl talking about?"

Marcus swallowed hard. "She asked about me, where my family was, where I was born, how long I had been in the army, if I had brother or sister. Things of that sort. She said she…" he stopped, censoring his words.

"Go on," Lucius directed.

"She said she was born in Cilicia and had a father and one brother. Her grand father died in the wars against Mithridates, having been killed at Amisus in the fire that destroyed the city. All their wealth was lost and she and her parents moved to Cilicia where they owned a farm. Then an itinerant teacher came through and much of her family listened to him and became Christians. Her father became a leading man in the area and led many to hear about the carpenter they call the Christ. Then…."

Lucius raised his hand to interrupt.

"Did she ask anything? Did she ask you anything?"

"Only two things."

Lucius leaned forward.

"And what was that?"

"She asked if we could remove the chains of their slaves, the newly arrived ones…" He hesitated for a moment. "And she asked if there was any prayer she could offer on my behalf."

Lucius straightened and motioned for the soldier to return to duty.

"Those people and their slaves. Most perplexing." I offered. My voice crackled like a dying fire.

"I should put them all in chains, Tychon. It is perhaps their plan to gain some small concessions in order to aid further concessions in the future. Or perhaps their young girls are set upon seducing our soldiers with tender words to gain escape. The softness of their words cannot be genuine."

His speech was rapid and more than a little nervous. I wondered how much of his mind was still in Campania, imagining how similar soft words had ensnared Julia and brought us all to ruin.

"Lucius, we have seen many insurgents in our travels. We have seen the rebels, the schemers, the liars and the weaklings. In Gaul, we saw tribal chiefs express fealty to Rome while gathering hordes of warriors to slaughter us. In Britannia, we saw tribes change allegiance when they thought us weak. Do these people not seem among the most harmless we have seen?"

"'Harmless', Tychon?" He turned to me, his eyes flashing. "When they can cause innocent victims of their preaching to believe their superstitions and be put to the sword? When they can threaten the order of the empire? 'Harmless?'"

He paused, and taking a deep breath, he regained his composure, motioning to the centurion to join us.

When the centurion saluted, Lucius spoke to him.

"Centurion, you are new to our ranks. What is your name?"

"Gaius Metellus, Tribune."

"And where are you from?"

"Brindisi. My father was a centurion for many years."

"Excellent, Gaius. You have the honor is serving in one of the best legions in the empire. Where is your father now?"

"He is retired in Brindisi and if we make port there, I hope to see him before we return to Judea."

"Perhaps you may be able to. For now I have a question for you. Who are the main leaders of this group you have brought?"

The young man hesitated and when he responded, there was a strange tone in his voice.

"There are several but the main leaders are an old man named Barnabas and a young man from Ephesus who accompanies him."

"Bring them both to me after dinner tonight, under guard."

He started to turn away but then hesitated.

"And bring Lydia and the older woman who accompanies her, from the lot we took from this city."

The centurion was motionless for a moment, as if wanting to speak but did not do so. He saluted and turned to go. I touched his arm and he stopped.

"Tribune," I said, turning to Lucius, "perhaps that young girl who was talking to the soldier should also be brought to us."

Lucius looked at me and then turned to the centurion, nodding. Gaius Metellus returned to his soldiers. We turned and walked quietly back to the edge of the camp.

"Tychon, why do you want that girl to attend?"

"Lucius, why do you want any of them to be brought to you?"

"I have my reasons, ones you might discern if your head were clearer. I want to interrogate them in detail." My head continued to throb. "And your reasons for the girl?"

"If you have your secret reasons brother, then I can have mine."

"She is under sentence of death, Tychon. Do not be foolish and think there is any hope there."

"She is attractive, Lucius. Most lovely. I would like to be near her. No more than that. It has been a long time since I have simply talked to a beautiful young woman. A very long time."

We found ourselves at the edge of the hill again, looking down over the busy streets and docks of Ephesus. The docks were filling up with new boats, transports for our party, and two warships for protection. Soon we would be leaving.

"Did you know, Tychon, that this city honored my ancestor, the general Lucullus."?

I nodded and hoped for silence. I knew the story well and I needed fewer words and more of the medicine we left in the tent. We had had this conversation the last time we were in Ephesus several years ago.

"Yes, 15 days of festival and celebration was held in his honor, called the Lucullea. He was famed for having relieved the Ephesians of the burdens heaped on them by the moneylenders and for his humane and generous treatment of them. He was honored and loved. He spoke of it often, I am told." He paused. "Fifteen days it was."

No long dead celebration would protect us this day. Those celebrations were a small note in my history, nothing more. The festive fires celebrating Ephesus' deliverance from Mithridates were now replaced by flaming crosses in a degenerate emperor's garden. And Lucius' long record of courage, ability and loyalty would offer no protection for any of us in the days to come. I knew it. And beneath his stoic demeanor, Lucius knew it also. But the chains of his ancestor's memory could not be removed as easily as those of the prisoners we guarded.

"Fifteen days" he said softly, the smoke of the general's celebratory fires fading, "Fifteen days."

That evening, after the dinner plates were taken away, fresh wine poured and his armor removed, Lucius settled in. The tent flap was open so we could enjoy the setting sun and he sat behind his desk and instructed Strabo to bring the prisoners in. I had recovered from my debauchery and now Lucius turned to me and spoke in a low whisper.

"If I am to bring Julia back to her senses, I must know a great deal more about these people and their strange beliefs. We have always been the most successful, Tychon, when we entered a battle knowing the disposition and intent of the enemy. This battle is no different. We will speak to them now and on the voyage. We will gain an understanding so I can restore Julia to sanity."

Before I could respond, the prisoners were brought in. There were the two men the centurion identified, as well as Lydia, the older woman, and the young girl. The girl looked not so young as I first thought but she was very lovely. She smiled at me and I smiled back, not caring what Lucius thought of my demeanor. He was the interrogator. I was the charming and worldly companion. And I would not allow the Shadow Wolf to come near me this night.

Lucius sat for a moment, fingering his dagger in distraction, placing it on the map in front of him then picking it up again. He looked at each of the four in turn, carefully, as if there were a message on each that could be discerned. The girl he left to me to survey.

"I called you here to give you an opportunity to defend your beliefs, which have been judged a threat to the empire. You are among those who have brought insurrection to Judea, incited violence among citizens and refused to honor the emperor. Rome is a fair and just empire and will not condemn you without a hearing. A formal hearing will be held when you are delivered but I wish to make a preliminary inquiry. Am I understood?"

They nodded, no one noting that such mild assurance was a sham and bore no relation to the certainty of the grisly execution that waited.

"So how do you defend yourselves? Speak."

The old man, Barnabas, spoke first. He was tall, stooped, beard all grey and hands trembling slightly, not from the cold or fear, I felt sure. He spoke quietly, taking frequent breaths, as the infirm do.

"Most honored Tribune, we are innocent of the charges against us and if a just trial is held, we shall be acquitted."

"So how will you defend yourselves?"

"With the truth, Tribune. It is the best and only defense of the innocent person."

"Are you so sure you know what the truth is? And what is your name?"

"I am called Barnabas, Tribune. And yes, we are in possession of the truth."

Unexpectedly the older woman spoke up.

"Or more accurately, the truth possesses us."

"And who are you?" Lucius asked.

"My name is Claudia Procula," she answered.

Older, perhaps the same age of Barnabas, she was most unremarkable in her dress and appearance. One would pass her a thousand times in the forum without noting her. It was only in the confidence of her voice, with a hint of exhaustion, that she was at all remarkable. It hinted vanished nobility.

"What do you mean by saying 'the truth possesses us'?"

"I mean that the one who is truth holds us fast in his arms."

"Truth is a virtue, an ideal, not a person."

"For some, it is that, Tribune. For those of us whom God has been gracious to rescue, his son and our Lord is truth. He taught us that he is the way, the truth and the life. No one can come to the God of all the world except through his son, our Lord."

"Are you a philosopher, Claudia?" She shook her head. "Then why is truth so important to you? Would that not best be left to men of philosophy?"

"Truth is what you seek, Tribune. It is what you charged us to speak and it is what you expressed uncertainty about. I am quite familiar with such uncertainty." Her last words were measured and heavy with echoes.

She said no more and Lucius turned to Barnabas.

"So what is your response to the charges?"

"Please repeat them, Tribune so I may address them directly."

"First, bringing insurrection to Judea. Second, disturbing the peace by inciting riots. Third, dishonoring the emperor."

"Tribune, we are not among those Judeans rebelling against Rome. We do not take up sword or dagger. We do not poison. We do not war. In truth those Jews whom you imprison and take with us to Rome would as soon see us dead as they would Romans. You certainly know that since you have removed some of our chains but keep theirs."

"And to the charge of inciting riots?"

The younger man, named Demosthenes, spoke up at this question.

"Tribune, if I may be permitted, I would like to respond. I am a citizen of Ephesus and I speak with authority, having been here and part of the crowd when Paul, the apostle, came here several years ago. I was not at that time a believer and most fiercely resented his teachings, as they were a threat to our beliefs and our commerce. If his beliefs took hold, pilgrims would stop coming to the temple and stop buying our statues. I was quite wealthy from these sales and his preaching threatened that. So we sought to kill him. There was a riot. But it was not at his incitement. He spoke the truth about God and his son and some, including myself, under condemnation by the truth, grew angry and violent."

I felt Lucius' sideways glance to see if I was attending this exposition. I was watching the young girl touch her belt. Her hands were very graceful.

"Your Paul was a most unimpressive magician, I understand," Lucius continued. "How did he manage to delude so many?"

The old man Barnabas spoke before Demosthenes replied.

"He was not of imposing stature, being small and stooped, nor a great orator. His voice was a bit shrill and he was not trained in the rhetorical school. But it would be foolish to dismiss his teaching for such reasons."

"But still he deceived you." Lucius' tone was getting a little shrill. I wondered if the young girl had a musical voice.

Lucius fell silent and then turned back to Barnabas.

"On the third charge, do you deny you dishonor the emperor?"

"How do we dishonor him? We pay taxes. We follow the law, except in those few cases when we are made to violate our beliefs by supporting a lie. So we are not guilty of that charge."

"But you admit there are occasions when you would withhold obedience from an imperial decree. Do you not?"

"Only when it would compel a lie."

"Obeying the emperor would not compel a lie, would it?"

"If the emperor, or his agents, ask us to worship him or acknowledge him as lord above all, then we could not obey since to do so would admit he is a god, above all men and worthy of worship. That he is not, that he cannot be. Likewise, if we were to swear to honor those gods Rome asserts, we would lie in asserting their divinity."

"So when we honor Jupiter or the divine Augustus, that is a lie?"

"Tribune, Augustus was emperor when our Lord was born." His voice was firmer now, deep, powerful, like the drum that calls legionaries to assemble. "After his death, he was esteemed divine and is so spoken of now. But his ashes are kept in the mausoleum bearing his name in Rome. Those ashes bear witness that he was but a man, perhaps a wise man or a powerful man when he was alive, but a man still. Has anyone ever been healed in his name? Has anyone been raised from the dead? Did he rise from the dead after three days? No. He is but ashes and such he will ever be. But those very miracles have been seen in the name of our God, in the name of his son, our Lord."

"Anyone can claim that these things occur," Lucius said.

"I have seen them with my own eyes, Tribune. And hundreds of our faith have seen bones made straight, illness cured, even cripples healed and limbs made straight." He did not look at me but I felt sure he had noted my withered arm.

"And the dead have been raised, Tribune, in the name of our Lord. There is one among us who was one of those so blessed."

Lucius started to respond but did not. I sensed he was about to demand the person be brought forth but for some reason, did not. The young girl looked at me and smiled. I maintained my heroic pose.

The discussion continued for some time, Lucius asking questions, challenging beliefs and the prisoners responding, first one, then the other, the women speaking as boldly as the men and often responding when Lucius challenged the truthfulness of their accounts. The girl said nothing, disappointing me. I imagined her voice would be musical, much like a lyre, and magical, weaving some web of beauty, but until I heard it, I could not be sure.

At last I grew restless and went outside, taking my wine with me. Finally, the Christians came out with their guards and returned to their fellow prisoners.

Lucius came out and stood beside me. The evening was quiet and in the distance, I heard the sounds of night birds and faintly, over the sea, cries of gulls.

"What did you think, Tychon?"

"Much to think on, brother."

"I trust our talk did not distract you too much from your adoration of the young lady," he said.

"No, no, not too much. But she will need my personal interrogation, I fear. And I do not think she is as young as she might appear."

"Fortunate for you, Tychon, if you are not to appear to be an old and reprobate lecher."

We went inside and settled in for sleep. As the lamps were trimmed, the lights were low but my bed still stunk of my drunken sleep the night before.

"Lucius, I have a question."

He did not answer.

"That older woman, the one who is like our aunt. Why do you think she is so much concerned about truth? She didn't talk about piety, or authority or loyalty, or anything except truth, like her personal lodestone."

In the dim light of the tent, Lucius rose on his arm.

"There is that similarity also to our aunt. That day in summer when our father died shaped all our lives, including aunt Alexia. The smells of that day, the dress of that day, the sounds of that day stayed fixed in her memory and years later she could tell us what we wore, what we ate, how warm that day was. The words spoken that day were etched in her memory as surely as if they were graven in stone. To the day of her death, those words were clear and fixed. As they are in ours."

His shoulders moved with a barely audible sigh. After a few moments he turned back to me.

"So it is with this woman, Claudia Procula. There was a day long ago that lives in her mind and it is that day that causes her to speak so much of truth."

His eyes seemed to be looking very far away.

"On that day, her husband sat in judgment of a carpenter charged with treason. The carpenter spoke of truth and her husband challenged him, asking 'What is truth?' He then condemned the carpenter to death. That carpenter was the Christ these people worship. Her husband, a Roman official, was the agent of their leader's execution. His name was Pilate."

I did not recognize the name.

"The night before, she had a dream and warned her husband about that Jesus and told him to have nothing to do with him. Her husband ignored her and had him crucified." Lucius paused, considering his words. "Pilate did not believe in truth. Now she believes in truth most fervently."

"And where is her husband now?"

"She does not know. He fell out of favor and was removed from his post thirty years ago. The very Roman authorities he sought to serve turned him out of office a few years after these events."

I felt Lucius' triumphant smile in the darkness.

"He left her some ten years later, after she became a Christian, left Judea. She has sought him for years. She still retains hope he will come to believe as she does."

I said nothing but lay back. In a moment Lucius did also. He took from his tunic the carved stone that hung about his neck. On it was the outline of the face of Julia. As always, he cradled it gently and held it to his chest. Sometimes when he thought I was asleep he would speak to it. The words were indistinct.

As I drifted off, I had one last question.

"How do you learn all this, brother?"

"The young centurion, Gaius Metellus, told me earlier."

"And where did he learn all these details?" Had our troops been talking to the prisoners against the rules?

"His father told him. He was a centurion in Judea when all this occurred and served in the Augustan cohort. He saw it all."

I turned on my back and closed my eyes.

"As a matter of fact, Tychon, his father was the centurion who crucified that Jesus."

A cool breeze lifted the tent flap and whispered over me as I pulled my blanket tight. In the shadows outside, a strange host was gathering

Chapter 8   The Voyage

The next several days were maddening.

On the first day, all soldiers were assembled before dawn and struck their tents, preparing to leave camp and board transports, which were waiting at the docks. Wagons were filled with the provisions we would take with us. Casks of wine, bread, figs, cheese, dried fish, beef, veal, lentils, vegetables, wild and domestic fowl, grapes, apricots, apples, and melons were included, along with honey and that special flavoring sauce, garum. Cooking pots, dishes, bowls, firewood, cleaning materials – natron, bath oil, soap – joined those supplies which our cooks and their quartermasters had purchased and requisitioned for our troops and prisoners. Medical supplies, sufficient to treat injuries or shipboard illness were included. Add to that the tents, furniture, horses, weapons and military equipment and moving just these 300 troops and 200 prisoners was no small effort but one which the centurions were accomplished at managing. We estimated eight days for the voyage, with only one stop, at Corinth, and all we were to eat or use had to be taken with us.

Then when we reached the docks, we were told the departure was postponed. In the darkness just before dawn, the captain of the largest ship, which we were to occupy, had seen an owl sitting on the mainmast rigging. This omen foretold a storm or pirate attack. So we returned to camp, set up tents and waited.

I spent the day ruminating on the deeply superstitious Romans. Every act or decision can be halted by the most random event. A bird flying overhead or perching on a famous statue. A chicken that refuses to eat before a battle. A misplaced lightning strike during civil turmoil. And no one is more superstitious than a ship's captain.

I grew more irritated on the second day, when a goat was seen wandering near the docks. It was a black goat, predicting large waves and storms. Departure was again postponed.

On the third day, the captain reported he had a dream the night before and in it, he saw his face on the moon. This omen had deeply disturbed the captain since it foretold destruction of the ships and their passengers. We did not leave that day.

During all this time, while the soldiers were content to await better augury, Lucius grew impatient, frustrated and finally, on hearing of the captain's dream, enraged. He did not speak while eating and when I sought to speak of more pleasant things, he was abrupt in his dismissal.

His patience and relaxed manner before Ephesus had reflected the time needed to collect the prisoners. Now, he was all for action and quick movement and he found delays intolerable.

At last, on the fourth day, we were ready to leave. The skies were clear, the auguries positive and no confounding dreams or ill-omened birds, or goats or floating ship wreckage were seen. Lucius called Strabo in before we struck tents and instructed him to tell the soldiers and prisoners not to sneeze while boarding the ship, not to utter any curses or use foul language and to stay silent and in their assigned places until we weighed anchor. He would not tolerate another delay.

We boarded two large ships, which were in harbor to deliver grain and pick up objects of art and commerce being shipped from Ephesus to Rome: vases, pottery, statuary, jewelry, ornate furniture, precious purple cloth, and the cloth called silk from beyond the end of the world. There was sufficient space in these two vessels for half again as many passengers as we numbered, so travelers seeking transport to Corinth and Rome took up the remaining space.

Lucius put half of our company in one of the transports and half in the other. For our ship, he identified the specific prisoners and left Strabo to distribute the rest between the two ships, making sure that the *secarii* were assigned to the second ship and under Strabo's close watch. When I asked, he said he wanted to use the voyage to question the prisoners at length. He then went on to assure me he had included on our ship the young woman I had singled out and trusted her companionship would lessen any boredom the voyage might cause. He told me her name was Sophia and smiled, knowing that her name in Greek meant "wisdom." I refused to show dismay.

After two hours of moving, loading and settling, we were underway. Accompanying our two ships were three warships to prevent pirate raiding and three other transport ships, which joined us for the protection we provided in the voyage.

As we cleared the harbor and the pilot boats dropped their lines and returned to the docks, a good wind filled the sails and we were moving quickly to the west in good seas. We went about our tasks, setting up sleeping covers on deck for most of the passengers, securing cargo below decks and standing at the rail to view the lovely water and sunshine. The prisoners were all unchained, at the order of Lucius and again warned against any disturbance, while guards maintained their watch.

Lucius set up our quarters in the one large cabin reserved for persons of importance and I unpacked my possessions, leaving my writings in their sealed trunks to protect against any damage from any leakage or storms. We had only the few items a soldier on campaign takes and it did not take long to unpack. At last, Lucius and I went topside and surveyed the receding city.

"It is truly a lovely city, Tychon. If I were a man who chose to live in a city, this is the kind of city I would choose."

"It is beautiful and civilized." I paused for a moment and then looked at him. "Do you think we will ever return here?"

Lucius said nothing for a moment.

"Tychon, do you remember that Gallic chieftain we fought who had the huge sword scar on his chest, the one we parlayed with at the river?"

"Yes, I remember. Artaxus was his name, I recall."

"Yes, Artaxus. What do you remember of him?"

"He was impossible to deal with. While we talked seriously, he smiled, and then laughed unexpectedly. He spoke to the air, as if talking to some god whom we could not see. He would close his eyes for long periods and neither move nor speak. Then he would stand and begin waving his arm about as if he had a sword in his hand."

"And what did we conclude, Tychon?"

"That he was mad. Out of his senses."

"Agreed, he was. And we had difficulty forming a strategy to defeat him since his actions were unpredictable and random. And when we did defeat him and his army sued for peace, we insisted the parlay could take place only if his head was delivered to us."

"And when it arrived and we unwrapped his head," I interrupted, shivering at the memory, "it still stared at us in madness, as if his mad god was still alive and viewing us through those dead eyes." I shook off the terrible memory. "But what has that to do with our danger?"

"Everything, friend, everything." His voice grew lower and I noticed most of the passengers and some of the guards were on the far side of the deck, out of earshot.

"Tychon, we serve a monster masquerading as emperor. Nero is a word that curses, a blight, a butcher, a madman. He does not govern the empire so much as plays with it and pillages it for his personal pleasure. He taxes provinces into revolt. He executes senators on a whim. He murders his own mother. He gelds a young man and pretends the youth is a woman and makes to marry him. He burns down that part of the city where he plans to build his Golden Palace and blames the Christians to deflect blame. He stomps his pregnant wife to death and then mummifies her so he can visit her and speak to her. He plays at being a performer, a singer, a poet and no one tells him he is unfit to clean a stage, much less play upon it. He plays at being a charioteer, and it is our loss that his injury in the race last year was not fatal. And he has Tigellinus, the prefect of the Praetorian Guard and a man of infinite cruelty, at his elbow, to encourage him in his evil and suggest new ways to bleed the state."

"And?"

"And as we defeated a mad man Artaxus by seizing the initiative and exploiting every opportunity, so we will do the same here. My plan is simple: take the prisoners, or most of them, to Nero. But if the time is not right, or the mood of the emperor has changed, or new crises arise, we will wait, or change. First and foremost I must see Julia. The rest of our plan flows from that."

In his persistence and determination, even in light of deadly adversity, Lucius was Roman to his core. Time and again, Rome has been defeated in battle, sometimes catastrophically, as when Hannibal defeated an entire Roman army in one day and killed over 80,000 legionaries. A lesser nation would have sued for peace. Rome is not such a nation. Instead it raised new troops, appointed a new general and went to battle Hannibal again. Rome's stubborn determination, her refusal to admit defeat and her drive to dominate all she touched allowed that small backwater city to become the capitol of the world.

And that determination flowed from all the noble Licinia clan ancestors, down through General Lucullus to my brother. That insistence on fighting against overwhelming odds was undiluted in his veins. We might die but we would never surrender.

But I determined to put aside such dark thoughts today. The day was beautiful and we should enjoy it. Accordingly I spent the first day gazing over the water, blue and smooth and sunlit. I composed poems to the loveliness of the sea and its eternal confidence while Lucius spent the day moving about the troops, encouraging, listening, and watching their endless games of dice amidst bawdy banter. His familiar affection for legionaries returned as he spent time with those in this world he most respected and the soldiers responded with smiles and affection.

Late in the morning as I was at the rail, putting the end to a particularly fine line of verse, I sensed a presence. A few feet down the rail, a young girl was leaning on the rail, looking at the water. It was Sophia. She was looking out with a thoughtful gaze and did not notice my staring at her for a moment. Then she turned and smiled.

"It is a beautiful day."

"Yes, Sophia, it is."

She looked startled. "You know my name?"

"Yes. And my name is..."

"Tychon," she interrupted. She moved closer and was at my elbow.

Now it was my turn for surprise. "How do you know my name?"

"Perhaps in the same way you learned mine, by asking."

"Ah, I thought perhaps you had heard of my writings."

"You are a writer? What do you write?"

"Poetry, philosophy, history."

"I thought you a soldier. Someone said you had accompanied Tribune Lucullus on many campaigns."

"You have been busy making inquiries." I smiled at her and to my delight, color rose in her cheeks when she smiled. "He and I have been in many battles. But now that is behind me since my wounds disqualified me from active service. Now I am his aide, and friend. And brother."

"Brother? You do not look like him in any way."

"Adopted. I am Greek. His father found me on a battlefield and took me to his home and I have been a part of that family ever since. And you?"

"I am Greek also." She turned back to the sea. "All my family are farmers. For many generations, we have worked the same farm. I was raised to herd, harvest, weave and cook. My father died a few years ago and now my brother and I work the farm with just a few freedmen."

"You have no husband?"

She said nothing for a moment.

"I had a husband. He died a few weeks after my father. I have never remarried."

"How did your father and husband die?"

I expected her to pause before answering, but she did not.

"My father grew old. He took ill, lay down and never rose again. He was not so very old as our family lives. He was only in his sixth decade when he died. It was not the farming that hastened his death. It was the taxes. The taxes wore him down more than the work of farming. And in farming, nature assists your efforts." She looked down in silence. "Tax collectors are not a part of nature."

"And your husband?"

"My husband was working with our sheep and one became lost. He tracked it to some high rocks some distance from our villa. In seeking the sheep, he fell from the rocks and was killed."

Her eyes shadowed at the memory. Her face was full but without excess, her eyes a blue-grey, hair short and irregularly cut. Her lips were full and expressive and I found myself wanting her to continue speaking. Her voice was soft and its rhythm, first strong then falling off at the end of a thought, reminded me of the summer wind that comes just before sunset.

"How did you come to be taken prisoner?"

"I was in the city when the soldiers came. I had left the farm to my brother's care while I went to town to be with the brothers and sisters and we were all taken." She sighed. "I do not know what has become of my brother. I pray he will manage without me and not be too frightened for me."

"Are you not frightened for yourself?"

"Sometimes, yes. But then I pray and am encouraged. After all, what can they do to me, Tychon? Chain me? Imprison me? Kill me?"

"Do you not fear these prospects, Sophia? Chains mean slavery. Prison is a dark and filthy end for anyone. And death is neither welcome nor painless."

She turned from looking at the sea and looked directly at me. Her eyes were serious and she leaned slightly toward me, as if her words were of great weight.

"Tychon, I have been a follower of the Christ since shortly after my husband died." She spoke slowly and deliberately. "Chains and prison are not welcome. I fear them when I think on them. But then I pray and sing and reflect on what our blessed savior underwent and I am comforted." She sensed my puzzlement. "No, not comforted by the things themselves but comforted by the spirit of God which gentles my heart. And comforted by the Lord who says He will never leave us or forsake us. He is with me in my prayers, in my work, in this ship now. He will not leave me in chains or a prison."

"Here, now, in this ship?" I smiled at her innocence. "I do not see him."

It was her turn to smile.

"Do you see your breath which goes in and out of your body, Tychon? Do you see warmth of the sun or merely feel it on your skin? No. But they are there. And love as well."

"What does love have to do with it?"

"God loves you, Tychon. I don't mean Jupiter or Hera or any of the gods you imagine exist and worship. I mean the one true God. He came on earth as a man and died for our sins. He knows our weaknesses and in mercy, he sent a means of rescue from his judgment, his son Jesus. And in that, he is loving."

"And he is here?"

"As surely as you and I are. Would you like to meet him sometime?"

I turned back to the sea and did not respond at first. She was so confident and assured and gentle that I could not scorn her beliefs. She was heading toward such a dark end, that I could not bring myself to mock. And I had not wanted our conversation to take such a turn.

Unexpectedly she reached out and squeezed my useless arm. It had little sensation to it but seemed to warm at her touch. Embarrassed I pulled back. She held on and tightened her grasp.

"It seems hard to let go of a thing, Tychon, even if that thing has been a burden for your life. Our Lord healed a man who was crippled from birth and depended upon begging to stay alive. He sought healing and our Lord had mercy on him and healed him. But I have often thought, as I prayed and thought about that man, how did he feel after being healed? What trade did he know? Nothing beyond begging. He had neither a wife nor children probably. Now he was healed, and adrift from all he knew or had lived. How was he to go on? Perhaps his healing was not just a miracle but also a new burden. But our Lord consoles us that his yoke is easy and his burden is light. It is the first step, like that crippled man, that is the hardest."

She released my arm and I turned away. I had imagined seducing and enjoying her, in some dark corner. Such thoughts had made me warm with anticipation. Her words had chilled those desires and I did not know what to say.

For a long while I was silent. I thought about that man she spoke about and his useless legs. I thought about my leg, once strong, once used for running and climbing and now always painful and slow. I thought about my arm, not able to move, lacking most sensation, useless for lifting a child or embracing a woman. In my poetry, I sometimes resented the able and the whole and sang dirges to my losses. In my other poems, and in my writing of history, I tried to find the pattern, the weave that would explain my losses, Lucius' losses, our family's losses, and our empire's losses. I was no nearer that design than when I started so long ago. And now this young woman seemed to be so certain of the design.

"How old are you, Sophia?"

"Thirty five. And you?"

"How old do you think I am?" I refused to face my evasion.

"About the age my late husband would be."

Now it was my turn to feel warmth in my cheeks, but only in my cheeks. I looked down. Her eyes smiled and held something I feared to name.

Luckily, the time had arrived for the mid-day meal. She went to rejoin her people and I went to our cabin. I liked her and wondered if such simplicity could expect to escape the gardens of Nero.

A little later, I felt the ship slow and went on deck. Everyone was gathered at the rail, looking in the direction of Ephesus.

A courier ship, small and lean and quick in the water, was approaching After a space of half an hour, it drew abeam of us and signaled for us to send the ship's boat. The boat was pulled close, a senior crewmember and two oarsmen got in and quickly rowed to the newcomer. A legionary from the new ship climbed into the boat and it returned.

Lucius went to him and they exchanged greetings. The courier handed Lucius several messages and indicated he would wait for a response. Lucius took the messages to our cabin, after gesturing for me and the centurion to wait on deck.

As the day seemed to grow dim and the shadows deepen, I felt a presence at my elbow. Thinking it Sophia, I fixed a smile and turned. It was the Christian, Timothy.

"A fine and quick boat, Tychon," he said, gesturing to the courier ship bobbing in the water.

I said nothing, thinking he might leave and be replaced. He stayed.

"There must be some urgency to these dispatches for this boat to be sent after us."

"Probably so." I wondered what he might be thinking. "How are your fellow believers? Have many of them been on a ship before?"

"Some, but not many. I have been on many ships and this is one of the largest. I hope we can avoid a storm but if we meet one, such a large ship should handle it well."

"That is why we chose this ship. My master does not do well in storms and if possible, he will always choose a larger ship. The captain says the Etesian winds favor us and we should have a smooth trip."

"I hope it is a peaceful journey."

I turned and looked closely at him. Slender build, the face of a youth, pale blue eyes, thinning hair, slightly shorter than me and a great deal shorter than Lucius and the look of man who could be trusted.

A motion behind me caught my attention. Lucius had come out of his cabin and was handing a dispatch case to the centurion from the courier boat. They bid farewell and Lucius returned to his cabin, gesturing for me to follow. As I turned to go, Timothy caught my arm.

"Sophia is a most modest and pure woman, worthy of respect. While I do not know your usual manner with women, I urge you to treat her most kindly and without guile."

I said nothing and inclined my head only slightly. It was an unusual request in the world from which I came but I did not find it surprising coming from this man.

As I entered, Lucius was studying the dispatch. Papers were strewn about the desk and writing materials indicated he had been busy with dispatches. He read for a moment more and then put it down, moving it across the table for me. I looked at him instead. His eyes were troubled but his speech firm.

"What is it?"

"War," he sighed, "civil war. Rebellion and marching legions and Roman sword against Roman sword."

Lucius gestured to the dispatch.

"There is the message from Vespasian. He received news some time after we had left and sent swift word to us to inform us. It barely caught us. But the news is some weeks old and much may have changed since he received it but it is clear. Civil war. Again."

"Who? Where?"

"Sit down. There is much to hear and much to think about." I sat and touched, without reading, the dispatch. Lucius told the tale.

The revolt began in Gaul. The governor there, Gaius Vindex, decided the grievance of the locals about being reduced to poverty by the continued increases in Nero's taxes was indeed justified. He declared revolt against Nero, but having only a few troops, appealed to Servius Sulpicius Galba in Spain to join him and declare against Nero. Galba hesitated. Nero sent Lucius Rufus Virginius, governor of Germany, with his legions to put down Vindex. He did so.

Then Galba put aside his hesitation and declared against Nero. His legions were now marching on Rome. The empire was once again facing civil war. Galba, a bachelor and a miser, a brutally strict commander who punished initiative as if it were mutiny, was leading trained legionaries to face the corrupt and vicious Nero. Rome was sinking into violence again.

Lucius spat on the floor.

"That is where we are now, brother."

I sat for a time and thought on these matters. The world we knew was changing each day. I had never been through a civil war and neither had Lucius. Our knowledge came from stories and from our father, who told us of the first civil war his grandfather fought alongside Sulla, and of the second civil war between Caesar and Pompey. But those were history. Now blood and the butchery was returning.

"Lucius, what of our plan? The prisoners? Our families? Surely we cannot continue."

Lucius gestured at the dispatches.

"Vespasian gives us leave to continue and leaves it to me to decide whether to go forward alone or with the prisoners and the soldiers as needed. He is going into camp and will neither attack Jerusalem nor withdraw. He, too, is waiting to see what happens. He asks that we take note of developments and send him reports. Also he asks that we contact his brother in Rome and ensure his son Domitian is safe."

"And what of the legions in Britain, Africa, Germany? Are they joining the Spanish legions of Galba?"

"No word on them."

"So what do we do, Lucius. How will we continue?"

Lucius got up and walked around his table to sit by me.

"My brother, we will continue as we have always done. In battle, there is a time for standing still and receiving the attack and a time to attack. We will attack. We are heading into the heart of the storm and only there will we know how to protect those we love. We are taking our prisoners with us, and the soldiers. If we do not need them, we will not use them. But if we do need to use them, we would be foolish to have sent them away. We are not Galba. We value initiative. And we will adapt. Our Seneca told us, 'Brave men rejoice in adversity just as brave soldiers triumph in war.'"

His words, as always, calmed me. At least for a time. I recalled another teaching of Seneca, "A man who suffers before it is necessary suffers more than is necessary."

He stood up and folded up the dispatches and returned to his chair across from me.

"I sent word to Vespasian to send couriers to us at Delos, where we will stop in two days, and to Corinth where we will lay over for a day and also to Puteoli, where you and I and few others will get off before the rest proceed to the port of Antium. I have written messages to friends in Rome to send us word of what is happening in Rome and messages to Antonius at our farm to send couriers to us at Corinth and Puteoli.

"Don't lose hope, Tychon. Civil wars are seldom concluded quickly. The wars of Sulla and Caesar lasted several years, stretching across nations, borders, and seas. They were mighty struggles and all the muscle and might of the empire was consumed by them. There was little time for small matters that must have seemed important before the first battle. War has a way of narrowing the sight. This war will be the same. There will be little time to spend on pursuing or burning Christians. And there will be much confusion and chaos. And chaos and confusion can be our friends."

I sat for a time, turning his words over carefully. At last, I stood and prepared to leave. I turned at the door.

"Do you really believe what you have just said?"

Lucius covered his mouth with his hand, feeling his beard gently as if to reassure that it was still there. His eyes looked up at me and seemed, in the dim light of the cabin, indistinct.

"I will save us, brother. I will save us."

I spent the rest of the day alone and slept on the deck by myself that night. Now that the awful truth had been revealed that an emperor could arise elsewhere than in Rome, how many men of ambition might now slip the leash and seek the throne themselves?

Chapter 9   The Storm

On the second day of our journey, we passed the island of Samos. I had a headache from a fitful night sleeping on deck surrounded by people snoring, grunting and passing gas and was slumped over the rail trying to settle my mind in the mist of the ship's wake.

A cup appeared before my face. Turning I saw Sophia. My smile was weak.

"Drink this, it will help," she said.

"What is it?"

"A little water, some herbs, a spice or two. It will help you, I promise." She smiled and looked terribly refreshed. Part of me hated her for it. I drank. It was not unpleasant.

"A bad night?"

I did not answer.

A second sip. The cords around my head slackened. Perhaps the drink had something to do with it. I tried to smile.

" I am ragged, dirty, uncivilized. Those miserable excuses for baths that we found in Judea provided no joy for me. They were too small, the water too cool, and there were no rooms to exercise, no gardens to relax in, and pitiful service of food and drinks."

Her amused smile silenced my petulance. I was not heroic. I summoned a feeble smile in response.

"Do you know this island we are passing?"

She smiled and turned to look at it. "No, what is it""

"It is Samos. An island of some reputation."

"Reputation for what?"

"Well, my young Greek lady," I warmed to the task of bard, "it is fabled for Pythagoras, the founder of the religion that bears his name, and a Greek, like you and me. He is also said to have been a mathematician. Also, Epicurus, the founder of the Epicurean philosophy was born here. And Aristarchus, an astronomer and mathematician who claimed our world moves about the sun. So this island is renowned for its thinkers, as you would expect for an island inhabited by so many Greeks."

"You are quite proud of being Greek, aren't you, Tychon."

"Aren't you?"

"I don't think of myself as a Greek. My mother was from Pontus. My father was Greek but taught us little about Greece, or Rome for that matter. He taught us planting and weaving and irrigating and a little carpentry. It was our friends on other farms nearby who told us of the glories of ancient Greece, of Agamemnon and Helen and Achilles. Later our mother taught us reading and writing but we were too poor to have much to read and too busy farming to have the time for such things. You see, Tychon, I am just a peasant farmer."

I looked at her eyes. They were more blue today, all sky and sunshine. I felt my head clear, then dizzy. Perhaps I was hungry.

"You may be a farmer; you are no peasant. To me."

She looked back to the sea. "Tell me about your brother, the Tribune, Tychon. I hear the soldiers talk of him with great affection. Is this normal in the legions?"

"'Normal?' No. Some tribunes and legates lead this way. Some do not. What you see in these soldiers is a thing Lucius most values and most readily gives, loyalty. He is always loyal to the troops and they are loyal to him. They also trust his honesty. His word is sacred and he will not break a promise he makes. That is why it is so difficult to pry a promise from him. Also, he is greatly respected, for his years of service and faithfulness but also for his age. Lucius is unusual in that he is much older than the normal tribune. The tribunate is usually a position for a much younger man."

"Why is he in this position?"

"We were called out of retirement by General Vespasian. When the emperor charged him to suppress the rebellion in Judea, he in turn called Lucius to join him, thinking he could use a steady hand. We had served with him before, in Gaul and Britain. Lucius was reluctant but finally agreed. Since he needed someone to guard his back, I naturally had to come to protect him." I waited for her to laugh at my weak humor. She merely smiled.

"And he did not mind leaving his wife?"

"He very much minded, but the friendship of Vespasian and his loyalty compelled him."

I paused, thinking of the awful consequence of that compulsion.

"And she is a good wife?"

"She is a very good wife. No one could ask for better. And among the women who have haunted our family for generations, she is one of the pearls."

"What do you mean, Tychon? Do you speak of your mother?"

"No, not my mother. Others." She looked at me with a question.

"Sophia, you are from a farm. You do not know Rome. And for that you should thank your god. It is a place that breeds ambition and in women, that ambition turns often to scheming, treachery and debauchery." Her gaze seemed rapt.

"It began with our great grandfather, the first Lucius Licinius Lucullus, as all our stories begin. It was from him Lucius got his name and we got wealth, estates and a legacy of treacherous women. The General's first wife, Clodia, was constantly unfaithful to him, even committing incest with her brother who was on the general's staff and undermined his authority in the Mithradatic war.

After he divorced her, the general married Servilia, who became notorious for her unending affairs also. She bore him one child, his only child, our grandfather.

"Finding no pleasure in his wives, the General used his vast wealth gained from his family and from the treasures of his foreign wars to build vast estates in Neapolis and Tusculum, accumulating a vast library of Greek writings, and indulged in legendary banqueting. But one of his most beautiful and lasting contributions was the Gardens of Lucullus, in Rome. He brought a model of lush public gardens from his service in the east. These gardens, with their winding walks, shrubs, trees, flowers, ponds and aviary, were a treasure to the Romans and one of his enduring legacies. To this day they are without equal."

"You must be very proud of them."

I looked at her and beyond her. "I wish they had never been built."

"Why? They sound beautiful?"

"They are, and from that beauty, our father died." I looked back at the ship's wake swallowed by the sea.

"You see, Sophia, beauty breeds envy. A beautiful wife breeds lust in other men. A beautiful estate breeds greed in the hearts of a neighbor. And a beautiful garden, with shaded walks and ponds and flowering trees and a carpet of flowers breeds envy among those whose hearts are wretched and vile. And such a woman was Messalina.

"After General Lucullus' death, the gardens were sold to the family of Valerius Asiaticus in whose hands they remained until the reign of the emperor Claudius. The wife of Claudius, Messalina, a wanton and debauched woman, wanted those gardens for herself. So she trumped up charges against Asiaticus, who was the most loyal of Romans, and had him executed. She then took the gardens for her enjoyments and her meetings with her army of lovers.

"But there was one problem she had yet to dispose of. Our father. He had been in negotiation with Asiaticus to buy the gardens back into the family. A sale price had been agreed upon and our father was contemplating filing a claim in court. If he were successful, he could possibly regain the gardens. Further, she hated our father for having spurned her advances years before. And she hated our mother because she had escaped Messalina's consort, the former emperor, Caligula, when he attempted to rape her years before."

Sophia's eyes seemed to be getting bigger as I told my too true tale.

"As your surely know, Caligula was the most debauched and cruel of emperors. You can know only the smallest part of his cruelty. In killing men, for instance, he instructed his torturers to kill the men slowly, slicing parts of the body and cutting off skin for a long, long time. He instructed the executioners 'Make him feel he is dying.' And his debauchery knew no limits, even to incest with his sister.

"But it was his banquets with noble families that threatened our family. Caligula had the habit of inviting Senators and their wives to dinner and then, choosing a particularly lovely wife, he would take her from dinner into another chamber, rape her and then return to describe what he did and how the woman responded. The Senators could do nothing, lest they be executed, just as they would be if they refused to attend the dinners. An emperor who insisted parents attend the tortures and executions of their children had no hesitation in executing an offending senator.

"So it was that my father and mother were invited to one of his dinners. Messalina was there with Caligula, and was certainly looking forward to seeing my mother raped and my father humiliated. And as if prompted, Caligula chose my mother. She went with him, and Messalina smiled at my father, as if to suggest revenge for his earlier rejection.

"Then my mother returned, just a short time later and went to my father. Caligula returned, enraged, and ordered both my mother and father to leave and never return. It seems that my mother, fearing such danger, had brought with her a medicine and when she and Caligula went toward the inner chamber, she took the medicine without his noticing. A few moments later, as he was preparing to remove her clothes, the medicine had its effect and she began violently to vomit. She vomited on his hands, over his body and all about the floor. The stench was overwhelming and Caligula was terrified. He was disgusted by vomit and could not abide even the slightest unpleasant odor.

"Our parents were dismissed and thought themselves safe, or so they thought. But Messalina's hunger for revenge did not abate and years later, after the murder of Asiaticus, decided to protect her new possession and settle a score. A false charge was brought against our father. Emperor Claudius was too feeble in character to resist his wife's insistent wheedling. He allowed the charge to proceed and found our father guilty. Narcissus, the emperor's most trusted assistant and friend to our family, persuaded the emperor to extend clemency to the family. So only our father was to commit suicide. We were spared."

For a time, she looked at me, trying to understand. In the fields and sheepfolds of her farm, such stories must seem the stuff of unreal night visions.

"And what became of your mother? And Messalina?"

"Our mother lived a few years after our father died. At the end, she walked the halls all night, talking to him." Perhaps, I thought, that is where Lucius learned talking to an absent loved one before sleep.

"And as for Messalina, she gambled and lost. All the years of her debauchery, she risked being discovered by Claudius. After all, when you are unfaithful to the emperor, it is not just adultery; it is treason. But she continued, year after year. She had affairs with nobles, slaves, gladiators, foreign nobles, traders, actors, mule drivers. She organized orgies for licentious noble women. She even challenged the leading whore of Rome to a contest to see how many men each could service in a night. Messalina won, servicing 25 men.

"But then she went too far. While Claudius was out of town, she actually married another man, whom she planned to make emperor, somehow. Narcissus found out, informed Claudius, who was reluctant to believe what everyone in the empire knew, but he was finally persuaded.

"Happily though, our family had a strange measure of revenge. Messalina, knowing her hours were numbered and death was fast approaching, fled to her most prized place, the Gardens of Lucullus. There she spent her last hours and when the soldiers arrived, she was there, in the garden, a dagger poised at the breast, which so many men and women had caressed, unable to stab herself. The centurion sent to see to her death saw her hesitation. He drove the blade home and died. She lost what she killed our father to gain. And the grass grew over her spilled blood and the Gardens returned to their unspoiled beauty."

As the sun moved higher in the sky and the sounds of the mid day meal began, she turned to me as we left the rail to eat our separate meals.

"Tychon, did Messalina's death bring your father back? Or bring peace to your heart?"

I offered no reply.

As I ate my meal alone, I recalled the history I had recounted. So much blood and waste and treachery. Sometimes memories lift up. These bore down a hundred weight, sad in their time, decades in their consequences. And I considered the Gardens, spores of deadly flowers floating down the years to threaten us. How good to be rid of that danger.

I spent the rest of the day alone, writing and staring over the water. After dinner, as the light began to turn to dusk, I put my writings away and put aside visions of beautiful girls bringing sweet meats to me in a garden of flowers.

The storm hit us at dusk.

Dinner was over and I was reading when the door to our cabin opened. The captain was shadowed in the dim light.

"Tribune, you may want to alert your soldiers. A storm approaches."

He was a short man, surprisingly corpulent for a man of the sea, with a graying beard, heavy brows and muscular short arms. His eyes were watery and vague, as if he had seen many threats and discounted most.

"A storm? This seems just a slight breeze."

Lucius stood up from his desk, a worried look in his eyes.

"It is not the breeze alone, Tribune. It is the smell." He saw our puzzlement. "A good storm can be smelled when it is quite far away. And this one has a strong smell. Have your men secure their belongings and the horses and have them be prepared to help out our crew. I will signal the other ships."

He turned and left without waiting for a response, calling crew members to him. Others were moving among the passengers. Their pale and frightened reactions reflected their reactions. Lucius turned to me and spoke, one dread replaced by another.

"I can't believe it, Tychon."

"What can't you believe, Lucius?"

"A storm," he said, speaking through gritted teeth, "a storm. This ship. Now. Us in a storm! The captain assured me we would have a calm voyage." His tone rose.

"He was wrong," I added unnecessarily.

He left the cabin and went to the centurion, Gaius Entellus. As they talked, I looked to the north. The clear skies had vanished and been replaced with something grey and wide, like a cover drawn over the sea and being pulled toward us. A gust of wind carried a coldness that had not been there before.

Over the next hour, the ship was alive with activity. The crewmembers pulled the mizzenmast down and stowed it. The ship's boat, bobbing along behind us in increasingly choppy water, was brought aboard and stowed. Deck covers for sleeping were stowed. Hatches were secured and loose cable coiled and put away. Below decks, the horses began to whinny and snort as they sensed the coming storm and rebelled. Tourists secured their belongings and began to huddle together.

Strangely the Christians did little at first. Gathering, they prayed and then went among the tourists, in groups of two, speaking quietly to them. They had few belongings to secure but after doing so, they acted very much as they had before, neither hurrying nor lingering.

At one point, I turned to look at the storm. It was much closer now and I could see it was going to be a big one, like the one Lucius and I met so many years ago on our way to Britannia and which laid him low for three days after it was over. That had been the storm that taught us that we could never approach a voyage without fear. Now it was as if the disturbance in our life had called its twin from the air to strike us. So much for the captain's divination.

At one point, as the ship began to wallow slightly in the waves, Sophia appeared at my side.

"Will this be a bad storm?" Her mouth was uncertain and I saw fear in her eyes.

"Nothing we cannot handle." I hoped my tone was reassuring. "This is a large boat and they do well in rough seas."

A strong gust pushed her back from the rail. She grabbed it with white fingers.

"Aren't you afraid?" She looked most earnest and almost embarrassed, pleading.

"Of course, we all are, but we persist. A good ship and a good crew are our best security."

"And God's mercy," she said.

"Yes, and that," I said without thinking. And wondered why I had said it.

She was silent for a moment, trying to look at the storm. It had now changed from a cover of grey rolling toward us. It now had slender dark clouds like fingers, reaching toward us, seeking to grasp us. Its knuckles flexed, reaching to grasp the sky and pull itself toward us, hungry and unrelenting. It wanted to clutch us and crush the feeble wood that was our hull and shatter our masts and rigging and sweep all of us into the sea and kill every man, woman and animal on board. I hoped she did not see that, or my face. She moved against my side, perhaps from cold or the shifting deck, then pulled away.

"Can you answer a question I have? A silly question."

"Yes."

"Why are the people who are travelers with us putting on jewelry? The women are putting on broaches and necklaces and fine gold. And the men are putting on jeweled rings. In a storm why would they do such a thing?"

Her curiosity at such a time was strange, and sweet.

I was not sure I should tell the truth. But it was impossible to lie to her.

"There is a custom to do such a thing in a storm. If one is swept overboard and dies, or if a ship is destroyed and all die, the gold may persuade that man who finds the body to give it a proper burial."

I looked to see her reaction. There was no fear, just a firm mouth.

"So bribery continues even after death," she said to herself.

We said little more and she rejoined the women prisoners and they stood silently, their lips moving with no sound.

Soon the storm was upon us. A heavy rain cut us off from all the other ships and we could see nothing beyond the rail. It was grey, then a darker grey, then black. The ship began to roll from side to side, waves hitting it with increasing fury. Waves washed over the deck and anything poorly secured disappeared over the side. People shrunk down, trying to hide from the onslaught. Others stood clasping the rail or a mast or anything that seemed secure. The numbers on deck were smaller than before and I wondered how welcoming the horses below decks were to guests. The wind was unrelenting, gusting first from one quarter, then another. Crewmembers were frantically moving about at the captain's shouted orders. The pilot turned one tiller, then another, trying to keep the storm behind us, but the ship kept shifting abeam and the storm would hit us from the starboard side until he tried again to move the ship.

I had wrapped my crippled arm with a rigging rope near the cabin and hung on with my good arm and watched as Lucius desperately tried to go about the deck to direct the soldiers helping the crew. He would move from one group to another giving encouragement and then would suddenly lurch away, stand quite still, then rush to grasp the rail or a rope and try to gain his strength to continue. I could not help him. No one could, or tried. He would clasp the rail with a desperate hold, wretch over the side, some of the vomit borne back on him, and then sag for a moment. Then he would pull himself erect and move, more slowly now, to another group of soldiers. After what was perhaps an hour of such increasingly feeble efforts, he was at the rail again, bent over, his head lolling on his shoulders. He had been there for some time and did not seem to be moving at all, unable to straighten when a dark figure moved to his side. Perhaps something was said but as the wind was screaming, I could hear nothing. Then the figure put his arm around Lucius and putting Lucius' arm over his shoulder, circled his waist and led him to the cabin. The normally strong Lucius was unable to walk and it was only the powerful arms and shoulders of the other that kept him up. He took him into the cabin and as he came back out, I saw it was Apollos, the Greek whom Lucius had struck at his arrest. He looked at me with a slight smile of encouragement and nodded for me to join Lucius and went away.

When I went inside, I saw Lucius was in a fearsome condition. He was on the bunk, his breastplate removed, his tunic soaked, his hair matted and vomit clinging to his beard. His eyes were closed and his breathing irregular. His face was strained and his involuntary movements indicated he was fighting the urge to wretch, as the small space of the cabin moved with the ship, up and down, side to side, rolling to one side, then the other. As I touched his beard, he flinched. I drew my hand away and saw something mixed with the vomit. Blood. I touched his forehead. It was cold, too cold. I had no skill to help him. I sat beside him and wondered how long a storm he could stand.

The storm had cut us off from the world. There was nothing I could see or know beyond the room, the waves crashing over us, the darkness just beyond the ship. That was our whole world and it was violent and unrelenting. There were no other ships, no islands, no coastlines, nothing except the constricted world of cabin and deck and rigging and frantic effort, and fear. Now the whole vast empire had shrunk down to our cabin and it was like a jail, cutting us off from even the fragile companionship of those on deck.

I tried to offer him water but he turned his head away, feebly. I covered him with a blanket but he still shivered and struggled not to vomit. Then he sat upright, frantically, and I got a jar beneath his chin before he threw up again. There was more blood now.

All this time, Boudicca had been watching me and seemed to be wondering why I was not doing something. I sat there for a long time, thrown back and forth, the ship dropping, then snapping back to smash my arm or back.

Then just as I despaired, the door opened. Timothy entered. He seemed even slighter in the pale light of the cabin, as if he could have been easily blown back to Ephesus by the weakest of these howling gusts. He moved quickly to the bunk.

Timothy stood beside Lucius, looking at him as a father might look at a sleeping son. Then he knelt beside him and began praying. Lucius, pale and shuddering, opened his eyes and looked at him, but whether he recognized him I could not say. Then, as Timothy spoke, he closed his eyes and turned his face to the leaking roof overhead.

"Gracious and eternal father, you have counted our days out as a man counts out gold. You are high above, beyond the storm and the sun. And you are here in this dark and threatening place." His voice dropped to a whisper.

After a few moments, he concluded.

"…You have put him in our path and your spirit is at work in his heart and mind. Shelter him with your wings and show him mercy…"

His words were swallowed by the howling winds. At last, he laid his hands upon the head and shoulder of Lucius, who did not move, then arose, and left. It was a very nice prayer but poor medicine to my suffering brother.

Then the door opened again. The woman Lydia, and the older woman, Claudia, entered. I struggled to my feet, lost my footing and stumbled toward them. Lydia smiled at me, for what reason I knew not.

"May we minister to the Tribune Lucius?" Her tone was gentle and I recognized it.

"What do you wish to do?"

"Make him comfortable and relieve his sickness with some medicines,' she said, gesturing to the bag she was carrying.

I paused for a moment, torn between protecting my brother from people who were his prisoners and a conviction that this woman and her companion were incapable of doing harm to him.

"Go ahead," I said and moved aside. I noticed then that the older woman had a jug of water with her and cloths, torn into long strips. I noticed Boudicca did not seem concerned at their presence.

They moved to Lucius' unmoving form and began their work. Lydia took jars from her bag and finding a cup, poured some liquids in it, added some green herbs from a small pouch and added water. Then raising Lucius' head, she helped him drink. As the cup touched his lips, his eyes opened and seeing their faces, directed a look at me. I nodded. He drank and laid back.

Lydia put her bottles away. The older woman soaked one of the small strips in the jug of water and began wiping his face, cleaning it of the vomit and blood that were in his beard. Then she wet another cloth and put it on his forehead. He did not move. I noticed some slight steam coming from the cloths when she brought them out of the jar. Somehow, in what manner I could not divine, these people had found a way to heat water in a storm.

After several repetitions, giving the medicine, placing cloths on his forehead, Lydia sat on the floor beside the bed and took his nearest hand in hers. She held it gently and looked at it. She stayed that way for a very long time, sometimes closing her eyes, her lips moving but with no sound I could hear over the storm.

The ship continued to roll, the storm roared its anger above us, and the sounds of tortured wood and metal, men moving about, and muffled cries continued. But in the cabin, it was quiet and strangely calm. When the ship twisted, rose and then dropped suddenly, she gripped the bunk rail with her one hand while not letting go of Lucius.

From time to time, they would give him more to drink, then put cloths on his forehead and speak quietly to him. His eyes would flutter and after a few moments, he would breathe deeply and rest. They would resume their places.

As Lydia held his hand and the older woman sat against the wall across from her, appearing to sleep but then moving her lips too, I felt an unexpected peace. It was as if our mother and aunt were truly back and the fanged creatures that haunt a child's dreams were locked out of this place. There were only the four of us and after a while even the sounds from above and below grew fainter.

And so we stayed long hours. The storm did not abate, the night passed and the cries on deck were overtaken by shouts and weeping. Perhaps some had been lost over the side. Perhaps the fear that death is near had been replaced by the terrible prospect of it being at your elbow.

Then a few hours after midnight, the creaking complaints of the hull around us lessened. The cries from outside faded. The boat rolled less, settled more, and I knew the worst was over. I struggled out to the deck and found quiet. As shards of moon light peered between rolling clouds, I could see the devastation. Soldiers, passengers, Christians, crew were scattered about, with no distinction or rank among them. They stood at the rail, they slumped against rigging, but mostly they sat or lay exhausted and drained. There was nothing to say, no words, only the slackening wind and the chilling cold. I went back to the cabin and stayed the rest of the night with Lucius and the women. Lucius was asleep.

The soft whispering of Lydia was the last sound I heard as I fell asleep and the first sound when I awoke.

Chapter 10　　The Market

The morning was as lovely and peaceful as the night had been horrible and dangerous. As I woke, I found Lucius awake but still. He was pale, his voice a whisper.

"The ship? Men?"

"I don't know. Do you want me to have Gaius Entellus report to you?"

He breathed deeply, closed his eyes and then opened them again.

"A few moments, then send him." He closed his eyes again.

I turned to go and then saw that Lydia and Claudia were standing at the door, their pots and medicines and cloths in their arms. I accompanied them to the deck.

I took Lydia's hand in mine, her wrist still carrying the red welt from her chains. It was the same hand that had held Lucius in the storm.

"I thank you for your care of my brother."

She smiled and squeezed my hand. I nodded to her friend, Claudia, extending a smile of gratitude to her.

"I have never seen anyone get so violently ill in a storm," she said, her voice touched by amazement. "He will need several days to get his strength back and should eat only bread for a time. No olives, no cheese and no meat. If you wish I can prepare a simple meal for him. But the worst for him is over."

I thought how wrong she was. As they moved to rejoin their group, Claudia hitched up a moment to regain her footing on the slippery deck and as she did, my aunt's profile reappeared, long gone and here, and reaching into tomorrow.

The ship was damaged heavily from the storm. Rigging was tossed about and torn, the main sail ripped, the railing smashed in places, shelter cloth scattered and unusable, and the ship's boat smashed beyond repair. Some of the passengers were wandering about, dazed and distracted. Others sat on the deck, staring blankly. The prisoners were in their usual groups, circled and silent. The captain, whose manner seemed no different in calm than in storm, was moving about, checking the condition of the ship and giving instructions to the crew. Seeing me, he pulled away from a crewman and came to me.

"Quite a blow, Tychon. Praise Poseidon he did no worse. A stout ship and a good crew." He smiled as if the storm's end and the strength of the ship was his personal achievement. "How is the tribune? I understand he does not endure these storms well."

"None of us do, I think. But he is recovering and if you want, I shall report to him any message you have."

"Tell him our ship is damaged but not seriously. We shall have sail again in a few hours and will set out to find the rest of our ships. The storm scattered us and we need to reform. That may take one or two days."

Still more delay.

"Was anyone lost?"

"No, none. Zeus was most kind." I wondered if the captain was always so inclusive of the gods to avoid their displeasure. He was not naming Hera, Hermes or any of the other Olympians. I supposed he would be sure to include them in later conversations with others.

I sought Gaius Entellus to communicate Lucius' instructions. He nodded and proceeded below to check on the horses. Later he came back and said two horses were dead, one having been so frightened it was thrown about and smashed its head and the other simply fell over, terror killing it. Their cavalry riders would be dragging their bodies topside later and throwing them overboard. I suggested that he visit Lucius in a few hours and brief him.

I went back toward the cabin but a hand stopped me. It was Timothy, with Apollos alongside him.

"How is the tribune Lucius?"

"Weak but well, thanks to the one called Lydia and her friend Claudia. I did not know what to do but they were most kind."

"Lydia is a fine woman," Apollos quickly asserted.

"I could not agree more," I said. "I am doubly in her debt, for the medicine she gave me at Ephesus and for my brother."

Apollos stared at me and his deep voice seemed softened.

"You would not have needed the medicine at Ephesus if you had not…" He stopped when Timothy laid a hand on his arm.

"God was merciful to us last night, Tychon " Timothy said. "No lives were lost and the ship can be repaired. We will pray we can find our other friends soon and that they are safe."

"Our good teacher Seneca once said, 'You learn to know a pilot in a storm.' That was surely the case last night. We have a good captain." I offered the thought cheerfully but saw in Timothy's eyes that he knew as well as I that Seneca had been speaking of a very different kind of storm.

I smiled, seeing Sophia coming toward us, smiling at us. Timothy and Apollos turned and saw her. Timothy smiled, Apollos glared, and both left. She joined me and we walked to the rail. I looked at her and saw her hair matted and still damp. Her dress was wet and her eyes tired.

"How are you, Sophia?"

"Better now, Tychon. I felt like the storm was trying to beat through the ship to get at me. It seemed personal. I felt anger from it. And then I felt it did not care at all what it was doing to us, as if we were nothing to it." She shuddered at recalling.

"Storms are like that. Sometimes it helps to remember they will end. That nothing like them is permanent."

She looked at me shyly.

"I would have liked it if you could have been with us to tell us that, Tychon. Your words would have comforted me."

My words failed. For a while I was mute and then began to talk to her of other things.

The rest of that day was taken up with repairing the ship, even the ship's boat, which wondrously was made seaworthy after the work of the ship's carpenter and crew. At the end of the day, the ship was underway and before nightfall, two of our squadron were located, but not the other large cargo ship carrying the rest of our soldiers and the other prisoners.

The next day we were underway, heading to Delos, our next stop. It would normally have been a long day's journey from where the gale hit us but the storm blew us south and it was two days before we saw land. By that time the rest of our fleet had joined us, except for the transport of our people.

Lucius was rapidly recovering, moving about, taking meals and talking to the soldiers and the captain. It was only in the cabin, as we were about to sleep, that I saw his exhaustion. He was pale in the light of the lamp and sighed deeply as he collapsed in his bunk. The last night before we reached Delos, he spoke to me before falling asleep.

"Tychon, were you here the entire night of the storm?"

When I responded, he turned to me. "Was she here through the night?"

"All night, holding your hand and praying for you."

He turned to the ceiling and said in a low voice, "Why did she do it, Tychon? She had no reason to help me. We are taking her to a sentence of horrible death. Why did she help me? Does she not know what awaits her in Rome?"

"She knows, Lucius."

"Then why?" He looked down for a time and finally sighed, a deep, long sigh. "Tychon, can I give her over? Such kindness toward an enemy does not merit death. When I would open my eyes, I saw our mother and our aunt. I felt her hand on mine and I could not speak. How can I…?"

A terrible dilemma was forming in his mind and he was just beginning to see its silhouette.

The next day we put in at Delos. A bustling port, with many ships and a busy dock, Delos was a port I had never liked and I avoided going ashore when I had the misfortune to stop there. Its temples to Isis, Hera and Dionysius were said to be beautiful. The Temple of the Delaines was reported as a classic example of Greek building. And the twelve marble lions lining the Sacred Way to the temple of Apollo brought visitors from across the empire. But I never went ashore. Even on board I could feel the misery the city held, defacing the beauty of her temples.

Our ships dropped anchor just outside the harbor entrance and we were delighted that our other transport was already there. Strabo came across and reported to Lucius, who was largely recovered, that they too had been stricken by the storm but had suffered casualties.

"The *secarii* were unchained on my instructions," he explained, "to help with the anchor. When they were finished, while I was working with the captain to bring down the main mast, they grabbed the soldiers nearest them and tried to jump overboard with them." He paused. "Three succeeded. They went overboard, the legionaries with them. Two were cut down. The rest were subdued and are in chains."

Lucius stared at Strabo. Lucius and I had served with his father and brother in the II Augustus in Gaul and Britannia. There was no finer family of soldiers in the empire. But Lucius had to be sure.

"There was no alternative to unchaining them?"

"None, Tribune," Strabo responded. "Everyone was engaged trying to save the ship, passenger and legionary alike."

"All right then, Strabo. Return to your men. You are a good soldier."

As he reached the door, Strabo turned.

"One more thing, sir. A small thing."

"Yes?"

"The *secarii* leader, Simon, the one you spoke to on the road to Ephesus. After he was struck down while trying to wrestle a weapon from a legionary, he lay bleeding. He motioned to me. I bent over to hear. He said, 'Tell the tribune I have seen again the dark haired beauty in the fire, the one struck by lightning. She stepped from the fire, her throat bleeding, tried to speak a word and then vanished. Tell the Tribune.'"

Lucius looked closely at Strabo and said nothing.

When Strabo left, I went topside and watched him make his way back to his ship. As I stood at the rail, Sophia joined me.

"What is this island, Tychon?"

"Delos."

"And what is it famous for? Mathematicians? Philosophers?" Her tone was teasing.

"Nothing so ordinary as great thinkers. It is said the god Apollo was born here. And the goddess Artemis also."

"Gods born here?" Her look was surprise and dismay mixed. "Do people still believe that? Do you?" Her question was laced with fear.

"Do you not believe your God was born in some miserable Judean village?"

She said nothing. My tone had been harsh.

"See those ships and skiffs bringing them to shore, Sophia? Filled with pilgrims going the temples of Apollo and Artemis. They believe. And they come from very long distances to worship. Gold enters the port in their purses and stays when they leave."

"And you?"

"I do not believe. It has been many years since I believed. Now it is too late for me to believe much of anything."

"You are wrong, Tychon. You may know much about many things but you are wrong in that. No one is too old, or too bitter, or too lost to believe. Our Lord came for the old, the bitter, and the lost. There are many sheep whom He seeks."

"Even those sheep?" I gestured toward the several large transports at the dock. She looked at the ships and then at me.

"Who are they?"

"Slavers, Sophia. They bring thousands of slaves to this place. They buy slaves. They sell them. Storms do not stop them. Famine does not stop them. Wars do not stop them. In fact, wars are good for them. Wars bring captives and captives become slaves. Every army has slavers following it, along with the prostitutes and thieves. As soon as the last body falls in battle, the slavers are there, buying the vanquished from the victor and whole cities and tribes from their officers. The victorious soldier sells his captured opponent and pockets the money and the slaver leaves the battlefield with hundreds, thousands of slaves. And most of them come here, to be sold and traded." As I heard my words, I felt a deep sadness within and did not know why.

"Are there so many here?" Her voice seemed so innocent.

"In this port, as many as ten thousand slaves have been sold in a day."

She was silent and then I looked at her. Her eyes were moist.

"So much suffering." She said no more and left to rejoin her prisoners.

As she spoke to Timothy, he nodded. Certainly he had seen this port before and knew it. He put his hand on her shoulder. Then he spoke to the one called Barnabas. Soon they were gathered in a circle and I heard the low hum of their prayers.

As I wondered if these people did anything but pray, my attention was drawn to a ship's boat approaching us. A young man climbed aboard our boat, sought out the centurion, gave him a message and returned to his boat. Gaius Entellus took the message to the cabin.

I walked over to the soldiers playing dice on the deck and watched for a while. The sun was lower in the sky and the fragrance of dinner being prepared reminded me that I had not eaten all day. Before I could identify the smell, something passed by me to the other side of the ship. Someone I did not want to see.

The barber had just exited our cabin. I left the game and quickly found Lucius in the cabin.

Inside, the light was strangely faint, the wick struggling to illumine. Lucius was sitting in his chair, behind his table. Maps were spread before him but he was not looking at them. A cup of wine was near his hand but he did not touch it. In his hand was a letter. He held it loosely. He was staring at something far off, much as he had when we sat beside the road, watching the horse die. This time his eyes were narrow.

Minutes passed before I spoke.

"I saw the barber leaving."

He said nothing. Leaving Caesarea in Judea, he had let his beard grow, as was his custom when not in battle. Now, many weeks later, the beard was gone.

His eyes came back from that far place, as the sound of a horse whinnying below deck seemed to call to him. He looked at me as if I had just entered the room and then he looked at the paper and then back at me.

"News, my brother. News from home." His voice was low.

"Bad news, Lucius?"

"Bad news, Tychon." He paused.

I moved toward him but he gestured to stop me.

"Lucius, what is it?"

He threw the message on the table.

"They are taken, Tychon. All of them, Julia, Antonius, the servants, the workers. Arrested. Marched away in chains to Rome. Beatrice, Callimachus, and the children of our servants." He stopped before naming Julia again. His lips started to form her name but he could not finish.

"When? Who?"

"Weeks ago. How long I don't know. This message has been waiting for us for some time." His tone was impatient, frustrated. "Who? Tigellinus' men, of course. Two dozen men came at dusk and gathered them all up. Some informer told Tigellinus there were Christians at our estate and he sent his men to deliver them up to Nero for…"

He could not continue. He slumped back into the chair.

I felt as I did back at the temple courtyard. I stood, unable to speak "So, now, Lucius...?

He looked at me with a cold smile. His voice was tired.

"Now, Tychon, we have no choice. There is no going back, only ahead. I will follow our original plan after making a few changes." He looked at the map on the table and pointed at cities with his penknife.

"We proceed to Corinth, then to Italy. We will go to Rome, the prisoners along with me, not so many as we have now. We shall send some back to Ephesus. We will take a smaller force of legionaries. We will go to our estate and then Rome. Then to the palace and the emperor."

His voice was flat, as if reading from a document he had seen too many times.

"Why send prisoners back, Lucius?"

"The plan I had will not work. I had planned to stop their arrests but now they are in chains. By the time we get there, Nero will have executed some or all of those he captured. I will not be able to save the dead. I may be able to save survivors if I can get to the emperor. And the Christians are my way to get to him. But I do not want us encumbered by so many prisoners. We can move more quickly with fewer and I do not want any distractions when we meet with the emperor."

I sat down. His eyes did not meet mine. In the silence, I understood. The storm had undone him. Soon he would find an excuse to release all the Christians.

"Tychon," he said, stroking the long deep scar on his bare cheek, "if my Julia is gone, then this plan is the only one I care to pursue. We must move quickly. Nero has butchered thousands and the rabid dog will not resist torturing and burning a few more. But if the threat of Galba does not slow him and if we are too late, I must then only get in the same room with Nero and his executioner, Tigellinus."

He met my question with dark eyes.

"Then, Tychon, I shall slit the throat of Tigellinus and Nero, I will gut like a pig."

Rome's relationship with Greece was an uneasy one, resenting it even as it envied it. For hundreds of years, Greece had been the master of the Mediterranean, establishing colonies in Asia, Africa and even in our lands. Its learning was the inspiration and guide to Rome's own meager efforts at philosophy and the arts. Its gods were stolen, given different names, and its dramas overshadowed our pitiful efforts.

So Rome resented Greece, even as it envied it. Romans bought Grecian art, drank Grecian wine and brought Grecian tutors to teach their children. And Rome always secretly feared Greece's sense of superiority might just be grounded in fact.

When Rome finally achieved dominance over Greece (I trust, Pausanias, your teachers have thoroughly instructed you in that part of your heritage), it was to assert an authority and mastery that would finally banish all fears of inferiority. And when Thebes was destroyed and Corinth burned to the ground, Rome's pride and power were on full display.

Years later, of course, Julius Caesar rebuilt Corinth, in the months just before his assassination. The new Corinth, like the new Carthage, rose from the ashes of an old enemy and was laid out in the orderly and regular way that was the mark of Roman order and reason. Greece might spawn new ideas but Rome had no equal in ordering the world.

But Corinth was the essential port of call for any shipping, as its isthmus cut days off travel time to Italy. Neither Lucius nor I had spent much time in Corinth, preferring Athens, with its crooked streets and beautiful art and ancient monuments, to the commercial and licentious smell of Corinth.

But haste was essential; so Corinth was our gateway of speed to Italy.

Our ships repaired and the fleet reassembled, we set out and two days later, Corinth came into view, its shining white outline on the horizon. I was wakened by the captain's boisterous voice rousting his crew to work and soon, all hands were busy.

Of all the port towns on the sea, Corinth required more preparation than any other. In addition to the usual tasks of pulling down the deck covers and stowing them, securing sails, retrieving the small boat and bringing it on board, there were the additional duties caused by the need to transport the ship across the isthmus.

We would arrive in Cenchreae, the port on the east side of the isthmus, in the Saronic Sea. The boat would be unloaded of all excess weight that could be easily moved and then it would be pulled from the water by massive hoists onto rollers to be hauled down the Diolkos, the paved road, to the port of Lechaeum on the west side of the isthmus where it would be deposited back in the water and fully reloaded and depart. Of course, the size of the boat, its weight and the difficulty it presented in being hauled the miles from one port to the other determined how much the Corinthians collected in fees. A captain had to balance the need to reduce costs by providing a lighter boat against the time and effort to unload and reload cargo and passengers.

In this matter, the captain was somewhat annoyed by the instructions Lucius gave. The prisoners were not to disembark, nor were their jailors. The horses below also were to stay onboard, along with their attendants. Tourists could disembark and enjoy the shopping for the famous black Corinthian pottery or seek the tender caresses of a temple prostitute at the Temple of Aphrodite, but their lightening of the load would be minimal. The captain would not enjoy quite so much profit as he expected and his look was dark and reproachful.

As the pilot boat came alongside, Lucius gestured to me. I came over to him and found him with Strabo. They had been talking but had finished when I came up.

"Tychon, Strabo will get off with us. He will go to the other ships as they come in and get reports on their status after he instructs them to keep prisoners and legionaries on board."

Shortly we found ourselves in one of the first of the small boats that removed the passengers. As we prepared to depart, I looked back at the ship. At the rail, alongside Lydia, Sophia caught my look and smiled. Her hand came up in a quick wave. I had not spoken to her for several days and I realized how much I missed the sound of her voice. I imagined she looked quite sad as we pulled to the dock.

"Where are we going, brother?"

"We will visit the provincial governor, who is here, and then get a drink at a tavern nearby."

As we walked to Corinth, the sun grew warmer in the cloudless sky, the hard paving stones of this most Roman of roads growing hotter, the air still and stifling, I realized Lucius was returned to that state which was his from the day we left Caesarea. He was confident, all doubt gone. He was measured, not hurrying when nothing was to be done, and quick when action was needed. His plan, however much he doubted before, was now firmly fixed. We passed over the wide and marbled streets to the governor's palace. It was situated near the center of town and was surrounded on all sides of its high walls by the offices of merchants and lenders and shippers who bought and sold all the wealth that flowed through this port. It was a river of gold that they ladled from one port to the other and they grew wealthy by skimming just a small part of glistening cup. I saw them move about in the shade of their porticoes, waving paper and contracts before buyers and sellers and captains. Their voices were demanding, bodies fat and sweating, fingers glistening with ruby rings and golden bracelets. These were not Romans; they had the stench of eastern luxury.

As I watched them, I wondered if any thousand of them could begin to match the wealth of our ancestor, General Lucullus. He spent more on a single banquet for two dozen of his friends than most of these men would make in their lifetime. Even in our reduced circumstance, as Lucius had given away millions of sesterces and thousands of acres of land to impoverished veterans, we had a great deal of that wealth. But our family was Roman to the core and not given to the luxury and ostentation that was the great blot on our ancestor's memory.

I was brought from my reverie by the voice of Lucius calling to me. He was coming from the governor's palace with a clutch of paper in his hand. He shoved them into his dispatch case and began walking quickly down the street.

When I caught up to Lucius, he rounded a corner and moved quickly to a tavern a short distance away. We entered its shadowed door and came into a cool and dark room. Tables were set about and the room was filled with smells of wine and beer and food, fresh bread and meat. These were smells I welcomed. I was Roman enough to favor bread as the staple of our meals but unlike most Romans, I enjoyed meat as more than just an occasional supplement to bread.

We sat down and Lucius looked around, searching.

"Who are we waiting for, brother?"

"A messenger," he replied.

"What of the messages you got from the governor?"

"Official messages, no more. Messages from Rome on the arrival of our prisoners, sent by administrators charged with such things. Messages from the ports and from the military authorities instructing us on feed for our horses and accommodations for our soldiers. And of course, your favorite, the *act diurna*."

He brought three issues of the *act* from his case and shoved them across the table at me as he gestured for wine. I had missed reading the *act*, the newspaper welcomed in every Roman camp across the empire. The last issue of the army newspaper I had read had been at Antioch, on the road to Ephesus. A soldier gets used to having that paper in camp and its fresh editions every few days provided reading for every soldier across the empire. I read each of its parts eagerly, even its reports of weddings, funerals, births and traffic jams in Rome, but like most soldiers I read its sporting reports with the greatest interest. The Greens were continuing to dominate in the chariot races but I continued to hope the Reds would finish the season strong. Avarus the young gladiator who so raised the color of Roman wives easily bested a pitiful opponent in his last match, having to kill the opponent when the crowd booed lustily for the loser's death. Strangely the report said nothing about Nero approving the death. It was not like him to be absent. I checked the dates; these papers were more than 10 days old.

After a time, we finished our wine and ordered another. Then another. Finally we ordered food and while I enjoyed some roasted lamb with grapes, Lucius ordered only some figs and bread. I could not bring myself to be so sternly Roman in the land of my birth.

An hour later, the messenger arrived. I recognized him but did not know his name. He gave Lucius an embrace, deposited his messages with him and then went to a corner where he sat and waited, ordering beer and bread.

Lucius opened the message and read it. In the dimness of the room, his color rose and there was a sharp intake of breath. He read the message again. Then he put it down and looked upward, eyes shadowed and unclear. I pushed my plate away and waited. What new shock was there?

We sat there in silence for a long time. I refilled my beer and waited. The owner took our plates away and I waited. The messenger in the corner had another beer and I waited. And Lucius was silent, eyes closed, not moving. Beyond, the sounds of the street seemed to dwindle. At last, I must have made a noise. Lucius looked up at me, opened his mouth and then spoke in a whisper.

"The emperor is dead."

The air seemed not to be moving and the wood of the table seemed insubstantial. I came to understand that I had not heard wrongly.

I had known the death of Tiberius, forgotten on his island of debauchery. I had known the death of Caligula, a time of rejoicing at a mad dog put down. I had known the death of Claudius, unsurprising and just. But this death was unlike those and I did not know it meant.

"How? When? Why have we not heard before?" My voice seemed a shout in the dark place.

"Suicide. The Senate declared him an enemy of the people and he stabbed himself in the throat. And the news has just arrived, on a boat just come to harbor. The word is spreading quickly through the city. Soon we will be awash in people and talk and rumors and endless confusion."

He looked about him and following his eyes, I saw the figures in the darkness of the tavern were growing in number and noise. Voices were rising, whispers punctuating the pauses, drink flowing.

"Just like that?"

"No, General Galba is marching on Rome and Nero's enemies found the courage to flee him. He was alone and the Senators, those sniveling dogs, finally found enough courage to condemn him."

"The miserable beast deserved much worse, Lucius. I would gladly have seen his skin peeled and his body boiled."

He did not answer.

Then he rose and moved quickly to the messenger and they talked quietly. Lucius' back was to me and I could not hear nor see the interchange, as the messenger's face was in shadow.

My mind blank, I chewed the meat without tasting it. The wine was tasteless. All I could see was the face of my dead wife. Would I be joining her soon?

After a time, Lucius returned. He picked up a piece of bread and began to chew it, ripping pieces off with his teeth.

"This changes nothing, Tychon. The chaos before is certain to be greater now. We can exploit that for our purpose. We merely have to locate the prisoners and free them."

"'Merely?'"

"Tychon, listen." He leaned forward and began tracing the grain on the table, as if he were drawing a map and outlining a battle plan. "There is one man whom we must approach, a man who was Nero's evil twin, encouraging him in killing and torture and rape, a man so greedy and drunk with power that he is fatally vulnerable."

I sighed. The horse was running and I could not dismount.

"Tigellinus."

"Yes, Ofonius Tigellinus. Breeder of horses. Criminal. Violator of women. Bully to those weaker than he. Craven sycophant to those more powerful."

"With Nero dead, there are none more powerful, Lucius. He is the prefect of the Praetorian Guard and that gives him enormous power."

"No, Tychon, you are wrong. You would be right if this were a normal time. But this is not normal. Generals are revolting, the Senate is surely frightened, citizens are confused. Tigellinus would be as powerful as you imagine if the normal order prevailed. But with a new emperor soon to be crowned, Tigellinus has to be careful, very careful, to be on the winning side. And remember, he is co-prefect along with Sabinus. So even the Guard may be split."

"And who is the winning side?"

"It does not matter to us. No one knows. The Senate does not know, the generals do not know, though Galba pictures himself in the palace. Once an emperor is dead and a general is marching on Rome, there are certain to be others who imagine they would look good in the purple."

He paused to drink wine.

"It is a time of chaos, Tychon. And, as I said before, chaos favors us. In this interval, between the death of one emperor and the proclamation of another, there is room for us to move. It will be brief but if we move quickly and remain outside the intrigue, we will be victorious."

"Do you have a plan? A new plan?"

"Soon, Tychon, soon. I think our opponent may be less dangerous than you think." I restrained a laugh.

As we prepared to leave, Lucius went to the messenger and spoke to him for several minutes. As we exited into the blazing sunlight, I asked Lucius who the messenger was. He gave me a name.

"And where do I know him from?"

"The farm, brother. He sought our help two years ago. He was being thrown off his land due to debt and we helped him out." He smiled at the memory. "He is now a very good farmer and his family is fed and clothed respectably."

"The Brotherhood."

"Yes, the Brotherhood."

Through the years, on leave at home, in camps on duty, then finally in retirement, Lucius had been a tireless friend of veterans and was always ready to help out someone who had served in the legions. Sometimes they would send a letter asking for help. Often they would show up at the front gate and ask to see him. Sometimes their whole family would come along, women and children and servants and cows and household goods piled into a wagon, like refugees from a battle. In a way, they were refugees and the battle they had lost was to a moneylender, a tax collector or a Senator looking to add another small plot to his vast estate by crushing a small farmer.

Through the years, Lucius had helped them, lending money, giving money, buying back plots of land which were seized, even training some of those who were not very skilled farmers in the ways of successful farming. These veterans, now numbering in the hundreds, were devoted to him. It was said that he could travel anywhere in Italy and most foreign lands and find a meal and a bed within a day's walk.

These men were the *evocati* to the empire, veterans who could be called back into service in time of emergency. To us, they were The Brotherhood, united by the scars of war and the generosity of one of their tribunes. Now he was calling on them for help. And we could not know how much their help would be needed.

As Lucius and I returned to the governor's home, I thought of all the provincial officials who were this day learning of Nero's death. I smiled at the thought. When emperors die, the foundation trembles and many an official feels the ground move.

Welcome to our world, governor of Corinth.

I did not sleep as long as I had hoped. Before the sun rose, Lucius shook me awake and over a breakfast of bread and figs, he sought to explain his plan to me. Lucius' plan seemed to grow as we talked, finding shape and texture.

The plan centered on Tigellinus and his unbounded avarice. He had begun his life as a breeder and seller of horses. He had grown up among horses and was quite skilled in identifying young horses of potential and strength. This skill brought him to Nero's attention, as the emperor was fixated on fame as a charioteer of renown, as well as becoming a great actor and singer of songs. Once imbedded in the royal household, Tigellinus set about encouraging the emperor's degeneracy and devising new forms of debauchery and evil. But throughout, he never lost his love of horses.

Now, Lucius proposed to take advantage of that affection. We would take two horses from the farm, thoroughbreds of the greatest value, to offer to Tigellinus. This was the ploy that would gain us access to him, regardless of the turmoil and uncertainty in Rome.

Once we gained access, Lucius would show him the authorization from Vespasian to conduct business on his behalf, with his full authority. The authorization, meant to be used to convey prisoners to Nero, was most broadly worded and could easily mean whatever the bearer said it was to mean. Such a sweeping conferral of authority spoke of the great trust and affection Vespasian bore toward my brother and now full advantage would be taken of it.

Lucius planned to make a political offer, based upon this authorization, to Tigellinus and when the prisoners were exchanged for the horses, the offer would be concluded. I asked what the offer would be.

When Lucius told me, I was astounded.

"You are going to tell Tigellinus that Vespasian is offering his army in support of Galba's claim to the throne if he can be formally designated Galba's successor to the throne?"

"Yes," Lucius coolly replied.

I sat for a moment, not believing what I heard. Finally, I burst out laughing at the sheer audacity of the strategy.

"Vespasian said no such thing and made no offer!"

Lucius looked at me with slight amusement.

"No he did not but only you and I know that. No one is privy to our meeting and no record of it exists."

"But where is the evidence Vespasian would even contemplate such a move?"

"His armies have pitched camp near Jerusalem and are not attacking. That could surely mean he has other plans, including packing up his army and heading to Italy to either support Galba or meet him in battle."

"Battle? You are going to tell Tigellinus Vespasian is ready to go to war with Galba for the throne?"

"If necessary I will tell him that. More likely I need only leave the offer stand as witness and let his mind and imagination fill in the rest of the implied threat."

"My brother, the whole lie could be exposed by a communiqué sent to Vespasian."

"That would take at least two weeks, Tychon. I will have the prisoners safe and removed long before then. And if Tigellinus learns of the lie later, how can he speak of it without seeming to have joined in a conspiracy to stop Galba ascending the throne. He will have to keep silent.

"And remember, Tychon, an animal like Tigellinus knows only two things: avarice and fear. The gold, the horses, the favor of Vespasian will sate his avarice. And the risk of exposure and the anger of Galba will be enough to stoke his fear. The goad of his greed is sufficient in any case, Tychon. For a man like him, greed is the lever he gives to others. "

"I thought you were going to kill Tigellinus."

"If Julia is harmed, my brother, be assured he will never live to ride those horses."

Silence followed as we ate the meager food sent to our rooms by the governor. I was as unsure of this plan as I had been of the other. But Lucius was convinced of his plan and would not be dissuaded.

Mercifully, we soon took leave of our rooms and went to leave the compound. The governor, a thin, pale and stooped man, hurried to speak with us. He seemed anxious to please and fearful he would fail.

"Have you heard, Tribune?" Lucius nodded. The governor sputtered.

"Rome is afloat in rumors. No one seems to know what is happening, who is in charge. Rumors say Germans are invading, General Galba is at the gates, Nero was killed and not a suicide. His mother's spirit drove him to madness."

"Governor, that last rumor might well be true," I offered, "He killed his mother and her spirit may have come back from the grave to haunt him. You have heard how he arranged for her bed to collapse and kill her and when that failed he put her in a boat designed to come apart when she was on it and when she swam to shore, he had her killed with a sword. She told her executioner 'Smite this womb.' Perhaps he began to feel that sword pierce him at night, or perhaps he saw his bed's canopy about to drop on him. A mother's hatred can reach beyond the grave, governor. There is much danger in the dark."

My words had the desired effect. He grew paler in the bright sun and more stooped, as if seeking to avoid a blow. Lucius was looking at me with annoyance at my malice. We both knew the governor was a placeholder, a weakling who could never be relied upon in a crisis. He was known as a corrupt man who left his mother to live in misery in order to pretend he came from nobility. My placing a maternal ghost at his elbow would certainly cause him to flinch even more quickly today. I enjoyed my tormenting but I did not have time to enjoy it further. We departed quickly and left the governor to stand in the courtyard sun, glancing about nervously at the shade.

We said nothing as we walked to the port. At our arrival, the centurions were shuttling the prisoners out of their enclosure and removing chains. There was a hum of conversation and the legionaries were relaxed. Laughter, which seemed out of place on board ship, now broke out among the Christians as they embraced one another, began praying together in groups of twos and threes and in some cases, dashed from the dock to the streets beyond.

Strabo approached Lucius and asked about the remaining *secarii*. Lucius told him they would be conducted back to Judea under guard and Vespasian could decide their fate.

After several hours, the centurions and soldiers completed their work. Two centuries of legionaries prepared to return to Judea. The third century, a little less than 80 men, as well as 20 cavalry, gathered their belongings and equipment and moved to the one ship that we would take home. Surprisingly, Lucius directed that the centurion Gaius Metellus join Strabo in accompanying us. When I asked why we were taking an extra centurion, Lucius merely smiled.

Unshackled and released, most of the prisoners had left the dock but a few lingered near the gate, talking in low tones. Lucius went over to them and a long conversation ensued. At one point, the conversation stopped and for a moment there was silence. Then a single word was spoken and the conversation resumed.

I went aboard ship and to the cabin. I brought out my favorite wine and sat on the deck, in a chair the captain usually occupied. I looked at the sun, beginning its slow decline, and wondered how many more settings I would witness. The wine was unmixed and added to my darkness. Thus it was that I did not notice her approach.

Her hand touched my arm.

"Are you so very lonely?"

I looked at her and frowned. "Lonely?"

"Just you and the wine bottle. No time with your brother or those you have traveled with."

"Sophia, I am often alone. Even when with people." I drank deeply from the bottle. "It is not so very bad to be alone."

"It is a very bad thing, Tychon. God did not mean for us to be alone. Alone is unnatural. Alone is cut off. Alone is death."

"No, young one, death is death. Alone is just a whisper of death."

She said no more and I drank again.

"I have enjoyed talking to you, Sophia. You are a bright flower in this place. You were headed for a dark place and now you are free. Go ashore and regain your life. You are well out."

"Well out of what, Tychon?"

"Well out of where we are going. We are going to a dark place, with much danger. It is likely we will not come out of it alive. You are well out."

"I am not well out, Tychon." She smiled and her smile irritated me.

"You will go home, work your farm and raise your sheep. You will be very far away from the death and the darkness."

"You are wrong, Tychon, very wrong. I am not going home. Not yet."

The wine bottle stopped midway to my lips.

"I am going with you."

"No, no, you may not go with me," I shouted, struggling to my unsteady feet, my voice more squeak than roar. "I don't give you permission to come with me, with us. Go home."

She smiled and took the wine bottle from my hand and dropped it over the side.

"I do not need your permission. I am simply going to Rome. I am free to go wherever I please. Your brother said so. And I choose to go to Rome. I am writing my brother to tell him I am safe and going to Rome for a time. He can take care of the farm. While I am in Rome."

"You are insane. A girl alone in Rome. Never been there. Doesn't know the city. No money. Confusion and danger all about. In the middle of a civil war. No one to protect you. You are insane." I found it a trial to stand and slumped to the deck.

"I will have protection, Tychon. I will not be alone."

"Oh yes, your god will protect you." I sneered and glanced about for another wine bottle. There was none.

"Yes, he will certainly protect me. But some of the others will also."

"What?" I asked. My mind seemed clouded.

"Tychon, I am not going alone. Several of us are going to take ship with you and your brother for Rome tomorrow. Timothy and Apollos and Claudia and Barnabas and Lydia and…"

She stopped and looked at me. I tried to speak.

"You all are free and you are going to Rome, where we were taking you as prisoners? You are mad! Why?"

"Timothy and the others have business there. And there are prisoners to be freed. The ones I understand you are searching for. They will be sold and dispersed in Rome if we do not save them from the slaver who took them.

"And Timothy has work to do there, and Apollos will be visiting the believers in Rome, and Lydia has business to conduct, and Barnabas will be…"

I raised my hand to stop her exhilaration. She ignored me and continued.

"It's all being arranged now, Tychon. Timothy and the brothers and Lydia and the others will all be coming with you. Your brother has agreed and there is no problem with it. I look forward to spending more time with you." She paused, a disapproving look shaping her lips. "But I do ask you show more restraint in your drinking. Your time is better spent."

I heard the voice of a long-dead wife in the reproof and shivered briefly in the warm twilight. As I drifted off to sleep on the hard warm deck, I felt the whisper of a dead carpenter and the warm words of a woman mingle with the night breeze. And I was at ease with the prospect of tomorrow, where the long fingers of a thousand yesterdays awaited.

Chapter 12   The Farm

The next few days were uneventful. The three ships in our squadron had no military escorts, those having returned with the main fleet to Judea with liberated Christians, Jewish revolutionaries in chains, and soldiers no doubt wondering why they were returning to that desert without having tasted the pleasures of home

I kept away from Sophia. Her smiling serenity irritated me and I found myself wanting to drink more when confronted with her remorseless intent to make me a moral person. She was a builder in search of an edifice and my sharp edges resisted the chisel.

So I took refuge in my books. First, it was Cato but his stern and Spartan character made me shudder. So I turned to the biography of Cincinnatus, the legendary hero of ancient Rome. He served twice as dictator, saving the republic from peril and afterwards, each time, he returned to farming. I cast him aside as too noble for my low mood.

At last, I turned to Pompey. Despite his role in our great grandfather's fall, I had always nursed a grudging admiration for him. He sought throughout his life to recapture his youthful success and fame. Always seeking glory, he finally led his armies against Julius Caesar in a civil war. Defeated in his final battle, he fled to Egypt, thinking to gain the assistance of Cleopatra's brother. Instead, the treacherous Egyptian courtiers sought to curry favor with Caesar and when Pompey's boat touched the shore, they stabbed him to death, in plain view of his beloved wife on the deck of their ship. Thinking to find help, he found death. Small men with narrow eyes and hidden blades now swarmed the man who commanded thousands and fought in desperate battles. I put the scroll away with a shudder.

We passed through two screens of ships, being challenged each time as to our business and where we were going with our hundred soldiers. Each time, Lucius spoke to the officer in charge and taking each aside, told a story that could be supported by our official documents, that we were being sent to protect the new emperor, Galba, from assassins traveling from the edge of the empire. Lucius told them the actual details would be revealed to the Praetorian Guard when we reached Rome. His astounding fabrication was believed and we passed to Puteoli, our destination.

In two hours, ships were unloaded, mounts saddled and we were on the road to our estates. I strained to keep up with Lucius, who drove his horse to run at speed and we left behind us the Christians and the legionaries on foot. Only the cavalry were with us and even they had difficulty keeping up. He ignored my pleading to slow down but I kept up, ignoring the throbbing in my leg.

Finally Lucius came to sudden halt, some few miles from his villa and I nearly ran my horse into his.

He was staring. Smoke, thin and fading like a disappearing dream, rose from beyond the hill. In that direction was home.

He spurred his horse forward and I followed. Beyond the hills, we saw it.

The farm lay in ruins. The smoke came from two barns near the main house, now smoldering. The vineyards to the west and east were trampled down, the olive trees stood still but several seemed to be smaller, cut by sword or burnt.

As we slowed to a walk along the long road leading to the main house, we looked about us in silence. The fields were green but now mottled with dead animals and blowing bits of clothes torn from bodies now long gone. There was the semblance of what we once knew but it resembled nothing so much as one of the many battlefields we had trod. The fragrance of fresh harvest was replaced by the smell of rot and ruin.

We stopped within the courtyard walls. The enclosure was broken down and the ground before the villa strewn with broken pottery, remnants of cloth and spoiling food, dead animal carcasses and the dark stain of dried blood, perhaps animal. The only sound was the pitiful lowing of a dying cow, lying partially hidden beneath a leveled vineyard pole.

Lucius sat in his saddle for a time, not speaking. I was mute, and unbelieving. Just that morning I had pictured the farm and home as it had looked when we left.

At last, Lucius dismounted and moved through the courtyard, pausing to pick up a shard of pottery, then looking for a moment at it before tossing it. He stopped at the sight of a broken statue and bent to pick it up. The head was that of our grandfather and its half face seemed to stare at us, puzzled and lost.

Lucius paused longer at one piece of stained cloth and as he picked it up, I heard a sharp intake of breath. The white cloth looked like part of a dress, its fine stitching speaking of wealth and position. Some of stain was not dirt but worse. His large hand encompassed it and he moved to the house.

The heavy oak door, nearly as tall as two men and wide as four abreast, was torn in half, one panel hanging limply on its hinges, the other flat on the tiled foyer. The gold and silver inlay had been pried loose and the engravings, so artfully depicting Hercules struggling with a lion, were defaced and unrecognizable.

Inside, the destruction continued. Statuary was broken and scattered about. Tapestries were missing. Murals were defaced and dried dung clung to the walls. The inlaid tile was scratched and layered in dirt and debris, and the stench of death was here too.

And in the center of the atrium was the pool, square and inlaid with beautiful blue and green tiles, suggestive of the ocean, catching the water running from the open ceiling above and meant to create a peaceful fountain of dripping water. Now the water was stagnant and mossy and in its depths, a dead sheep lay, bloated and rotting. And at the edge of the pool, near the surface, was the body of a young boy. His dark hair was matted and hid his face, and the jagged wound that had been his throat was now an angry white.

Lucius pulled the young boy from the water and clearing space, lay him down. He turned him over. A low moan filled the room.

It was the grandson of one of our oldest servants. He had seen four summers when we left but would never see seventh birthday, as he lay limp and cold.

Lucius sat there for a long time, holding the boy, his eyes closed. I went to the other rooms, pausing in my old bedroom that I had shared with Lucius. Its quiet peace was now gone in the chaos. Clothes were strewn about, parchments tossed about or burned, ragged remnants floating in the thin air. The mural over my bed, which showed Achilles triumphant over Hector, had been defaced and obscenities scribbled over it.

In the library, books were cast about and an obscenity scrawled on the map of the empire painted across one wall. The windows to the garden were closed and the library seemed not a place of learning but the abode of the dead.

The kitchen was stripped of food and any tools of value. The larger dining room contained two more bodies, servants killed, their bodies bloated and wrapped in flies and vermin. In the smaller dining room, three slaves were dead, recently killed, and a dog stood chewing on one arm until I struck it and drove it away.

Our parents' bedroom, where our father died, was strangely intact, with little sign anyone had been there. I sat there for a moment and remembered. Then I went outside to see the rest of the devastation.

The gardens were dead and dying, the fountains silent and lifeless. The outbuildings showed the scars of invasion. The bathhouse was pillaged, its rich tiles defaced or stolen. The workshops for making olive oil and wine were stripped of everything and stood empty. The one remaining stable had been damaged but not burned. The storage barns for grain and wine were empty and one was burned.

As I returned to the house by the flowered walkway, I saw the body of an old veteran legionary, who had probably been visiting and seeking help from the family, nailed to a makeshift cross in the herb garden near the kitchen. The awful wounds on his arms and shoulders testified to the resistance he gave to the marauders.

Bile came to my mouth and I thought of Nero and Tigellinus as I spit it out.

When I returned, I found Strabo and the cavalry in the courtyard. The riders were finding water and resting their mounts. Lucius was with them, still carrying the boy.

"Send the cavalry out, Strabo. Some of this destruction is recent. Find who did it and bring them here."

After Strabo and the cavalry departed, Lucius and I stayed outside, no longer wishing to visit our old home in its tortured state. I took the body of the boy from him and placed it beneath a shaded arbor that was surprisingly intact.

The sun was dark red and low to the horizon when Gaius Metellus and the rest of the legionaries arrived with the Christians. They set about making camp and the Christians settled near the house. Timothy came to Lucius and put his hand upon his shoulder. He stood like that for a time, saying nothing, and then joined the others, who were walking about the near area, setting vineyard poles aright and picking up the ruins. All were silent.

As the sun hid behind the edge of the world, Strabo and his men returned with four men. They had the look of bandits. The area between Rome and Campania was notorious for banditry and with the breakdown of order upon Nero's death, it was certain to be a deadly fate for the unwary traveler or the undefended estate.

Lucius went to the chained men.

"Were you the ones who did this?"

No one spoke at first. Then, without warning, Lucius seized the biggest man, a burly brawler with a long scar on his neck and an expression devoid of fear, and drew him away from the others.

"Unchain him."

Strabo took his chains off and stepped back. As the bandit rubbed his wrists where the chains had cut flesh, Lucius backhanded him. The bandit instinctively swung back at Lucius. Lucius dodged and smashed the bandit's nose with a quick sharp right hand. The sound of broken bone mixed with an animal howl from the bandit as Lucius quickly drew his sword and slashed his left leg. The bandit sagged to the ground, blood gushing from his leg, bone broken and life draining. Lucius turned to the others.

"Who is your leader?"

They all pointed at the man on the ground.

"And who killed the boy and left him in the pool?"

Again all fingers pointed at the man on the ground.

Lucius pulled a small piece of cloth from under his breastplate.

"This was in the young boy's hand. He tore it from the tunic of his killer. It does not match your leader's tunic. All of you are guilty and will pay."

With that, he walked over to the youngest of the bandits, a young man not much older than my son. His face was that of an animal, furtive and scheming, now fearful. And his dark shirt was the same color of the cloth Lucius held and its sleeve was torn in the same shape. As Lucius placed the cloth back in its place, the young bandit grabbed at Lucius' sword. Lucius' right hand gripped the boy's throat. There was a strangled cry from the boy and he fought to get loose but Lucius grip was too tight. At last, Lucius threw him back and gestured to Strabo. Strabo came forward and put the boy with two soldiers.

Lucius started to turn to the third bandit when something caught his eye. He bent over the bandit on the ground, now mewling in pain, and took from his tunic something bright. It was a legionary medal. He held it up for me.

"There was an *evocati* nailed to a tree in the side yard, there," I said, motioning.

Lucius went to the side yard and returned a moment later.

"This came from his tunic," he said, holding it up for the bandit to see, "and you sealed your death when you butchered a man who served his duty protecting homes from vermin like you."

The bandit started to speak, but Lucius' sword cut off his voice and head.

A gasp went up from the Christians, and then muttered shock. Silence held the rest of us as the legionaries dragged the dead bandit into the spreading darkness.

Then as Lucius turned away, Timothy approached.

"Tribune, do you mean to kill them?"

"Yes," he replied, his tone cold.

"Please reconsider. Is there no lesser penalty?"

Lucius started to answer but his eyes strayed over Timothy's shoulder. Lydia had caught his eye. He stared and then looked back at Timothy.

"I shall think on it."

As we moved away, I thought of the old veteran who was crucified in our garden and I thought I heard the cries of burning bodies in Rome. The Shadow Wolf had become our companion again.

" That dead legionary veteran in our garden, brother, was crucified alongside the flowers our mother tended."

Lucius looked at me with the empty eyes of a man lost.

"Have them all killed, Lucius, leave none alive. This is no place or time for mercy. Or if you do not want to, let me tend to it. With one arm, I can slit throats very handily." I paused and remembered the legionary's face. And the boy's. "Let me do it, Lucius."

Lucius slowly shook his head. Strabo had the two men tied and guarded.

As the sun set and camp fires were set, Lucius sat alone, peering into the flames, unmoving but for fingering the cloth and the medal. A little after dark, Lucius went to Strabo and spoke to him. Strabo asked a question and Lucius shook his head. Strabo assembled a small squad and the bandits were taken away. Later, distant shrieks, the flames of a fire, and Strabo and the soldiers returned.

Food was prepared and we slept under the stars, in a strangely beautiful night. The gathering darkness hid the scars and we could pretend we were children again, all full of hope.

Chapter 13   Repair

Early the next morning, I left our home. My sleep had been fitful, fragrant harvests clashing against sounds of the dying. I would wake in the darkness, hearing the movement of legionaries at the watch, and reach for my sword before realizing I was safe. Then I would hear the cry of a young boy begging for mercy and waken to hear nothing. So the night passed.

With a single cavalry rider, I rode to my farm. Three hills over, along the meandering path of a shallow stream, beyond the stand of yellow wheat on the hill marking the boundary, I found my farm. It was strangely quiet in the early dawn but it seemed unmolested.

This had been where I brought my wife and saw my son born. It was a small farm and only a handful of servants worked it. I farmed wheat and olives in rich soil. The wine I produced was neither acclaimed nor scorned. Spurning family aid or help I was a moderately successful farmer. I enjoyed farming, a great deal when I began, less after my wife died and my son neared the age when he would leave for the legions.

In the dark of some nights, as I lay alone in my room with my son asleep, the servants in their rooms, I felt the kind of loneliness a man feels when there is little to engage his wit, his energy, or his hopes. I was learned and educated but the walls were the only audience to my expositions. I judged my wit sharp and clever but the animals of the yard were little impressed. And my hope slipped away in the twilight and was slow to return with the dawn. Perhaps, I thought, I should sell the farm and move to a nearby city, perhaps Capua or Neapolis, and open a tavern. Often it was the imagined smell of food and beer, the boisterous shouts of ex-legionaries and the clever banter of visitors with the one-armed owner that escorted me to a smiling sleep in the dark hours.

Now the land seemed strangely alien, as if an invisible hand had reshaped it ever so slightly in my absence. The breeze seemed not to blow by the line of olive trees to the west of the near field quite the way I remembered. The stream seemed farther off to the right than I recalled. The house seemed a deeper tan than I saw in my memory. Even the noise of sheep seemed fainter. As I dismounted a motion caught my eye. A man moved from the shadow of the nearby barn and after a moment looking in my direction, he suddenly ran toward me.

"Diomedes," I shouted.

My farm manager rushed to me, smile on his dark face, more wrinkled and much older than when I left him. He grasped my good arm in both his hands and began to weep.

"Master Tychon, thank Jupiter you have returned. I was about to give up hope."

"I am here, and we will make things right. Tell me what has happened."

He wiped his tears and blew his nose. Taking a deep breath, he sat on a pile of rough logs at the edge of the main gate and gazed at me, hand trembling.

"It is all right, Diomedes, Lucius has returned with me. We have soldiers to protect us and no one will raid this farm again."

He nodded and, between sips of water, told the story.

After someone betrayed Julia and our family, the soldiers rode in and arrested Julia, Antonius, Beatrice, the author of all our woes, and the servants. The only ones who escaped were those in the fields or traveling to market. Those in the fields fled to the imagined safety of Capua or Misenum and were not heard of again. Some went into hiding, living off food smuggled to them by Diomedes.

"They came at midday, master. Twenty or more, with chains for the prisoners and a dozen wagons to take them and all the loot they could carry. They laughed as they butchered the cattle, raped the women and cut down anyone who tried to resist or flee. One of them smiled as he looked at the burning buildings and said 'Our master will not have to bid much to buy this rundown shamble; let us reduce the value still further!' And so they went about their pillage, master, and we could do nothing but hide."

After the soldiers left, Dioceses had taken charge of both estates as best he could with the few servants left. There were far too few to keep up both estates. The result was that my farm was well taken care of but Lucius' began to degrade. The few cows remaining were not well fed and died. The wheat fields needed harvest, but too few harvesters were available, so the wheat rotted and died. Swatches of vineyards grew heavy with grapes and then collapsed when they were not picked. The stream was fouled with dead animal carcasses and several fires broke out and burned barns. Servants, fearing arrest, were reluctant to spend much time in the fields and their fear caused Dioceses to plead for their help.

Then the first bandits came to bring more rape and ruin. The process repeated as legionaries, hearing that the Lucullus estate was unprotected, raided it on several occasions, carrying off anything of value they found, destroying at random what was judged worthless. Then the bandits came again and with them, the final despoliation.

After a while, his story became a whisper and his head hung low. I knew he felt he had failed me, and Lucius. I sat beside him and put my arm around his slumping shoulders.

"You did well in a terrible time, Diomedes. You were left alone, with few to help you and you were heroic in your efforts. I am in your debt and will always be."

I felt his shudder at these words and he turned to me with tears in his eyes again. He could not speak and I could not either. We sat that way for a while.

Then the horses whinnied and shifted their pose and I stood up and looked down at the retainer who had served me so faithfully for two decades. Faithfully.

We walked the grounds and inspected the damage. His work had been fruitful and only a little more work would fully restore the farm. I embraced him, promising to see him soon after the rescue of Julia and the household. I said nothing to indicate I might never complete the promise.

As I came in sight of the villa and saw new horses and strange faces there, I slowed to a fast canter and studied the newcomers.

Four of them, *evocati* from their look. Dressed in civilian tunics, they looked heavily dressed for a warm day, certainly concealing swords beneath their cloaks.

As I approached, the group moved open and Lucius was in the center. They continued talking and Lucius looked at a parchment one of them apparently had brought to him.

I dismounted and approached. Lucius introduced me to the men. They were indeed ex-legionaries and had brought news.

"Tychon, these faithful friends have brought news. Brave men all, they have information on the changing affairs of our empire." He gestured to the oldest of the group, a grizzled veteran marked by scars and a blind eye. His voice was that of a centurion used to shouting orders.

"General Galba approaches Rome on a slow march of death. He lays waste to those towns that resist. He kills those who do not celebrate his march. He leads soldiers who hated Nero but they do not love him. And he is surrounded by advisors who control his contact with the outside world and block the counsel of wiser men."

"Who are they?"

"Vinius, Icelus and Laco." He spat the names. "All men of disreputable character and insatiable greed. That a man as tight-fisted and suspicious of other men as Galba should have as his counselors men of such dishonor and avarice is beyond understanding. A dark cloud precedes the general. Citizens and Senate are uneasy."

"Is there opposition to him in Rome?"

"Nothing worth mentioning. Those who loved Nero are hopeful one of their own, a certain Marcus Salvius Otho, will succeed Galba. The old general Galba will not last through a harsh Roman winter, so the story goes, and Otho may be the one to succeed him. He accompanies him on his bloody trek, seeking to ingratiate himself, bribing officers to support him and trying in every possible way to make others forget his association with Nero on his drinking and whoring expeditions."

Lucius showed a tight and hard smile as he spoke.

"General Galba ran for forty miles in full armor just a few years ago and bested the youngest of his legionaries. It would be foolish to assume he is in his dotage and near his tomb. This Otho may have a long time to wait to don the purple."

All smiled and nodded and then the leader spoke.

"After we water our horses, Lucius, we will take our leave."

Lucius nodded and turned back to the villa, where several legionaries were putting in place and securing the mighty doors to the foyer. I then noticed the other repairs done in my absence. The courtyard had been cleared, the bodies of the dead animals and young boy removed and there were sounds of work from inside the villa. As I listened to the now familiar sounds of Christians singing, the soldiers at the door parted and Sophia emerged.

She was carrying a basked filled with broken pottery. It was a large basket and looked very heavy but she carried it with ease. She did not see me but was looking at the growing pile of debris in the space beyond the yard. Her face was smeared with dust, her hands covered with what looked like the dried blood of animal or human but she moved with energy and grace. I delighted in seeing her and then had the awful reminder of her youth. Thought vanished as she turned to me and smiled.

I gestured greeting to her and called Lucius aside. We sat in the shade of the one standing arbor and I told him of my morning. He expressed gratitude for my farm's protection and deep respect for Diomedes and his work to keep his estate safe. Then he sighed and looked at me with a look of amazement.

"Do you know what sound I woke up to, Tychon?"

"My leaving?"

"No, nothing so ordinary, brother, you have always been an early riser."

I nodded, ignoring the irony.

"No, I woke to something most amazing. It was not even light, you were gone and I thought perhaps the men were changing shifts when I realized the sounds were coming from inside our villa. I got up and took my sword, thinking perhaps bandits were skulking about. I went inside quietly and what do you think I saw?

I shook my head. Animals? Cows grazing in the library?

"The Christians, Tychon. The Christians." He looked at me in puzzlement.

"They were working, indeed had been working for a while. They were moving about, cleaning floors, draining the pool, cleaning it and refilling it, picking up debris, washing walls, and gathering up broken pottery, putting books back into library shelves, sweeping cobwebs, putting windows back in place."

I did not know what to say.

"All of them, brother. That Timothy was in charge, barely audible as he whispered directions to the others and working alongside them with such calmness of manner. And Lydia, getting her beautiful gown filthy with blood and intestines.

"Then the other Christians arrived and joined in just after light, before eating. The old man Barnabas, working and then taking rest, ignoring my asking him to stop. Claudia, working without stopping and smiling the whole time…"

He paused and a strange look came over his face.

"And Apollos. What a beast! He lifted loads twice his weight and never asked anyone for help. He manhandled one of those door panels, which it took three legionaries to manage. And he never…"

Lucius paused and looked down at the ring on his finger.

"Wondrous. I don't know…"

At dinner, the *evocati* ate with us, and then left for Rome. As the last plateful of steaming food was consumed, Lucius turned to Timothy.

"Timothy, why are you helping clean the home of someone who chained and led you to death?"

"You are in need," Timothy's eyes softened with memory. "Tribune, days before you arrived, several of us were praying and fasting. One night, three of us, separately, had a dream. We were placed in chains and all about us was singing. We knew our prospects and we knew we should make no effort to escape. We knew there was work for us to do, the Lord's work, in the place you would take us."

"So your god told you about this estate, the storm, the destination of Rome?"

"No, Tribune, the dream was not a prophecy; it was comfort. He reminded us of the gospel we were to take with us when in chains. We do not know the future, only our need to follow and be faithful."

The silence hung, the fire crackled, and the ashes rose to the sky. The darkness held no menace and for now, we were safe.

Chapter 14   The Appian Way

The emblems of the might of Rome fill every corner of the empire. Law and courts. Legions and military outposts. Cities laid out in order. Resplendent baths and reverential temples. Monuments of victories and statues of emperors. Aqueducts bringing fresh water from far mountains. Circuses and entertainments.

And highways. Begun in Italy and expanded throughout the empire, these roads are marvels of the engineering and construction. Other nations have roads, haphazard in direction, unplanned and unsigned, washed away in heavy rains and impossible to navigate in ice or mud. Rome has highways, carefully laid out, artfully planned, magnificently engineered. Each highway is a proclamation that Rome is inevitable, irresistible, and invincible. Roman roads do not conform to the land; they insist the land conform to them.

These roads, my son, do not flood, do not wash away and will remain for centuries after you and I are in our graves, as a marvel to those who built them.

These monuments to Roman civilization enable trips to be reduced from months to weeks, from weeks to days and from days to hours. Originally planned to enable Roman legions to move quickly into hill country to suppress resistance to Roman rule, the roads provide quick passage to government officials, as well as businessmen and tourists. Every road has mileposts, marking distance to the next city. Couriers, working in the Cursus Publicus, the official government communication service, traverse the roads quickly, bringing news to the far reaches of the empire. Post houses, providing changes of horses, are to be found every ten to fifteen miles and every thirty miles or so, inns provide sleeping accommodations and rest for the horses. Truly, a man who travels a Roman highway for the first time must be in awe of the might and skill that is the best of Rome.

And we now began our trip to Rome on the first highway of the empire, the Via Appia. Along the way, we passed by thousands of post holes where the soldiers from the army of Spartacus hung crucified after Rome crushed his rebellion, an ever-deadly testament of the futility of resistance to the empire. The blood from their tortured bodies had long since seeped into the stones and whispered to us as we left Capua and raced toward Rome.

If Lucius had his way, we would have made the trip in one day but my leg and the physical limitation of the horses made it two days. We traveled in the company of the young centurion, Gaius Metellus, ten cavalry, and twenty-five legionaries, who were now mounted. Timothy and Lydia also rode with us, leaving the rest of our party at the farm.

Before sunrise, we had started our journey. I slept well but an early morning shower woke me and I found Lucius up, gathering the travel party. As I watched the leave taking, I realized that I would not be going back to war after Julia and our friends were rescued. No matter the promise to Vespasian, I was returning to my farm. Ahead was my last battle, a final one, for family, and I was entering it with a weak leg, one arm and less quickness than any veteran legionary should have. I was tired of war.

Soon we were on the road to Capua to join the Via Appia.

Now, hours later, our horses were frothing and tired. We had come a long way and without rest, leaving even the newly mounted legionaries struggling to keep up. Finally I prevailed upon Lucius and we stopped, and in a few moments, some of the sweating legionaries joined us. Gaius, the young centurion, looked exhausted and it was apparent he had little equestrian experience. Legionaries might consider riding a lark but for serious travel, they much preferred walking. But the twenty-five miles a legionary can travel when needed would make our journey twice as long as Lucius would allow; so foot soldiers would become temporary cavalry.

We were midway between post houses so we fell out in a copse of trees beside the road. The morning rain had passed but the air was heavy and the trees dripped on us. There was a small stream farther back in the trees and the legionaries took our horses there to water. Bread was broken out and shared and we rested on the damp grass. Shafts of light broke the shade, and a light breeze cooled us.

Soon Timothy and the rest of our party arrived and joined us. Lucius gave them a cursory glance and returned to his solitary thoughts, sitting apart from all of us and eating nothing.

Lydia dismounted and came to sit next to me. She offered bread and figs. I took them and thanked her.

"Tychon, I notice you rubbing your leg. Does it hurt much?"

"Riding aggravates it a great deal. I am much better off walking." I realized I was not answering her question. "It hurts some but it feels much better once I dismount."

She was silent for a while, eating and drinking and looking at the far sky, with its fluffy clouds and shifting colors. I realized I knew very little about her.

"How did you come to be in Ephesus?"

She turned to me with a gentle smile.

"I come there often on business, and to visit my family."

"What is your business?"

"I am a seller of purple."

"A woman of wealth." A woman of wealth and grace. I wondered how old she was. "Is your husband about?"

"My husband died several years ago. His family had been in the Tyrian purple business for many generations and after he died I continued the business."

"So you are stuck with the terrible odors that come from dead mollusks as they rot in those huge vats you put them in for harvesting the purple."

She laughed and leaned toward me.

"Do I smell that bad?"

I smelled nothing, not even the perfume a wealthy noble woman would wear at all times. I shook my head.

"We milk the snails, Tychon. We do not crush them. Crushing uses up the snail and creates an odor that is overpowering. Milking them means we can harvest year after year from the snails and we only need a large number of people to milk the millions of snails needed to produce even a small amount of purple. You see, we take them…"

I interrupted, lest she describe the dreary details of a process I need not learn.

"So you have a vast number of slaves to create this wealth."

"No, not vast wealth, Tychon. Wealth, to be sure, but not vast. And no army of slaves. Freedmen, much like the tenant farmers I am sure you employ."

"Freedmen? You pay these people to milk the snails? Slaves would be so much cheaper. Why freedmen?"

"Freedmen work harder, Tychon. They spoil fewer. And they sing."

"Sing?"

"Have you ever heard slaves sing, Tychon? On the rare occasion they sing, the songs are heart-breaking laments. My workers sing and their songs are not laments. I have freed over a thousand men and women in the last four years, and I would have freed more if the empire did not restrict how many can be freed in a year."

"Do you require them to become Christian before you free them?"

She laughed again, her voice full of merriment.

"What do you think of us, Tychon? Do we seem so horrible? Do you think we eat the flesh and blood of babies? Or hold secret ceremonies to call down curses on the empire and its senators? Or seek to overthrow the emperor? Or evade taxes? Or…"

I held up my hand.

"No, none of that."

"Then why ask if we make believing in our Lord a condition of freedom." When I made no answer, she continued. "Some of my freedmen, Tychon, are

Christian but their faith is not a condition for freedom. Belief in our Lord is no small thing, Tychon. It is not to be taken lightly or done on a whim. To believe and to commit is to have your world change totally; if it does not radically change, immediately or over time, then likely you are not truly a believer."

Her voice became a whisper as she leaned toward me.

"Belief is especially hard for someone who thinks he has no belief in any god, or for a philosopher who thinks religion a hole where the frightened and the ignorant hide.'

She paused, and then looked at Lucius.

"Do you think your brother would like something to eat?" She gestured with a piece of bread toward Lucius, who was brooding and perhaps conversing with the Wolf.

I shrugged my shoulders and nodded toward him. She got up and approached him. He was turned from her and she stood for a moment beside him, then spoke. He turned at her word and took the outstretched bread and figs.

She returned and sat beside me.

"Has your friend Claudia truly been looking for Pilate, her husband, all these years?

"Yes."

"How did you meet her?"

"I met her years ago, at Corinth, at a service in the house of a friend, Phoebe. Claudia was traveling to Germany to look for him and was staying with them until she could earn enough to continue her voyage. She and I took an instant liking to each other and she has been with me ever since, except when she leaves to search for him."

"Why does she search? I understand he wants nothing to do with your god and divorced her because of her faith. Why does she not remarry and relinquish her dream."

"She believes he is still her husband and she cannot let him continue on that dark road." She put her hands flat against one another and slid her top hand off the other, like a man sliding over a cliff. "You see, Tychon, everyone of us is born to die. Everyone is born in the darkness of sin, rebels against God. We cannot buy our way out of that death or avoid it. I know you Greeks believe in Hades, a dark and dismal place where dreams disappear and human glory ends in despair. That is a small shadow of the true pain and hopelessness that awaits each of us if we die in our sin, without our Savior. And Claudia does not want to let him go into that place, where the wails of pain and suffering will never end. She wants to catch him before he goes there. She loves him and prays she will find him and he will repent."

"Has she not found him yet?"

"She has found him twice since we met."

"And?"

"Once he ran away, screaming for her to leave him. The last time, he beat her and left her in the street, telling her he would kill her if she came after him again."

"And she still persists?"

"The shepherd goes after the one lost sheep, Tychon. Our Lord told us that he was the good shepherd who comes after us. He seeks all of us."

I started to declare I was no sheep but a warrior and a poet. Her kind eyes silenced me and I said nothing. Then Lucius rose and we remounted and moved quickly down the Appian Way.

That night, we stayed at an inn at Terracina. We were less than sixty miles from Rome. Dinner was quiet and our company was divided. The legionaries ate in one corner, the Christians in another and Lucius and I by ourselves. In the dim light, Lucius' face was shrouded.

"How is your leg, brother?"

"I have had worse pain, brother. A good rest will restore it."

"I am sorry we have had to move so quickly and that our speed has hurt you."

"I understand, Lucius. It could not be helped."

Before I could say more, a figure appeared from the shadows and approached Lucius. He was small, and young, quick in movement and sly in manner. A messenger surely but from whom? He handed Lucius a sealed letter and after a coin was pressed into his palm, he vanished back into the shadows. I was wondering if there was a tavern where I could drink and eat quietly, without the interruption from one of Lucius' endless informants.

Lucius inspected the letter carefully to assure it had not been tampered with or opened and resealed. He opened it and tilted it to the light from the oil lamp. He read it twice and then put it beneath his breastplate.

"Our host is waiting. He has enough room for our party at his villa and will have the information we need when we get there."

"You have still not told me if he knows the full story of our business and our wretched prospects."

"I could not commit the details to writing, Tychon," he sighed, exasperated at my continued pessimism. "He understands it is delicate and dangerous. And as a good friend, he will help."

As I finished my dinner, I thought of my parting from Sophia this morning. As the horses were being saddled and we prepared to mount, she approached me.

"You are leaving early, Tychon.".

"Yes, my brother is most impatient to leave." She was looking down and her shoulders were slumped. "I wish we had spent more time together since our time aboard the ship."

She looked at me with large eyes, now sad.

"I also, Tychon. I enjoyed our time together."

"Lucius and I have been quite burdened, Sophia, and I had not the time…"

"I understand, Tychon," she interrupted. A fragile smile came to her lips. "We will see each other soon, Tychon, but I am not sure if we will have time alone, as we did on the ship. And I… I miss hearing about the islands we passed. And I am sure there is much of this capitol you could tell me about, its history, its people, their ways. So much a peasant from the provinces could learn from you."

"No, not a peasant, Sophia. Much more than that." I swallowed hard. She placed a firm hand against my face. It seemed suddenly small and fragile.

"I pray for your safety, Tychon. And the safety of your brother. And the safety of your family."

"Thank you for your prayers."

She turned to go and I caught her arm.

"I value your prayers more now than when our journey began."

She stood for a moment and smiled, then nodded and left.

We finished our dinner and went to our room. I was not sure I could sleep but then exhaustion overcame pain and I fell asleep as Lucius was turned to the wall, his wooden image in hand, no doubt telling Julia her rescue was near.

Chapter 15   Rome

The next day, our party divided. Timothy and Lydia departed before breakfast after a hasty farewell. We had a quick breakfast and rode swiftly toward Rome, the horses strong from a night's rest, and we spoke little. Before noon, we passed over the Pontine Marshes, with their foul-smelling and stagnant pools, and I saw Lucius' face harden, the smell of corruption now near. Then we moved through the Alban hills and came in sight of the capitol.

From a distance, its buildings gleamed white in the sun and seemed most beautiful. Here was the center of the world. From here, all roads radiated to far nations and peoples, offering peace and civilization to all who would submit. And for those who resisted, the legions would compel submission. And once part of the empire, a nation may not withdraw. What the empire gained, it kept.

As our horses slowed in the traffic entering the city, I thought of Caratacus, the rebel leader in Britain in the first war we waged there before our final clash with the mighty warrior queen Boudicca. Caratacus, like countless rebel leaders before him and after him, was crushed by the relentless power of the legions. Taken in chains to Rome, he was most eloquent in his defense and Emperor Claudius pardoned him. Amazingly he settled on a small farm not far from ours and spent his remaining days cultivating his orchards. I remembered his words when he first saw the gleaming marble temples and rich splendor of this capitol: "And can you, then, who have got such possessions and so many of them, covet our poor tents?" The question has been asked by peasants in a hundred lands and answered a thousand times with the sword.

We came to the Porta Capena, entrance to the heart of empire. As we passed into the city, I saw again the beggars at the gate, many of them Jewish, and I thought of the dead *secarius* and his dream and prophecy, and in the warmth of the midday sun, I shivered.

As we moved toward the Circus Maximus, the crowds grew thicker. Wagons filled with goods. Slaves hurried on errands, to get food, or carry messages. Rich and poor mixed together in the flow of the streets, the one riding in carriages or litters, the other on foot, stepping in the offal and garbage, which was accumulating in a city in crisis. Vendors still cried to passersby and in the alcoves and small squares, lawyers still argued their cases before judges while the curious stared or shouted insults. Yet fear and unease mixed with the normal stench.

Faces turned toward us and eyes narrowed. Were we part of the army of Galba? Perhaps we were assassins or Nero loyalists seeking revenge. Lucius looked neither to the left nor to the right but continued until we reached the side street, before the Circus Maximus, which took us to the large villa on Caelian hill, which was our destination.

We came to it finally and turned in at the large gate. The walls were unusually high and the gate almost as large as ours at our villa. Two servants waited for us and recognizing us, they threw open the doors and all of us entered the courtyard. Gaius and the legionaries were led to a large guesthouse and stables that were in the rear of the property and Lucius and I entered the home.

We were once again in the presence of an old acquaintance, one whom we had not seen in several years.

He came from the back of the home and smiled as he approached.

"Lucius Licinius Lucullus, my old friend, welcome."

"Titus Flavius Sabinus, my most revered friend, it is good to see you."

They embraced and separated, staring at each other, no doubt assessing how the years had changed the other. As they exchanged greetings, I considered the man who now held our future in his hands.

Titus Flavius Sabinus, old friend to our family, was a rich and revered nobleman of Rome. We first met him during the first war in Britain, where he served as legate in Aulus Plautius' army. Later he was consul and for the last eleven years had been *praefectus urbi* under Nero. The prefect led the urban cohorts, fifteen hundred men responsible for the maintenance of order in the city and if need arose, military action. Like legionaries but more highly paid, these cohorts served as a kind of balance to the Praetorian Guard, that most powerful and dangerous fixture of Roman politics. No one knew more about Rome and what was happening in its back streets and temples and villas than the urban cohorts. And therefore, Titus Flavius Sabinus knew as much as anyone about what we were facing.

And as important, Titus Flavius Sabinus was General Vespasian's brother.

"And how is my brother, Lucius?"

"He is well, Titus Flavius, and sends his warmest regards. He is now at the gates of Jerusalem, his army is well supplied and he has his son Titus as a chief and well-regarded commander. The harsh Judean landscape has made him eager to be home in Italy but otherwise he is quite well.

"He has sent us here and wishes for us to complete our quest even as we keep him informed of political matters as they develop here. He also asked me to assure that his son Domitian is safe in these dangerous times."

"Would you like to see him, Lucius?"

Lucius shook his head.

"I am in a hurry, Sabinus. I must dispense with the social amenities for now. Please forgive me. I feel confident you are a most powerful protector of your nephew."

"There is nothing to forgive, old friend. In your circumstance, I would follow your course." He smiled and turned to me.

"Tychon, my old friend, it is good to see you. You look well and I hope when this matter is finished you will read to me your latest work on the history of our empire."

I assured him I would and as he took Lucius' arm and we moved into the library off the main hall, I noticed a stiffening of Lucius' movement. No doubt, like me, he was feeling the strangeness of this moment. Our loved ones were in peril and we were conversing amiably about memories and histories. Was there not a need for urgency, for speed?

As we entered the library, Titus Flavius closed the door and turned to us. Before Lucius could speak, he held up his hand.

"I know you want to move quickly, Lucius. You want to rescue your wife and your family. But we cannot do anything tonight. Tomorrow, if we are fortunate, we will be able to move."

"But…." Lucius interrupted.

"Lucius, Tychon, sit, and I will explain."

We took seats in the richly appointed room, lights gleaming in wall mounts, casting the brilliant colors of murals and books in sharp relief. Wine was brought and Titus Flavius folded his hands on his desk as he spoke.

"Lucius, this a terrible time for our city. The city is full of prisoners, strangers with the looks of assassins, thieves and bandits masquerading as businessmen and all manner of trouble and crime. General Galba is moving slowly toward Rome, killing along the way. Refugees fill our streets, loyalists to the late emperor are plotting an overthrow of Galba before he even arrives, and order is barely held together." He sighed, worn down by the litany of troubles.

"Chaos is the firstborn son in a civil war, Lucius, and my troops are straining to maintain order when no one knows what will happen next. Yesterday we nearly had a riot over a rumor that grain shipments had been cut off and starvation was imminent. Old friends of Nero are fleeing abroad, sowing fear, encouraging revenge, or seeking to ingratiate themselves with Galba. You may have heard of one of them, Marcus Salvius Otho. He is in General Galba's travel party even now and has told many that he will soon be named heir to the emperor."

He paused and looked carefully at Lucius.

"And another schemer is the one you seek, Ofonius Tigellinus.'

Lucius leaned forward at the name.

"Tigellinus is moving about the city and nearby towns, fearful of being set upon by Otho's men or others seeking to ingratiate themselves with the new emperor by killing one of Nero's most bloodthirsty companions. He is seeking to parley with representatives of Galba while avoiding the daggers of his enemies. Therefore it is very difficult to locate him."

As Lucius started to speak, Titus Flavius raised his hand.

"From your message, I understand the urgency of moving quickly. But tonight we do not know where he is. My men have good information that he will be back in the city tomorrow and in a place where we can reach him. Tonight, you rest. Tomorrow I should receive the confirmation where he will be and you can move."

It was silent for a moment. Lucius sighed.

"Old friend, I appreciate your help. Forgive me if I seem ungrateful. I cannot abide the thought my beautiful Julia may be suffering this very night and may be only a short distance from this place and my protection."

"I understand, Lucius. If there were not so many refugees and so many people flooding the city, we might locate her without dealing with Tigellinus. But only he would know where she might be."

Titus Flavius put his hand on Lucius' shoulder.

"And it is possible, my friend, that he will have forgotten or never knew the details of her capture. He may not be able to answer your question."

Lucius turned his head up to face Sabinus. There was spittle at his lips.

"In that case, Titus Flavius Sabinus, he will die."

A strange look passed over the prefect's face and was gone.

We rose and went to our rooms, after promising Titus Flavius we would join him at dinner. I had thought we had left the Shadow Wolf behind in the country but now I feared his true den was this city.

When we entered the dining room later and took our places on couches, along with Titus Flavius, his lovely wife Arrecina Clementina, and their two children, I noticed several guests who seemed not at all the wealthy patricians normally present at dinners here. One or two looked like merchants, one was obviously a craftsman and two looked like neither patricians nor equestrians. As the servants began to bring food to us, peacock tongues from the look of it, with some sweet sauces, I turned to my wine. It was fine and familiar and I was relieved to find it strong and heady. Then I heard a voice.

"Tychon, will you not add water to your goblet?"

I looked to my left. There she was, settling on the couch next to mine.

"Lydia!" My arm jerked and almost spilled my drink. She laughed.

"Here," she said, taking my drink from me. "Let me hold it while you calm down."

"But what are you doing here? I thought we would not see you again soon. And are you acquainted with our host?"

"We made a brief visit to old friends but they were absent. So we came here. Our host is a friend and he invited Timothy and me. So I am a guest, like you. Timothy asked me to carry his regrets. He has been delayed."

"Timothy! What has he to do with Titus Flavius?"

Lydia smiled again. She thought I did not notice her adding water to my goblet. Obviously she and Sophia were of one mind.

"Timothy and Titus Flavius have been friends for some time."

She handed me back my wine. It was not nearly so strong now. "You mean…?"

"Titus Flavius is one of us, Tychon. He is a Christian."

"A Christian?" I stuttered. "This close to Nero's inner circle?"

"This close." She seemed amused at my alarm.

I looked at the other guests now with renewed interest. Were they Christians also? Was this traitor's nest so near imperial power?

"And who are these men? Are they of your religion also?"

"Yes, they are Tychon, and I will introduce you to them if you wish." She leaned around me as she said this, to include Lucius, who said nothing but was deep in thought.

At last he spoke to Lydia.

"And who are they?"

"That one there is a merchant from Alexandria, those two are brothers from Judea and that one, Tychon," she said, nodding toward a small and very intent man with a serious mouth and piercing eyes, "is a writer I would like you to meet. I told him about you and he asked if he could meet you and examine your arm."

"My arm? Why would a writer be interested in my arm?"

"He is also a physician, Tychon, as well as a writer. He saw you enter today and said you reminded him of someone from long ago with a similar condition."

What cripple might he have been reminded of? I did not like the thought and drained my cup.

Lucius rose and went over to settle beside our host.

"The Lord is present in all this, Tychon." She was looking very serious.

"The Lord? Where, Lydia? I do not see him."

"Don't be fanciful or scornful, Tychon. You are too intelligent for such."

"Lydia, my brother and I studied under Seneca and learned that our emotions must be governed by self-discipline and yet we fail each day in that effort. I am beyond help and want nothing but peace to write and work my farm."

"It is not your emotions that need first attention, Tychon. And you can never govern yourself successfully. That is very hard work and fails in the end. It is your heart, Tychon, and the darkness that lives there needs cleansing and light and you cannot accomplish that yourself."

I started to tell her my soul was not so evil but then I saw her eyes and her knowledge, and I would not pretend to her.

"If there is darkness in me, Lydia, it can never be cleansed. There is too much blood and death there."

"Never too much, Tychon. There is one who can cleanse it, my friend. He is even now at your elbow."

I said nothing and resisted the urge to look to my side. Only a cushion was there. So I sat in silence for several moments. She continued to look at me. Before I could fully understand, her voice broke in, low and peaceful.

"In time, Tychon, in time." She refilled my cup, with a great deal of water.

"And in this room, Tychon, another first heard of our Lord, Tychon, not so very long ago. Someone you know."

I turned to look at her. She was smiling. My eyes asked and Lydia answered.

"Yes, Tychon, this is where Julia came to hear the word of God and believe. It is in this home that your brother's wife, Julia, first came to church. And this is where she first heard about our precious savior. This is where it all began."

Chapter 16   Waiting

Again, we waited. Again, Lucius could not abide it.

We rose before dawn, put on our armor, and waited. We ate breakfast and Lucius went to see that the legionaries were armored and ready. All was in readiness, and we waited.

The early morning saw the usual supplicants come to Titus Flavius' door for gold or favors. These poor and needy showed no surprise that so many soldiers were in the courtyard and ready for action.

Then came friends of Titus Flavius. We stayed in the rear of the house, not wanting to meet anyone and wanting only to be on our way.

"Nothing has changed in this city, Tychon. The refuse of empire still depends upon the meager provisions of patricians to survive. This empire never changes because Rome never changes."

Lucius was standing in the garden behind the main house, his hands gripping the shoulder plate near the cloak around his shoulders. His face was calm but the way he shifted his weight every few moments and would not sit betrayed him.

"The city breeds them, Tychon, as it breeds disease and rot. As it breeds vile and small men who care not a bit for the masses except as they can be used to further political ambition." He spat on the ground and looked at me.

As he spoke, I recognized the tone, the one from long evenings and dark discussions of the death of Roman virtue. I looked through the window, into the library. On its wall, the mural, all red and brown amidst the shadows, depicted the infants Romulus and Remus being suckled by a she-wolf. I knew these two figures well but here there was something terrible. In a flash, I gasped in understanding of the Shadow Wolf that had been stalking us.

It lived before Romulus and Remus, before the Republic, before the Empire. It filled men with ambition that swallowed honor and greed that strangled virtue. It hid from sight. It lurked in the darkness at the edge of perennial night. I opened my mouth to tell Lucius who it was but could say nothing. He was settling into that calm I had seen dozens of times before battle. It was a mixture of determination and anger and a firm grip on the *gladius*. This morning, Lucius did not look his age and his eyes glistened. His strength flowed to me. I could do or say nothing that might distract. It was enough to know that the den of the Shadow Wolf was in this capitol.

A little while later, Titus Flavius came to us.

"I am sorry, my friends, I could not come to you sooner. The capitol is awash in rumors and many seek me out to learn what I may know."

He sat beside Lucius.

"My troops are reporting in, Lucius. So far there is no word where Ofonius Tigellinus will be or when he will be arriving. I will keep you informed."

With that, he left. We went to join the troops and gave instruction to Gaius to let them take their ease. Soon gambling was underway and we passed time watching the play. The veterans were relaxed, having faced many battles before and knowing that the laughter of gambling competition is a fair way to await death.

Then, in late afternoon, the message arrived. Titus Flavius called us to the library.

"Ofonius Tigellinus will be at the Domus Aurea this evening. He will transact business there and leave the city before daybreak. His personal bodyguard will accompany him. He has not received word from Galba accepting his pledge of loyalty and he is worried. His bodyguards never leave his side, even when he is engaged in violating some young...." Titus stopped suddenly and then changed tone.

"Lucius, let me send a guide with you, one of my household staff, who is most familiar with the Domus. Have you ever visited it?"

Lucius shook his head.

"It is large, Lucius, with hundreds of rooms. You could spend the whole night looking for him without success. That is one of his protections, and your difficulty. But my servant knows his habits when he visits there. He was taken to Tigellinus there a few months ago and knows the man, sadly. He will be a good guide for you."

"Thank you, old friend, for your help." Lucius stood and embraced him.

"Don't be so quick, Lucius Licinius, to thank me. There is one provision I need to discuss with you."

He paused and gestured to sit.

"The young man I speak of, your guide, is not just a servant. He is a brother in the Lord." He waited a moment for us to consider. I looked at Lucius and he at me. Neither of us knew what was being said. Titus understood our puzzlement.

"He is a Christian, friends. A Christian. My brother in Christ." He waited a moment before continuing. "And there is a moral issue that may handicap his being of service to you."

Lucius' eyes grew wide and he opened his mouth to speak. Titus raised his hand.

"Wait here, I want them to explain it to you."

Titus rose and left the room. Lucius and I could say nothing.

"'Them?'" I finally exclaimed.

There appeared a moment later three figures. Titus Flavius. A young boy not much older than my son, fair of skin and hair, handsome except for the jagged scar on his cheek, red and recent. And behind them, a slender man of youthful face, with the red mark of a rope clear on his throat.

Titus stood to the side and closed the door behind them. For a moment, there was silence.

"Timothy? What have you to do with this?" Lucius stood and confronted the preacher.

"Lucius, it is good to see you again." Timothy spread his arms to grasp Lucius, who made no move. He dropped his arms and raised his voice slightly.

"Titus Flavius has explained you want to see Ofonius Tigellinus and this young man can take you to him this evening." He paused and continued, looking squarely at Lucius, who was glaring at him. "This young man is a believer and has been for some time. I have come to know him and we have corresponded. He has asked my counsel on many matters over the months and I have welcomed the opportunity to pray and worship with him."

"And?" Lucius interrupted, his voice impatient.

"And now," Timothy responded, "he is concerned that if he takes you to find this man, he will be a party to murder."

The word hung in the air and we understood immediately.

Lucius' hand dropped to his sword and his voice tore the air.

"Timothy, I have fought many battles and killed many men. I have cut men in two and slashed a hundred throats. I have run men through with javelin and sword and smashed their brains with clubs and the edge of helmets. I have waded through blood and spilled guts up to my knees and I have watched as a thousand prisoners were put to the sword and then gone and eaten a hearty dinner. I have seen kings boast of coming victory over my army and then kicked their severed heads aside after the battle. I have no fear of murder, or invisible gods or the threats of pale preachers or weakling women or smooth cheeked boys. In my wars, if a young boy refused to be a guide, I would think nothing of executing him rather than plead with him or ignore his insult. So do not preach to me or threaten me or plead for my mercy. I will have a guide and I will go where that beast is and if I slay him, that is no one's business but mine. And if this boy seeks death from an insult, let him say so."

"There will be no blood spilled in this house, Lucius Licinius Lucullus," Titus Flavius interrupted, his voice menacing.

Lucius and I turned to look at him. He stood in the light and he might have been marble. The air was alive.

Lucius turned back to Timothy and they looked at each other without pause. Lucius could have killed Timothy with a single blow but I was not sure who was the stronger. At last, Timothy spoke.

"A simple promise is all we seek, Lucius Licinius. No more than a pledge from you. I know you are a man of honor and a man who will keep his word.

And all of us want to reunite you with your wife and household. But I have counseled this young man and he has taken my counsel. He will guide you to the man you seek but only if you promise not to murder him."

Lucius stood without moving, or taking his eyes from Timothy. I cleared my throat and spoke to Timothy when he turned to me.

"'Murder' you say. But if we are attacked, can we not defend ourselves. Can we not kill if set upon? Would you have us defenseless when confronting a man of such violence?

"So you are a lawyer now, Tychon, in addition to being a poet and historian," Timothy was almost smiling now, to my amazement. "Of course we demand no man give up the right to defend himself. Murder is quite another thing. It is an act of deliberate and cold taking of life, not to protect but to punish wantonly, for gain or revenge."

"But Tigellinus, Timothy? A vicious and brutal man, who ravages young men and women, who rapes and tortures and seeks the death of believers such as you. Would not the world be better off and your flock safer if we slit the throat of this beast? And are those marks on this young man evidence of the violence that beast inflicted on him?"

"Yes, this young man was ravaged by Tigellinus, beyond what you can imagine, and wounded. But you see, Tychon, he," pausing, Timothy smiled at the young man, "has forgiven Tigellinus and will not be party to his murder. Would you poison your soul, Tychon, to get your revenge? When his body lies dead, will your soul be dead also?"

I knew there was no moving this man.

Lucius turned and walked to the window facing on the garden. For a long while he stood there, unmoving. Then he turned.

"You have my word, Timothy. I will spare the life of that beast if I can."

Timothy moved to embrace Lucius but a slight gesture from Titus Flavius stopped him.

A moment later, they were gone.

"One more battle, Lucius. One more for me. One more for you?"

He did not answer.

We left the library, gathered our troops, the black horse we had brought from our home, our young guide, and set out from the lighted and warm house into the shadowing streets.

Chapter 17   House of Gold

The Christians in Rome had much to fear, my son, and it is not surprising they hid. At first, they were insignificant, another religion among many. They were not so violent as the Jewish revolutionaries who led revolts and battled Roman legions. They were not so numerous as to threaten established customs. They were small, and peculiar, and far away from the center of empire.

Then it changed. Their faith spread from Jerusalem and Galilee to Syria, and Damascus, and then Ephesus, gateway to the west. In Roman ships and over Roman roads, it moved to Greece and Macedonia and Africa. Borne like seed in the wind, it landed in our homeland and took root. From its blooms more seed was carried on constant winds to welcoming soil in distant lands.

Its adherents were like nothing ever seen before in the empire. Women were believers and were treated as equals in this strange new faith. Slaves filled its ranks, alongside the poor and the crippled, the uneducated and the barbarian who knew neither bath nor perfume. And when these followers of The Way were starved, they sang and prayed. When they were torn apart by animals, they sang and prayed. And their last words, always songs and prayers.

And so at last, this religion, which first confused Romans, then made them fearful, spread quietly into the inner reaches of the capitol, ever nearer to Nero and his inner circle. And when Nero saw the population grow resentful at his excesses, he looked for the opportunity to direct their anger at the Christians.

A fire provided him his opportunity. One among many that were commonplace in this dirty and overcrowded city, it was unusual in its speed and intensity. Hundreds of homes were destroyed and the center of the capitol became smoking ruins. And from those cinders, a conspiracy was born.

Tigellinus, Nero's companion in evil, whispered in Nero's ear that this was the perfect chance to shift the blame for this catastrophe to the Christians. Nero did so and the persecution of the new religion accelerated. Hundreds died in the weeks and months following.

Then rumors spread that perhaps it was Nero who started the fire. After all, it was announced that rather than rebuild the homes and shops that had been destroyed, Nero planned to raise a new palace on the 125 acres of smoldering ruins.

This would be the greatest palace in the world, lavish beyond imagining and beautiful beyond description. Over the next four years, Nero set about executing his vision. The palace, Domus Aurea, the Golden House, would be set in the space between the Palatine and the Esquiline Hill. It would feature land made into a country estate, with a lake, woodlands and fields, with pastures, vineyards and exotic animals from the farthest reaches of the empire. The palace itself would be filled with ornate galleries, costly murals and statuaries of marble and gold. The main street to the palace would be a mile long, in a triple colonnade. And at its entry, which all would pass through, a 120 pure gold statue of the emperor would proclaim him as emperor of the whole world.

Its extravagance and costly luxury were an affront to Rome, its history and its values. Its cost was borne by everyone in the empire, all being taxed to pay for this butcher's indulgence. When the Domus Aurea was completed, the empire's treasury was empty and the emperor had less than a year to live.

It was dusk when we left for the Golden House.

The young man said little and we moved quickly. Rome is not a city to travel after dark. If the cutpurses do not set upon you, the wagons bringing goods into the city will run you down. And if you escape those dangers, there is always the risk of getting lost in the warren of unlit and crooked streets. Lose sight of a landmark and you could wander all night without any idea of where you are. But this servant moved with confidence and we came to the Sacra Via, the main road leading into the Domus Aurea, before many minutes had passed.

The crowd thinned as darkness approached and there was only the stench of the muck under our horses' feet and the solemn dirge of thousands of voices behind shuttered windows. At last we came to the colonnaded entrance, which stretched up the hill. As the last sun disappeared, its light shone off the golden leaf of the entrance and we saw the blinding glow of yellow that gave the house its name. We passed beneath the high marbled arch and there in the pale light was the towering statue of the dead emperor, stretching hundreds of feet over us, placed on a magnificent marble base, his wreathed face more lovely than it had ever been in life, his legs more muscled and lean than he could ever have fancied. And in his hand he held the orb of authority, a symbol of the world he had ruled so recklessly. As the last sun's rays touched the orb, glinting and trying to warm the dull gold ball into life, I thought of his body, now dust. Where would Christians consign him after death, to Hades as we thought our destination, a dull and dark place where we forever wander aimlessly and sadly, or was there a more terrible destination for the butcher? The air chilled my ruminations and I turned to see that all our legionaries were behind us. They were comforting.

We paused to show our pass to the Urban Cohort guards and passed into the grounds beyond. Fields stretched off to the south, vineyards heavy with unharvested grapes, wheat rotting untended and pastures with herds of sheep. Beyond were enclosures for the wild animals. A large animal of brown spots on white, with an incredibly long neck, was eating from the very top of a tree. Leopards and tigers were kept nearby, along with the heavy hided animal with a horn on its forehead we had seen so many years ago. Strange animals abounded, some lovely, others nightmares.

Then we passed along the lake, large and serene, looking natural and not created, with magnificent boats floating at anchor, awaiting an emperor who would never come. Water birds floated on the surface and nearby geese made noises and moved about. In the distance I heard the snorting of swine and the lowing of cattle and wondered who was tending this wild collection.

We skirted the hall of antiquities that contained so much of the art and statuary Nero collected. Praetorian Guards were stationed at intervals, protecting the rich treasures that lay within. As we passed, they studied us carefully, likely wondering what so many legionaries were doing there at twilight.

We made our way to the east wing, where our guide indicated Tigellinus was. Stopping outside the entrance, Lucius instructed all to dismount and leave their horses with a guard. Gaius and ten men would accompany us. Another ten men would take the horse to the location on the backside of the complex which the young guide showed them on a map he had drawn. Lucius and I led the way and moved down the corridors behind the guide.

On each side of the wide and dimly lit hallway were countless rooms. Our guide explained these were rooms for parties, sexual encounters or drunken feasts. There were no bedrooms in this immense complex since this was a place for feasting, drinking, debauchery, violence, art and entertainment, not rest. We at last came to the one very large dining room, rectangular with high ivory fretting and having an odor to it that I could not place. Our guide explained that this was a room for large parties, as noted by the dozens of couches and purple cushions, the numerous serving tables and large silver goblets inlaid with jewels. The special guests invited to feast in this room would be treated to showers of flower petals, which would be released from the hidden devices in the ceiling at the emperor's pleasure, along with perfumes sprayed from hidden pipes in the walls. Rotting flowers and stale perfumes combined in a cloying stench.

We passed through the corridor and into the octagonal dining room, with its lavish alcoves for assignations and sexual activity, notable for its open circular ceiling, through which the stars were shining this night. All in this room was green marble and rich gold. Even the large wine urns were coated in gold and the utensils, surprisingly not stolen, were also gold. The murals on the walls displayed athletic contests from Grecian mythology, with the heroes and gods all made to look much like the late emperor. Gems accented the depictions, emeralds staring from the eyes of Apollo, large ruby drops of blood flowing from Hercules' wounds, mother of pearl fingertips pointing from Juno and Jupiter toward a rosy cheeked Nero, gilt in gold and glaring upon his unworthy subjects from a throne of gold.

How many slaves and poor farmers of the empire died to pay for that mural?

A few steps off the corridor leading to the pasture where the horse was, we came to the room where the prey waited. Our journey was nearly over.

At the entrance, a small man greeted us with an air of suspicion. He was not unlike a thousand other functionaries we had dealt with through the years. Fearful of displeasing his master, he would adhere to the strictest letter of the law and revel in his authority. He looked at our credentials, glanced up as if he could determine from the paper if we were truly the officers meant to carry these messages and returned them to Lucius.

"Only you may enter, Tribune, no one else. Your soldiers must wait outside. Only on these conditions will the revered Ofonius Tigellinus see you."

I swallowed my retort to this beetle of a man and threw my cloak back so he could see my dead arm.

"Surely the revered one would not object to the tribune's lowly assistant accompanying him."

The functionary studied me, deemed me no threat and nodded. He put his hand on the door and glanced at Boudicca.

"The dog goes with the men. The honorable Ofonius Tigellinus does not like dogs."

He must resent the resemblance, I thought. The door opened and closed behind us. I heard our men moving off down the hall, with the young guide and the small man, and then their voices were no more. They were now too far away to hear us if we called. We were alone.

The room was richly decorated, walls gold gilt and open to the reflected light from cleverly placed windows high in the walls, statuary of marble surrounding the room, furniture of rare woods and ornamented in silver and gold, dishes of gold, and even the richly carved door through which we entered was gilt in gold. Yet the room had an abandoned feel. It was cold, with a whisper of wind and papers on the desk ruffling slightly as the man at the desk turned from one page to another, making notes and speaking to himself in a low whisper.

It was Tigellinus as I had remembered him. He was bent over the table, his dark hair curled precisely, in the manner of a court familiar, hands clean, nails polished and glistening even in the dim light. He was a handsome man, regular of feature, tall and thin, but his eyes, studying us quickly before turning back to the papers, had the searching look of the man who seeks out in others the place of greatest pain.

At last, those eyes rose to rest on us and I saw the fox in them.

"What do you want? I am very busy."

Lucius presented our credentials and spoke of our mission. We were here to carry word of assassination plans against General Galba, which would certainly be of great interest to the new emperor. And for our efforts we sought only to purchase a small number of Christian prisoners in Rome to add to those we have brought with us from Judea, looking to profit from their resale elsewhere. As Lucius laid out our convoluted proposal, I looked at Tigellinus' guards. I realized at once that we were in great peril.

These were not legionaries guarding Tigellinus. Nor were they Gauls, whom we had heard he favored for personal protection. These were Germans, the warriors whose deadly force had driven the Gauls from their homes and forced us to battle them to keep them out of Roman lands. These were the nightmares our enemies feared more than us. These were the warriors who ambushed and slaughtered twenty thousand legionaries in two days in the Teutoberg forest, roasted the survivors alive and so terrified the emperor Augustus that he gave up any plan to annex Germania.

And now they were here, their glossy fur cloaks concealing long heavy blades that would cleave a man in two with one stroke. These were frightening enemies under any circumstances. If there was trouble, Lucius faced them and Tigellinus with only a one-armed brother.

There were three of them. One was tall, a good head taller than even Lucius, with scarred face and lip that hung down at one side. One was shorter, with a white blind eye and the smell that comes from a man who never bathes. The third was slightly hunched, with strong short arms and eyes that never left me. All were unsmiling and studied us with a blend of contempt and challenge. There would be no surprising them.

As I fingered my dagger with my one good hand under my cloak, I wondered how Lucius was going to get us out of here before our fraud was discovered. Our dice were thrown and we had no choice. Dead or bloodied?

As I stared back at the Germans and wondered which one would come at me, I heard Lucius say something that caught my attention.

"Our general would smile most favorably on your cooperation, Tigellinus."

Tigellinus put the papers down and smiled at Lucius, without opening his mouth.

"'Our general,' Lucullus? 'Our general?' This set of orders is signed by Vespasian. He is not 'our general.' Our general, and emperor I should note, is Galba. I trust you are aware of that."

He paused and looked at the Germans, his audience. They did not smile or even look at him. Their eyes stayed on us and their looks said they wanted to kill us, for amusement perhaps. Tigellinus held up the orders.

"I do not see Galba's name on these orders. These orders are meant for a dead emperor, to deliver unimportant people on the authority of a distant and unimportant general. They are not fit to wipe my ass with."

With that, he held the orders over the open flame and tossed the ashes to the floor. The Germans almost smiled.

A long silence. Then Lucius spoke.

"The emperor is dead. But the general is not so unimportant as you may think. Emperor Galba will certainly need his soldiers, and his good will at some point. And that good will may be slow in coming if his honor has been insulted by a third rate functionary acting as if he were part of the inner circle of the emperor's court."

The words struck home and Tigellinus rose, his eyes bright and angry. Lucius continued.

"If such a functionary were to be cooperative in a matter such as this, no offense would be taken and at such time as the legions of Vespasian would be required to assist Emperor Galba, they would be provided willingly and might just be the winning margin in some future conflict."

Tigellinus stood rigid, balanced between anger and ambition, between a man of honor outraged and a lackey. It was one-sided. He sat down and hinted at a smile.

"What use do you have of these prisoners now, Lucullus? And why would you want them, if there is no emperor to deliver them to?" Lucius had already explained this but now had to repeat it to Tigellinus, who apparently only paid attention to what people said when they were offering him a bribe.

"I have made an investment of time and effort to bring these people here and I cannot be left with nothing to show for it. I want the prisoners here to sell into slavery, along with the one hundred I have already brought with me. Together they represent a substantial amount of gold to a slave trader, especially if I see them in far off countries where there is no civil war."

Tigellinus' eyes took on a luster and he was angry no more. The whiff of gold was sweet. He sat down.

"And what is my part of this?"

Did this man not listen to anything that had been said?

Lucius smiled and his voice was reassuring.

"I have a matched pair of stallions. Dark as the night, strong and fast. Excellent bloodlines. Perfect for the races. The Greens could use them in the upcoming season. Worth much and free to me from the prisoners I have taken. They would be my gift to you for the prisoners. Along with gold."

Lucius touched the heavy bag at his waist and its thick bulk drew Tigellinus' eyes. He smiled, a tired smile, certainly one Nero had seen often, just before the rape of a child or the torture of a resisting man or woman. His eyes seem unfocused, as if recalling such things and his head tilted slightly to the side, as if hearing a plea for mercy. His smile grew at the memory and a flush rose, then vanished. He finally sighed, perhaps sad such things were not to be had this evening. But there were the horses. And the gold.

"I think that might be adequate, so long as the horses are as you have described them."

"I have only one with me," Lucius said, gesturing with his head to the place where the horse waited outside with the legionaries, "and I will deliver the other, along with a second payment of gold, after I have removed the prisoners. Please go outside and assess whether I have not truly brought you a fine stallion."

Tigellinus grunted assent and rose from his seat, said something to the guards and went out the door, one guard with him and the two staying with us. He returned in a few moments, his eyes shining in the pale light of the room. He sat at his table and began moving papers as he spoke.

"So which batch of prisoners are you interested in?"

"The ones taken from the farms of Campania a few weeks ago." Lucius' voice was controlled and even.

Tigellinus looked through several lists before pulling one out and smoothing it out on the desk.

"Ah yes, this group. Not very large. Nothing very notable. They are marked for sale, those that are left, who still may be at the prison. You will pay me the gold you have and I will sign the release and you may have the prisoners that are still there. If they are gone, I will relinquish claim to the second horse and retain only this one as a deposit on future transactions we may have." He smiled, pleased at his sharp dealing.

Lucius moved around the table to look at the list. The one-eyed German moved aside as Tigellinus nodded permission and Lucius bent over the table. From his look, I knew he recognized the names. We were near.

As Tigellinus scribbled a note and exchanged it for the bag of gold, I spoke for the first time and my voice sounded timid to me.

"You said 'those that are left.' Are some of the prisoners already sold?"

Tigellinus sought to be reassuring.

" Some were sold earlier. But no, I was not speaking of those. I was speaking of one who died. "

Lucius' head moved slightly.

"Only one? How? I should not think we would want diseased prisoners for sale."

"No, no. No disease. I had to kill one."

My mouth was dry.

"Understandable if a man is not used to chains." Lucius spoke slowly, as if speaking to a person with no wits.

Tigellinus smiled and sat back in his chair, proud.

"No, no man. A woman." He waited with his smile, eager to tell his story. "She was quite lovely, dark brown hair and slender. My friends," he said, gesturing to the Germans, "saw her and brought her to me several nights ago. They know I appreciate more than just good horseflesh. It was in this room that I took her, there on the floor. She did not fight me, much as I wanted. I slapped her, beat her and kicked her, showing her my method of softening, before finally taking her. She cried, she seemed to be praying but I couldn't tell since her mouth was full of blood."

He stopped to laugh, as did the Germans, then continued.

"I was going to pass her to my friends, since they enjoy wearing down a beaten sow but her praying, or whatever it was, was most annoying. So I slit her throat."

Lucius lifted his head to look at Tigellinus. His voice was a croak.

"You raped her and then slit her throat?"

"Yes, but it was just one prisoner. The rest are yours."

There was silence in the room. Even the breeze from the window died. Lucius stared at Tigellinus, who drew back. He sensed the change in the air, as did the Germans. I moved a short step forward, and then another as the short German watching me turned to see Lucius. There is a moment before battle when the hourglass sands pause and the air stills. I sensed it, Lucius sensed it and the Germans sensed it. Death was near.

Lucius bent back over the list, his right hand moving inside his cloak as if he were adjusting his tunic.

"Ah, Ofonius Tigellinus, she was the most important of the prisoners. And you have killed her. She was the one person you should not have harmed."

"And why is that?" Tigellinus' voice was a sneer. The short German put his hand beneath his fur and turned to me.

"You should not have hurt her, Tigellinus. She was the only thing standing between you and this."

Lucius moved in one swift motion, dropping his cloak on the desk and bringing his *gladius* out. Before Tigellinus or any of us could move, he struck Tigellinus across the face with the flat of the blade so hard Tigellinus flew out of the chair into the wall amidst a spray of blood. In the back of my mind, I knew his jaw and nose were broken and he would not move for a few fateful moments. As he hit the wall, Lucius drove his heavy war sandal's spikes into his groin. A short quick blow and Tigellinus' ear was gone.

The room filled with shrieks of pain and the tall German was on Lucius' back, one arm pulling him away from the screaming figure while the other arm fumbled under the bulky fur cloak to bring his sword into play. He blocked the way of the one-eyed German who moved around the desk to strike at Lucius from the other side. The desk was large, the crumpled form blocked him and he could not reach Lucius, merely bring his sword across to strike him.

The hunchback came at me, his cloak back and his sword out. In this small room, it loomed larger than it ever had on the battlefield and I felt terribly unprepared. As he circled me, he smiled. With only one good arm, I was no match for him and he knew it. So I did the cowardly thing. I submitted.

As I saw the melee of three figures out of the corner of my eyes, Lucius striking down again and again at an unseen figure on the floor who was screaming and begging and two figures striking my brother, I took my helmet off and went down on one knee. I bowed my head slightly, opening my neck to the sword. I looked down and saw his feet approach. Curses in German came from the corner, with the sound of sword on leather and metal and screams. The feet stopped in front of me and I noticed how dirty they were as I sensed a sword being raised. I waited for a moment. As the sword reached its peak, as he readied to separate my head from my body, I spoke two words, "Vastung chank" loudly, as my hands raised my helmet. I knew he heard the words, "Rat eater." He bellowed and the sword went higher, as they it always does when rage erupts.

I shoved my helmet on, and lunged forward at his shout, driving the metal crest of my helmet into his mouth. I felt it go deep into his jaw and bone cracked. When I drew back, his mouth was gone, only a dark hole and blood where it was. The pain was certainly unbearable but brief for a German warrior. He recovered and lunged at me, wild with pain, off balance. I stepped to my left and my good right hand came from under my cloak with my sword. I brought it across his throat. Blood gushed, he went to one knee and in trying to get up, he stepped on his long fur cloak and stumbled, falling on his back. He struggled to rise but was weakening fast. I thrust through his heart. My blade broke. His blood was everywhere.

The three had lurched from behind the desk and now were separated. The one-eyed German was nearest me, facing Lucius, back to me. The giant was facing me, on the other side of Lucius. Lucius was trapped between them. He had shaken out of the German's grip and now his sword was out, moving back and forth between them. They had removed their fur cloaks and I saw a dozen battles in dark places, screaming and shouts and the dull, dead sound of metal plunging into body and the terrified scream of horses. It was quiet here now, with just heavy breathing and the shuffling of feet and the moaning of some kind of animal in the corner.

Now the giant was looking at me and I knew one of them would be coming for me. One-eye was facing Lucius and did not know I was alive and behind him. But the moment flashed and the giant shouted a warning to one-eye. He spun and saw me. He moved forward toward me, a smile of anticipation. My hand came from my cloak and he saw the dagger. His mouth opened but before a warning came, I threw the dagger. He moved his head slightly and the knife went wide. A squeal came from across the room and I saw the dagger had lodged in the giant's shoulder. I pulled the broken blade from the body at my feet and one-eye circled me, the hunchback's body between us.

Lucius and the giant faced off. Covered in blood, Lucius looked thirty again. He moved with grace and half-bent, edged closer to the German. Even to a German, a barbarian used to blood and slaughter and hacked limbs, Lucius' murderous smile must have been terrifying. In battle there are no smiles but here a blood-drenched madman muttering promises of gutting death in flawless German was cornering him.

One-eyed lunged at me and I moved to the side, he could not rush me so long as the body of the hunchback was between us. The floor was slick with blood and one slip or trip on the corpse and I could impale him with the stub of my sword. So he lunged and circled and lunged.

Suddenly there was a guttural shout from the giant as he swung at Lucius. Lucius parried but the force drove him back a step and he slipped in the blood of the moaning man and went to one knee. The German swung overhand and when Lucius met the blow, he raised his hand for another blow. Lucius rolled to his right, and lashed out at the German's leg. The hamstring popped audibly and the German screamed as his leg gave way. As Lucius struggled for footing in the blood and stood, the German lunged at him. Lucius drove the German's blade to the right and brought his own sword up under the arm of the German, the force of his blow cutting through the fur and tunic into the armpit. Another scream and the German dropped his sword and stumbling on one leg, drove at Lucius, his massive bulk now looming. Lucius moved to his left and drove his sword into the upper chest of the German. Bone shunted the blade to the right and it went deep into the chest. The German grunted weakly and fell face down. He did not move.

Lucius flipped the body and pulled his *gladius* out. He moved behind one-eye, coming at him from his blind side.

"Rat eater," he bellowed and as one-eye half turned, he struck him across the throat while I drove my broken blade into his side. He fell and twitched, then was still.

Silence. Only breathing, heavy and labored and pained. Then a gurgle from one eye and then silence. Exhausted, Lucius and I looked at the bodies and then each other. I tried to smile but couldn't. We faced each other, spent and amazed. After a moment, we heard a sound. Tigellinus.

Lucius went to the moaning figure at the wall and dragged him over near the door, to a place with little blood.

Tigellinus opened his eyes. Terror had replaced arrogance and through a torn mouth, teeth and blood dribbling over his chin, he tried to speak.

Lucius looked at him and brought his sword before the cripple's face.

"You killed my wife, Tigellinus, and now you will die. I had thought to save her but you made that impossible. So prepare to die."

Lucius rose and prepared to deliver the deathblow.

"Lucius," I said, laying my hand on his arm. "Remember the promise."

He looked at me with narrow eyes.

"Why should I spare him? He has killed hundreds and relished their suffering. Now he shall pay for one. He should suffer a hundred times worse."

"Lucius, the promise." My voice was almost a cry. This moment, Lucius, my brother of honor, might disappear.

Lucius' breathing slowed and he stood over the fallen man, undecided.

At last, he knelt beside the man and spoke in the voice one uses to tell a secret to a child.

"In a moment, we will leave and you will never seek to follow or find us. Your handsome face is wrecked beyond remedy and your bones are broken, but you will live. It will not be much of a life but you will live. But if I hear you are seeking me, or this brother of mine, or any of our family, I will find you again and I will be free of any promise to spare your life. Then, in that dark night when I find you, I will remove your manhood and leave you to bleed. I will remove your feet and your hands also. You will probably die but even if you live, you will not walk or eat or live in any way like a human. Because you are not human. You are a dreadful thing, a monster of nightmare. So you will live a nightmare life. You deserve to die but you will not, tonight."

Lucius thrust Tigellinus aside and as he did, his leg, bent at several angles from the broken bones, fell into view. I looked down. Around his thigh Tigellinus was wearing a leather thong, with a small golden coin attached.

"Where did you get this?" I tore it free from his leg and held it before him.

Tigellinus stared dumbly at it as if seeing it for the first time.

"From her. From her. I got it from her. Take it. Please." His words were bubbles of blood and tissue.

There was a moment of silence. In the distance, I heard voices.

Lucius knelt beside him and took the thong from my hand. His voice was quiet.

"Describe her. Be very careful of what you say. Leave nothing out."

Tigellinus went to bite his lip but he had no teeth and little lip.

"She was beautiful. Quite beautiful." His tone was pleading. Even in his agony, he was searching for the right mixture of flattery and scheming to rescue his life. "She was slender, as I said, with dark hair and dark eyes. She was beautiful. Muscled. Not in an ugly, peasant way but strong."

Lucius looked at the leather thong, and then at Tigellinus.

"Go on."

"She was dressed in simple peasant garb, not as a fine lady. Her eyes and her …"

Lucius interrupted him.

"Why did the Germans pick her for you?"

"They said she had the mark of a witch and would know secret things of value."

"The mark of a witch?"

Tigellinus took a breath, choked and spit out clots of blood and teeth.

"Her hair. It was witches' hair."

Lucius stopped breathing for a moment. He glared at the man who was not so much a man, waiting.

"She had that white streak in her hair. They said it was from lightning striking her and filling her with dark powers. All such witches in their land are killed or used for secret divinations but here she would be harmless and I could…."

"You are sure there was a white streak? Where exactly?" I interjected.

Tigellinus raised a bloody hand to my face and marked the exact place where the white streak was.

Together Lucius and I stood and looked at each other.

"Beatrice," I whispered.

At that moment, the legionaries rushed in, Boudicca leading the way. He came immediately to Tigellinus and sniffed him repeatedly before looking at Lucius to see if he should finish the work begun. Lucius shook his head, retrieved the bloody prisoner slip from the desk and prepared to leave.

Before we left the butcher's room, Lucius bent over the prone figure.

"We are going to leave now, Ofonius Tigellinus. I have left you your hands and feet and your genitals. We are going to retrieve the prisoners. If we meet any resistance, if there is any treachery, from you or your soldiers or anyone, I will come back here and make you into a monster for the world to see, just as I said I would. If I cannot find you here, I will look until I do find you. If I am detained or imprisoned or killed, one of my men will find you and do to you what I have promised. I have smashed your face and broken a dozen of your bones. Your knees are both broken and inside you are bleeding. You may die before the dawn. I do not care; I will have kept my promise. If you live, hide yourself. If I hear your name on anyone's lips, I shall find you. Find a hole, crawl in it and live out your days. And hope that we shall never meet again."

And so we went out of the room, leaving one who had delighted in others' pain to savor his own.

At the octagonal room down the corridor, we paused to speak to the legionaries. Gaius Metellus looked at us with some wonder. We were covered with blood and bits of bone and tissue. The battlefield had come to the palace of marble and gold.

"It is not our blood," I said. "We need to get to the prison. Quickly."

"Yes, quickly," Lucius said. He started to move, then his knees gave way and he fell to the floor.

Before I could move, Gaius had bent, removed Lucius' armor and then we saw. There was a deep wound on his chest where the German's sword had cut through the breastplate, several ribs appeared to be broken and smaller wounds, made by a dagger, were leaking blood. His tunic was soaked with blood and I saw now he was pale, paler than I had ever seen him.

In a dozen battles, I had seen wounds like this. If no doctor was near or a great deal of blood was lost, such wounds were fatal. Lucius had lost a great deal of blood.

He opened his eyes.

"Julia, you…" He looked at me.

"I will, brother. I will find her and protect her."

Hearing that, he closed his eyes and was unconscious.

Chapter 18   The Prison

The legionaries were experienced in transporting badly wounded men and moved to action without being told. A litter was fashioned from the inlaid wood couches and satin purple pillows softened the trip for my brother.

"Gently, gently," I found myself saying as we exited the Domus Aurea and hurried to Titus Flavius Sabinus' home. The soldiers moved ahead quickly, clearing the way, their horses and swords knocking aside the few travelers in the darkness that impeded our progress.

Still it was almost half an hour before we moved through the gates and carried the barely breathing figure into the large bedroom facing the garden. Titus Flavius was there and gave orders quickly. Water was heated and there appeared the small man who was at dinner, who had expressed such an interest in seeing my arm.

He ignored the noise from outside and the murmuring within the room. Lucius' armor and tunic had been removed and the man examined him closely, probing the large chest wound, pushing on the dagger wounds to see how much blood was coming and seeming surprised there was so little. He gently touched the ribs and bent to hear the breathing. He looked at Lucius' eyes and his fingertips and then covered him. Standing, he gestured to me and Titus Flavius to step outside. His expression was grave.

"You are his brother?"

"Yes."

"Is there an army surgeon near?"

"No."

"Regrettable. I shall be honest with you. An army surgeon has a greater knowledge of such wounds. Such a surgeon has seen a thousand of these wounds and can tend them in his sleep. As a physician, I know enough to cleanse and stitch and bind but I cannot say that my care will be as good as one of your surgeons. But I will do my best."

"Could we not send for an army physician?" Titus Flavius asked.

"If these wounds are not tended very quickly, Titus Flavius, this man will die of a certainty."

He looked to me. I nodded. He turned to go but hesitated at the door and as his assistant entered the room with instruments and water and cloth, he spoke to me with a sad voice.

"It is not likely, Tychon, that your brother will live the night. He has lost much blood and his body is growing cold, as bodies do before death. We will try to keep him warm and we will dress his wounds and insure no further bleeding. But I have never seen a man with such wounds live more than a few hours. Prepare yourself."

He entered the room, the door was closed and Titus Flavius and I stared at each other. We went back to the library and sat. He gave me a goblet of wine and I gestured for him to add more water. I sat for a time, thinking of the farm and how we played as boys. We would take our wooden swords and play our games. I would be Hannibal and Lucius would be Scipio Africanus. I would outwit and outfight him until at the end; his skill and cleverness would defeat me. I always played Hannibal.

"Why do you always want to play Hannibal? He lost the war," he once asked me.

"But for most of the war, he won. And his victories were glorious."

"But in the end," Lucius laughed that bright summer day, sucking on a fruit, lying on his arm glistening with sweat, "in the end, he lost."

He rolled over on his back and looked at the scuttling clouds. "And no matter how many times we play, brother, Hannibal will always lose. The might of Rome, brother, the might of Rome."

In the library, I whispered that to myself.

I looked at our host and he looked at me with a concern that was deep and real.

"He must live. We are so close." My voice was stammering.

I told him of our encounter with Tigellinus and the prospect of rescue. I told him that three Germans lay dead in Nero's Golden Home and there was also there a shell of a man who had killed so many. And I told him Lucius had the beast's life in his hands and spared it to keep a promise.

"He kept his promise, Titus Flavius. Will that buy some favor from your god?"

Titus Flavius smiled a sad smile and laid his hand on my arm, which was trembling.

"I will go with you, Tychon, to the prison. Have your centurion assemble your men. I will take a few from my cohort and we will go get the prisoners."

"Should you not stay here, Titus Flavius, to see after my brother?"

"Tychon, your brother is in good hands. If I am here, I can do nothing to save him. But if I go with you, I may be of some help to save the one your brother is most desperate to save. If we bring her to him, we bring him a medicine that is stronger than any salve the best physician can apply to him."

We rose to leave and at the door, I caught his arm.

"I don't know the physicians' name, Titus Flavius. He has my brother's life in his hands." My voice caught and I felt wetness on my cheek. " And I do not know his name."

Titus Flavius looked at me and I thought I saw tears there.

"He is an old friend and a good man, Tychon. His name is Luke."

Our rescuers were assembled, a squad of cavalry with Gaius Metellus, and a half dozen Urban Cohort troops with Titus Flavius. We passed beyond the gates and we moved quickly from the Palatine Hill and soon passed along the darkened streets. Soon we passed on the Via Nova between the House of the Vestals on our right and the palaces of Caligula and Tiberius on our left. How strange, I thought, that a house containing women committed to virginity for life in service to their gods should be across the street from palaces filled with debauchery and perversions of the worst kind.

We turned right at the Temple of Castor and Pollux and left into the Forum, now shuttered and dark except for shadowy figures scuttling to avoid the flickering torchlight of our outrider cavalry. Perhaps they were the spirits of victims from the mad Caligula or the vicious Tiberius whose death prompted the citizens of Rome to cry "To the Tiber with Tiberius," wanting his body dragged through the streets and thrown into the river as so many of his and Caligula's reign had been.

As we passed the imposing Temple of Jupiter Optimus Maximus, I looked at Titus Flavius and felt reassured. There were few men in Rome who commanded authority and power in this strange time and one of them rode beside me. He glanced at the Temple and in the shadows of the uncertain torches of our cavalry, he seemed to shake his head, perhaps sharing my dark thoughts about noble ideals laid low by vicious emperors, and a sad shadow flitted across his noble features. Perhaps he too had once believed in the Empire.

At last we came to the Temple of Concord and drew up our horses. We dismounted and moved past the Temple. I paused for a moment to look to my left at the Gemonian stairs, the famous place of execution for the dishonored. It was here that prisoners were strangled and thrown down the stairs to lie and rot. Dogs would come and eat them, passersby and children would defile their bodies and only after several days would workers place hooks in their bodies and drag them to the Tiber. I had the flash of a young girl with a streak of light in her hair lying here and I recalled her executioner lying in a dark room with bones broken and barely able to breathe. It was justice.

Across the steps from the Temple of Concord was the Mamertine, the most notorious prison of Rome. In it, prisoners of the empire held no hope of redemption or rescue, just cold, and blackness and the day when a swift sword would bring an end to their misery. The entrance was guarded by two of Titus Flavius' men. Inside were a half dozen legionaries, who regarded our armed band with suspicion.

"I have come to take prisoners you have," Titus Flavius said, with the calmness and faintly bored voice that said this was an unexceptional transaction. They were unpersuaded.

"Do you have authority?"

The questioner was an old centurion, and his eyes played over our group as he spoke. They settled on Gaius Metellus, wearing the cross crest of the centurion, and there was a glance that said young pups did not merit the rank.

"I am the Prefect of the Urban Cohort, as you certainly know. I have authority over all prisoners in an emergency. And I have written authority."

With that, he produced the written paper from Tigellinus. The centurion took it, drew back slightly when the saw the blood on it. He looked at Titus Flavius, then again at the blood stained document and then at us.

"Was there some difficulty in getting this authorization?" His gesture meant to indicate the blood.

"Not at the end," Titus Flavius replied coolly.

The suggestion of bloodshed was as good as a bribe. With a smirk of satisfaction, the centurion told us where the prisoners were and waved us through. The guards opened the main door and Titus Flavius, two of his men, and three legionaries with Gaius went with me. We passed by the cells on the first floor and moved to the lower cell.

Its opening was a large hole, a covered grate that breathed death and disease as we neared. There was no light below and as we moved the grate aside and prepared to descend, the smell of excrement and rot, tempered only by the freezing temperatures, rose from darkness.

Titus insisted on being the first to descend and did so, holding two torches. When he reached bottom, he put both torches into stanchions on the walls and called for more. Three were tossed down to him and soon we could make out the figures. I swallowed hard when I saw. There were only four people there, not the dozen I expected. And Julia was not there.

I was lowered next. A sound greeted me as soon as I touched the soiled straw that covered the damp and filthy floor. It was a voice.

"Tychon, is it you?"

A figure struggled to his feet and stumbled toward me. It hardly seemed human, all hair and filth and rags. But it was human, someone I thought would be dead. It was Antonius, manager of the estate and Julia's father.

I embraced him, although embarrassed by his filth and degradation, he tried to push me away. The man who carried me on his shoulders when I was a child was now captive to the embrace of a one-armed man. I swallowed hard with the memory and for a time we did not measure, I held him there. He would not be taken again.

At last I felt Titus Flavius' hand on my arm. He pulled us apart.

"This is Antonius, our manager, our friend, Julia's father," I explained. Titus Flavius nodded.

"Where is Julia, Antonius? And the others."

"Gone," the old man sobbed and looked at the top of the hole, as if expecting them to appear.

"Where? Who?" I blurted out.

"I don't know where. A man came and had papers saying he had bought us. They took everyone except us." He gestured at the others, old and weak and not worthy of the chains that would bear them to market. There was no profit in such as these.

"I tried to hide Julia, Tychon. I had her dress as one of the others, cover herself in filth and look as worthless as she could manage. But their leader saw through it immediately and took her first of all of them. I tried to stop him, Tychon, I begged him but he beat me and said he had power of life and death over me and I should not tempt him to kill me."

Antonius thrust his swollen face at me, revealing the deep gash on his neck from a ring or whip handle.

"We shall find her, Antonius. We shall find her." I took his hand. "When did they come?"

"Two days ago, Tychon. They must be far away now and I fear we shall never see her again. The empire is so large. She could be anywhere."

"The empire is not so very large, Antonius. There is nowhere this man can hide. We shall find them." I hoped he believed me.

We lifted the four of them from the cell and went to leave. The veteran centurion greeted us with a knowing smile.

"Not so many as you hoped for, prefect of the urban cohort. Slim harvest, eh?"

He was most fortunate Lucius was not there. Titus Flavius merely smiled.

"Do you know the slaver who took the other prisoners? Or where they were bound?"

"Bound? I am not sure. And one slaver is much like the other. After all, I am not a jailer by calling; I am a soldier who fights. I merely serve here until the matter of emperor is settled."

"Do you not think it is settled now?" I asked.

"Perhaps my crippled friend you do not know that there are those who think another should be emperor, not the old man who now nears the city."

"And who might be your candidate?" Titus Flavius asked.

"His name is Marcus Salvius Otho, and you would do well to seek his favor, old man." He sneered at Titus Flavius and I smelled the heavy wine. It had made him insolent and rash. This was a good thing.

I reached into my pocket and brought out a handful of coins. I held them out so he could see they were almost as much as a half-year's pay.

"You may be a place holder for now, centurion, but you should be comfortable until your exceptional talents and loyalty are recognized by Marcus Salvius Otho."

I paused to give his addled brain time to assess the coins.

"So who was the slaver and where is he bound?" He finished his counting and his dull eyes met mine.

"He is headed toward Brundisium but said he had other stops to make. He did not say what they were or where."

"And what is his name? What does he look like?"

"I don't know what his name is. He calls himself Vindex but no one thinks that is his name. He crosses our palms with gold and we could care less what his name is. Of course, " he paused to belch, thinking to observe the rules, "he always has the authorizations and pays the official prices to the proper authorities. He pays us only to compensate for the cost we have of turning them over to him. He takes prisoners and sells them. He dresses well and pays well and smells pretty."

He chuckled and belched again. He must have been drinking the entire time we were with the prisoners and well before we got there. Perhaps it was the drink that allowed him to tolerate the awful odor that filled the air, now augmented by the foul stench from his mouth.

"Where was he taking them from Brundisium?"

"The mines perhaps. After all, they were prisoners."

Even in the chill of the prison I shivered. The mines.

"Which mines?" Titus asked.

"A mine is a mine is a mine. How should I know?" His speech was slurring more and drool was next. Where was his cheap wine hidden, I wondered?

We did not want to leave knowing so little. So we stood there while the horses and riders and rescued prisoners waited.

"Can you tell us who knows more about him?" I shook the coins and he came alert, slightly.

"No one knows much about him. He is a regular, the usual jailor told me before he left. But he is a kind of ghost. He comes, he goes, and we do not know where."

"So there is nothing you can tell us."

"No."

I frowned my disappointment in his response and gave him only half the coins. Titus and I went to the door and were preparing to exit.

"Noble Romans, a moment," he called.

We turned and looked at him.

"He said something that was peculiar." I stared at him without moving, then held the coin bag for him to see. "He said this would be partial payment of an old debt. I looked puzzled and he restated it. He said it was a very old debt."

I tossed him two coins. Suddenly quick, he caught them.

"And there is a thing that may help you identify him."

"Yes?"

"A mark. A curse, my mother would say. A sign the gods have marked him as a warning. His hand," he whispered, as if the gods might mark him too, "his wine hand, all red and dark and when he raises it, you cannot take your eyes off it … it is cursed."

I tossed him two more coins and we left the prison. The air outside was now very cold

As we returned to Titus Flavius' home, I was alone in the darkness. Julia was swallowed up in the Empire's vast darkness and I did not know where to begin searching. The one who was always at my side to guide us would be destroyed by the news and I could do nothing for him either. I was no help for anyone I loved.

As we dismounted and the horses were led away, I stood in the courtyard gloom. Outside the walls were a thousand streets and roads and Julia, if she were alive, was traveling one. Inside, I feared the physician's words. The light of the door that opened to us seemed no more warming than the gloom beyond the walls.

Titus Flavius gently took my arm and led me inside.

All was quiet. Servants moved about without making a sound. Doors were opened quietly and closed quietly. Steps made no sound and no voices echoed. A deathwatch.

I returned to the library, alone. Romulus and Remus and the wolf stared down on me without pity. The wolf had nursed them and was perhaps watching years later when one brother died and the other lived. My wine goblet was still there. I left it. The room was darker and colder now and that was good. It was cold on that field where a dirty and terrified child wandered lost among the dead and dying. Perhaps he had not traveled so very far after all.

I remembered a time when I was angry with my father. I was very little at that time and felt quite the prince. I do not recall what it was that angered me but I was certain I could punish the one who loved me most if I hid myself. So I went into one of the rooms used for storage and hid. No one went there. It was musty and filled with old furniture, broken and waiting for repair, covered in cloths. There was a space under an old table where I could lodge, and as I settled in, I was sure if I spent but an hour there, my father's anguish would drive him to regret denying my wish. His stern rebuke to me would melt and he would grant me what I wanted.

It was early evening when I hid away and as the time passed, the evening grew late and the house grew quiet. Servants went to bed, the dogs quieted, the animals of the farm fell asleep and I was alone. The room grew very cold and the darkness seemed to make it colder. I shivered. I wrapped my cloak about me but after a time, it could not keep out the night vapors. Soon I was very cold and the darkness seemed to be drawing me to a strange land far from home. It was a land of strange and frightful creatures like Medusa or the Hydra. And I was alone and without a weapon, or even food or water.

At last I knew that my father was not coming. He did not care if a half-breed orphan lived or died. I had only imagined I was truly loved. I would stay there and die, only being found in a hundred days when I had become no more than bones. Or I could leave and find my way back to the universe of my family and be humiliated in front of my father and beaten by my tutor.

I began to cry quietly. I came to understand that my family was all I really had and whatever I had wanted was nothing compared to those I loved, even if they did not love me in return. I knew then that it was my folly that had brought me here. I repented of my wickedness there in the dark in the cold, not knowing what I should do.

There was a sound in the room and from under the table, I could not see what was moving. Perhaps it was Medusa and if I looked out and saw her face, I would turn to stone. So I stayed quiet and tried not to breathe. Perhaps she would pass by and find another wicked little boy to turn to stone.

"Tychon, are you in here?"

It was the voice of Julia, soft and warm in the cold room.

I leapt from my hiding place, smashing my forehead on the sharp edge of the table. I staggered toward the dim light of her lamp.

"Yes," I blurted, trying not to cry.

She stood there in the doorway, small and beautiful, her long brown hair flickering in the pale light. Her eyes seemed to shine and I was so relieved that this night I would not turn to stone.

"We have been looking in all the rooms for you, Tychon. We looked outside but could not find you. We looked in the barns and the baths and the wine press. We looked in the vineyard and the arbor and everywhere. I am so glad to find you. We were worried that you might have gotten injured. Or worse. If we could not find you in these rooms, we would have to tell your mother and she would have to tell your father when he returns…"

"'Returns'?" I interrupted. "He has gone from home?"

"Yes, he was called away several hours ago on some Senate business."

I breathed deeply. I would be spared humiliation and a beating. And I knew that my father's love was unchanged. I moved outside into the hall quickly, to be in the light. Almost at once, Lucius was there. His smile was broad and then disappeared.

"Brother, we have been looking everywhere for you. I am glad to find you." His hand touched my shoulder and squeezed. "But you appear to have been wounded in your adventure." He gestured at my forehead. I touched it and my hand came away bloody. A deep gash was leaking red down my face and onto my tunic.

They took me away, awakened a servant to clean and dress my wound and for some time, I bore the scar of my abortive refuge.

In the library, I touched the spot where the scar had been and looked to the dimly lit doorway to see if any young rescuer was at hand. Nothing.

Then, almost magically, there was a woman there. Not so young and hair not so long.

"Please come get something to eat, Tychon. It will be a long night."

I rose without complaint and accompanied Lydia to the dining room. Food was set out for us and I lay on the couch without taking any. Lydia stood over me and looked at me with sorrow.

"I am very sorry your brother is hurt, Tychon. Please know that I and others are praying for him."

Seeing my expression, she touched my arm.

"Our prayers might seem like just words, Tychon but their power is more than you can imagine."

When I rose to go to where my brother lay, Lydia blocked me.

"Luke asked you to be brought here, Tychon. He will be out to see you in a moment. He is a fine physician and your brother is in excellent hands."

We sat without talking and after a few minutes, Luke joined us.

"Your brother is alive, weak and not far from death. He has not moved nor has his condition changed since you left. He is still pale, but his body is getting no colder. We have him covered and additional braziers have been brought into the room for heat."

"I want to see him," I said.

"Of course," he replied.

We went to the room and when the door opened, a wave of heat like a smithy's forge struck me. The room was warmer than any room I had ever known but when I touched his forehead, his skin was cold as a corpse.

How pale he looked, like an ancient with few days left, his hair flat against his head and his lips slack. I reached under the covers and took his hand and it was as cold as his forehead. I dropped it and stepped back.

"Is he…?" I asked.

Luke quickly stepped forward and put his face against Lucius'.

"No, he is not. Yet." He looked at me with compassion. "Leave, Tychon. Go get some rest. If there is a change, I will come get you."

I returned to the library. Lydia started to follow but I closed the door behind me and was alone. The hours passed, the chill grew as the lamps went out and the room's brazier guttered, then died. In the darkness I could not see, nor did I want to see, the wolf and the two brothers doing their business. I did not want the hungry eyes of the beast to see me in this hour.

Somewhere in the dark, I fell asleep. As I lay on the couch, wrapped in my cloak, I dreamed, scenes cluttered and crowded. Our ancestor Lucullus vanquished a tall and menacing Mithradates in front of the temple of Artemis and crowds gathered to praise their liberation. As he turned to accept the laurel crown, his face became Lucius. Then I saw our father at the side, standing in the atrium that awful summer. He spoke to us of bravery and went off to die in our mother's embrace. He re-emerged from the room, his face now Lucius. Then laughter and voices as Julia walked with Lucius through the vineyard. Then he left Julia and dug my body from the dead pile and carried me to the surgeon and put a dagger to his throat. As he worked on me, Lucius turned his sword on advancing Germans until Boudicca appeared from nowhere and guarded me while Lucius took blow after blow, and bled.

And then as the awful swords struck death at Lucius, light came around us and enveloped us, and warmth like that of rising summer sun bathed us. A surgeon appeared and I sat up, and Boudicca made a noise of a puppy content. The surgeon was gone and in his place was someone else, a woman. Older than the surgeon, she radiated such light I could not see her face but only her outline in the surgeon's tent. She appeared and smiled at us and I saw that Lucius was bleeding no more and I was young again, and whole. From under her skirts she brought candies and offered them to us and said something that sounded familiar. I looked first at the candy and then at my brother. Lucius was there beside me, and Julia also, and they looked at me with their still young faces. They laughed and nodded to me to accept the gift. I turned to take the candy and then started. It was not our aunt. She was someone else, but I could not remember her name. And it was not candy. Her hand held three objects wrapped in beautiful purple cloth. I knew which one was mine. I laughed, a free laugh such as not sounded for many years, and I took mine. Holding it in the palm of one hand, I unwrapped it with the other and was unsurprised when I saw it was a pearl. I wrapped one arm around Lucius and the other around Julia and was about to ask her how I could use both arms when she spoke my name.

"Tychon."

And again.

"Tychon."

My eyes opened.

Lydia was there, in the brightening light of morning, standing by the door. Outside there was the noise of a home awakening. And something else.

"What is it?"

"Something good, Tychon. Something very good."

I ran past her to the room where Lucius lay. The door opened as I approached and I felt no blast of heat.

I went into the room and to Lucius. He lay still, not moving, eyes closed. I looked at Luke.

"Touch him," he said gently.

I touched his forehead and then reached under the heavy covers to take his hand. His skin was not cold and there was the beginning of warmth in him.

"He has made it through the night, Tychon. He may live and if he does, it will be not as the result of anything I did. He was as near death as any man I have ever seen and I did not expect he would live. If he recovers, it will be an answer to the hundreds of prayers that have gone to the throne of God this night. Many have prayed for him, Tychon and it seems their petitions to the most high are being answered."

I sank to my knees beside the bed and looked at Lucius and remembered my dream. His face seemed to change as I looked at him. The lines, which had grown so deep and hard, now seemed to soften and I recalled the face in the dream that smiled and wanted me to take the gift. Was this the gift? No, I seemed to hear.

After some time, Luke came and pulled me to my feet.

"We will give him something to drink and care for him, Tychon. Several of our company have offered to care for him and we will not leave him alone. He will be well cared for. There are matters of urgency for you, I understand."

I nodded and looked around the room. Luke's assistant was there, along with another, younger man who had been at the dinner. He smiled at me and held the door. I moved around Boudicca who was lying at the side of the bed and had the look of someone who would not be moved. I gestured to the dog to come with me, planning to feed it. Strangely, it looked at Luke, who nodded. It got up and walked out beside me.

"So you have added him to your growing company of friends? Have they invited you to attend their rituals also?"

Boudicca did not respond but gave me a look that said he understood my jibe.

After feeding the dog and leaving it with a servant to take outside, I ate briefly and went to find Titus Flavius. He had just completed greeting and visiting with the supplicants and was in the garden.

"Good news, Tychon, I understand. Your brother is a strong man and I am praying he will recover."

"Thank you, Prefect, for your kind words and your help."

We sat and for a moment enjoyed the sound of the fountain, surrounded by red and yellow flowers, struggling to counter the noise and movement just beyond the walls. The city was awake, moving and coiling, racing, stumbling and grasping. Its labors were the signs of life.

"How will we find her?" I could not restrain myself.

"We will find her, Tychon. There is nothing I will withhold in searching for her. We will look and seek and we will find her, no matter how long it takes or how far she has been taken. You have my word."

"But the mines, Titus Flavius, I have been to the mines in Spain. They are the abodes of death, entry rooms to Hades. The mines in the earth swallow men up and poison them and shafts collapse on them and no one lives. The very air that hovers over mines poisons and kills the birds that fly over them. The mines are death, slow death, and agonizing death. If Julia and the servants have gone to one of those, there will be no records, no names, and she will die without tomb to mark her…"

"Calm, Tychon, calm. You are an intelligent and clever man, so use your mind. Your emotions are ruling your thoughts and your teacher Seneca would not approve such fear overwhelming. Use your mind. Do you think the slaver would pay money to buy prisoners and then transport them to mines in Africa or Spain? He would never make a profit doing such. She is not destined for the mines, I am confident, despite the bleary tales of a drunken prison guard. I have sent word to all my troops in the city to look for this man. My cohort has experience in finding men who seek to escape; they know where to look."

"But what if he resells her before we find him. Or decides to…"

"Do not fear, Tychon, he is nearby, I am certain," said a voice from behind me.

I turned to see Claudia Procula. "His parting comment, which Titus Flavius relayed, means he has a debt to settle and he will stay here until it is."

"How can you be so sure?" I asked.

She smiled and touched me on the arm.

"I am quite sure. This man called Vindex is no stranger to me. I shared his bed and life and have been searching for him many years. Trust me, I know the ways of my husband, the former procurator of Judea, Pontius Pilate."

Chapter 20   Interlude

A few times each lifetime, the ground beneath your feet tremors, shifts or drops away and nothing is ever the same again. Changes whisper, hint, slip by undetected. Sometimes they appear, seem inconsequential, then cause a sharp intake of breath. So it was as Lucius recovered.

Two days saw a change in breathing and a shift in color. The breathing was no longer the rasping of a man near the end. The color had become pale, instead of white. Then no change.

I stayed in his room, taking my meals there and sleeping on a couch placed there for me, just as he had sat beside me when I was retrieved from the dead pile and stitched back together. I spoke to him all day and most of each night, telling childhood stories of games in the fields, classes and hidden secrets, beatings by the tutor, dinners and feasts, summer dreams of daring adventures, races won and lost.

I recounted tales of our freezing in Britannia or fighting through tangled forests in Gaul. Often I would remind him of narrow escapes, bold tactics and the stolid defense of the legion's front line. I challenged him to contradict my version of our adventures and waited with expectancy for his lips to form corrections. His lips did not move. And I told more stories.

Each dawn I rose with hope that he would speak and each late night I would fall asleep alone and fearful. How long would he remain like this and what should I do if he never awakened? He was always the leader, the one who drove forward, waving his sword and I came along to protect his back. The sword of leadership was not shaped for my hand.

Each day I heard the reports from Titus Flavius and they brought no hope. His troops had checked exits, interrogated slavers, searched prisons, compounds, farms, and found nothing. Pilate had taken his prisoners from the Mamertine and vanished. The ports did not see him, neither Ostium nor Puteoli nor even Brundisium. The taverns on the Via Appia had not seen such a man. Titus even interrogated the post riders who travel all roads in all directions from the capital to the farthest reaches of the empire. There were no main roads they do not travel and a company of prisoners led by a man with a brilliant red hand does not easily escape notice. The post riders had not seen such a company.

"How could he disappear so completely?" I asked one day, exasperated and fearful.

"I do not know, Tychon. But since he has not been seen on the roads or at the ports, then it is likely he has not moved at all."

He sat in his study, behind him the busts of his ancestors and one of Augustus, whom Titus Flavius alone respected of the emperors. Arrecina

Clementina, his lovely and gracious wife of many years, stood by his side, her expression one of deep sorrow for me. I was not sure if it was my fear or my weakness she felt such compassion for.

"What do you mean?"

"I mean if the fox does not run, he must be in hiding."

"He is still in Rome?" I remembered Claudia Procula assuring me he had not left.

He nodded. He had gone to ground. We had the resources of the empire and we could not find one man, or his prisoners. I thanked him and left.

I spent a restless hour in the room with Lucius, pacing, talking, then sitting quietly. Boudicca looked at me as she might a lunatic. Luke returned and agreeing with the dog, he suggested I get out of the house for a while.

I gathered my moneybag and without putting on any armor save my sword, I was about to exit the door when a voice called me.

"Tychon, are you leaving so soon?"

I turned and saw a man of middle years with a youthful face and a rope burn on his neck.

"Timothy, you are a most welcome sight," I blurted out, without thinking. A smile unbidden came to my lips and I took his arm with my hand, squeezing. I frowned in surprise at the thought of how much I had missed the man.

"Are you going far, Tychon and when will you return?" He stood there with his cloak over his arm, obviously just having arrived.

"Not far," I replied, "just getting out for a short while. Physician's orders."

"May I go with you, or would you prefer to be alone?" He was putting on his cloak.

"You are most welcome." I smiled and was again shocked at my pleasure.

We left and made our way toward the Forum by way of the Via Sancta. At the Forum, we skirted the hundreds of vendors and stalls and the crowds of slaves, merchants, artists and lawyers, Senators and soldiers and foreigners rushing about, each so intense and determined. We turned on the Vica Jugarius, on the way to the Halitorium where I thought to buy some cabbage.

"I want to buy some cabbage, Timothy," I explained as his look questioned where we were going. "I grow tired of the meat and the fish Titus Flavius serves each night. I yearn for vegetables, pears, and figs. The cabbage here is most delectable."

"Have you always enjoyed vegetables?"

"Yes," I said, recalling long nights lingering after supper as children, eating cabbage dipped in vinegar or chewing on apples until our stomachs hurt, telling tales of the heroic and legendary feats we would accomplish when we were grown and serving in the legions.

"I have always like cabbage, though not as part of Cato's regimen." I smiled when I said it and looked at Timothy to see if he understood the joke, seeing that Cato felt eating cabbage and bathing in one's urine would cure most illnesses. Timothy frowned, either from puzzlement at my words or disapproval of a crude reference.

"Also, I want to get some *garum* for my fish. I like a sauce made from tuna and Titus Flavius serves mainly the expensive kind made from mackerel. I am used to the watery kind we use in the legions and the awful *garum castum* they use in Judea has ruined me for the expensive kind. The Halitorium should have a good selection."

We passed beneath the Temple of Jupiter and I moved to the side of the street and sat on a stone. Timothy hesitated and then left the flow of people and sat beside me.

I looked around and was silent. I felt Timothy looking at me.

"This place is special to me, Timothy. It has been for many years. This spot appears on no map and will never be noted except by Lucius and me."

The sounds of the crowd faded as we sat there. Another sound grew loud, a retinue of soldiers and Senators appearing from the mists of those days, walking down this street, the emperor in the lead. He was young, so very young, and he walked with a kind of awkward lurching, sometimes bumping into the person next to him or just behind and talking ceaselessly, proclaiming, declaiming and disputing with a tone or a glance. And there was in his eye the fleeting darkness that marked Caligula as mad.

"My brother was here that day, Timothy. He was buying something and talking to a young man he had met once, a few months before. The young man's family was not so noble or wealthy as ours and had fallen on hard times. The young man did not look or act like a patrician, with a square face and the solid stocky build of a wrestler. His hands were big, his fingers thick as sausages and his neck twice the size of normal. Yet here he was this day, a young man working his way up the *cursus honorum*, hoping that some day he might achieve that which so many young men his age desired, honor and glory and the esteem of men.

"His job this year was as aedile. Now there are many things an aedile does but the one thing that brought him here this day was his duty to keep the streets clean. This street, filled with merchants, travelers and animals, was notorious for being filthy, deep in animal waste and human offal and garbage. He was directing a crew of slaves cleaning the street and as he was speaking to my brother, Senators and the court of the emperor appeared.

"The emperor stopped and called the aedile to him.

"'You call yourself an aedile!" He screamed at him. "You are a disgrace to your office and to Rome. Only a pig would allow such filth and dung to clog our streets. You are a pig, an awful disgusting pig with your thick neck and peasant's body and stupid look. Perhaps your mother pushed you out the wrong orifice and that is why you love living in this muck!' His retinue burst into laughter while the young man shrank under the assault.

"Then the emperor motioned to a slave and taking from him a small shovel of dung, he stuffed it down the young man's tunic, saying 'If you like it so much, take it with you, pig.' He wiped his hand on the young man's tunic and whispered to him 'If this street is not cleaned up, I will have you castrated, pig.' And with that, Caligula moved on and the young man was left in the street.

"All around, the people had shrunk away, terrified the mad emperor would turn his wrath on them. But Lucius had not moved from the aedile's side. 'Come, let us get you cleaned up and see what we can do with this street.' He took the aedile to a nearby home of a friend of our family where he could wash and dress. Thereafter, Lucius and the young man became very good friends. Not long after that another soldier stabbed the mad Caligula because he had humiliated him because of his battle wounds.

"Years later we all served in the same legions together in Gaul and Britannia. That is why that young man, Vespasian, sought Lucius out when he was to go to Judea. Their friendship began here, in the middle of dung and offal and garbage."

The sounds of the street returned, Caligula disappeared into the collective memory of Roman madness and we sat in silence for a time.

"And look where it has brought us, Timothy. Loss, death, suffering, destruction. If Lucius had shrunk away with the crowd, then…"

"Consider, Tychon. Vespasian stood there, covered in filth and taunted by the emperor. Your brother had a choice. He stood with the outcast, the one scorned. He cleaned him up and did not abandon him. And there was forged a friendship that endured."

"That friendship, that loyalty has put everything at risk for my brother. Was it worth it"

"My friend, there was a carpenter I know who did the same thing, and still stands by the castoffs of this dark empire." He paused to let me consider that man and when then he continued. "And we are very near the end, I believe."

"My brother? He will die."

"He too is in God's hands, Tychon."

I said nothing.

"You are the near the end also, Tychon. There is just a little more to come."

Timothy rose and started toward the Halitorium. I grabbed his arm and turned him back to face me.

"Do you mean we will find her soon?"

"I do not know that."

"Then what are you speaking of? Surely not Lucius' death!"

"No, Tychon, I am not speaking of death, but life. Not Julia's, not Lucius'. Yours. Your new life is not far off."

He pulled away and moved down the street. He stopped and turned back to me with a smile. I joined him for the last part of our journey.

Chapter 21   Awakening

As the summer month named for emperor Augustus waned and the evening air grew cool, farmers took their harvests to Rome and sat in taverns humming with whispers of conspiracy. Speculation birthed rumors as the army of Galba snaked its way to Rome, feeding on prey each day. In October, General Galba arrived. His arrival was as bloody as his march.

At the Milvian Bridge, marines from the fleet at Misenus met with him. They had had been formed into a rough army unit to help protect the city and now sought recognition from Galba. He roughly dismissed their request and unleashed his troops. A thousand marines were slaughtered and the remainder drew lots to see which tenth man would be executed. This brutal punishment of decimation, long discarded as proper punishment, multiplied hatred among the legionaries and the city felt its dread confirmed.

Galba thus began his reign, which would not last half a year.

And through all of this, the search for Julia continued.

Twelve days after our battle in the Domus Aurea, Lucius opened his eyes.

The sun came through the window and touched his darkness as it had done each morning. I was sitting on the side of the couch and to my amazement, his eyes fluttered, stopped, and then opened. I sputtered his name and his eyes, unfocused and watery, looked at me, empty, then worried. He tried to move his mouth but I shook my head. His searching eyes moved past my shoulder but then came to rest on my face.

"Do not try to talk. You are very weak and need to rest. I have everything under control and you should not worry. Close your eyes and rest."

My lie tasted bitter but he believed me and closed his eyes. He slept for another twelve hours, waking at dusk to take some water and wine and then went back to sleep.

And so it continued for another twenty days. Each day, he was awake for longer periods but seemed exhausted after each effort. He had lost much weight and seemed gaunt and grey from being inside. Luke saw him each day for the first two weeks but then left for a time and the family physician replaced him.

In the home, the daily routine continued but there were more faces I did not recognize and many of them, I felt sure, were Christian. Lydia had left on business after the battle and Timothy also, on other work. I missed Lydia's warm words and Timothy's soft strength.

Each day I thought of Julia, what we might do to find her beyond the net Titus Livius had cast, and what I must tell Lucius when he recovered. Each night I fell asleep thinking of Lucius, Julia, and, increasingly, Sophia. Their faces and voices filled the long hours from dusk to dawn and I wondered if those Christians were still praying for us.

I wondered where Sophia was, here in Rome or far away and how she looked and if she was safe. I spoke with no one about her; I felt strange thinking of her so much. What did the likes of me have to do with someone like her.

In the last week before October, took solid food, for the first time since our bloody encounter. Two days later, he was helped to sit up. Four days after, he was helped to stand but despite determined effort, he could not stay upright. Three days later, he stood, with assistance and two days later, took his first steps. Each improvement saw him exhausted and sleeping long periods but there was no going back. My brother would live.

Throughout this period, his weakness prevented many questions. I would silence him each time he was about to ask a question. I would reassure him but his recovery must soon overwhelm my evasions and force the truth. I refused to tell him how many weeks had passed and I was dependent on his weakness and confusion to shield me.

"What shall I say to him?" I asked Titus Flavius and Luke, who had returned. "If he learns she is still lost, he will surely try to leave to find her. I do not want him to die in the effort."

Luke smiled a tired smile. He had been closeted with Titus Flavius every day for a week, working together long hours into the night. I did not know what so focused their attention but the dark marks under his eyes and his sluggish movement told me he was exhausted.

"Tychon, he is not so strong as to be able to make it to the street. A search is beyond him. You do not need to trouble yourself about him flying off to look for her."

"It will not always be, Luke; he will recover and very soon press me. What am I to tell him?"

"The truth, Tychon," Titus interjected.

My look spoke a question and Titus answered it when he rose from his chair to go to his desk and hold up stacks of messages from his desk.

"These are reports, Tychon, from across Rome, and from across Italy and from across the empire. These are messages from my urban cohorts, from legionary posts and camps across the peninsula, from foreign contacts in Sicily and Egypt and Africa and Syria. Scores of Roman officials and soldiers are alerted and looking for her. And your friends, the *evocati* also are looking and their messages come each day. We have put the engine of the empire to work for us and while we have not found her yet, we will. The fox has not raised his head yet, but he will. And when he does, he will be seen and we will know."

There was a welcome confidence in his voice. We sat for a time, the three of us, Titus Flavius reading messages to me, answering my questions, offering reassurances as Luke struggled to stay awake. Finally I felt I could tell Lucius how everything that could be done was underway.

Later, as we rose to leave, I stopped Luke.

"You look very tired."

"I must indeed. Titus Flavius noted it also, earlier. I think I will rest for a while."

He turned to go but I caught his arm.

"Before you go, I have two questions for you."

He turned back to me and gestured for us to sit on the benches sitting in the hall, between busts of Julius Caesar and Cicero. They paid us no attention.

"Luke, you may have heard of an old legionary saying, 'Do not make your physician your heir and you will live a long life.'" I smiled but Luke yawned.

"Luke, I do not share that legionary sentiment about you. Some physicians may be burial details with a bag of medicines but I have great respect for you and therefore I think you will speak truth to me."

I hesitated again. To speak of a dreadful thing can give it a life, which may bring it to you in the night.

"Do you think a man can die from loss, or disappointment?"

He looked very much like my father when he answered.

"Tychon, a man can die of many things that do not injure or maim. A heart can be wounded with fear, or loss, or dishonor and the body will follow to death. I know why you ask this. And Lucius is most blessed to have such a caring brother. But I can say with some confidence that so long as there is any question of her living, he will live and get stronger and his love will strengthen him to find her."

He paused for a moment before continuing.

"Love causes the most amazing sacrifices, Tychon. A husband can love a wife and never give up looking for her. Just as a wife may never give up on her husband and may spend her life searching for him."

In a moment, I saw Claudia Procula's face, and I was encouraged. I breathed a long breath and rose to go to Lucius. This time Luke caught my arm.

"And your second question?"

"Perhaps you will not want to answer it. You are a fine physician and you have taken very good care of my brother. Your business with the prefect is certainly a matter of privacy for you both but I am very curious. You have spent many long nights with him and I am wondering what task has so engaged you?"

"Tychon, you are an historian, are you not?"

"Yes."

"Well so am I. I am writing a history, a history of a man who was also God, our Lord. It is the record of his teachings, his works, his power and the good news he brought to all of us. I have completed the first part of it, his actual life and death and resurrection. I am now almost finished with the second part of it, the establishment of his church and the men and women who are even now carrying his message to the farthest parts of the empire."

"And Titus Flavius, what is his role?"

"He is the one I am writing it for, Tychon. He is the patron who supports my poor efforts. I travel the empire, interviewing those who walked with our Lord, confirming their stories, verifying details and compiling a true history of his redemptive work. Titus Flavius provides monetary support and puts me in contact with officials all across the empire. Doors are opened, ways are made easier."

"And he does this for what reason?"

"He loves the Lord, Tychon. He wants the truth to be carried to all those living in darkness. He is not an apostle, nor a teacher, nor a pastor. But he has wealth and influence and he uses those to assist us in telling the good news of eternal life. And he does that because he loves Christ and loves the father who sent Him. He is 'Theophilus.'"

"'Theophilus,' god lover." A fine Greek word.

"Indeed, Tychon, he is such. He has lived through the reign of emperors good and evil. He is a man of renown and honor and above reproach. And when he became a Christian, the kingdom had a new outpost in this city, from which the truth can flow. The story I am writing is a beautiful one, Tychon, and a most powerful history." He paused to consider. "Would you like to examine this history?"

Now it was my turn to pause.

"As an historian, Tychon, you could be most helpful to me in pointing out any unclear passages. Yours is a trained mind and your experience would aid me."

Seneca would have shaken his head in disgust at how easily my vanity enticed my agreement.

"Send it to me and I will be happy to read it."

"Much of it is almost indecipherable, I am afraid, Tychon, with my marginal notes and abbreviations. Would you permit me to read it to you and then provide a written copy later, when I have a finished?"

"Yes, that would be fine. When would you like to start?"

"As soon as your brother is a little stronger."

I nodded agreement and as we separated, Luke turned to me with a smile.

"Let us do our work in your brother's room. The reading will strengthen his mind and engage his heart. It will be a time for his healing in both body and spirit."

That all was to come but on that first day, as I returned to Lucius' room, I did not tell him of what Luke and I had agreed. When I entered his room, he was standing. And for the first time, when he opened his mouth, his words were not the weak and feeble mutterings he had been uttering for the past few weeks. His voice was stronger and clearer and I knew my dissembling was done.

"I am up, Tychon, and I am recovering. Now tell me, without the sauces of rhetoric, where is Julia?" His eyes had new clarity and they were fixed on me. I hesitated for a moment and discarded any idea of evasion.

"She was taken from the jail by a slaver, brother. We know who he is but we do not know where they are. We have everyone looking for her and Titus Flavius has his entire cohort searching. The veteran brotherhood is also looking. She has not left the country, we are reasonably sure, but we are still watching all ports and exit points."

"A slaver? No, you cannot be right. A slaver?" He sagged onto the bed. "Not my Julia, my precious Julia. Not a slaver." He was near tears.

I sat beside him and put my arm around him.

"We will find her, Lucius. The fox will bolt and we will snatch him."

"But how, Tychon? There are hundreds, or thousands of slavers. How can we hope to find one among so many?"

As he spoke, he weakened, the words like drops of water gushing, then slowing and finally dripping, leaving their broken cup empty.

"He is," I hesitated, wondering what effect the knowledge would have, "distinctive."

He looked at me with the question. He held himself up with a stiff right arm gripping the bed.

"His hand, Lucius. It is wine in color. Purple. It is distinct and unusual, especially for a slaver who dresses in fine luxury and jewels." I waited.

At first, Lucius said nothing. He stared at me, uncomprehending, eyes dull. Then he understood, and flaring, tried to stand. He wanted to shout but could only whisper.

"Him! The one on the road. The *telones*? That one? He is the one who took her?"

"He bought her and took her and the rest of the household staff."

"'Bought her,'" he repeated again and again, his voice lower each time.

For the next hour we talked. Again and again, I explained all that was being done. Again and again, he questioned whether we had done all that could be done to prevent them leaving the country. I told him of Pilate's long flight from

Claudia Procula and her confidence he had not yet fled the city. At last, he paused in his interrogation

"Is this, Tychon, what it has come to?" He was sitting on the bed, his head low and his voice lower. My arm was around him and he felt like a frail and gaunt child, facing a long sickness and a slow recovery.

The day grew late and Lucius began to slump. He was looking down the long days to a terrible outcome and he was not sure if he would live beyond it. At last he lay down and his eyes searched the deep darkness. I could not hold on for very long to the cheerful reassurances and any moment I feared he might see my heart but mercifully, exhaustion dragged him into sleep.

His eyes were closed for just a moment and then flashed open, in a sudden rush. He pulled me close to his whisper.

"The dead zealot's prophecy, Tychon. Lightning where there was no storm. Beatrice's hair. A mouth with no words…it was true….if I had believed, I might …" I drew back and stroked his head gently, coaxing him to rest.

His grip on my hand relaxed and his eyes closed again, a deep sigh releasing his struggle. I sat back and looked at his sleeping form for a long time. This was my brother, my friend, and I could not give him back what he most sought and treasured. He had saved my life and would have died that I might live but now I could do nothing to help him.

Through my tears, I saw the Shadow Wolf reappear in the gathering dusk. I had always wondered at its color and size and now I made out its form perfectly. It appeared not in my dreams or the gathering darkness of the camp or the solitary evenings in our tent or cabin. It strode into the light in this home, blinding those who lived here to its presence. It was not so much a stranger, as I thought, but an ancient figure stirring in the depths of our hearts and the menacing world about us. It fed on death and despair. It had never died but merely slept, waiting for the smell of blood and terror to awaken. In the places of light, it had merely assumed another figure, harmless and toothless, masked as ambition or honor. It was not young but quite old, not alpha of a pack but a solitary hunter. Its teeth were as white as they had been millennia ago when it was born and its appetite for the noble and the virtuous was unsatisfied after many feasts on the bodies of the reckless and the unwary.

In its forms of war, or politics, it was ennobled in verse and celebrated in song but it was a killer, pruning the herd of men of those who clung to traditional honor or morality, ripping apart the innocents who flee the onslaught of evil, but feasting mostly on those large and powerful men who catch its bloodthirsty fancy. It was their treacherous plots that called it from its den to assume its disguise and move about the corridors to slake its thirst.

In this home, this refuge from noise and filth and the violence of the city, it showed itself in the library. Its face was in the mural, turned from feeding the two young founders of Rome to look at me, daring me to alert others to its presence. It knew, as everyone who had ever sat in that room and seen its face had learned, that one of the brothers she was feeding was fated to die while the other would live. I recalled her face and knew then that the reason I had never made her out in the shadows was that she wanted us to come to her city, a city born of treachery and blood and violence, before exposing her identity.

Which of the faces was mine, I wondered? The one who died or the one who lived? I continued wondering as I left the room.

As October dawned and then waned, while our eyes were on a recovering brother and each day brought no new intelligence that would lead us to Julia, the city buzzed with the activity of Emperor Galba's agents.

The profligate Nero had exhausted the treasury of the empire through the millions of sesterces he spent on the Golden Palace as well as the expensive gifts he lavished on his adoring sycophants. Galba set his men to recover those riches and his agents harried the friends of Nero, the Senators, merchants, artists, performers and debauchees who populated his court. Their efforts were unavailing. The riches were now in statues, estates, and jewelry. Only a dribbling amount was recovered

The efforts did yield a bountiful harvest of hatred, however, and later, when Galba cut back the grain allotments to the poor, the empire teetered. Those who had predicted violence on the death of Nero were prophets.

Luke was right.

Lucius was strong and his heart was strong. He slept well that revelation night and all the next day, rising only to eat one meal before going back to bed until the following morning. When he arose the next day, he greeted me as I entered his room with the servants bringing his food.

"My brother, I am sorry for all the pain I must be causing you. It is no light thing to sit at a bed and watch another prepare to die, and the worse is if that person is a loved one. I have always been most fortunate in having you as my brother."

"Lucius, you may recall what Seneca taught us: 'Sometimes even to live is courage.' There has never been a man of greater courage than you."

And so we sat to eat. His color was good. His appetite was stronger than usual and we even laughed as we told war stories, his memory always accurate and mine occasionally. He sat at a table, having sworn he would never eat from a couch again after his long imprisonment in his bed, awaiting death. When we finished eating, Lucius took my one good hand.

"Brother, I want to thank you for saving me in our fight with the Germans"

I laughed and squeezed his hand.

"I would normally be happy to take credit for such a bold move, Lucius but I cannot. I was not aiming at his shoulder. I was not aiming at him at all. I was aiming for the other German and missed. It was just random. Random."

"Random?" He considered for a moment and his voice was serious. "I do not think so."

As the servants cleared our dishes, I told him of Luke's readings I had arranged. Lucius sighed and refilled his cup. The color in his cheeks was more pronounced.

"Tychon, is this necessary? You are the historian, not I. You love the stories of the past. I want to hear the stories of today. You want to hear of philosophies and theologies. I want to hear of what new vine grafting has been successful. You want to hear about half-naked nymphs in the forest and I want to hear of fat cows herding in my meadows. What have I to do with the history Luke writes?"

I did not want to mention the obvious reasons for hearing about this new faith and its personal connection to our condition. Instead, I was bland.

"Indulge me. I think you will find it more engaging than you think. And I do not think there will be any half-naked nymphs."

And so it was that each day, Luke would come into Lucius' room and read to us. At first we would sit, I in a chair, Lucius in his bed or sitting up, Luke pacing about, reading and pausing, waiting for questions or commentary. As Lucius became stronger, he also would stand and walk about the room or we would go into the garden to hear the story of the carpenter known as Jesus, the Christ, the infant religion's title for the redeemer. We were told of his miracles and his teachings and those who opposed him and finally killed him, only to see him rise from the dead and confound their plans. Luke would read, we listened, we questioned, we scoffed, we argued and later, we sought to understand.

One day, several days after we began, we were sitting in the garden and the day was well on. Gaius Metellus had joined us that day, as he often did, to listen to the reading, along with Arrecina Clementina. Surprisingly, she spoke often, more boldly than a proper Roman wife would be expected to, and demonstrated a remarkable grasp of Greek language and Judean history. Her remarks sometimes countered an argument of Lucius or sought clarity in Luke's story but always were offered with a smile and a disarming gentleness.

The warm afternoon had begun to give way to the cool of the season and the time for the evening meal approached. Only one servant was nearby, bringing wine when we gestured, leaving us alone otherwise. Gaius was sitting underneath a tree in the garden, listening but saying nothing while overhead, a solitary bird sat on the limb chirping, and then swooping to the fountain for a quick drink before resuming its solitary vigil. Each time it moved, we looked at it until finally Lucius spoke.

"Luke, in your story, your carpenter talks about a raven and how your god feeds it."

"Yes?" Luke paused in his pacing to look at Lucius.

"He says that if your god feeds him, then he will take care of our needs, food and clothing and the like. Do you really believe that? Will he magically appear and present me with bread and figs each morning?"

Luke sighed and sat down, smiling at Lucius. The bird paused, listening for the reply.

"No, not so simply as that, Lucius. Our Lord was talking about the concerns that trouble all men. It is not for men to sit down, cross their arms and wait for a divine being to fill their bellies and clothe them. But the Lord who loves us and died for us does not want us to get caught up in the possessions of this world and become fearful and anxious. Instead he wants us to seek his kingdom and trust that our ordinary working effort will be blessed by our loving father."

"Ah, yes, his kingdom." I interjected, happy to challenge Luke on that word. "I still do not understand 'his kingdom.' Where is it? Where are its soldiers? Where are its battles? What are its medals?"

Luke tapped his chest in reply.

"The kingdom is here, Tychon. In my heart and the heart of every believer, who follows the Lord. And it is everywhere a believer walks and in every deed of a believer who glorifies our god. Its soldiers are we who believe. We who follow the Lord are ambassadors of the kingdom, warriors and physicians for the kingdom. We carry the word in our hearts and in our minds and on our lips. We are citizens of that kingdom and its king is our Lord. The battles are here, in this garden, and in the dark streets of this city and the far lost corners of the empire, wherever men seek life and light and truth. Its medals? There is only one medal and it is eternal life."

For a moment, there was only the singing bird. Then Lucius' brow furrowed.

"A battle in this garden?"

"Yes." Luke's voice was solemn.

Lucius' eyes narrowed and his mouth sought to frame a question.

"The battle is for you, Lucius," Luke said, and then turned to me, "and for you, Tychon. The angels of the lord are gathered about, the Holy Spirit is here, the Christ is at your elbow and he seeks you both. It is a battle for your hearts and your lives."

"But I thought you said your messiah said to love your enemies, not battle them," Lucius said, confused.

Luke paused for a moment. And then continued.

"Lucius, Tychon, consider. You are legionaries sent on a mission to rescue Roman citizens taken captive by a foreign power. He has enslaved them and will kill them. He has a powerful army and powerful weapons. You organize a rescue with your men and you assault the prison where they are held. Now the king was very clever. He took some of the prisoners and telling them lies and bribing them, he made them into guards.

"Now when you assault the prison, will you kill all the guards or just the king's own men? Would you not try to subdue the Romans acting as guards without harming them? After all, they are prisoners too, but are blinded by the king's lies."

Lucius considered for a moment, then conceded he would try to spare the Roman guards who had been duped.

I thought of a question but before I could speak, Arrecina spoke it.

"So some of those you preach to are good people, some are wicked and some are deceived?" It was her turn to be confused.

"No, Arrecina Clementina," Luke smiled at her, "there is only one kind of person, the wicked. In the heart of every man born of woman, there is wickedness. We do not have to teach our children to lie but a great deal of effort must be spent to teach them to tell the truth. Thievery is always easier than work, drunkenness more comfortable than prudence, violence settles disagreements quickly and lust flows from a man like sweat."

His was a tired sigh.

"We are all those guards in my story. Only the king, the enemy of our souls and prince of the power of the air of this world, and his legions of demons, are the enemies of our souls."

"So it is not just legionaries that battle."

"No," Luke said, "it is shopkeepers and artists, sellers of trinkets, slaves who sweep the street, cooks, and physicians. There is no enlistment period, either; you serve until your death, with battles every day and no truce, ever."

Even the bird stopped singing as we considered what he had said. This was too much and my head began to hurt. Lucius seemed untroubled but puzzled. At last, he spoke.

"But there are only some who can enter this kingdom, you have said before. So there must be those who cannot enter because they have too much evil in their hearts. They are beyond the gate and the kingdom's gates are closed to them."

His hand dropped to his waist, as if to touch his sword that was not there.

"No, Lucius, the wickedness of our hearts does not put us beyond the reach of the grace of god. It was the wicked the lord came for, the worst of the worst. Any man or woman may seek and find forgiveness, so long as they are sincere and truly seek new life. And no man of violence is beyond God's grace. All can approach the throne of grace. They enlist by truly and completely believing in the Lord."

Lucius looked unconvinced. Luke glanced at Gaius and then at Lucius. He took a parchment from the middle of a stack sitting beside him and began to read.

"After he had finished all his sayings in the hearing of the people, he entered Capernaum. Now a centurion had a servant who was sick and at the point of death, who was highly valued by him. When the centurion heard about Jesus, he sent to him elders of the Jews, asking him to come and heal his servant. And when they came to Jesus, they pleaded with him earnestly, saying 'He is worthy to have you do this for him, for he loves our nation, and he is the one who built us our synagogue.' And Jesus went with them. When he was not far from the house, the centurion sent friends saying, 'Lord, do not trouble yourself, for I am not worthy to have you come under my roof. Therefore I did not presume to come to you. But say the word and let my servant be healed. For I too am a man set under authority, with soldiers under me: and I say to one "Go," and he goes; and to another, "Come," and he comes; and to my servant, "Do this," and he does it.' When Jesus heard these things, he marveled at him, and turning to the crowd that followed him, said 'I tell you, not even in Israel have I found such faith.' And when those who had been sent returned to the house, they found the servant well.

"So, Lucius, his faith was what opened the gate to the kingdom for this centurion, not faith in the empire or faith in a wooden or marble figure but faith in the messiah, Jesus. His sword and warrior's past did not disqualify him. The ground at the foot of the cross does not admit of higher or lower place. And no one's hands are too stained with blood, or violence, or greed to be turned away."

"Faith, Luke? How does one get that faith?" My question was our question.

"It is a gift, Tychon, a gift from God and no man can merit or gain it on his own. No sacrifice or pilgrimage or flagellation or gold will gain it. Labor all you will, nothing will gain but the free gift given by your Father in heaven."

Arrecina spoke now.

"And faith is often such a small thing, at first, Tychon. It is not always a storm that throws you into the kingdom but a small breeze that bears you there. A gentle thing."

Luke glanced at another parchment.

"He said therefore, 'What is the kingdom of god like? And to what shall I compare it? It is like a grain of mustard seed that a man took and sowed in his garden, and it grew and became a tree, and the birds of the air made nests in its branches.'"

The bird signaled his agreement.

A servant came to tell us the evening meal was ready. As the servants lit torches to illuminate the garden, we rose and prepared to enter the house. I caught Luke's arm and held him back as the others entered the house. We sat under the tree apart from Gaius who was waiting at the door to accompany us. As Lucius drew abreast and was about to enter, Gaius stopped him and began to talk to him. I could not hear what they were talking about.

I started to speak but could not. There was a long silence as we sat there and at last, Luke spoke.

"Is it what we have spoken of this day, Tychon? Are you troubled?"

"No, not troubled. I want to ask a question and I fear to."

"There is nothing to fear. The Lord knows what you want to ask without your words."

"But I have lived unlike you, Luke. I have bedded women and burned homes and slaughtered men. I have marched and fought and never retreated. I have borne thirst, heat, cold and pain. I have swallowed fear. And I have seen that fear in men's eyes before I cut them down. But I have never presumed on any man or asked anything I did not think I merited. Whatever I asked for, I earned. Never would I presume, never."

I stopped, my words having poured out without my thinking. Then they came again.

"And now, after so many years of struggle and violence and crushing losses, you have been speaking of something different, something that I never dreamt I could contemplate. It is like a dream that beckons you not to wake up but to lie back and dream until your last breath. And I do not have any claim to it, no merit, no value. It is beyond me, and yet I …"

Luke took my good arm.

"Is it Sophia? Your brother?"

"No," I whispered, my eyes growing moist, "it is this."

I touched my arm, the one that once was fully mine.

"You told the story of your messiah healing a man with a withered hand."

"Yes."

I sat there, fearful to form the words.

"Is it possible…?"

"Yes, Tychon. It is not beyond God's reach, nor is his love shortened. The spirit blows where it will and no man can say where it came from or where it is going."

"But I am not a believer, Luke. I see the truth in much of what you are telling us, about the evil hearts of men and I hear the wonderful stories about sacrifice and taking another's sin and all the terrible pain your Christ suffered. But I am not one of you. So how can I come to you and ask for my arm to be healed? Would he not want to know why I want to seek healing?"

"And why do you, Tychon? Tell me and omit nothing."

I looked down in the darkness of the tree's gathering shadows and my voice sounded weak and childlike in my ears.

"It haunts me, Luke, the image in my mind of Sophia and me together. I see us on my farm, working together in the fields, trimming trees, pruning vine branches and herding sheep, directing servants and watching the sun set and the children play. And in all those scenes, I have two good arms. They wrap around her and draw her to me. They lift our children over my head and they pull a horse's neck toward me as we ride together.

"And I can never bear the thought of being there with her with only one arm. But I cannot ask because I do not believe."

Luke took my crippled arm in his two hands and smiled.

"There may be some stirring of the Spirit in your heart, Tychon, or you would not even speak of these things. And there was just a little seed of faith in that man with the withered arm. He had only enough faith to believe our lord could heal him and enough faith to come to him to ask for healing. It was not a robust faith of the centurion who knew the power of our lord to heal with a word. It might seem like little faith, but it was enough for God."

The bird had left, the night was dark and I could say no more. There was something stronger than my desire to be whole again. It held me in check, and I did not want to know what it was. Luke held my useless and cursed hand as he might someone whose recovery was unclear.

"Tychon, one arm or two does not matter. Faith in the savior is the only essential. Seek the giver, not the gift, and you will find peace."

He turned to go but stopped.

"Tychon, a man may hold his wife tightly with just one arm."

And I fought to believe Luke's words but as I fell asleep, the Shadow Wolf seemed to smile at my presumption. Lucius had unleashed the beast when he embraced revenge and hatred. I was a part of it and could I escape the consequences?

I did not answer it before I fell asleep.

Chapter 23   The Visit

The year bore on to the end and Lucius' restlessness returned with his vigor. He took to pacing the corridors, early morning and late at night. He found it increasingly difficult to sit for any long sessions with Luke or listen with patience to Titus Flavius recitals of reports from his men.

I moved to my own room and each day, when we gathered with Luke in the garden in the late morning, we found ourselves dressing more warmly and after a time, the servants lit braziers to keep us warm. Arrecina seemed to want to go inside but Luke and Lucius seemed to feast on the cool air, even when their breaths began to show. I finally persuaded Lucius to move inside and thereafter we met in the library, my position firmly set so I could not see the mural.

At last, when Luke departed to visit a church in Puteoli, the sessions were suspended. Lucius grew withdrawn, unsettled and nervous.

One day, I suggested we walk the streets and find a meal at a low and common tavern, preferably one frequented by legionaries. Lucius quickly agreed.

The day was unseasonably mild and the sun shone brightly. For a long time after we stepped outside the gates of our lodging, Lucius stared at the blue sky, unstained by the usual brown clouds of smoke, and breathed deeply, drawing something from the rough stones beneath his feet and the warm sun that bathed him. At last we stepped off.

"What have you heard from the villa, Lucius?"

"Antonius is regaining his strength now that he is back at the farm and working. He reports that the restoration of the main house is complete and the barns and out buildings nearly repaired. Your farm is fully restored also but there was much less repair needed, thanks to Diomedes' faithfulness."

"Did Antonius hire more workers or did the servants who fled return?"

"Some of the servants have returned but," he paused and looked at me with a question "the bulk of extra hands has come from the Christians." He paused and a sliver of a smile appeared. "Apollos chief among them."

I moaned. Must that man join us on this pleasant outing?

"Quite the leader, Antonius says, and disputatious. He argues with Antonius on the proper diet for the cows and the quickest way to reinforce the barn supports, and Antonius says he is right more often than wrong."

Seeing my discomfort, he continued.

"And he is strong, able to work longer than the most experienced farm hand and seems never to eat or drink much. A kind of pack animal, Antonius says."

"Strong back. Weak wit." My whisper was smothered by the cry of merchants.

"And Antonius says another of the Christians works as hard but she does not argue so much as sing."

"She?"

'The day is lovely. Perhaps we should visit the baths today." Lucius was working to conceal a smile.

"The baths will be there another day. Who is 'she?'"

He would not look at me and I could only see his curly uncut hair above his cloak.

"She is the one you no longer speak of, Tychon. Her name has not been spoken for many, many weeks. Why do you now ask?" He turned, and his face was gentle. I turned away.

"I have no reason to speak of her. I do not think of her so much."

Lucius laughed, a sound not heard in a long time.

"You are the empire's worst liar, Tychon. If there were a contest of failed liars, you would be the unquestioned choice of every nation and every tribe. Your eyes shift when you lie. Your mouth purses and relaxes again and again. Your voice rises and becomes a young girl's."

I was not offended by his words but thankful that for a time recently, I had been most artful in deceiving him.

"It is not that you think so little of a certain person, my brother," Lucius whispered, "it is that you think a great deal. And there is something you can add to your meditations."

He looked around as if conveying a state secret.

"You need to know she will be here within ten days."

I stopped suddenly, and a woman with a basket ran into me, cursed my stupidity, my ancestry and suggested terrible futures for my children

"She is coming here? In ten days? Why?"

"Why shouldn't she come here? She has been working hard at the farm after her return and wants to see us."

"Return from where?"

"She has been to Ephesus and other cities near there. She has set matters aright at her own farm. There is no mystery here, no riddle. She wants to see us." He smiled, slightly. "Or perhaps not 'us'."

With that he turned into a merchants' store to look at newly carved statues of Emperor Galba. Their prices had been reduced by half. I joined him and after we had listened to the owner lament that he was compelled to reduce the prices still more to clear out the inventory, we returned to the streets.

The day continued sunny and we spoke little. Perhaps Lucius was able to enjoy the day itself and avoid the Wolf's taunts. I spent the time thinking of our visitor. How would she look, after all the hard labor at the farm? Would she be exultant to see me? Or even know I was there? Would she have forgotten things she said about us? Had someone else caught her eye?

When at last, I returned to the street, I saw we were rather near the prison. In the sunlight it looked no less deadly. Its dull and simple lines could not conceal the dread and pain that seemed to whisper from its rough-hewn joints. Its thick walls hid misery and a thousand unheeded cries for mercy cut short by the axe. This was where the one called Paul, whom Luke so often spoke of, came to die. I shuddered and jumped when I heard our name called.

We turned and were greeted by a messenger who had been seeking us. Lucius unwrapped the note and thanked the messenger who stole away from this place. Lucius studied and looked at me with a small smile.

"Titus Flavius has asked us to return. Guests are coming," he paused, waiting for my reaction and getting none, continued "important guests. The emperor, he says."

Again I moaned. How important could it be for us to attend at the visit of an emperor who was trailed by the Furies, and could not offer enough sacrifices to Jupiter to extend his reign beyond the next few weeks? Why could we not just continue our pleasant walk? I was hungry, and did not want to chat amiably with a doomed emperor.

Lucius read my mind and reminded me tersely that we had an obligation to our host. So we retraced our steps to Titus Flavius' home.

As we neared it, a servant intercepted us. Outside the walls were a dozen Praetorians and legionaries not of our company, along with the litter of the emperor.

"Do you wish me to announce your arrival, Tribune Lucullus?" he asked.

Lucius stood, considering and then nodded approval. The servant moved ahead and we followed behind. Before he could enter the gate, the emperor, his courtiers and guards emerged and moved toward his litter. Seeing us he stopped and motioned his party to pause as we drew abreast. He stepped forward, a large and old man, with the look of an underfed vulture, sharp eyed and squinting, with no trace of humor or mercy. His lip protruded as he spoke and his neck forced his face toward us, cold eyes assessing the state of decay of its next meal.

"Emperor Galba, my deepest respect and honor to you," Lucius said, bowing slightly. I did similarly.

"Lucius Licinius Lucullus. A man of a noble family. A man of wealth and a warrior. Your name is respected, Tribune, and your service. I have an important question for you and I have not found the time, due to the perilous state of our empire's finances, because of the profligacy of the late emperor, to raise it before now. But Jupiter be praised, you are here and I now demand an answer."

I looked at the man's dead grey eyes and his pursing lips and thought the man more Charon bearing the dead to the underworld than Achilles or Hector. There was the stench of the sepulcher about him. Lucius looked at him with a level gaze and if the old general thought this was another cowering legionary or Senator, he would learn otherwise.

"And what is the question, emperor?"

"Where is Ofonius Tigellinus?"

I tried not to gasp and thought that it was good that the question was not addressed to the worst liar in the empire.

"Emperor, is he of interest to you?"

The old man's eyes widened. It was unusual for someone to challenge a question an emperor's inquiry.

"His person has been of use to one of the empire's leaders," he gestured toward one of the Three Pedagogues who lurked in the lengthening shadows near the litter, possibly the small craven one with a pallid complexion and bulbous eyes.

"I did not know this Tigellinus was missing, emperor. And I do not know enough about him to say where he might be."

The emperor stepped forward and put his skeletal finger on Lucius' chest.

"You, Lucius Licinius Lucullus, were seen meeting with him. And no one saw him after that. The room he was thought to have met you in was covered in blood and signs of violence. Do you care to say what happened?"

Lucius looked down at the finger and did not reply until it was withdrawn.

"I offered to sell him a horse. He did not take it. I left. Where he went, I do not know." I pondered his answer. It was a creative mixture of truth and omission.

Emperor Galba considered for a moment. Something in his eyes said he was testing Lucius and keeping a promise for one of his cronies, no more.

Without a farewell or any gesture or word, Galba turned and left. As his company formed up and processed behind his litter, a man of middle age and middle build separated himself from the herd and came over to us. His manner was nervous but his smile was warm.

"Lucius Licinius Lucullus, a man I have long looked forward to meeting. I wish we had the time to spend over food or some particularly fine wine from Spain I have. I would very much like to become your friend and make you mine. I am Marcus Salvius Otho and I have the privilege to serve as a counselor and advisor to the emperor. In the years ahead I feel sure we will have great need of a patriot and nobleman such as you."

Finishing his speech, he smiled a well-used smile and raced to catch up with the courtiers.

"So that is Otho," Lucius said slowly, "I had expected someone larger."

"Oh he is large, brother, in ambition and financial need. He was calculating how much to borrow from you to pay his creditors. As a patriot, you should be relied upon for 50,000 sesterces but as a patriot and nobleman, at least 100,000 sesterces. As for me, I did not rate so much as a glance; poverty makes you invisible."

We went inside and saw Titus Flavius waiting for us. He was slumped on a bench in the atrium and gestured for us to join him. Titus Flavius spoke to us in a low tone, the words slow.

"Bad news, my friends: I have been replaced. The emperor came to me today to say I am no longer urban prefect. The city now is the responsibility of Ducenius Geminus and the urban cohorts will be his, not mine. The emperor feels," he paused, looking to the shadowed corner, "that my service is not what is expected of someone serving him. He is replacing me with someone he feels will bring better order to the city. One of his courtiers no doubt."

There was silence in the atrium as he finished. As prefect of the city and the urban cohort, Titus Flavius was our eyes and ears in searching for Julia. Further, his troops guarded exits from the city and surrounding villages and the slaver Pilate could not move without the cohort learning of it.

Now that was ended.

For a moment, no one spoke. Then Lucius looked at all of us with a quiet determination.

"We shall search with the legionaries. They are not so expert but they…"

Titus Flavius cut him off with a raised hand as he produced two scrolls from his toga.

"You do not have the legionaries, Lucius. General Vespasian has sent both of us instructions. All but a personal guard are to be turned over to Domitian immediately."

Color drained from Lucius as he took the scroll handed him and read. I read with him, as the winter cold filled the atrium.

Vespasian indicated that the increased uncertainty in the capitol made it necessary to increase the security of his son Domitian. In light of Lucius' injury, he felt certain it would be several months before Lucius would recover and would have no need of the cohort while convalescing. Domitian would domicile and direct the troops with the aid of the cohort centurion. He went on to express his hope Lucius would recover quickly, but gave no indication he wanted or expected continued service from either one of us henceforth.

After reading, Lucius said nothing. Titus Flavius assured us that the *evocati* and his servants could assist but neither Lucius nor I said anything. In the vast capitol with all its holes and dark corners, we would not be able to find Julia.

Arrecina sat with us for a time, saying nothing and then retired to her room, certainly to pray, as was her habit. The servants were quiet, fully appreciating the change that had taken place.

Previously we had thought darkness was behind us and light was ahead. That was no more. I thought of the dangers we were now exposed to without the weight and authority of the urban prefect or our legionaries to protect and aid us. Later, in the garden, I could not contain my fear any longer.

"What shall we do, brother?"

Lucius looked at me as he sat down. His face was serious but not grave. There was a good color to it and I knew he was almost at full health, recovered and ready for another battle.

"We shall do what we have always done, brother. We will search and ask and seek and when we learn what has become of the slaver and my Julia, we will move."

I started to speak but he interrupted.

"Please, Tychon, I know our reach is dreadfully short. But we will use what we have and hope for something like the miracle Luke keeps talking about. We will not relent. We will find Julia."

It seemed weak drink but there was no other. I sat in silence, searching for the bird in the tree, but sadly it seemed to have also abandoned us.

Chapter 24   Reunion

The unforgiving cold of winter settled on us like a pall. A strangeness gripped the home as days shrunk into grey tedium. A day began with retainers and clients appearing at first light. Voices and shuffling feet filled the courtyard and the atrium, interspersed with voices praising a patron so generous. After their departure, there was the first meal of the day as we all gathered, and afterward the sounds of dishes being cleared and servants leaving on errands.

But then the sounds of activity disappeared. Where before there had been preparations for the city's prefect preparing to leave on official business, the constant urban cohort officer reporting on disturbances, violence, rumors, thefts and the search for Julia, now there was silence. The master of the house was just another Senator and nobleman, no more urgent business demanding his attention, and scant visitors.

We had contacted two dozen of the Brotherhood and given each an assignment. They were to monitor comings and goings in the city, rumors in taverns, public slave sales, and maintain contact with old friends in the city cohort. But there was still nothing. The fox had not moved yet.

Titus Flavius joined us for our readings from Luke and for a time, we did not confront the dismal prospects that lay ahead. One day, while we were gathered in the library, Luke seemed more than a little distracted. The questions we asked were answered more cautiously than usual. Finally, he turned a sad face to us.

"My friends, I have been thrice blessed by the months I have spent here. My host, Titus Flavius, forever known as Theophilus in my writings, has been more supportive and committed to our cause than anyone in the empire. His honorable and holy wife, Arrecina, has provided a hospitality and care for me which is a model for every Christian wife in the empire. And I have had the opportunity to meet new friends." He paused for a moment and looked, first at Lucius and then at me. His eyes seemed cloudy with tears and he looked down at his parchment.

"So it is with sorrow that I must leave you."

Silence followed, then puzzled looks and a jumble of questions.

"Where do you go, Luke?"

"Will you be gone long/"

"When will you return?"

"Who is going with you?"

Luke waited for a moment. Questions ceased and he smiled.

"I am going to Cyprus, my friends, to the city named Larnaca."

"And your reason for going there must be important," I observed.

"Yes, Tychon, it is very important. Barnabas has written and urged me to come there as soon as possible. A friend of ours, and of our Lord, is near death again."

Titus Flavius spoke as Luke sat back in his chair.

"The man he goes to visit, Tychon, is named Lazarus. His story is well-known among believers. He died and our Lord raised him from the dead. He later went to Cyprus where he carried the word and established a place for believers to learn and worship. He has been there for a long time. His sisters, Mary and Martha, went with him and aided in the spread of the gospel. Mary died a few years ago and now it is for Martha to care for her brother. He is ill, near to death, and Luke goes to see him and Barnabas, who is now with him."

Arrecina, who had been so very quiet during our morning meal and in our time with Luke now rose and left, turning her face away. Titus Flavius followed, and the three of us were left alone. Lucius moved to sit next to Luke.

"There is so much more I would hear from you, Luke. Your words have come to be a comfort to me."

"Lucius, I must go. There is a copy of my writings that Titus Flavius has. You may read them as often and as long as you want. Study them. Learn from them."

He put his hand on Lucius' shoulder and smiled.

"But Luke, when you read those words, there is something…" He paused and his voice caught. "And you saved me…"

Luke squeezed his shoulder and got up.

"Lucius, I am merely a man, chosen to record what I saw when I accompanied the apostle Paul and what I have learned from others of the life and work of our Savior. I am the least in the kingdom and merely a slave to our Lord's will. It is not my skill or wisdom that touches you but the quickening of the Spirit, moving you to a place no man's words could take you. And I was a tool in the hand of our heavenly Father when you were near death. He brought you back from death's edge and I was honored to be there.

"Besides," he said, touching Lucius' shoulder, "I will likely be back before very long. And in my absence, I will write to you."

Luke gathered his papers and left the room. We sat alone and watched the fire in the brazier die and felt the winter creep into the room. The new year was now several days old and after months of searching, we were no closer to finding Julia.

Lucius slumped in his chair, staring at the dying embers, his cloak gathered about him. He seemed to shrink into the gloom as the fire died and he did not move.

"It is hard to believe Luke will not be with us, Tychon. His leaving removes something constant I have come to treasure. Something we both have come to treasure. Timothy comes and goes and Lydia is gone on business and has been for some time. I find there are moments I want to see or talk to one of them and they are not there." He sighed. "What has become of me?"

I gathered my cloak to me as the chill of the room deepened.

"You spoke of Luke's words, Lucius. They have come to affect you more than I realized. Have you become the philosopher now?"

Lucius laughed, a tired and short laugh, without looking at me.

"No philosopher, Tychon, never a philosopher, playing with ideas like a child babbling to speak his first words, to impress the listener. But these words, when he reads them, stir something within me. An hour of his reading passes like a moment. The words, even when he has told the story before, seem new and touch something here," he reached into his gathered cloak and touched his breast, where the sword had sought his heart.

"Watch it, my brother, or soon you will find yourself on your knees praying to their god."

"'Their god' my brother? Just theirs? And are the knees not quite suitable for praying?" He turned and looked at me and then beyond, as if seeing two women on their knees in a moonlit room.

The next day, I left the house and walked the streets alone. The cold weather had driven many indoors but there were still vendors, bundled and frosted, to call to me as I passed, offering hot food or warm drink, worn slaves or tired prostitutes, statuary or jewelry. The forums and marketplace alcoves offered the usual trials and lawsuits for public enjoyment and there were a few hardy lawyers who were unaffected by the cold but fought the air with frosty breath, hot words and rhetorical flourishes. The crowds were sparse and the taunts of shivering spectators seemed to lack their usual vigor and scorn.

None of the noise, smells or faces stilled my thoughts. The cold stabbed, and my cloak was weak defense. As I glanced down the alleyways and tight confines of crooked and dirty streets, I thought again that perhaps we might never find Julia. Months of searching had revealed no hint of her path, her destination, or her owner. She was gone and it began to seem we would never find her. The movement under my feet was perhaps not a chasm opening but a sealing of the hole that had swallowed her.

Had she been spirited out of the city before the guards were posted? Had she provoked her owner and Pilate slit her throat and thrown her into the Tiber? Was she in chains in some dark room less than a few minutes walk from our home? Had she been sold to some house of prostitution and violated by customers who even now passed by me without notice? Perhaps she was now in some mine, with its pestilential vapors, drawing her last halting breath.

My breath stopped and I rested against a fountain, suddenly weary. Moisture from my forehead ran into my eyes and I knew I was sweating. In the cold of the first month of the year with a chill winter wind enveloping me, I was sweating.

I sat on a low stonewall and watched a vendor across the small space of the square banter with passersby. He was selling bread, a single loaf, claiming it was fresh and warm. From where I sat it looked moldy and as hard as the desperation in his voice. It might be that this pitiful bread was all he had to buy food for his family and if it did not sell, then he would have to feed the noxious specimen to his children. The crowd thinned and with no audience he turned slightly and looked at me. He gestured, holding the bread up like a sacrificial offering, with both hands, raising it slowly till it was level with his quivering lips, an offered dread communion. Frozen, his eyes stared and seemed to grow cold.

I nodded slightly and he did not move for a moment, unsure. I nodded again and he rushed across the square, ready to babble some price and assurance as to its value. I took the bread without speaking, saw it was not moldy and had been warm not so very long ago. I took two gold coins from my purse and passed them to him. Shocked, his eyes grew large and he stepped back like a man who was a stranger to good fortune. He held up a coin in each hand as if introducing them to each other. He looked at me long and hard and then as I rose to leave, his words followed me "May the Lord bless you."

As I rounded the corner, I thought I heard him say, "May he lead you to what you are seeking." I spun, came back around the corner. He had vanished. I moved to the center of the square and looked about. Gone.

I touched the bread in my cloak. He had been real, not a ghost.

I walked further, past the Circus Maximus and heard the screams of thousands cheering their teams. No weather could dampen the spirit of the crowds at chariot races and so long as the horses could gain footing and sufficient slaves were at hand to carry off the maimed and dead, the races would continue through weather foul or fair. As there are some politicians who thrive in time of fear and tumult, so there are charioteers who prefer the mud and the churn to fair weather and dry track. I heard the crescendo of cheers that signals the end of the race. Who won, I vaguely wondered?

Soon the chill grew too much for me and I turned to go back. I clutched the bread and wondered why, then puzzled that the bread still seemed warm.

When I entered the house, there was a different smell to it, a difference in light. From the grey and cold street, I walked into light, warmth and a sweet smell. The servant who opened the door for me was smiling. It was a strange smile, knowing and secretive. His eyes clung to me, watching me move through the atrium until I passed to the dining room, from which the sweet smells came. A meal was underway and I was late. There were voices and laughter, a strange sound that I had not heard so much these last months. Lucius' serious injuries and long recovery had silenced that sound and now it was back, I felt the pain of its absence.

As I was near, I stopped and did not move. A voice, male and soft and smiling, had asked if the meat was familiar. A woman's voice answered "no" and then there resumed the sound of eating and music from a lyre.

I was frozen by the word. The girl had made me a statue.

Without realizing it, I had pulled my cloak over my useless arm and had moved to the side, into the shadow of the large statue of Augustus. A moment later I turned to slip out but I did not see the chamber pot alongside the pedestal. My eyes were on the dining room and as I turned, my foot kicked the pot. It skittered across the marble floor, a metal clanging call to arms. It hit the far wall and proceeded to upright itself, spinning and clattering as it settled to rest. I stood transfixed, unable to take my eyes off it, willing it to be silent, and failing. When at last it stopped and silence returned, I looked up and in the doorway I saw six faces staring at me.

Lucius was smiling, a broad and relaxed smile. Titus Flavius' head was angled, quizzical and curious. Arrecina's face was concern and curiosity. The musician stood with his lyre cradled in his arm, his face a frown of irritation that I had interrupted his music with such discordance. Timothy's smile was that of a greeting. And Sophia stood at his side, hands clasped together to keep them from flying away, eyes wide and hair now grown longer and embracing her face tenderly. Her look was inexpressible, with excitement, tinged by hesitation, with flashes of embarrassment and warmth of color that I could not bear.

No one spoke for a moment. Then Lucius moved to me.

"My brother, you have outdone yourself in declaring your entrance in a most daring and dramatic fashion. You could have simply instructed the chamberlain to announce you. But I suppose the drama of the capitol's ways has awakened your flair for stagecraft."

Titus Flavius cocked his head further and looked at Lucius with a disapproving tightness of the lips. This was no time for such raillery, he seemed to say. Then Arrecina spoke to me, while looking at her husband, checking his instinct.

"Are you quite all right, Tychon? We have been worrying about you and were about to send servants to look for you."

"I am fine, dear lady," I answered, trying not to stutter.

Timothy strode forward and embraced me, kissing me on the cheek and drawing me to the dining room. A servant slipped behind me, removed my cloak and before I could quite speak, I was on the couch, reclining in front of dishes clean and apparently designated for me. To my left was Sophia, who had not spoken. I looked at the food set in front of me and sighed. Peacock.

I was still holding the loaf of bread and I placed it on the table, as the others pretended not to notice. I motioned to the wine steward, gesturing for four parts water. At my left there was a slight smile.

"It is good to see you, Tychon." Her voice was rich and soft. My memory had not failed me.

"It is good to see you also, Sophia." I took the wine and sipped it as she smiled, her teeth white against the dark tan of her skin. "You have been out in the sun and working I understand."

"Yes, I have," she smiled with pride, "and the work has been wonderful." She paused and looked at me with pleasure.

"Good friends, good work, the wonderful fatigue that comes after a day of hard work and little rest. The house is restored, and clean, and the barns and outbuildings are rebuilt and stocked. The harvest is done and the wine ready, the olives pressed and oil stored." Her words tumbled to a stop and she touched my arm.

"And I spent time at your estate also. It did not need so very much and when we were nearly done at your brother's estate, Apollos suggested I go work at your home." She pierced a piece of peacock and started to eat it, then put it down. "You have a lovely farm, Tychon, so very much like mine at home but larger. And in your home, there is a warmth and…" She halted and leaned back.

"Thank you for tending my farm," I said. "It is not always easy to work about a strange place."

"It felt not so strange, Tychon, but rather like something I belonged to, or was meant for." The words came too quickly for her and she lowered her head and considered the peacock meat without touching it. "I should say it reminded me of you, Tychon, each corner of the house, each field and grove."

I moved to drink again, the words hanging in the air. I drained the cup and gestured for a refill, signaling with two fingers.

I could not think what to say. My thoughts were cluttered with the image of a man that once had two good arms. I stuttered and was silent. Sophia waited. I stuttered again and only could think to inquire how good the prices were for the early pressed olive oil. Conversations continued until Lucius excused himself from the party.

"Go to your brother, Tychon," Sophia urged, "he looks forlorn and must surely be thinking of Julia."

I left the room, put on a cloak and joined him in the garden, shivering in the sharp winter breeze. Lucius had waved off a servant with a brazier and we stood there among the drooping plants and leafless trees. It was Britannia cold, with sharp gusts and grave chill creeping into hands and feet, the whisper of the shroud for the unlucky, the solitary. No legions at our side on this battlefield.

I put my one good arm around his shoulder and we stood there. When his voice came, it was a whisper.

"She is most likely dead, Tychon."

The words came from nowhere and had never been spoken. Instinctively I spat a denial and he looked at me sideways, a look of appreciation.

"She is dead, Tychon, and I can't go on."

"You can't stop, Lucius. Not now. Not you. You have never given up and you will not give up now, not when we may be very near finding her. You are Lucius Licinius Lucullus, born of a noble family and your family never surrenders. It fights on. She is alive. You must find her."

"My family never surrenders." Lucius looked at me and pushed me gently away to stand full square in front of me, grim and bitter. "Oh they surrender, Tychon, they surrender. My father surrendered when he took poison. My aunt surrendered when her spirit died. My mother was a ghost of a mother after my father died. And my great grandfather, he surrendered magnificently, retreating into wealth and decadence and lavish dinners and books and scholarship, his companions the ones who drove him there. Surrender? I am merely continuing a tradition."

"Oh who is now the dramatic player, brother. Who is playing the part of pathos, looking to summon a tear or a lament? Or is the part not pathos, but cowardice?"

Lucius lunged forward and grabbed me. Before I could protest, he raised me off the ground and held me in the air before him, his face red, perhaps with cold. He held me there for a time and then put me down, his breath visible and rapid.

He pushed past me. Inside he passed by the others and went to his room. Inside the dining room, I heard praying. The voices were low, muted. I could not make out the words and went to my room.

I lay on my bed, the room dark except for the small brazier and its glowing coals, which grew bright with the breeze and then dull red in the still of the deepening evening. This was where I belonged, away from the peace and beauty of the dining room, with the smell of savories and the sound of voices reaching toward a god who must be deaf to such as my brother and me. Next door there was no sound, except for a dog's claws on the marble floor as it paced off the room and guarded the figure lying on the bed, his eyes certainly open and staring at the ceiling.

I pulled a cover over me and soon drifted into a twilight place.

Our old horse trainer, Callimamachus, was leading a horse. The horse was dark brown, with a white streak on its head. It moved in synch with Callimachus and I spoke to my companion, "he is not limping as he used to" and then "Callimachus, that is, he used to limp." No one answered me and I waited while the horse was bridled and then saddled and then mounted. As he mounted, Callimachus seemed to grow younger and became the strong youth I had never known him to be. He walked, then cantered, and then trotted the horse around the yard. Voices of approval and laughter came from the windows of the main house. They were the voices of our father and mother and they spoke excitement and encouragement. I looked over to the house but they were nowhere to be seen. I turned back to the figure on the horse and now it was Lucius, young like I was, not more than ten summers. "Look at me, Tychon," he yelled, "I am ready to race and none will outlast me." He laughed at his own boasting and then rode to me and stopped. He gestured and I came to him. He leaned down and whispered so that no one could hear, "Never surrender, Tychon, never surrender."

"Tychon." The words came again but the voice was not Lucius'. It was Sophia.

"Tychon, up quickly."

I was in the bedroom and the coals were dead in the brazier. It was almost dawn. I threw off the cover and stumbled to my feet. She took my hand and dragged me to the atrium.

In the bright light of the atrium, I blinked. Everyone from the night before was there, except Lucius. And at the side, there was a stranger, an old man I had never seen before, slightly run down and dirty, eyes nervous and mouth weak. As I rubbed my eyes Titus Flavius produced a parchment, small and weathered, and held it out, in my direction, without giving it to me.

"It is a message brought by this man," he said, nodding to the old man, "and is for Lucius. He will not come to the door. I thought you had best receive it and deal with whatever its contents are, before we force the issue with Lucius."

With that, he passed me the parchment. I took it, read it and my breath stopped. It was simply addressed, in a hand I knew well.

"To Lucius Licinius Lucullus, from his loving wife, Julia."

Chapter 25   The Message

As the new year's freshness faded, so did the emperor's time. Even if he had a seer's vision, there was little he could do to slip his fate. Despite his distinguished pedigree and wealth, he was a man singularly unfit for the throne. Inflexible, more comfortable with harsh discipline than mercy, and lacking any political skills or vision, he did little to win the trust of the army or the people.

So when legions across the empire were to swear their annual oath of loyalty to the emperor, two legions stationed in Upper Germany boisterously refused. Galba's statue was toppled and the two legions set fire to a dry peace.

Learning of the rebellion, Galba too late sought to gain support by naming a successor. But displaying the same insensibility that led to this crisis, he named an anemic aristocrat, Lucius Calpurnis Piso Licianus. Despite his impeccable lineage and correct character, the star-crossed Piso had neither welcome reputation among the people nor any military achievement to curry favor with the army. He was a small cup of water thrown on a spreading inferno.

I started to open the letter and then stopped. I looked at the expectant faces around me and saw, beyond the concern and restrained elation, a hint of gratitude that it fell to me. Each seemed poised to take a step back, fearful of the dread blow that might soon fall. I thought for a moment and then turned to Titus Flavius and Arrecina.

"Please leave me for now and let me decide what to do. If you would, attend to this messenger and feed him. Do not let him go until I have had a chance to speak at length to him."

They all turned to go. I caught Timothy's arm.

"Please stay with me."

We went into the library and sat. Servants brought two braziers as the night was getting bitterly cold and frost hung on our breaths.

After a time, I held up the stained, small letter.

"I do not know what this is, Timothy. It may be a breath of hope. Or a final word of farewell. Perhaps death to my brother. What shall I do, Timothy? If I open it and it is certain death, how can I pass it to Lucius? If it is hope, then what right do I have to be the one to first see it? And can we endure more hope only to see it evaporate?"

"You have been meeting with Luke for several months now, Tychon, have you not?"

My face must have shown my impatience at such irrelevancy but before I could challenge, he raised his hand.

"Tychon, I do not know what the spirit is doing in your heart but I do know that your heart is not so hard as you think nor is the spirit of our Lord sleeping but active and about the business of leading you to a place you do not think you will go."

He raised his hand to silence my objections again and I saw the iron that lay behind his youthful face and gentle manner.

"The Lord has barely begun a work with you, Tychon. There is much yet to do and I think it begins this night."

"This is about Lucius, my brother, not me. This is a time for action and movement."

"This is precisely the time for reflection, Tychon. There are moments in all our lives when we find ourselves on the edge of the dagger, poised to tip one way or the other. And in those moments, God is at hand. This is one of those moments."

I said nothing and he pushed the letter back to me.

"Trust God, Tychon. This moment, trust him."

I took the letter.

"Give your brother the letter, Tychon. Julia is God's child and nothing can ever separate her from His tender care."

I stood at the door, frightened. Then I went into the hall and passing by all the faces with their questions, I went to Lucius' room. I knocked and waited. I heard Boudicca come to the door and stand there, panting.

"Lucius, it is Tychon. Open the door."

Silence.

"It is important, Lucius."

Silence. Then a shuffling sound and the door opened. A face, eyes red ringed, hair askew, clothes hanging limply, then a voice, from darkness.

"What do you want?"

I said nothing but handed him the letter. He leaned out to see it in the light of the atrium and reading it, he drew back. He snatched the letter, almost tearing it, and shouted for a light.

Getting two oil lamps, we went into his room and nodding at the faces in the hall, I went in after Lucius and closed the door. We were alone in the cold circle of light.

He sat on his bed and opened the letter. It was short, as I could see from standing against the wall, and he read it quickly. At the end, there was a gasp and then a deep sigh. He turned to look up at me, eyes full of tears. A tired, shocked smile dropped the years away and the young man who ran in fields and chased cattle with me returned.

"She is alive, Tychon, she is alive."

He turned back to the letter and held it in front of him, lest his tears stain it, reading it again and again, turning it this way and that, as if seeking a hidden code or message. Then he held it to his face, seeking some fragrance of her, and finding none, smoothed the page, caressing it tenderly.

"Alive, alive," he whispered.

I sat beside him and held him as he read it again, and again. I do not know how long we were there but at last some noise from outside shook me from my reverie and I opened the door and looked out at those waiting.

"Julia is alive," I announced.

A chorus of cheers and thanksgiving erupted from the small band, now including all the household staff, and all rushed forward into the small room. Voices rose, questions flowed and Lucius sat there in the center of the clamor, looking about as if dazed, and finally passed the letter to me to read.

"My dearest Lucius, my husband, my love,

I am alive and well. I know you, my husband, as I have never known another before, and I am sure you are searching for me. Be assured that if only the smallest crack should appear in the wall of my prison, I should become a mouse to escape through it and rush to you. But I am imprisoned by the one who took me from the jail. My eyes were covered when I was taken and I found myself, along with the others from our farm, at a home in Rome. We were kept there for a time and then moved again. So we have moved several times since, always in the dark night. The man who took us, notable for his wine-red hand, has given us several names and I do not think any of them is his real name. Our current place is in the city and we reside in an outbuilding near the wall. Several guards watch us and we are never left alone. I am one of four left, including Pallas, Damia and Callimachus, but I have heard the slaver say he is about to sell them, keeping only me. The slaver has not abused me but seems to take a particular delight in reminding me that you cannot find me. He hates you and will not say why. On more than one occasion he has said he will make sure you never find me and will leave you to feel the loss that he has experienced at the hands of the empire he served so well. I do not know what to make of his ravings but perhaps you do, since he wants you to suffer or to pay some debt he thinks you owe. Do not fear, my Lucius, our Lord has kept me safe and I trust him to keep me safe this day. How I wish I could hold you in my arms and tell you of the wondrous joy our Lord's grace has comforted me with during this terrible time. I shall try to get this letter to you soon and know that my thoughts and prayers are with you each moment of each day.

Your Julia"

Then scribbled at the bottom of the page, as if written in haste and without looking at the page, were these words:

"Sometimes, for a day or so, there is a very strong odor of onions from beyond our room."

When I had finished reading, the small audience looked at each other. Where was she? A wall? Onions? I knew Rome so little, nothing came to mind.

Then a voice, from beyond the room.

"The onion market. Every second week."

The party divided and standing in the doorway was Lydia, the light from the atrium framing her tall and slender form.

Her face, dimmed in the shadow, was smiling and she moved to embrace first Timothy, then Sophia, then Titus Flavius and Arrecina. She turned to open her arms to me and embraced me, kissing me on the cheek, then stood over Lucius, hands extended. Looking at her with tenderness, he rose and let her kiss his cheek and stood for her inspection as she held him at arm's length and studied him.

"You look well, Lucius Licinius, and it seems the Lord has rescued you from the death bed for more work. I am most grateful to God, and most pleased to see you."

"Most gracious lady, I am glad to see you. I only wish you could see me not just when I am seasick or mortally wounded."

His manner seemed light, his face was fixed in a smile and he cupped her hands in his, as he used to our mother when they talked. In a moment, I saw a tender care pass between them and an older woman reunited with one who was, in some new way, her son. I realized I did not know if Lydia had children and if so, was there a son, for surely if there was, he now had a kind of brother. I stepped back, as if intruding on a private moment. Titus Flavius broke the silence.

"The onion market."

Lydia turned and letting go of Lucius' hand, went out to the atrium. We all followed.

"Yes, that must be near where she is being held," she said, her voice certain and loud. "We would do well to go there quickly."

"One thing first," I interjected, "we need to speak to this messenger and find out any more of where and from whom he received this letter. We must talk to him."

"I will do so," Titus Flavius volunteered, "and the rest of you wait here."

He and Timothy left for the kitchen, where the messenger was being fed. We sat in silence, Lucius and Arrecina and Lydia in one group, Sophia and I in another. Lucius kept looking at the doorway to the kitchen, standing up and then sitting down again. Boudicca lay at his feet, watching and assessing if his master was about to move.

"Do you think we will find her there?" Sophia whispered to me.

"I hope so. We have searched for months and never been so close. Now we know her prison, or the neighborhood it is in. But…" I looked at her full in the face and then turned to hide. Her hand touched my chin and turned it to her.

"What is it?"

"The smell of an onion market carries far and there will be many houses near there that might hold her. We need at least twenty men, soldiers most of all, to seek out all the houses and at the same time. If we just go house to house, we may raise enough of a disturbance to alarm the slaver and we do not want him sneaking away. We need at least twenty men and we do not have them. We did have them and did not have need of them. Now we have the need and we have only a few servants and…"

"…A few women," she finished my thought and smiled. "We can knock on doors as artfully as you and Lucius, Tychon. And we might indeed be more skilled in assessing if the one who answers the door might be concealing your friends."

She smiled a broader smile and took my hand.

"I can be most clever, Tychon, without seeming so. My family always sent me to market with the family's produce because I was a good bargainer and yet seemed not so very shrewd when I dealt with the sharpers and the cutters."

I smiled back at her, at first in amusement at her claim and then at the likely truth of it.

"You should not go with us, Sophia. There may be danger. She said in her letter there are guards. We do not know how many and there may be violence."

"Tychon, I am going. There is to be no more discussion of such. You will be there if there is violence, and Lucius and Titus Flavius. Three men to protect and rescue me if need be. Rather more than enough I should think."

Two and a half, I thought, but then knew she had read my thoughts before they formed.

"Yes, three men, two of them experienced warriors, will be enough."

She seemed quite pleased with her assessment of the battlefield and the warriors needed to deal with it and sat back, folding her arms, very pleased with herself.

"And when we return, Tychon," her mouth was narrow and fixed, "you and I have some words to speak to each other." She looked at my widened eyes. "Or if you do not wish to speak, then I will speak for both of us."

Titus Flavius and Timothy came out of the kitchen with the messenger behind them and we rose. As we started to move closer, Sophia caught my hand and turned me back to her.

"When I was working at your farms in Campania, I had a great deal of time to think and there are several things that I decided."

Before I could inquire further, she turned me back to the others and pushed me forward.

"This fine man brings us this most important letter with no expectation of anything beyond our gratitude," Titus Flavius announced, "but I am giving him a most generous reward for his diligence."

The messenger jingled a pouch at his waist and smiled, toothless and elated at his bounty.

"He received this letter from a man in the street who grabbed him while his overseer was distracted and slipping him this letter, told him to take it to the home of the urban prefect. He gave him a single coin and told him lives depended upon his delivering his message. First this messenger went to the home of the new urban prefect, and being turned away, realized the one who gave him the letter had not known of the change in prefects and then came here."

"What did the slave look like?" Lucius asked, leaning forward.

The messenger spoke up, his voice thin and weak.

"He was small and limped."

"Callimachus," I whispered, in unison with Lucius.

"Where was it this took place?" Lucius bent closer to the messenger, almost in his face now.

"Near the Circus Maximus. He and two others were being taken to the slave market."

"When did it take place?" My voice was as thin as the messenger's.

"Two days ago. Yesterday I went to the new prefect's home and then yours today."

Lucius moved quickly to his room, without speaking, and reemerged a few moments later in full armor and ready for battle. Without speaking, I did the same and Titus Flavius gathered his servants and Timothy, Arrecina, Lydia and Sophia waited for us in the atrium. In the early light, we were on the street, a dozen of us walking swiftly to the Circus Maximus and then westward to the onion market in the shadow of the Temple of Jupiter.

Lucius looked at me as we neared our destination. He patted the letter stuck in his tunic, a promise of our victory. I hoped it was so.

Chapter 26   Blockade

As we passed through the forum, pushing through crowds of spectators heading to the chariot races, we heard the clatter of horses rise above the sounds of vendors and street noise. Turning we saw two dozen cavalry, riding at full speed from the direction of the Praetorian Guard camp. Wearing the distinctive markings of the guards, they were bent for attack, scattering pedestrians like dolls and knocking down and trampling the infirm or the slow. And they were headed for us.

I grabbed Sophia and pulled her to the side, into an alcove filled with lawyers and litigants. Lucius grabbed Timothy and Lydia and pushed them into a doorway and Titus Flavius, Arrecina and the servants dodged to safety.

The horsemen screamed "make way, make way" to no one in particular as their eyes seemed fixed on something ahead.

In a moment, the twenty horses were gone and the dead and dying on the street were the only markings of their progress. Moans mixed with cries for help and pedestrians huddled in doorways or porticoes dazed and unmoving. Arrecina's voice rose in a demand to all the statues frozen in shock.

"Help the wounded. Everyone. Move and see to the injured. Someone find a physician. Move, now."

Slowly the statues came alive. I looked at Sophia and after determining she was untouched, I joined Lucius and Timothy in seeing to the injured. The wounded were carried to the side and covered. Some physicians arrived in a few moments and the dead were piled into a corner of one alcove. Titus Flavius had disappeared in the direction of the riders after a few hurried words to Arrecina. After surrendering one old dead man to his son, I went to Arrecina.

"Where is your husband?

She looked at me with sadness in her eyes, her carefully arranged hair now in disarray, hanging over her eyes, her hands and arms and dress stained red and for a moment, she seemed very frail. Then the strength returned.

"He said something serious must be happening and he went to see what. I think…"

Her voice was drowned out by a piercing scream.

It was the scream of someone who had witnessed a horror. Soon several screams joined it. Motion from the direction of the riders.

The crowd had reformed in the street and now the clatter of hooves split them again, half to our side of the street, half to the other side. And in the center of the parting, a man, running. He was alone and stumbled as he ran. He caught himself and tried to run faster, glancing over his shoulder and then turning his head from side to side as he ran, as if seeking someone. As he came near us, his eyes fixed on Arrecina and seemed to flicker in recognition. His gait faltered and he stumbled again, then gained his footing and lurched toward us.

The sound of horses grew as he ran and came into view, the Praetorian Guard right behind him.

He almost made it to us. As he opened his mouth to say something, the spear of the first horseman ran through his back and came out his stomach, spilling blood and gore on the pavement and snapping off as the cavalryman's horse shied to a stop. The man stood for a moment, with an expression of shocked surprise, then stumbled and fell forward, the shaft of the spear pushing him to the center of the street where he collapsed, blood spilling out his mouth and nose.

"So much for blood sucking parasites," the cavalryman shouted. He dismounted and went to the body. For a moment he stood there and then drew his sword and in one swift motion, severed the head from the body. He raised it to eye level and spoke a curse to it before holding it up for us. He turned it to Lucius, who had moved to our place and the Guardsman smiled as we recognized it.

We had seen that face not so very long ago at Titus Flavius' home. Its look then was the smug assurance of powerful greed. It was the face of Titus Vinius, consul, one of the Three Pedagogues, advisor to Emperor Galba. It had been said that in the six months since Galba rose to the throne, Vinius had spent every day and every waking hour devising ways to enrich himself. Now those thoughts dripped away with the trail of blood on the uncaring stones.

The horseman remounted and holding his trophy near him, he rejoined his troop and moved in the same direction we had been heading. The headless body lay where it had fallen and no one approached it. Stunned, the hundreds of people near us stood without moving, the only sound the continuing screams from the distance. At last, out of the crowd, Titus Flavius emerged and joined us. His face was grave and ashen.

"The emperor is dead," he announced flatly. His breath was strained and he sat on the wall of the alcove, his hands shaking.

We all gathered around him, Arrecina sitting beside him and taking his hand, Timothy behind him, resting his hand on the old man's shoulder.

"He headed to the Praetorian camp this morning to try to put down a revolt. The cavalry caught him and cut him down."

"And what of his other advisors," Lucius asked, nodding attention to the body in the street, which now had gathered spectators who circled it, women inspecting the handiwork of the spearman, little boys poking the corpse, men rifling it to find a few coins, others stripping rings from his fingers and scuttling away with their booty.

Titus Flavius looked at the body, for the first time, and drew a deep breath. He shook his head and muttered something we could not hear.

"They have fled," he added in a louder voice, "Piso to a temple where they are chasing him now, the others disappeared."

"And the new emperor is named?" Arrecina asked.

"It is Otho," Titus Flavius responded. Looking at us each in turn, he sighed again. "At last he has gotten what he has so long sought, the throne. It may not be so easy to retain it."

Soon the street was filled with troops, some on foot, some cavalry. They were posting at each street corner and square. As we made our way from the forum toward the market, we were stopped at the street leading toward the Onion Market by a company of cavalry, over twenty in number, their swords drawn and their faces grim.

"The street is closed. Go back." The centurion on his horse directed his words to Lucius.

"We are on important business, soldier. I am Tribune Lucius Licinius Lucullus and this is Titus Flavius Sabinus. You may not be aware that we are on important business which gives us clear passage."

"The street is closed, Tribune. Go back."

"We are on important…" Lucius started again but was stopped by the cavalryman dismounting and signaling silence. He was of medium stature and something caused me to rest my hand on my sword.

"You may be a Tribune, and this old man may think himself a very important person," he nodded toward Titus Flavius, "but nothing of that matters. The street is closed and you can drag your sorry company back where you came from. The Guard is in charge of this city and you can kiss my ass if you want but you will not pass this way. You will have to go visit your whore another day."

His mouth began to form a sneer when Lucius' fist smashed it. Blood flew and the cavalryman stumbled back against his horse. He stood upright, smiled a bloody smile, spit a tooth and his hand dropped toward his sword. Lucius was on him, slamming his sword hand so quickly the *gladius* never left the scabbard. As the man swung his free hand at Lucius, Lucius stepped inside the swing and drove his helmeted head into the man's face. More blood flew and out of nowhere two other cavalrymen jumped on Lucius' back. I pulled my sword and smashed the back of the head of one with the handle. He sagged to the ground and Lucius' elbow came back to smash the other Guard on his back. He kicked the collapsing Guard under the horse and turned to greet two more Guards. One he threw his shoulder into, sprawling him on the ground under the horse with the first soldier. The horse was wide eyed and began rearing with the men under it, wild cries filling the air. The second Guard drew his sword and moved to the side to slash Lucius. My sword caught his in mid swing and with my foot, I swept his nearest leg from under him. He sat down hard and Lucius' knee caught him in the forehead, knocking him back on the stones.

By now, the crowd who had been inspecting the body of Vinius had formed around us, watching the unscheduled gladiatorial games. Lucius and I stepped back from the mayhem and stood back to back, facing the half dozen soldiers who surrounded us. I took off my cloak and moved my sword side to side, inviting attack. I felt at home.

"Stop," a voice called. The Guards froze and a second centurion stepped forward, stepping between them and us. He was short and muscled, with the determined look and scars of a man not new to the ranks, nor unready for fighting. He looked at his troopers. He looked at us. Then he laughed.

"My Praetorian Guards. Chosen as the finest soldiers in the empire and committed to the protection of the emperor. And you are bested by these two men." He smiled and glanced at us, then at the rest of our party. "Or did these lovely ladies inflict some of the damage on your pretty faces?"

He laughed at himself but no one joined in. So he turned to Lucius and me.

"Nobleman, no one attacks my soldiers. You are both under arrest. Surrender your weapons now or I will take them from you myself. And do not think you will be dealing with some raw recruit if you take me on. I will gut you here in front of your ladies if you do not drop your weapons now."

I did not move but Lucius did. He grabbed the breastplate of the centurion and jerked him forward at the same time as his sword came up under his chin. The man's eyes flared in amazement at the speed of the move and he rose on his toes to keep the point of the *gladius* from biting too deep into his throat.

I knew Lucius was just a hair's width from killing the man. He was in a mood to kill and he would assault the whole troop, killing as many of the twenty as necessary to cut through whatever stood between him and Julia.

The blade slowly rose, the centurion rose until he could rise no more and a spot of blood appeared and formed a single thin line down the blade.

Then a hand, a man's hand, came to rest on Lucius' sword hand and gently pulled it down. Lucius turned slightly, catching Timothy from the corner of his eye. Timothy whispered, "No, Lucius," and continued pushing. The moment hung, the sword paused. Then Lucius took it from the centurion's throat and stepped back.

The centurion touched his neck and drew fingers of blood to inspect it.

"I have endured worse at the hands of our Guard's barber."

"Junius," a voice spoke. It was Titus Flavius stepping forward. "You have been promoted again, I see."

The centurion turned and seeing Titus Flavius, he smiled, a warm and relaxed smile.

"Titus Flavius Sabinus, my old commander, what puts you in this company?" He gestured toward all of us, his gaze coming to rest on Lucius. "Is Rome so empty of hotheads that it must import some to disturb the peace?"

"Not so, my old friend, this is Lucius Licinius Lucullus, a Tribune from the army of Vespasian. He is visiting me and we were on our way to see about a matter of great importance in a neighborhood not far from here. Your troop would not let us pass."

"We have our orders, Titus Flavius, and you cannot pass."

Titus Flavius took the centurion's arm and led him away from us. They spoke for several minutes, at one point the centurion glancing at Lucius and then shaking his head. At last, the two embraced and the centurion went to tend to his men. Titus Flavius came to us, a sad look on his face.

"He will not arrest you, Lucius, nor you, Tychon, in light of the regard he holds for me from his years of serving in the Urban Cohort. But he cannot let us pass. And even if he did, there are several more detachments now erecting blockades on our path. And no passes are allowed. The new emperor has given orders the city is to be secured."

He paused for a moment and then continued.

"We must go back to my home for the night."

Lucius started to argue and then checked himself.

We began to walk back to Titus Flavius' home, our steps no longer quick. As we neared the door to the courtyard, Sophia spoke up.

"If no one can move about this night, then no one can move Julia from her prison this night. We are frozen but so are they."

She smiled. We looked at each other and I smiled. Why had we not thought of that? It took Sophia to see the obvious. My Sophia.

The atrium seemed cold when we entered. The two servants left behind greeted us and took our heavy cloaks and lit braziers, putting them in the library as we entered. Boudicca emerged from the room she had been locked in and came to Lucius, sniffing the blood on his scabbard, looking at him in disapproval that he had not been along. Figs and wine were brought and we ate in silence. Titus Flavius sagged into the chair at the end of the large table and we took seats at the table, except for Lucius. Head bent and lost in the shadows, he paced to one end of the room and then back, pausing to warm his hands at the brazier, then resumed pacing.

"There is nothing for us to do tonight," Titus Flavius spoke, his words directed at Lucius. "Tomorrow, if the streets are opened, we will go immediately to the market neighborhood."

The group said nothing. Arrecina stared at her husband, her face calm, sighs loud in the quiet room. Sophia looked down, eyes hidden in the thickening gloom. I could not seem to get warm. Lydia sat away from the table, Timothy was unmoving, eyes almost closed, head forward, hands clasped. Lucius continued to pace, a sentry.

The room grew warmer and Timothy raised his head and glanced around as if discovering for the first time we were there.

"There is something very important we can do tonight. The streets are closed but not the way to our Lord. We must pray."

With that, he moved to the door. Lydia followed, then Arrecina and Titus Flavius. Sophia's eyes fixed on me.

I must have pulled back. Her hand reached out and took my arm.

"Do not despair, Sophia, the morning shall be better, I am sure," my words were thin and feeble and out of the corner of my eye, I saw the ghost stop, look at me with a question and then turn back to his patrol.

"It is not tonight or tomorrow that saddens me, Tychon. It is that when I go to join them in prayer, you and your brother," she nodded toward him, "will not join us."

Lucius stopped and came to us, sitting across the polished and smooth table from us, his hands spread out and straining toward her.

"Is it so very important? To you?"

"Yes, Lucius, it is," the words struggled and were barely audible. "It is, at this moment, so very important."

"It is like a time in my childhood," she breathed deeply "when some of our sheep were lost in a storm. The lazy herdsman had overlooked three and my brother and I went looking. In the storm, there was much thundering, great darkness, only occasional lightning. We had almost given up hope when a pause in the thunder let us here their terrorized bleatings.

"They had wandered to a very deep ravine, as deep as ten men and full of rocks, which had killed other men or animals who came upon it in the dark."

"We looked down and saw the body of a sheep, barely visible except for the dark blood on its coat. We searched the shadows of the ravine, looking for the other two. But we could not see them. At last we saw them, but could not believe what we saw. Barely visible, standing at the far edge of the ravine were the other two sheep, pitiful and a mere step from death."

She looked at me and smiled.

"You know sheep, Tychon. They are stupid, stubborn and always managing to get themselves into trouble their small and contrary minds can never help them escape. They would stay there, bleating and crying and waiting, until finally they would die of thirst or hunger, or take a false step and fall to their deaths.

"We had to take a narrow path, no wider than a man, around the ravine, taking more than three hours. We put the sheep on our shoulders and carried them back on the path, nearly falling several times from the icy and wet stone. When at last we rejoined the flock, we were in wonder at the event. How could those sheep have made it to the far side, in the dark, in the storm, on such a narrow and slippery path? They should have died and there was no explanation.

"But I remember," she said, turning to Lucius, "how I felt as I looked across to them. They were so very close but there was a deadly space between us, and their bleating was so loud, so sad, and they had no way to come to us. No more than fifty feet from us, yet they were a world away. Not to move, or to move carelessly, was to die."

"So it is important to you…" Lucius began but was interrupted.

"Important to me but more important to you, Lucius, and to you, Tychon," she said in turning to me, "your eternal life hangs on what you decide. Believe in the Lord and there is life. Stay where you are, like those sheep, and you will starve or fall to your death. Between us is that deadly space. You cannot come to him but he wants to come to you."

"You may cry out but there is none to save you apart from our Lord," a voice came from the door. It was Timothy, come to find Sophia.

Lucius turned and faced Timothy and his shoulders sagged. There was a long silence and a strange stillness.

"I believed at one time, Timothy. I believed in Rome, with its proclamation of honor, nobility and virtue. I saw scheming politicians and vicious cruel emperors gnaw at the vitals of the state and kill its virtue. And at last Rome killed my father and I loved it no more. Then I believed in a philosophy taught by a wise man, named Seneca, and this empire of ours forced him to die and he is now just a memory. I believed in a quiet life with the wife I love and now she is taken from me. And now you would ask me to believe again. You ask me to believe in a religion, when Rome is already filled with religions? You would ask me to believe in a religion that led my wife to chains and untold suffering? I do not think I can believe again."

Timothy took a step inside the room and came into the light. He looked at Lucius as Luke had when my brother lay dying.

"No, Lucius Licinius Lucullus, I would not have you believe in a religion, I would have you believe in a god-man, a Savior, who created you and died for your sins, the evil and the hatred in your heart, the darkness that haunts your days." Timothy's voice was a blunt hammer. "I would have you turn away from the empty promises that deceived you, the evil and wickedness that cripples and maims and disfigures the newborn, the strong warrior, the feeble old man. From our first cry, Lucius, we are taught to lie to get the trophies of this world. We scheme, betray and we kill. And even the noblest things we do are shot through with pride, vanity and that empty honor that pretends it is eternal. You are called to a much higher and eternal life, Lucius, and this is the place and this is the time: turn from death and the evil that stains and warps the soul. Turn to the savior and life. Let the Lord bridge that deadly space."

"I listened to the stories, Timothy, that Luke told us." Lucius was plaintive. "I read his account of the Christ. At times, the words touched me. But in the darkness of my room they seemed like tales told children. The lame made whole, the blind given sight, the dead raised, thousands fed with a few fish. Fantastical tales, Timothy, for children." His voice was sad.

"Yes, they are children's tales, Lucius, but we are all children, offspring of the most high God and what bright and talented children we are. Like children separated from parents, we have grown up far away from them and we have grown crooked in our separation, foolish and selfish in our lonely journey, but we can never know whose children we are until we know the truth, until we turn from the wickedness that infects our hearts, and follow the savior."

Lucius said no more but sat back, looking into the embers of the brazier.

"This is the time, Lucius, the door is open. Surrender to that which is moving in your heart. Believe." Timothy looked at Lucius and at me, nodding slightly to convey the words to both of us, then turned and left.

Sophia looked at me and her eyes spoke a dreadful question. She touched my dead arm and raised the useless hand to her lips. I started to pull back but her grip was firm. I saw her lips touch that dead thing but felt nothing.

She got up, paused, and went with the others.

Lucius rose and started to leave. I stopped him.

"Do you want to believe, brother?"

He was slow to answer.

"If Julia were here and I could talk to her, then perhaps." He did not know what to say so he stood to leave. At the door he paused and turned to me, his eyes dark in the shadows.

"And besides, brother, I could not believe this night even if I chose to. There is one thing left I must do first."

He waited but I said nothing. His hand went to his belt, to the *gladius*, which had seen him through every battle. Its handle caught the light of the brazier and I knew.

The room grew cold again and he left, leaving me to carry on my conversation with no one.

"And what of you, Tychon? Do you want to believe? Or are you cursed?" There was no answer. And so I went to my room.

I stared at the ceiling, as the house around me grew quiet. Through the window, I watched the moon rise, full, bright and touched only by long fingers of clouds sliding by, slicing in pieces, disappearing, revealing the light unhindered, its orb undiminished. In years past, the full moon brought dread to me as I rested on the eve of battle and felt its fearful emanations turning men into beasts and beasts into the forms of men, preparing to tear us to pieces and leave us drowning in our own blood.

Once, on a cloudless night, the moon had disappeared just before we faced the Gauls, its light shriveling to half, then a quarter, and then becoming black with radiance only around the edge. As its light disappeared, we heard, beyond the camp and our sentries and fires, a wave of noise, fierce and frightened, low at first and then growing as some unknown beast ate the light of the moon, consuming it, leaving only the terrible darkness. The voices of the Gauls rose and then rose still more, moans mixed with prayers, shouted not whispered, from a thousand voices lurking in the woods waiting for the dawn and death. Then another thousand joined the chorus. I sat up, with twenty thousand troops around me moaning and praying and wondering if the curse of the moon was falling on us as well. Should we slay some animal and beg our gods to spare us in the morning, just as the Gauls were doing?

Some of the legionaries did just that and fresh fires bloomed in the darkness as sacrifices were made. Prayers to Jupiter mixed with imprecations to Minerva and Mars and Juno and any other god who might proffer protection. And when the prayers were at their peak and the volume of sound inside the thick walls of our camp equaled the voices of our enemies outside, the curved knife moved and a sliver of light appeared, then a wider slice and finally, after a time, the moon was restored. Prayers inside and outside the wall slackened and there remained only the muttering of thanks from the few who remembered to thank Jupiter and his fellow gods for deliverance.

But through it all, I had not prayed. I was not one to pray. The gods had been only interesting stories and I learned at an early age to keep my disbelief to myself lest I bring censure upon my adoptive family. My fellow legionaries might believe the gods intervened to restore the light but I was more interested in the measured cadence of the movement of the light disappearing and then reappearing than in the prayers. The regularity of the moon's change seemed to me not to be linked in any way to the volume or power of the prayers and if they were in some way joined, I felt sure there were sufficient acolytes fill the absence of my pleadings.

Now in my room, the only light was the full and bright white light of the moon outside and the dull red coals of the brazier inside. And whispers. Timothy, Sophia, Luke, Arrecina. Sheep. Blind men. Cripples. Images of warm loaves, baskets of fishes, and dead men watching new dawns. Behind them, another serpent hiss: scorn, trap, delusion. The moon disappeared and I smelled it. The fragrance of a woman, a woman I took many years earlier, as a young man. She was voluptuous, earthy, smelling of fresh wine and just turned earth, willing to indulge all I wanted and could imagine. Here, she said, is your life and your pleasures. Not the pale and anemic offerings of these half men and dried up women afraid to savor the flesh. Her fragrance grew stronger and I was now fully awake, hungry, restless.

Then the moon broke from behind the cloud and the room filled with light. I looked at the light, almost squinting, and the fragrance faded. And was gone. The room was silent now and the voices gone.

I rose and, filling a brazier and drawing a cloak about me, went to the garden.

The night was silent and there was no wind and the only sound was the occasional bark of dogs in the distance, killing rats or warning of intruders. I sat on a bench and shivered, the cloak providing little protection. After a time, the embers in the brazier began to die and I prepared to leave. A rustle behind me stopped me.

"You need more wood, Tychon." It was Timothy.

He stepped forward, arms holding new wood. He opened the brazier, put the wood in and sat beside me. He said nothing and stared at the fire rising and the sparks escaping into the sky. Both of us moved closer to the fire and warmed ourselves. I turned to look at him and in the dim reflection, his face was a child's.

"You could not sleep?" I asked him.

"I slept for a time but there are nights when I sleep very little." He looked at me with a look that seemed like pain.

"I have a question for you, Timothy," I said, turning back to the now still fountain. "Why did you say this was the time for us to decide?"

At first he did not answer and then his face turned toward the moon.

"I said it because I have prayed for you and your brother every night since we first met. I knew the spirit of the Lord was at your side from the first. He is near every man but I knew He was especially close to you both and that conviction has grown each time I see you and your brother. And tonight I knew you were at the point of deciding."

My look at him asked why.

"You know better than I, Tychon. You are a thoughtful man, a man of learning and experience. You are a man who knows his own heart and mind. Except one part is hidden from even your stern examination, the dark part that embraces the cynical and discards the noble. It is that dark part that every man has, the deepest part of his soul, which eludes the noblest philosophy, whether from Seneca or Plato, and dresses itself in worldly wisdom, ambition or false honor, but it always is pride, just in different garments."

I opened my mouth to answer but it was too dark and too late.

"How long have you believed, Timothy?"

"For many years, Tychon. My grandmother believed, my mother believed and they both taught me. I cannot remember a time when I did not believe."

"And do you never dream of throwing it all off, and bedding a woman and getting drunk and running a man through with a sword. Or even stealing a purse. Or betraying another. Never?"

A chuckle broke the silence.

"I have seen men do all those things, Tychon, and I have seen the wreckage that follows. Bedding a woman? Who is not tempted by such thoughts? Stealing, hurting, betrayal? Of course I am tempted. Those are sins common to all men, and all women, to young and old. But as the years pass, my friend, those temptations lose their allure more and more. And as I see men shipwrecked by sins of this world, they no longer beckon as they once did. And I am not a man who does not sin, Tychon. I may not kill or steal but there are other sins, a word of contempt for the weak, a kindness delayed or shoved aside, a thought of violence or lust …these are no less a part of me than any man. And each day I repent and pray and strive to be faithful to the one who gave his life and forgave me. And forgives me each day."

He looked at me and I did not respond, but a small whisper formed and escaped my lips.

"But surely there are some beyond his reach, Timothy. He would not forgive the truly evil. Not Nero, the one who kills his mother, gelds his lover, stomps his wife to death and burns your friends as entertainment while he banquets. Surely not Nero!"

"Nero, also, Tychon. No unrighteousness is so great that the Son of God cannot forgive it. He has already paid the price for all those monstrous deeds."

I laughed, a dry raspy sound in the dark. The wood crackled and there was silence, even the dogs quiet now, in that hour of the night when men draw their last breath. Minutes passed, thoughts and clouds floated and I finally brought myself to the thorn.

"Could…would the savior you described heal me?" I did not meet his eyes.

"The savior heals those who believe in Him and follow Him and live their lives in Him. There is no sin, no shame He cannot heal."

"No," I interrupted, "I mean my arm." I tried to lift it to show him but it was dead. "He healed all those people, the lame, the blind, even the dead. Can he heal me, my arm?"

He heard the pleading in my voice and he moved closer, touching the dead arm.

"He may, Tychon, in his infinite mercy, he may. But even if he does not, it will be nothing compared to the healing of your heart, your soul, that will come if you truly believe and follow him, turning from your sins, your attachment to this world, and becoming his follower, with one arm or two, in sickness and old age and weakness, trusting and coming to know him better each day. You cannot trade your heart for the promise of a new arm. The only exchange that is critical is trading your sin and heart for his forgiveness and a new heart."

I knew he was waiting for an answer and so we sat there in silence for a long time. I turned over all the arguments I had formed over the last months and recalled the stories of little girls raised from death and blind men given sight. Time passed, the moon sunk lower in the sky and doubt snapped at me. It told me that I was not the sinner these believers said all men were. I was loyal to my brother and I had never raped a woman. And the men I killed would have killed me. Then I began to remember. I recalled the letter from Julia that began our journey and a brawler who took a blow across the mouth and did not strike back. And the women who nursed Lucius when we were taking them to certain death. And a beautiful young woman who loved me and would not harm me or deceive me.

I saw, in my mind, the crucifixion of a carpenter. And something warmed in me as the moon almost touched the horizon. I tried to speak but could not.

At last, a slight breeze blew and, letting go my doubts, I felt wonderfully weak. I fell to my knees on the hard stone of the garden, weeping. I rested my one good arm on the bench and my head lay on my arm. My tears wet the marble of the bench and I heard a low moan and came to understand it was me. As I wept, my mind cleared. I lost one thought and then another as they vanished with the night. I saw the darkness that was in my heart and mind, the things that had seemed so very wise, so very clever, so very attractive. They showed themselves now. They were dark lies and they had attached themselves to me.

I knew then that there was a darkness deeper than the lies. It was in my heart and I carried my own Shadow Wolf that fed on violence and lies and death. I drew back and felt it tear at me to stay but it were slipped loose and its voice faded. The darkness seemed to clear and I saw only that carpenter on that cross, that Roman cross set for criminals who took life. Now it held the one who gave life. And I imagined him looking at me as one of those criminals. And speaking to me.

And I knew, somehow, it was all true. Its truth seemed to grow and brightened and reached out to me and I reached out to it with both hands. It came to me, and then passed through my grasp into my body and mind and I felt its warmth, unlike any warmth of fire or human embrace. It brought understanding and light was growing, but not blinding. It illuminated and shadows fled. It spoke, of peace and forgiveness And the light spread and warmth washed over me that I had never known before.

I believed. I had never seen the carpenter or heard his voice but I had heard his brother's voice in this garden and I had read his words. And I believed.

My tears slowed and stopped and the warmth remained and the light steadied into a flame in my heart, and all around me were words and they were Timothy's.

"…and so Father, accept this child of yours into your kingdom. As your precious Son was raised from the dead, so raise this precious child from the ashes of the world of the enemy to new life, in body and mind and spirit. Heal him, I pray. And teach him, keep him in grace and perfect peace and let him serve you faithfully. Help us to minister to him as he ministers to others. And may he live all his days in obedience, faithfulness and peace, to your glory."

I opened my eyes. The sun was just beginning to rise. We had been there in the garden all night, which seemed but a moment. I rose and turned to Timothy. His face reflected the rising sun, and his smile was only overshadowed by my own.

I embraced him and wept. He held me for a very long time and he wept.

"Thank you, Timothy. My friend."

He stepped back from me and shook his head.

"I am not just your friend, Tychon. I am now your brother."

He dried his eyes as I dried mine. He smiled again, almost playfully.

"Is there not someone you want to tell?"

I smiled and turned to race inside. I ran to her room and began pounding on the door, calling her name. At last the door opened and her sleepy eyes looked at me and widened.

I said nothing but the tears came again. Tears welled up in her eyes and her head tilted to one side, as if seeing someone familiar but new.

I laughed and pulled her to me, embracing her, trying to speak, and I held her firmly with both my arms.

My precious Pausanias, the blessing of my autumn years, that day was my second birthday. Like my first, it was a quiet place at the edge of war, a place where there were no screams of dying men but the thin cry of new life. And it was not a day which only my long dead parents could recall, but a day that I recall as vividly now as I lived it then. It seemed but a brief moment, and I did not want it to end. There was laughter, joy and tears, a festive meal, endless words, seasoned silences and faces moving about me, arms hugging me. It was as if we were in a palace and the courtiers had just announced the birth of a prince. But never for a moment did I feel like a prince. I was a criminal, locked in a nameless prison from birth, never knowing it was a prison until I saw the world through a barred window and escaped through a door to the beauty that lay beyond.

There was a word I used that day when I sought to describe my journey. "Random" described that strange series of events that brought me to that garden, with that man to fill the brazier and the hours, with words that warmed beyond the glowing wood. As I have reflected on that night, as I shall always do until I take my final rest, the wood Timothy brought was priceless and came from far away. It burned but beyond the brazier. And when I would use the word "random,' Timothy would correct me, along with Lydia, and tell me that there was nothing random about the line that pulled me here. "The god who directs the path of the sun and moves the seasons has no difficulty leading a warrior and historian to a garden in the center of Rome," he said at one point.

And several times each hour, I sought to find something to touch, something to lift, something to hold or embrace. And each time, afterwards, I would look down at my new arm and thank God for his mercy.

Watching me, smiling at my happiness, silent as I babbled and laughed and lifted servant children and bowls of food, my brother never left my side. The curfew had been extended and these festivities, celebrating my new life, were a welcome respite from the continuing frustration of our search.

With Lucius on one side and Sophia on the other, one arm through his, one arm through hers, I processed to the garden and then the library and then the dining room, the kitchen, the atrium, courtyard, stables and then back again. It was such a day and as I now lie still in the long nights of pain and old age, the details of that day return and comfort me. It began with an embrace and ended just so.

Sophia held me for a very long time, letting her tears flow and then stop. She pulled back from me and took both my hands in hers and raised our arms above our heads and laughed, a loud and raucous laugh, which filled the hall and her room and stirred the house to life. Soon the hall was full of people, servants and cooks and tutors and Lucius and Titus Flavius and Arrecina and Lydia and Timothy.

Several times, she tried to speak but could not, nor could I. We who had spoken so much were now speechless. Smiles replaced words and thoughts became embraces. Soon we turned to those about us and each embraced me and called me "brother." Lucius, my always brother, was the first and the quietest. His eyes were filled with tenderness and his words broke as he said "My brother, you have taken on a new citizenship beyond your birth or your adoption. This one will last for a very, very long time. I am most joyful at these events." He reached out and touched my arm, squeezing it and inhaling deeply. He started to say more but did not and smiling, stepped aside for the embracing arms of Arrecina. And so it went for some time, even the servants lining up to shake my hand and steal a glance at my arm, which reached out to place a hand of friendship on each one's shoulder.

The day began with worship. It was already light when we gathered in the atrium, and Timothy led the service. These services had been held each day of my time there but they had begun much earlier, before the sun rose and the affairs of the day began. As I would awaken in the morning, I would hear the quiet singing, the reading of the sacred story, the words of teaching spoken by Timothy or Barnabas or Titus Flavius, the sound of words spoken over the bread and the wine and final blessing before everyone dispersed.

This day, I attended the service for the first time, and Lucius joined me. The sacred writings lasted a long time and after they were concluded, Timothy stood up and spoke to us, his voice quiet in the early dawn but his eyes searching each of us out in turn. He spoke for a time and said many things that explained what we had heard and how the darkness that dwelt in each man's heart could only be banished by the light of the savior's sacrifice. Then he turned to the one story that stood in the middle of the readings, the story of the centurion. He retold the story beautifully and we listened as one hour became two, then three. And finally he spoke looking at Lucius and me.

"My brothers and sisters, we are all like that centurion. We have blood on our hands, from our weapons of war and our weapons of wickedness, from cutting strokes to curses, from men slain to men defamed, from women raped to women lusted after. None of us need think our lives are purer than the warrior's. The blood of our guilt reaches to the bridles of our horses and none of it washes away without the savior. When we are washed clean in the water of our baptism, the blood is taken away. And the centurion was contrite and faithful and we can be no different."

As he spoke, I looked at Lucius. I wondered if the words brought to his mind the blood that reached the bridle of horses on the night of the Asiatic

Vespers. Would the general Lucullus even have sat in this place and listened to these words, which commanded contrition and self-abasement? Would the general who fell at Julius Caesar's feet and begged for his mercy have fallen at the feet of an unseen Lord and begged for mercy? I thought not and marveled that a random series of events had brought this descendent of the great general to this place. Lucius leaned forward at the final words of Timothy.

"… And we do not know our fate, brothers and sisters. But as our days are many or few, let the tanner and the smithy, the cook and the servant, the warrior and the shepherd, the wife, the student, the farmer all glorify the God who saved them."

After the service, we gathered for a festive meal, Sophia on my one side, Lucius on my other. As we ate, the noise of the city outside rose but was not so loud as it was before the curfew. No supplicants came to the door and we were isolated again.

Sophia turned to me.

"You are a very brave man, Tychon."

I started to agree and speak of the many brave things I had done on the battlefield but checked myself.

"Not so very much, Sophia. Not so very much."

She smiled, as if she knew what words I had swallowed.

"I could never have asked for a miracle as you did, Tychon. Never. I don't know how you found the courage."

"There was a great reason, and it gave me whatever was necessary to ask. There was someone for whom I needed two good arms. If there was such a person for you, you would have the courage."

She smiled and lowered her eyes.

"There is such a one, Tychon, so perhaps I would. I would."

She took my hand, my newly good hand and squeezed until my fingers were numb.

Hours later, as the singing and praying concluded, I looked to Lucius to gauge his reaction to a particularly clever remark I had made and saw he was gone.

I went to his room and he was not there. I went to the garden and he was not there. Finally one of the servants directed me to the courtyard. I went out and found him at the front gate, looking through the grating to the empty streets beyond.

I stood beside him without speaking. He never took his eyes from the darkening road that stretched into the heart of the city and the lights that began to flicker on in the gathering darkness.

"She is out there, Tychon. She is cold and lonely and I cannot get to her."

"Patience, brother, patience."

"If I had only not left the farm, but stayed…"

"'There is no person so severely punished as those who subject themselves to the whip of their own remorse.'"

He turned to look at me and the darkness of his eyes did not come from the onset of the evening.

"And our teacher Seneca died, Tychon, despite all those noble sentiments." He sighed. "I should have said no to Vespasian, friendship or not. What good did it do for us to be there? There were others that could have fought in our place. And I lost my wife and now my command. I have no troops. I have no wife. And I do not know what the future will bring."

I wanted to tell him that his Julia had found a treasure beyond measure. I had found it too. And I found Sophia. And now I had two arms. Yet I could say nothing. My blessing was mine and not his. His shoulders were broader than mine and bore a crosspiece much heavier.

We returned to the house and the evening was spent in front of the fireplace, all of us, sitting or lounging, wrapped in warmth and thoughts. I sat with Sophia and we said nothing. There was one last great contest that loomed out there in the empty streets and it was approaching, I thought, in the shadows. It had come down from the mural in the study, resumed its form in the shadows of the night and it was that which Lucius sniffed in the darkness by the gate. It was moving about out there and it was hungry for another meal. I knew now it was not Lucius' body or mind that it sought to destroy. It was his heart. If it had been my heart it had sought, I would sit back and allow it to waste its assault, leaving to the power in my heart the work of its vanquishing, a breath sufficient to send it flying. But Lucius had no such protection now and the wolf would make for him surely on the morrow. There would be no shifting in the dark, no feints or tricks. It would be the final battle and Lucius and the slaver, who was this day's form of the wolf, were the combatants.

I felt my eyes grow heavy. I reached my new hand up to rub my eyes. Satisfied it still moved, I lay it in my lap and felt sleep envelope me.

I do not know how long I stayed like that but I was brought awake by movement, light and the shuffling of feet. I looked around and saw everyone by the door to the hall, Titus Flavius in the middle, holding a document, all gathered about him and reading it also.

I struggled to stand and found Sophia leaning against my shoulder, deep asleep. I touched her face and lowered her to the couch. She did not stir and I went to join the others. As I approached, Lydia turned to me.

"The curfew is being lifted, Tychon. At sunrise tomorrow."

I looked at Lucius and he looked at me, half-smile, half-grimace.

"And Titus Flavius has been reinstated as city prefect, effective tomorrow. He will once again have the urban cohort," Lydia finished. She touched my arm and squeezed encouragement.

Timothy and Lydia and Arrecina began to pray thanksgiving. Lucius took Titus Flavius aside and I joined them.

"Titus Flavius, I purpose to leave at first light for the market district. How many men can you spare from the household staff?"

"Lucius, these are servants, not fighters. Let me send for cohorts tomorrow. I can give you 50 or 100 if you need them."

"I cannot wait for them, Titus Flavius, I go at first light. Tychon and I will go alone, or with as many servants as you can give us."

Titus Flavius started to argue but did not. He understood. He nodded and we were left alone.

"The last battle, Tychon."

"The last battle, Lucius."

We embraced and went to our separate rooms.

That night, for the first time in my life, I found myself on my knees, and I spoke not to a god of thunderbolts but a God who became a carpenter and was nailed to a cross by an empire I had once served, with the permission of a man whom we now went forth to find and defeat. Could I strike him down when the moment came? As a warrior, I gutted men without a thought and watched their intestines spill out while I hacked away at the men beside them. I fingered my sword in the dark and spoke to myself as well as to the One whose ear I sought.

"So what is this *gladius*? Weapon? Or relic?"

The coals of the brazier popped and sizzled but released no answer.

I lay down and was fast asleep. In my dreams, I heard Luke's whisper "Go and tell John what you have seen and heard: the blind receive their sight, the lame walk, lepers are cleansed." And the crippled are healed.

Chapter 29   Discovery

The day dawned bright and clear, with a hint of warmth. I felt it as I rose, a warm breeze through my window and the sound of a bird in the garden. Lucius was dressed, buckled, armed, and ready to leave before I had eaten my bread or my figs.

As I finished up my quick meal, Lucius assembled a handful of servants to accompany us, Titus Flavius asked one last time if we would wait for him to assemble a hundred men and Lucius declined. Sophia came to the dining room and sat beside me.

"I want to go with you."

"No, you must remain."

"If you can take servants, you can surely take me."

"No, you must remain."

She started to speak but I silenced her with a quick kiss.

"I have not found you only to put you at peril where we are going." I paused to take the last bit of fig. "And if you were there and if there is trouble, I would be looking to protect you and that might cost me dearly if Lucius or I were to fall."

She was silent for a moment and then reached inside her tunic and brought out a piece of wood, carved into a crude cross. She handed it to me and closed my fingers, those on my restored arm, around them.

"Our Lord goes with you, Tychon, even if I cannot. Come, let us pray."

We rose and went into the atrium where everyone was gathered. Timothy, sensing the urgency burning in Lucius, quickly began.

"Lord God, creator and sustainer of life, bless and protect these men as they go forth. One of your sheep is stolen, Lord, and they seek her. Help them to find her and bring her safely home. Gird them with courage and fill them with your spirit to guide them. Protect them as they protect others. We pray in our Savior's name, amen."

Everyone said amen and the group broke up. Lucius bent to Boudicca and took his protector's face in his hands.

"Last battle, old friend. I cannot take you with us. Much as I need you this day, you might frighten away that one who can lead us to Julia. You must stay and guard the ones here since I cannot. Be the watch guard here. You have always protected me; now protect our friends."

Boudicca looked at him quizzically but went to stand between Timothy and Lydia, looking at Lucius with head cocked.

Titus Flavius bade us blessing and we left.

Wisely we had chosen to walk, not ride, as the morning's streets were unusually crowded with citizens escaping the prison of homes under curfew. We did not speak for the thirty minutes it took to get to the merchant district. The smell of onions and leeks was strong in the early morning air and we set about asking who might have seen a strange man with a scarlet hand, walking the streets, renting a home or building, eating or trading at the numerous vendors. Every merchant, vendor, litigant, artisan and citizen shook his head. No one had seen such a man. We had not a whiff of his presence. We would have been better off waiting for the Cohort. They had more men and their questions might have forced better answers.

I moved toward Lucius, ready to suggest we send a servant back to Titus Flavius and have him bring every man he had assembled to help us. I had taken but a few steps when a hand seized my arm. I pulled my dagger and spun to find a young girl, younger than my daughter, standing before me. Poorly dressed, the mark of a slave upon her, hair matted and dirty, bright eyes wide with fear as they gazed at my weapon. In that moment it was no relic.

"What do you want?" My voice was impatient and I instantly felt regret.

Her mouth opened and small bubbles of fear formed at its corners but no words came.

"What do you want?" My words were softer.

"I have a message for you," she responded as she shoved a folded parchment at me.

I opened it and read. I looked around and saw no one familiar. I read it again.

"Stay here," I instructed her. She nodded and became a statue among the swirling crowd.

I pulled Lucius aside and showed him the message. He read it slowly, aloud, as we walked toward the girl.

"Lucius Licinius Lucullus and his half-breed brother, Tychon

As you certainly know by now, I have your wife. Her name is Julia, or at least that was the name she gave me before I silenced her. Your other servants have been released, as you know, but she remains my guest and will be such for only a short time longer. If you wish to free her, you must follow my instructions precisely. If you do not, this lovely flower will be plucked from the beautiful garden of your life and her fragrance will be lost to you forever. If you obey, and how hard that will be for a man of your noble lineage, so proud of his ancestor's acclaimed contributions to Rome's history and beauty, you will see her again. And if you return to me that which you have stolen from me, then she will be restored to you and you will be together again. Follow this girl to the place she has been instructed to bring you. No one, save the half-breed cripple your brother, may accompany you. Do not think you are able to deceive me or can reverse this matter; obey, and your wife lives."

Lucius stood still for a moment, looking at the girl, then the note, then the girl. For a moment, I thought him ready to smile.

"Where are you taking us, young girl?"

She looked down and her voice was weak and uneven.

"I am not permitted to say."

"And if you were to say?"

She looked at us with fear.

"Then my mother and father…their lives would be forfeit."

Lucius reached out and touched her shoulder.

"It doesn't matter, young girl."

Then he stepped away a few paces and stared at the note carefully, intently. He looked at the clear skies and drifting clouds and signaled the servants to approach.

"I'm sure we can get the truth from her, Lucius, I know we can."

"It doesn't matter, Tychon. Trust me." He paused. "As you always have."

I said no more. The servants gathered around and Lucius spoke in a loud voice.

"Return to your master's house and do not follow us. I have received this note and will follow its instructions. Find me a pen."

A pen was produced and Lucius wrote a quick note to Titus Flavius on the back of the message and gave it to the oldest servant to carry. As soon as the servants cleared the square, Lucius returned to the young girl.

"Take us where you have been instructed. Now."

She headed east out of the square, at a quick pace, and we followed. A few minutes later we moved to the Forum and toward the prison. As we reached the neighborhood of the prison, the girl stopped. There were few people about, lounging in the colonnades that framed the steps.

"Why are we stopping here?" I asked the young girl, who said nothing. I repeated the question to Lucius.

"Look about Tychon. A dozen doorways front on these stairs. Any one of them can have someone watching us. And watching the steps below to see if anyone is following us. The slaver is quite clever. If we are being followed, he will know it. And we don't know who is the one watching us. Clever."

Just then, a young man stepped out of a doorway a few feet beyond the prison entrance and motioned to follow him. A nod of his head dismissed the girl and she disappeared into the crowd. I wondered if either parent would survive.

Several more minutes and we reached the top of the hill above the Forum. We were at the base of the Pincian Hill and ahead lay the place where I suddenly knew our journey would end. As we walked up the long stairs at the top of the hill, I thought of that day long ago, when a small child wandered about a battlefield, tripping over dead men and severed limbs, crying and lost and dirty and hungry, and the man who saved him. A man of noble family, whose lineage stretched back to where we were now headed.

We paused at the arch at the top of the stairs. The young man, thin and resembling nothing so much as a raven, produced a bag from under his cloak and opened it.

"Your weapons, or she dies before you enter."

Lucius handed over his sword and dagger. I handed over my sword.

"Your dagger, cripple." He sneered and a fleeting thought came: I could slit his throat. The thought vanished as quickly as it came and I passed over the dagger. He took the bag and motioned us to enter. I felt guilty at the violent impulse.

As we passed under the arch for the hundredth time, I looked up again and saw the words "Horti Lucullani" and felt the past open like a door as we entered the broad swath of grass, now browning in the winter cold, that stretched before us.

We were now in the Gardens of Lucullus. Our great grandfather's ghost had called us home.

Beyond the arch of this famous and familiar place, the past merged with the present. The immense expanse of grass in front of us formed a half circle, with one path forming the bottom of the circle and the top half radiating out in three paths leading to the colonnade which outlined the top of the circle, its marble columns gracefully spaced and its back wall open to the buildings and gardens beyond.

This was the villa and gardens that General Lucullus had built with the wealth he brought back from Ephesus in his battles with Mithridates. These were the gardens Messalina coveted and secured through the death of our father. These were the grounds where she fled when exposed as the treacherous empress she was. And there, in the main house ahead was where she was executed for her treachery.

As we moved ahead, to the right path, leading around the main house, I wondered, not for the first time, how different our lives would have been if these gardens, this expanse of beauty, had never been constructed. Our father would not have been forced to kill himself, and the awful flow of events that shaped Lucius would not have occurred. What would both of us have been then? Were those events random?

These were the questions of the philosopher, or the tavern drunkard who imagines another life would have seen him rich and renowned. Our world was what it was and this garden played its part. No garden in the empire, no garden in the world except perhaps in ancient Babylon, could rival its beauty, with its flower gardens, filled with sweet fragrances, rare and beautiful trees and shrubs, ponds, sculptures, frescoes and small temples dedicated to a half dozen gods. We passed one now, a small temple dedicated to Jupiter, which sat at the mid point of the half-circle, as we moved toward the colonnade that led to the area of libraries and studies.

I had always paused at that place as a boy, staring at that temple, and only later, when I had seen the Temple of Artemis in Ephesus, did I come to think that this was our family's Ephesus. Perhaps it was such, and the road, which had led us from Ephesus, had now brought us back to it. The beauty of this Ephesus welcomed us this day as prisoners, not captors.

"Where are we going?" Lucius touched the arm of the young man.

He turned, sneered and said nothing. Another quick and guilty thought imagined him on a battlefield, facing Lucius.

Passing beyond the colonnade, we moved into a garden of regular paths and marble figures, plots of gardens and high fir trees, cypresses fencing the far reach of the land and still green in this cold season. Moving again to the left, we moved beyond the library to a wooden building that sat behind a few trees near the edge of the property. As we neared it, I smelled its use. A barn, for horses.

As we approached, the door opened and a figure came out.

He was large, as large as the Germans we had fought, and looked to be one of their race also. But he wore no fur cloak, just a homespun Roman cloak. He carried the long heavy sword of the German and pointed it at us.

"Their weapons?"

"Taken and bagged."

The German grunted and stepped closer to us. He sniffed us and made a face that said we stank. I smelled him as he drew close to me and knew he had spent too much time in the barn. He nodded and the young man moved behind us.

As the German held the sword to our throats, the young man tied our hands behind us, pulling the rope tight so that it cut into our wrists. Lucius and I submitted, knowing there was nothing we could do. Our captivity was complete. We were shoved through the doors of the barn.

Inside it was warm and after a few moments, the stench was not noticeable. The light was feeble, coming from three oil lamps placed near the stalls, the smithy and the door we entered. A rough table sat in the middle of the barn and single chair behind it. The walls were covered with a few bridles, leather saddles and horse gear. Three stalls had horses, and they neighed as we entered, wondering at our scents.

We were shoved to stand in front of the table. There was no sound, only the horses' loud breaths. I looked around and saw no place Julia could be held, no room, no place except the stalls. Then I heard it, the light breathing of a person, a person asleep or unconscious. I turned quickly to Lucius and looking at me, he heard it. His eyes widened.

"Julia, Julia," he shouted. He paused. "Julia, it's Lucius. Julia."

From the far stall, the last one, came a muffled sound, a voice stopped by something. Without thinking Lucius turned to move there. The flat side of the heavy sword struck him across the shoulders from behind and he went sprawling to the floor. The German moved in and kicked him in the ribs. Lucius grunted and stumbled to his feet. The German jerked him back and stood him in front of the desk.

"What is your name, German?" I asked.

He turned to me, hoping to find a reason to hit me.

"Ercanulf," he said, proudly.

"How fitting! It could be nothing else," I said, remembering the German word for wolf. I had spoken truthfully but obtusely. My strange reply must have caused his poor head to hurt as he sought to understand what I meant. His distraction allowed Lucius to clear his head and I was hopeful he had something in mind to deliver us.

Suddenly the back door to the barn opened and a figure came in. Moving through the shadows to the light, he carried himself differently than that day on the road. Pontius Pilate, once governor of Judea, the man who sent the Christ to his death, now a tax collector and moneylender and slaver, was across the table from us. He was the same man who had curried favor before but now, with us helpless and allied with an outcast group of Christians, he assumed a different face.

"Well, we are together again. Take your ease. We have much to talk about."

He gestured and two bales of hay were produced for us to sit on. The young man moved to our left, holding a dagger, and the German to our right, resting the point of the sword on the ground and studying us.

"Bring my wife here, Pilate, and I will talk to you as much as you like," Lucius said in an even tone.

Pilate smiled a threat and reprimand.

"Lucullus, you are no longer the high minded tribune here. Your general has abandoned you, your army belongs to another, your estate lies in ruins, and your friends are far away. You have nothing except this small dirty space and whatever I deem to give you. So do not think you are a patrician giving orders to the peasants or a soldier who fears your voice. I do not fear you, so do not presume to tell me what I should or should not do. Your life, and the life of your wife, are mine to send to Hades or set free."

"That is not a new role for you, Pilate," Lucius' voice was modulated still, and I waited for it to change but he continued. "Another man's life was in your hands several decades ago and you gave it over to the mob. And your foul deed is now the stuff of legend."

The words cut and Pilate rose from his table, leaned on it toward us, his reddening face as scarlet as his hand which pointed at us like a thick spear.

"You dare to lecture me, you who were born rich and famous and never have had to face his world turned upside down." Pilate spat the words and spittle formed at his mouth. "Never have you had to face dishonor and dismissal from your post despite having been the most loyal of governors and seeking nothing but the best for his emperor. You presume to lecture me when all was handed to you at birth, prestige, position, and power. My family is as ancient as yours. But we never existed for you, or for your ancestors. I…"

Lucius cleared his throat loudly and Pilate stopped, breathing heavily and beginning to sweat in the warm air of the barn.

"My wife?" Lucius said evenly.

Pilate said nothing for a moment. He breathed deeply and smoothed his clothes as if gaining composure after his outburst. Then he made a magnanimous gesture with his hand to the young man, who went to the far stall and dragged a figure from the shadows. She stumbled and he held her up, shoving her to the table and down upon a bale at Pilate's side. The moments passed in silence as Lucius leaned forward, his eyes fixed. The silence was unbroken, as he seemed unable to move or speak.

She was dressed in a dirty and torn tunic. Her skin was caked with mud and her hair matted and unwashed. Her face was uneven, one side swollen from a blow and caked blood was at the corner of her lip. Her hands were tied in front of her and there was the telltale red chafing around the tight rope which said she had been tied repeatedly but not constantly. Her mouth was stopped with a dirty cloth and she tried to speak but could not.

Yet beyond all the dirt and abuse, she was as beautiful as ever and her dark brown eyes shone even in the feeble light. After the young man removed her gag, she coughed and breathed deeply. She leaned forward to Lucius and a smile flowed into a broad grin.

"My husband, my prayers have been answered. You are here to bring me home." Her voice was a hoarse croak.

"I am here, Julia. At last and forever, I am here." The words were thick and heavy and as he spoke them, tears formed in her eyes.

Pilate raised his scarlet hand and grasped Julia by the throat. He squeezed, tightly, and she coughed. He released and she coughed again, to breathe.

"You will speak when I direct you to," he smiled, lips thin and pinched.

"Do not touch my wife, Pilate; I may forgive what you have done up to this point but not beyond," Lucius sat back and squared his shoulders.

Pilate looked at him in disbelief. Again his face grew crimson.

"You continue to presume, Lucullus! You continue? You are tied, helpless, solely mine to kill or free. And you presume still? Perhaps you would like me to show you what can be done to her, by one of these," he gestured to his two men, "by way of soldierly ravaging, or beating. Would you like that?"

"He has not raped me, Lucius, only beaten me a few times."

Pilate's scarlet hand came up, quick, and smashed across her face. She fell backwards off the hay and hit the floor hard. The German laughed and lifting her up to sit, he pulled her hair to hear her cry out. She looked at us, blood running from her nose, dripping from her chin onto her tunic.

At seeing the blood, Lucius lunged to his feet and rushed at the German. Before he had taken two steps, the young man tripped him and he went sprawling. The two henchmen lifted him up and dropped him beside me.

"That I cannot forgive, Pilate, for that you will pay." Lucius spoke to Pilate even as his eyes turned to Julia. His mouth was tight and his words heavy with menace.

"Forgive, forgive? Who are you to forgive? I…"

Lucius interrupted again, his voice becoming calm. His quick change of tone puzzled me. What was he about? His speech was controlled, muted, much as one speaking to a small and simple child.

"You said there was something I could do to secure my wife's release. Tell me what it is and we can be done today quickly. Tell me how much gold you require and it will be delivered to you."

Pilate laughed, a hard sound without mirth.

"Gold, no, not gold, Lucullus. Great Jupiter, not gold. I have something more precious than gold you must pay me. Anyone can pay me gold. Gold I can get, for slaves, for taxes, for rent. But only you can pay me what I require. Only you."

He sat down now, the preliminary skirmish over.

He sighed, sat back, a governor again. His elbows on the armrests of the cracked and stained chair, he looked at Lucius over interlaced fingers, crimson and white stripes, clasping and unclasping.

"Imagine my pleasure, Lucullus, when I found you on the road to Ephesus. For a very long time, I have been owed something by you and then, there you were. The gods delivered you to me, you and your half-breed cripple of a brother all proud and calm and riding horses bought for you by the empire, traveling a road paid for by the empire, all of it coming from taxes I raised. I raised the taxes and my revenue filled the emperor's coffers but never did he honor my work." His voice rose, a lifetime of resentments finding voice. "You and your kind regard us like a pestilence and something to be swept from the barn. You hold nothing but contempt for me, and it showed in the haughty speech and dismissive tone you used with me on that road. And I knew then that fate had put you in my path and you would pay me what I was owed. Then when I found your wife in the prison, I knew she was the key to my justice."

He breathed deeply, satisfied. Gesturing to the young man, he arose.

The young man hesitated, and gave Pilate a questioning look. Pilate frowned and nodded an order. The young man shook his head. The German grunted and went to the third stall. Guttural words, then a rustling and a harsh whinny.

He led out a horse, a dark black horse, eyes red in the lamp's light. It was the horse I had seen in Ephesus, the horse who had looked at me with menace, who haunted my dreams, who now stood here and looked at me, then Lucius, then Julia, as if deciding the order of our fates.

"This is my latest purchase, Lucullus. I bought him in Ephesus. He is of noble blood, strong in leg, powerful in heart and fast, fast as the blink of an eye. And he was half the price of any lesser horse." He waited for us to ask the question but Lucius and I were silent.

"He cannot be ridden," he at last answered our unasked question. "Several men have tried and were crippled by the effort. Two men were killed, and he was on the verge of being killed himself when I found him."

He walked to the horse and raised his good hand to pet it. It turned its huge head to him and his bright red eyes glared at him. Pilate lowered his hand.

"This horse was a gift, Lucullus. I have a friend whom I have known many years, a friend who has helped me in many situations and to whom I have always been loyal. He is a lover of horses and I bought this horse to give him as a present. If anyone could tame and ride this horse, he is the man. After I took your wife and others from the prison, I went to deliver the horse to him. He was gone.

"And for a time, my people could not locate him. Then at last they did and I took this horse to him." He sat again and stared at Lucullus with eyes not unlike the beast now pawing the ground.

"Imagine my surprise when I found my friend no longer the vibrant and capable young man I left him. He was not going to ride horses again, much less train them. He was not so young anymore. He was grey, his hair shot through with white. His body, which had been so beautiful and could sustain his insatiable desires with a dozen young girls at a time, that body was now crippled and broken. Now he can barely walk and each step is pain. His face is scarred and twisted and his words are barely to be heard. He is no longer human, Lucullus, just bone and skin and pain.

"When I saw him, I could not believe what had happened to him. It had been just a short time and a calamity like this could only have come from something, or someone, of vicious inclination. I learned that he had been found at the emperor's Golden House, surrounded by the slaughtered bodyguards he always had with him. Since the reign of Galba was beginning, no one could be interested in searching for his assailants. I asked him who did it and what do you think he said?"

In the light, his eyes seemed almost the color of the horse's. Had they glowed this color in the governor's palace when he questioned the carpenter?

Neither of us answered. Pilate seemed disappointed.

"When I asked him, repeatedly, what had happened, he would only answer 'The wrong girl, the wrong girl.' What do you suppose he meant by that?" Pilate produced a dagger and touched Julia's throat with it.

"And when I asked him who had done it, what do you suppose he said?" He pressed on the dagger point and a drop of blood appeared on Julia's throat.

Again we said nothing.

"He could not answer," Pilate paused for drama

"His eyes would grow wide, then fill with tears, and he would shake his head violently, and only a deep moan would be heard."

He leaned across the desk.

"But we know who it was, don't we? You and your crippled brother were seen. I added that charge to your bill of justice, Lucius Licinius Lucullus, warrior, butcher, patrician, heir to what is mine."

"And what of the exchange you offered?" I asked, tired of the delay.

Pilate turned to me, snarling.

"This is for your brother and me to discuss, not you, cripple. Your turn to die will come soon enough. The rest of your body will be as dead as your arm soon; so enjoy your few breaths."

I was irritated at his words. His pretension of power seemed so shabby in this barn. I could not resist speaking.

"Pilate, I have read of your judgment of the savior. Did you not admit he was innocent and yet you condemned him? Were you such a coward you could not withstand the mob's shouts? And why did you not listen to Claudia Procula when she told you of her dream and urged you to release him?"

Pilate stopped and then moved around the table. He struck me hard across the face.

"Do not speak of that time or that man!" His face was red again and his spittle flew at me. "I do not want to hear his name or her name, or the questions! Or would you prefer I have your tongue cut out?'

"But she said…" I stopped when I saw the color drain from his face as quickly as it came.

He looked wide-eyed and glanced about, looking for ghosts.

"You have spoken to her? You? When? Where?"

I smiled and he struck me again. The blow was not so hard as countless others I have felt. He hit me a second time. A little blood this time.

"The exchange?" Lucius asked again, his tone of boredom a false trail for Pilate to follow. And follow he did.

"Exchange, exchange, is that all you can say?"

Pilate breathed heavily, catching his breath. He strode away and the two men followed him to the far corner. The horse tried to follow but tethered to the table, he snorted angrily.

"Are you all right, Julia?" Lucius' voice was low.

"I am wonderful, Lucius. I am so happy to see you and I know now my prayers have been answered. Oh Lucius, tell me you received my letters and you know I am now a Christian."

"I know. I have read your letters so many times they are near tatters. But no word you wrote is as sweet as beholding your face here, in this place. Know that I will never leave you again and no force will keep me from holding you in my arms. I love you, Julia."

"And I love you, my Lucius. Please tell me you believe in the Lord and are a follower with me. Tell me."

"Almost my Julia, but not yet." Fearful of disappointing her, he added quickly, "But Tychon is now one of the faithful."

She turned to me, a wide smile framing her words.

"Oh blessed be God the father that is true. I want to hear your story, Tychon. You and I are now brother and sister in a new and eternal way."

"And he must tell you of the young woman who has stolen his heart."

Julia's tried to smile but winced at the pain from her face She was about to speak when the three returned. I wondered how Julia and Lucius could speak so amiably when we were so near death.

Pilate sat and looked at Lucius. He seemed disappointed, perhaps that we were not cowering or begging. He had been looking forward to feasting on our fear and pleading. We offered neither. The young man produced a goblet of wine and Pilate drank deeply.

"A feast, Lucius Licinius Lucullus. This is a feast for me. The road to Ephesus was the invitation, the taking of your wife the first course, and now comes the main course."

He sat back, pleased with his literary skill.

"You may think me a petty man, Lucullus. Perhaps you think I am seeking revenge for your brutal butchery of Tigellinus. You would be wrong.

"Or perhaps since you treated me as you would a captured slave on the road, you think this is my revenge. But you would be wrong again, Lucullus. You see, you owed me payment long before we ever met." His goblet was refilled and he began to speak. The words told me he had prepared this speech a very long time ago and each word had been chosen with care.

"Three generations ago, Lucius Licinius Lucullus, my family was one of worth and promise. My father was an equestrian, not so far below the aristocracy your ancestors belonged to. Equestrians might not be revered as highly as one of the ancient families like yours but their wealth and skills would soon open doors to them and their heirs. In one year, my great grandfather made over one million sesterces from properties, estates and lands he owned. The next year, he would have doubled that and the year after doubled it again. Our daughters would marry into your class and their children or grand children would serve as legates of legions or even Senators. Our path was charted, the way was clear and Pilate would be a name of renown soon."

He paused, having warmed to the subject, and stared into the goblet. He studied the wine and his expression said it had gone sour.

"But then the world moved and that day of renown was snatched away, Lucullus. You remember the civil war between Marius and Sulla, do you not? Marius the old warhorse, seeking power once again after years out of power. And Sulla, the ruthless and powerful new general, who opposed him. First one faction ruled Rome and prosecuted the other's supporters. Then the other one would take Rome and reverse the list of prosecutions. Blood ran, families were destroyed, lands seized, fortunes confiscated. And dreams died. My family supported Marius and when he was in power, we gained land and gold that it would have taken us decades to accumulate. Then Sulla came to power and all of it was taken from us. And that fortune and those lands we had held before the war were seized also. Because we backed the losing faction, we lost our wealth, our farms, our slaves, and our servants. We lost our future. From tens of thousands of acres of land, we finished with one small plot of land and from gold goblets like this, we went to wooden goblets and hard labor. My grandmother was reduced to working in the fields like a common slave. We fell, Lucullus. We fell fast, we fell far, and we fell hard."

He finished the wine and the goblet was refilled. The wine was not mixed yet his speech was not slurred. His growing rage was diluting it.

"And you are the agent of our destruction, General Lucullus. You were the one general who stood with Sulla when he invaded the sacred city of Rome. All Sulla's captains were loyal to the state and refused to countenance such a violation of a centuries-old understanding. Rome was never to be invaded by the legions of the empire but Sulla did, and with your aid, Lucullus. You helped him write those proscription lists that executed people, seized land, stole fortunes. Your seal was on the documents that dispossessed my great grandfather and threw us aside. Equestrians with money have a hundred horses and ride them, Lucullus, but equestrians with no money are dogs, filthy animals with no prospects."

"You are speaking of my great grandfather, Pilate, long dead. I am not the man you are speaking of." Lucius spoke slowly, unsure if Pilate were mad or speaking a part in some strange dramatic production.

"We went from horses, herds of horses, like that one," Pilate continued, unheeding. He gestured to the black animal standing and listening, nostrils sniffing as if a different scent was now abroad, "but then we became dogs, rooting for sustenance."

"And do you know something, Lucullus? We owned a large piece of land in Rome, a beautiful land with a flowing stream that came from a rock high above the Forum. Cypress trees bordered it, and wild flowers abounded among its several ponds. We had great plans for it, lavish plans that would proclaim our position. It cost us tens of thousands of sesterces and it was the envy of all. We would erect a villa on it, a wonder and beauty that would proclaim our wealth and status. It would become a center of culture and honor as we rose in the ranks of the aristocracy. But it was not to be. Sulla came and we were stripped of everything. We were forced to sell it. My great grandmother cried, her husband cursed. He cursed you, General Lucullus, and never a day went by he did not renew his curse. Another citizen claimed the land and we moved to a farm." His speech came faster now, mouth twisted, spittle and words mixed as the words tumbled out.

"Then a few years later, you bought it, Lucullus, with the gold you brought back from your war with Mithridates, and you built this park on it, a lavish park with trees and gardens and pavilions and colonnades and libraries and a magnificent villa. And you built a barn there too, a place to house fine animals and work animals, a place where those whose gold you stole could work like slaves and clear the barn and brush the horses and eat a few crumbs that fell from your table."

Lucius and I turned and looked at each other. Pilate was lost in the story told him from childhood. He was his distant ancestor confronting our distant ancestor.

"The exchange," Lucius said quietly, his tone meant to calm.

Pilate was gazing at the roof of the barn, as if trying to locate something misplaced. He shook his head and turned back to Lucius.

"Ah, you see at last, Lucullus. It is simple: return to me what is mine."

Lucius leaned his head to one side, assessing how mad this man was. I believed I already knew.

"Pay me back for those years, Lucullus. Pay me back for what I have lost. You robbed me when you took my land, my fortune, my prospects. And my honor. You stole my honor and without honor, no man can live."

"How was your honor stolen, Pilate?" I asked, now genuinely confused.

"When you dismissed me from the governorship of Judea." He addressed his answer to Lucius. "You sent me away when all I had done was restrain those wretched Jews. I was disgraced, my dreams were smashed and I had nothing left."

He shoved the young man aside, rushed to Lucius and struck him across the face.

"You must pay, Lucullus, the bill is long due." His voice was rising and the German was looking at him with puzzlement. "We faced ruin. Now you face ruin. We were robbed of what was ours. Now you will be robbed of your family, your life. I want this land, this garden, your farms, your gold." He was sputtering now and his eyes were wide and unfocused, something dark behind the flittering glances. Then his voice was rising. "And I want those years you have stolen. And I want my honor you have taken. Give me my honor!" His voice was a scream now. Then he stopped suddenly.

His breath came in short gasps, as a man who is drawing near death, and his body was shaking, unable to release the ghosts that battered to exit his body. After a time, his shaking stopped, his breath slowed and he wiped his eyes to clear them.

Drawing himself up, he resumed his place at the desk. Lucius and I glanced sideways at each other. His outburst had answered our question. Lucius was looking at Julia, who was wide eyed with shock at his outburst and in her eyes I saw terror at being at the mercy of a madman who thought her husband was his long dead ancestor. The past and the present had come smashing together and we were caught between.

Lucius sat for a moment, thinking, his head lowered. His mouth was moving slightly, as it did when he was considering an idea for the first time, but there was something strange in his expression. His shoulders grew slack. His mouth relaxed and he turned to me with a soft look. His face seemed relaxed and when he turned to Pilate, he spoke quietly, each word deliberate, as if speaking to a fevered and terrified child.

"Pilate, the past is gone and has no control over us, unless we let it. Our life is today, not a century ago, not thirty years ago, today." His eyes shifted to look at a place above Julia's head, seeing something I could not discern. Then he breathed deeply and sighed, a long, long sigh. His mouth curled slightly, a look of strange contentment in his gaze.

"I cannot return this land to you if I wished, Pilate. It has been a very, very long time since this land was in our family. The emperor now owns it, and I have no claim to it. For the rest, I could certainly give you land or gold. But you would have to release us to allow me to do so "

Lucius' words hung there. He seemed to be waiting, and there was a peculiar calmness about him. It came to me what had just happened. Sophia's face came to me and I felt sorry I could not speak to her once more to tell her what had just happened.

"Ah, you think to outwit me, again." Pilate's eyes glittered as he imagined he had caught Lucius in trickery. "You omit the honor. The years lost. Do you propose not to give those back to me? What kind of fool do you think me to be? Because Seneca taught you ... oh yes, I know he was your tutor, I know very much about you ... because he taught you, you think to trick me. Do not deceive yourself. I will have my honor restored or she will die this hour."

He turned and pressed the dagger against Julia's throat.

"Stop!"

Lucius screamed and rose from the hay. He ran at the table and was halfway across it, when the German grabbed him and threw him back. Picking him up at Pilate's gesture, he laid him on the table and held his throat up, inviting Pilate to move.

Pilate released his grip on Julia and turned to Lucius.

"What will it be, General Lucullus, my honor or your blood. I had thought to kill you after you watched me slit your beloved's throat but now I fancy the reverse." He turned to Julia and stood back for her to see Lucius. "Shall we see how bravely your husband dies?"

"Please," Julia pleaded, tears flowing and voice nearly a shout, "please do not hurt him. Take me and kill me if you will but do not harm him."

Lucius' voice was firm and surprisingly gentle.

"Let the past go, Pilate, it is beyond recall or remedy. Do not let it imprison you. Let it go, Pilate, shed its weight."

Before he could say more, Pilate clasped his hand over his mouth. His other hand, the scarlet one, laid the dagger across his neck again. I lunged forward and felt my new arm move in the bonds. Tied more loosely than the other, it might get free if I could work it a bit. Before I got to the table, the German's fist smashed against my forehead. I went to the ground and could see nothing. I could only hear. A voice, a new voice. Yet one I recognized.

"Stop, do not harm him."

There was long silence and I pushed myself to my knees. Behind us, near the door, in the shadows, was a figure. She spoke again

"Do not take his life, I beg you. Spare him. Spare them all." She moved forward into the light, Claudia Procula moving toward the object of her quest.

There was a scream. It was unlike any I had ever heard before or after. It was a scream of a man who sees his darkest terror made flesh and watches it approach him in a dark and lonely place. Pilate had summoned history and now history was moving toward him in a homespun tunic with a tender smile and he was terrified.

"Stay away from me," he screamed, backing away from Lucius, nearly knocking Julia over in his haste. The young man moved to intercept her while the German looked on, confused.

"Stand aside and let me touch my husband," she admonished the youth firmly. He stepped aside meekly.

Pilate now circled, attempting to keep the table between them but Claudia came directly at him. Lucius had sat up and was about to stand when the German pushed him to the ground. As he fell, Lucius' legs were thrown in front of Pilate, tripping him. He fell, hard and in front of Julia. As he sought to rise, a hand reached down and took his scarlet hand and pulled him up. Claudia held the hand and regarded it with a sad and long look. Pilate pulled the hand away and pointed the dagger at her.

"What are you doing here? Why will you not leave me alone? Am I some fugitive that you pursue me from town to town, from Philippi to Spain, from Syria to Macedonia, and now from Judea to Rome? Why will you not leave me alone?" His tone was now that of a child who is tired and cannot understand what his mother is asking him to do.

"You have run too long, my husband. I want to be with you and together we can find peace at last. I have never been anything but your wife and I will go to my reward as your wife. Please return to me and put behind us the past. We are not so very young, my husband, but the few years we have left should not be spent running. Come, take my hand."

She reached out and he jerked back in terror and screamed. Battle. At Pilate's cry, Lucius struggled to his feet and moved toward Julia. The German turned toward him and raised his sword to cut him down. As I jumped forward, tearing to loosen my ropes, I hit the table, which jerked sideways and struck the horse's chest. There was an awful screaming whinny and the snap of tether. The horse made to kill us but the German was between us. The German turned, Lucius pushed Julia back out of the way and Pilate jumped back, from all of us.

The horse reared, its legs pawing at the air, and as it lurched forward, one paw came down on the German's head. There was a sickening sound of breaking bone and the German fell against the desk and slumped to the floor.

As the horse continued to strike the dead German with its paws, Pilate grabbed Julia and backed away, holding her in front of him. I had finally loosened my bonds and went to Lucius and untied him.

All of us stood still for a moment, with no sound but the horse repeating its blows on the dead body.

Pilate began to move away from us, toward the door we had entered. Julia was being dragged with him and he held the dagger to her throat. He was cornered and yet we could do nothing; there was too much space between us and he could kill her before we reached him.

"There is no need for more blood to be shed here today, Pilate. If you free her, I will let you go. Do not harm her. Please." Lucius' voice was calm. No one spoke for a moment.

The boy had disappeared but in front of us, as we approached the door, was the bag. I retrieved our weapons and handed Lucius his gladius. Pilate continued his slow retreat.

"Lucius, even if he does kill me, do not harm him. Your soul is in the balance and even if I die, we will be together." As she spoke, tiny drops of blood appeared on her neck from the dagger touching her skin as Pilate backed toward the door. "Believe, my love, and follow our Lord. Then all will be well. This man's death will not count for what you would lose by killing him. If you spare him, you will be at the doorway of eternal life."

"Shut up, slut," Pilate snarled. "Your magic incantations cannot protect you."

"Please stop," Claudia begged now, her eyes full of tears.

"Do not do this, Pilate," Lucius' voice was low.

Lucius was now within striking range. I saw the slightest of movement as his hand tightened and I did not know if he could lunge and kill before Pilate moved.

It was then he looked at the *gladius*, holding it up like something of great worth and weight. I watched as he threw it to the side. It made a dull sound as it hit the floor.

Lucius said nothing. I said nothing. Pilate was within two steps of the door. He knew the door was at his back and even in the guttering candlelight we saw his triumph. He smiled and brought his scarlet hand back with the knife. We had lost.

As his hand prepared to strike, there was a swift movement from the door. Something silent and dark and large flew through the air.

Boudicca's teeth caught Pilate's hand and held it. There was a shriek and a growl and Pilate was torn from Julia and pulled to the ground. He rolled about, trying to loosen the dog but to no avail as the beast held firm and bit more deeply. Boudicca's massive head whipped side to side, tearing at the hand. As we rushed forward, we could see blood flying in a storm every time Boudicca's head moved. His paws clawed at Pilate's face and caught it several times.

"Boudicca, back," Lucius commanded and the dog released and backed away a short distance, its breath short, its muzzle crimson, its eyes fixed on the figure on the ground, now moaning, now whining, a mass of blood and torn clothes.

In a moment, Claudia Procula was on her hands and knees at her side, whispering to him, holding him and dabbing at his bloody face.

I untied Julia and she rushed into Lucius' arms. He kissed her and held her for a very long time. Over his shoulder I saw her eyes. They were closed and bathed in tears. I knew his were also.

"Never leave me, my love," she at last whispered.

"I will go no further than a voice can call, my darling," he replied. He looked at me and opened their arms. I entered and both held me close. Now I too had tears.

"I knew you two would find me."

"He did all the work. I merely protected his back."

There was a noise and suddenly the barn was full of figures. The Urban Cohort had arrived and Titus Flavius passed into the barn in a flurry of movement. Behind him was the young man, in chains.

We talked and we embraced and we touched one another to be sure it was real. Lucius held Julia close and would not release her. Then I saw Sophia come through the door, along with Lydia and Arrecina, with Timothy and Apollos in tow. She ran to me.

"Are you hurt?" She asked, her eyes narrow.

"Not now," I replied. I laughed, she laughed and I held her tight, with both arms.

Finally, Titus Flavius came over to us.

"What do you want me to do with him, Lucius?" He gestured toward Pilate, now sitting at the table where he had presided just a short time ago. His head was down and Claudia sat beside him, holding his hand in hers. In my years of battle, I had never seen a hand so mangled. It was useless now and I thought perhaps it might lose its scarlet hue now that was just a useless appendage. I felt a twinge of sadness for him at the same time I wondered if that was the same hand, clean and unmarked, that pointed to our Lord, all beaten and bloodied and not so much man as flesh torn and savaged, and said "Behold the man." I thought it surely must be and I turned to see that Boudicca, across the room and standing beside Timothy, did not take its gaze from Pilate.

Lucius did not answer at first but looked at Timothy and Apollos standing a few feet away. One he had struck and bloodied. The other he had put in chains. They said nothing and their faces were calm, even blank. They waited, with Titus Flavius.

"Find out from him where he sold the other prisoners from our estate, so we can reclaim them. Then let him go, Titus Flavius. Parole him to the care of his wife."

Lucius sighed, a deep sigh, and in that moment, I understood that we were leaving that barn with a great deal less and a great deal more than when we entered.

Reading my mind, Lucius spoke to me.

"A thing laid down is not so heavy as when carried far."

"Seneca?' Titus Flavius asked.

"Lucius Licinius Lucullus," I interjected.

As we left, Titus Flavius took Lucius' arm.

"What of the horse?"

Lucius smiled, then laughed.

"Do with it what you want. I will be happy if I never see a black horse, ever again."

Titus Flavius looked puzzled but said nothing.

Lucius stopped at the door, motioned for us to wait, and returned to the desk where Claudia and Pilate sat. He bent over and said something to Claudia, and then turning to Pilate, he whispered something to him. Pilate let out a low moan, perhaps from the hand.

"What did you say?" I asked when he joined us.

He merely smiled as we left, and I realized I did not know how the Urban Cohort found us, or how Claudia and the wonderful Boudicca had found us. I knew Lucius would enjoy hiding the answers for a time. But I also knew Sophia would tell me quickly. I exited smiling and holding Sophia by the arm. Behind us we left only an elderly couple sitting together in the warmth of a small circle of light.

Chapter 31   Rest

It was no time before Sophia told me what she knew. When Lucius read the note from Pilate, he surmised that Julia was being held somewhere in the Gardens of Lucullus. Pilate's note described Julia as a flower being torn from a garden and referenced Lucius' lineage and ancestor's accomplishment. Nothing so commemorated our ancestor as these gardens. Lucius thought this was a man thinking himself clever and providing allusions his enemy could not decipher. So Lucius told Titus Flavius to wait two hours and then come to the Lucullan gardens with his forces. A little later, Claudia Procula arrived with Apollos and hearing the instructions, she slipped out before the others. When she was missed, servants looked everywhere for her in the house and in their haste, a door was left open and Boudicca escaped and followed Claudia. Random developments, I might have said before.

We returned to the home of Titus Flavius, spent and joyful. We did not know it would be the last time we were ever to be in that home.

"So why did you instruct Titus Flavius to wait for two hours, brother? We might have been killed in that time. They could have been there on horse in less than half an hour." I was lying on the couch in the dining room and servants were preparing a lavish meal, without peacock I am pleased to note, for all of us. When I posed the question, Apollos and Timothy, who were reclining to our left, and Lydia and Sophia, reclining to our right, paused their conversation to hear the answer.

Seeing his audience, Lucius did a most unusual thing. He preened.

"It was foolish of Pilate to make such a reference. It was not subtle enough and it took little thought to link flower, garden and ancestors and conclude she was being held near a family garden. And since the Lucullan gardens are the finest in the world, the link would expose the location. Only in his mind was it a difficult puzzle."

"But why two hours?" Apollos asked.

Lucius raised his hand in the gesture of a tutor explaining a very important detail to a slow-witted student.

"I could not be sure that there would not be several more points where we would be passed from one guide to another. And I could not be sure that Julia would be at the gardens as soon as we got there. She might be brought later. So the cohorts arriving too soon might frighten Pilate away and we would lose our advantage. Time was needed."

He paused to let the explanation have its weight.

"And I thought we could keep him engaged in talking for some time. The hostility in his note revealed something personal, a grievance he had against me. And when a man harbors a grievance, he never tires of talking about it. That was a weakness that would give us time. And time would allow the noble Titus Flavius to arrive and rescue us."

There was silence for a moment before I registered a logical objection.

"But as it was, my most clever strategist and solver of riddles, my warrior brother whom all Britons fear, it was a close thing." I replied, noting Sophia's peering into my wine cup to see if my loquaciousness had its source in my drink, "Did you not reduce the margin of error a bit too much? We were only saved by a woman and a dog at the last moment. It was just random chance Claudia arrived here at that time and also that a servant left Boudicca's door open."

"Random chance, Tychon?" Timothy asked, smiling at me. As I looked at him and nodded in understanding, his smile widened.

Before he spoke further, Julia spoke.

"My Lucius planned it perfectly, Tychon. God did not bring these people here by chance," she nodded to Timothy," and God can use a dog to save as surely as he can use ravens to provide food to a prophet."

We all laughed but I knew nothing about prophets and ravens. Timothy smiled at Lucius.

"Lucius, you spared Pilate. That was not the act of a warrior."

Lucius looked at Timothy for a moment and then spoke.

"In that room, Timothy, something happened to me. I have been a warrior all my life and have killed and maimed hundreds of men without a second thought. But in that barn, I saw that the madness that fevered his brain was a torment I knew too well. It came to me that I could relent and release those memories and dark vengeance. I remember someone Luke had told us about, a man of high renown coming at night to hear about a new life. Something inside me shifted. It was like a flame being lit in a very dark place. I understood that his history had borne down hard on him and his memories became a jailor in his soul. I knew that prison and was convinced we might both be freed, of the evil that those memories nurtured. As Pilate ranted and screamed and condemned me and my ancestors, citing every injustice, every evil they had committed, I understood that the placement of those crimes on me was a rough kind of justice. So when he pointed at me and judged me guilty, I saw in a flash that I sat where the Nazarene had stood that day but he was innocent and I was guilty. When I heard Pilate' words and their condemnation, I saw and believed that the Nazarene had been me there and taken the place I deserved. I saw his hand gesture and I knew that was the hand that now bore a stain that no washing could remove. I believed and I surrendered. I believed from that point on, Timothy, I believed. I felt the ghosts of past wrongs begin to fade away as I forgave them. We were enemies no more."

He glanced at me and together, like children responding to a tutor, we nodded. All was silent as we thought about the terrible and wonderful events that now reached their climax.

"And what is next, Timothy?" I asked

"We will instruct you, brothers, in the faith. You have been given a new birth but like a child newly born, you need to learn. A child must learn to eat, to walk, to talk and finally stand on his own. You cannot declare a child a man because he manages to guide some small morsel of food to his mouth. It takes time and teaching. We will teach you. You will be in a class of catechumens, with others like yourselves, and you will learn the words and the teachings of the disciples and most importantly, the teachings of our master, the Son of God, whose truth is the only truth. Then when you have completed your studies, you will be baptized and be welcomed to the table of our Lord for His supper."

He smiled and nodded encouragement.

"If we are again to be students, Lucius," I said, turning to him in a stage whisper, "then will we be beaten when we do not learn our lessons well?"

Everyone laughed and Timothy the loudest.

The evening continued and it was one we did not wish to end. But finally it did and most of the party retired to their rooms.

Lucius and I, with Julia and Sophia, were most reluctant to leave. The evening continued for us and we talked until finally the yawn of a servant reminded us it was time to go. As we sat up on our couches, Lucius turned to me with sadness in his voice.

"My brother, did we not slay men without number? Did we not rape and pillage and burn and destroy? Can there be anything we can ever do to make up for those acts? Will those faces whose lives we cut short with the sword haunt our dreams and curse our children?"

I said nothing but Julia spoke up, her sweet voice a balm, just as it had been that long ago summer in the fields and the vineyards of our estate.

"There is a debt beyond measure, my beloved, that all of us owe. But we are acquitted the moment we turn our lives completely and utterly over to him. He paid the price for those dead and ravaged at your hands. And he paid the price for the hateful thought you will have tomorrow and the pride you will feel the day after that. You are forgiven, Lucius. Accept that. Walk in the light."

Lucius nodded and smiled. "What a learned woman is my wife."

"So what shall we do first at the farm, my husband," she asked, taking his arm and leading him to their room.

"I think I want cherry trees in our orchards, Julia. Their smell in the Gardens of Lucullus reminded me of how much I loved them as a child. Perhaps we can have 20 or 30 of them. And I want to graft some new vines to produce a wine I had in Judea that was quite delicious. And we can…" He stopped, surprised at his exuberance.

Julia held him close and turned to me.

"And what will you be doing, Tychon?"

I pulled Sophia to me.

"We will be married and then…" I could not think of more than that. I was tired and thinking was burdensome this evening.

But Sophia had been thinking about our future a great deal.

"And then, Julia, we will improve the land, repair the house and expand it. After all, we will need the room for the children." Her voice was filled with laughter.

"Yes, just so," I answered slowly, seeing several small figures rummaging through the manuscripts in my library and spilling them on the floor. I sighed.

"And we will have service each morning, just as the sun rises, won't we?" Sophia asked.

"Indeed we shall," Julia responded, and after a moment, "but where shall we meet? Your farm or ours?"

"It does not matter," Lucius said, "it is not the place we meet but who is there with us. And that we are there together."

Together we all exclaimed "Amen" and we all fell to laughing.

And so we bade goodnight to the servants and went to rest in untroubled sleep.

Epilogue

And so, my son, the end of this story has come. I hope this tale has not lulled you to sleep. Keep it and pass it along to your children and your children's children. And dear reader, who picks up this story many years hence, when my bones are long in the grave, know that these people were not so different from you and their legacy is not just in these few pages but also in the lives they touched ever after.

I retired to our farm and true to the prediction Sophia made, we were married in the spring, just after Lucius and I completed our catechumen class and were baptized. The farm was expanded and our home also, putting in those rooms you no doubt remember from your infancy. Sophia is a wife any farmer would rejoice to have. She has always worked alongside me in the fields, kept a table that was the renown of the district, and is the most loving and gentle spirit a man could want. Even now, in my final years, she assists me in rising in the morning but never treats me as a man of fragile frame. She comes to me, extends her arm for support and always says, "Give me your strong new arm."

Lucius and Julia returned to their estate and after our children returned from Asia, they joined us in working the fields. Lucius' network of brothers among former legionaries grew and changed. Before, Lucius had assisted them with gold and temporary help. Now he offered them small plots to use to learn farming and after they had shown whether this was a life they could succeed at, he would help them buy farms elsewhere for their work. Over time, Lucius sold off much of the land that his great grandfather had accumulated in order to give money to those in need. And to the veterans in need were added the believers fleeing persecution from the emperor. Lucius provided refuge, money and safe passage to Asia and the frontiers and no one was ever turned away from his door.

Timothy returned to Ephesus, Apollos continued his work and is even today, in his final illness, a beacon of truth and strength to those who come to seek his instruction. Lydia worked for many more years and her wealth grew even as she spent it in helping churches in need and the poor among them. She continued to visit us for many years and there was never a time her unannounced appearance did not bring delight.

Claudia Procula nursed Pilate back to health over several months. He resisted all her entreaties and continued to curse all politicians and all Christians as the source of his misfortune. In a letter to me many years ago, she told me that at night, he would wander the halls of their home, muttering to himself, "Give me back the years." At times, and without warning he would look down at his useless hand, which now was a shrunken, dark thing like a rotted fruit, and weep uncontrollably. One morning Claudia came home from the predawn service of believers and found him gone. Rumor was he had fled to Gaul and after working with Lydia for a time, Claudia went there to find him. Neither of them was ever seen again. Stories came back that they were in a remote Gallic village, living out their final years peacefully, but I am not persuaded.

The years were harder for those whom we left in Rome. Otho committed suicide after his armies were defeated by those of Vitellius. Vitellius became emperor and spent his brief reign in gluttonous dinners and an easy tolerance of his chiefs stealing and punishing the citizens and patricians of Rome. Since it was Vitellius who removed Pilate from power in Judea many decades earlier, his ascension to the throne contributed in no small part to Pilate fleeing, I suspect. At last Vespasian decided to make his bid and while he was preparing to go to Italy, one of his chiefs leading an advance army defeated Vitellius. In the melee that followed, Titus Flavius, Vespasian's brother and our friend, died.

Vespasian settled in as emperor and for ten years, ruled the empire. We met him one final time, shortly after his ascension to the throne. Lucius and his old friend embraced. There was warmth and an easy familiarity between them, but by this time, the emperor knew Lucius was now a Christian and that made a difference. Although Vespasian never persecuted us as he did occasionally others, because of past friendship, there was a gulf between them that no kind messages from one to the other could span. When Vespasian died after his ten years on the throne, his son Titus became emperor. This was the same Titus who finished the war in Judea and destroyed Jerusalem as a home for Jews, burning their temple to the ground and driving the Jews out in their diaspora. He also left us alone, not so much from respect as from our being so negligible a part of his great plans. Those plans were cut short as after two years, he died. And to the consternation of all, Domitian became emperor.

He is even now emperor and his persecution of Christians, as well as his unseemly habits which are a restrained echo of previous emperors, makes him a person many fear and all dread. But our time with him is not yet up and so it will require another book, if I should survive, to continue our tale and the wonderful sovereignty of our Lord in leading us in His ways.

Allow me to conclude this tale with a conversation I had with Lucius on our voyage to Ephesus a few years ago. Lucius had been delivered from his dread of sea travel and it was a pleasant voyage. He had visited Timothy several times over the years and walked the streets of our favorite city with him. Timothy was pastor at Ephesus, along with the apostle John, the one remaining disciple of our Lord Jesus and the author of a gospel I had come to love as much as that of Luke, which had first lit the fire within my soul. John was an

*old man when Lucius met him for the first time and was completing a new
writing which described the end times.*

*It was a bright day on ship, with a breeze every sailor treasures, and we
were on the deck at the rail, much as we had been that fateful journey so many
years before. It was a day when one feels young, no matter the years and I did
not know then that I had so little time left with Lucius before he would be
called home. If I had known, I would be able to call to mind the several long
conversations we had on that voyage. But I do remember one and I will tell
you a portion of it as my parting gift. Grace and peace to you, my son.*

The boat was moving swiftly over the water and Ephesus beckoned. We
had been talking since breakfast, first about our farms, then our crops and our
maintenance, then our children. We spoke little of the larger world, or the
emperor Domitian, his intrigues, his distrust and hatred of the patricians and
his determination to humiliate them at every opportunity. Nor did we speak of
the Christians on board our vessel whom we were accompanying to Ephesus
for their safety. We spoke instead of dirt and fertilizer and things that grow
and bloom, beautify and nourish.

Then we fell silent for a time, listening to the waves rush by the ship.
Lucius straightened, pushed his chest out and breathed deeply. He turned to
me with a tone that told me there was something he needed to tell me.

"Did you rest well, Tychon?"

"Yes, of late I find my rest is always good except when I have an ache or
pain, which seems too often these days. Sophia says I complain too little and
she never knows when I am suffering."

Lucius laughed.

"Oh the lord has done a work in you, brother. You complained all the time
when we were in war."

"I did not," I responded, assuming the long comfortable role.

"In Britannia you complained about the cold, the drizzle, the ugly natives,
the rotten food. You complained constantly. And then you followed that up
with boasting how brave you were in the last battle." He was smiling.

"You make me sound like a weak and unworthy soldier."

"You were a fine soldier, Tychon," the smile replaced by a serious tone,
"and the best brother a man could have. You have always had my back and I
would not stand here today without you."

There was silence, with just the waves and the sun and the breeze.

"And did you sleep well, Lucius?

"Yes," he hesitated, "but I did dream."

I turned to see a look I could not recognize. I waited.

"Do you dream as you used to, Lucius?"

"No, I do not, my brother. When I do dream, which is not often, it is a dream about the farm, pruning and planting and harvesting. Or I see Julia working in the home, or Lucia when she was little, playing in the field. It is good to dream sometimes but it is also good not to."

"Why do you say that? Are not dreams ways that God speaks to us?"

Lucius looked beyond me toward Ephesus as he replied.

"I asked that exact question of John, the apostle, when we were together on my last visit to Ephesus. He was telling me of the dreams he had regarding the end times and I told him of my dreams years ago." He looked at me with the look of a teacher about to make a point. "He told me that dreams can be just our own imaginings and not the voice of God. Or they can be assaults from the enemy meant to delude us, confuse us, tempt us."

"But what are we to do then?"

"He said that we are not to seek dreams or visions for those are things of pride, a lusting after control of the Lord's work and we then make our schemes the Lord's work. If the Lord wants to, he will use dreams or visions to speak. But that is very rare and we must not let the worm of pride drive us to presume that our cravings are the stuff of God's blessings. That is a wicked thing, he told me."

I considered his words. I breathed in the sea air and felt young again.

"And we have done many wicked things, Lucius. In our youth we were the most wicked of men."

"Yes, we were brother. And I more so than you."

"I offended God and man each day, Lucius and you were no worse than I."

Lucius smiled at me and I noticed the deep wrinkles made so manifest in the bright sun on his dark tanned skin.

"What was worse, Tychon, your bedding every woman who crossed your path, or the terrible anger I held in my heart? I did not know how much I hated those who I thought had wronged me, who dishonored General Lucullus, who took our father from us. It has only been through the years that the Spirit has shown me the darkness and violence my heart harbored all those years." His voice dropped and was barely audible over the waves. "Rather like Pilate's."

"Have you heard anything of him?"

"No, only rumors. I hope to hear someday that he accepted forgiveness and found the peace of the Lord."

We were quiet for a time as we recalled that long search and the final violent end. As in every such recollection of those events, my hand went instinctively to my restored arm.

"Do you think, Lucius, of the events of those days without marveling at the infinite care of God in bringing them about?"

"Never, my brother. If I were to change any twist or turn of that path, we would be hurtled into the darkness of no return and we would not be here today. And those I am able to serve would be lost also."

"Your farm never seems empty, Lucius. Every time I visit, it seems more like a small village than an estate."

Again Lucius laughed.

"There are many needs, Tychon and they find their way often to my door, especially since Domitian has determined to strike at believers. They need money, some of them, or they need a place to hide, or they need a place to go. I was led to a place of redemption and if I can share that with them, the Brotherhood will truly have earned its name."

He laughed unexpectedly and for no reason I could determine. My look asked and he turned to answer.

"It occurs to me, Tychon, that a good deal of the wealth that our great grandfather brought back from his wars in Parthia is now being used to send fugitive Christians back to the East to begin new lives. The wealth he gave us is flowing back to its source!"

He laughed and coughed for a time, his winter cold now stretching into spring. At last he stopped, breathing deep and catching his breath.

"Forgive me, Tychon, I have become an old man, I fear."

"We are both old men, my brother. And there is something old men do."

"Yes?"

"They lose their hold on the head of a conversation and grasp only its tail."

He puzzled for a moment and then smiled.

"Yes, the dream." His manner grew serious. "I dreamt of a horse, Tychon, a black horse."

The wind picked up and sails snapped.

"Which black horse," I asked.

"All of them, Tychon. The one that fell on me in Britannia. The one who died on the road to Ephesus. The one meant for Tigellinus. The one Pilate had. It was all of them." His tone was almost frightened. "Its eyes were red and it was in a field with me, a fenced field and I could not escape. I have not dreamt of that horse since our day in the barn with Pilate."

"Pilate, ah, what a figure." I looked at the horizon and remembered the storm. "Do you think Pilate was mad, or merely evil?"

Lucius considered for a moment.

"Tychon, when the wickedness of our hearts has consumed us and left us only bitter memories and a hunger for revenge, then there is not a hair's breadth of difference between evil and madness."

" So what happened in your dream, Lucius?"

"The horse meant to kill me, Tychon. And I did not know why. What it was and why it haunted my dreams has always eluded me. Until now."

I waited.

"You see, Tychon, the horse is very much like your wolf. It is powerful and dangerous and it seeks to slay us even while beguiling us. We think we can ride it and for a time, we do."

"The empire," I exclaimed, proud of my understanding.

"Not just our Roman empire, Tychon. It is every kingdom of man, every scheme that springs from our dark imaginations, every dream that promises hope but bears only rotted fruit. They spring from poisoned soil and yield only death. The horse in my dream sought to kill me and I could not escape it. And then the other came."

"The other?"

"The white horse."

I waited.

"It appeared from nowhere, Tychon. One moment it was not there and then it was. It approached the black horse, which drew back. It did not raise its leg or attack the black horse. It merely breathed at the black horse, a soft and long breath. The black horse shuddered, made a terrible noise and vanished. I was alone with the white horse. It looked at me, its eyes brown and warm, and then it too vanished."

He looked at me with a wrinkled smile.

"And I think I know where it came from."

"Where?"

"Just before falling asleep, I was reading the book John gave me when I was last at Ephesus, the story of the return of our Lord. Do you remember it?"

I thought for a moment and then it came to me.

"The white horse."

"Our Savior rides the white horse, Tychon, at the final time."

For a moment we were silent, deep in thought.

"So he will be the one who cleanses."

Lucius sighed and gazed deep into my eyes.

"You remember the last moments with Pilate?"

"Yes, and I remember you never told me what you whispered to him."

"I think I should tell you, brother," he smiled, "you have been most patient."

The wind picked up and his voice rose to be heard.

"I told him 'Pilate, I forgive you. And the Christ you condemned will forgive you also, if you ask him.'"

I recollected the scene. And his moan.

"He has already cleansed you and me, Tychon and he will do so to the world at the end."

I laughed and my laugh was loud in the pause of the wind.

"Well I am glad he will do it. You and I, brother, are not the warriors we once were and we are not up to such a task."

"Indeed we are not, Tychon."

"That leaves me the time to walk in the fields with my Sophia at sunset."

"And I am free from trying to do more than what is put before me each day and doing it well, to His glory."

"Such as having to decide where to put more cherry trees in your field!"

"There is that, there is that," he responded, smiling.

"Those cherry trees that General Lucullus imported and that you now plant so lavishly on your estate, Lucius, is it their fragrance, their beauty or their history that you most love?"

"Each and all," he answered.

"And will there be cherry trees in heaven, Lucius?

The breeze caressed our faces.

"I certainly hope so, Tychon. I certainly hope so."

Gentle Reader,

If you have enjoyed our story of great love and rescue, lost souls, and lives made whole, please tell a friend and leave a rating at Amazon so others may have the opportunity to share your experience.

My next book is in the works and will be set in our time. It's another story of a woman who has disappeared, whose life seemed full of light and laughter until a dark figure from her past found her. Her disappearance confounds her young fiancé and friends as investigation reveals she is not who everyone thought she was, and may indeed be a murderer. Her only hope: a detective and his partner, a blind cleric and a young woman who believes no one is beyond redemption.

Feel free to email me at plmillernc@yahoo.com and share your thoughts and reactions to this novel.

God bless.

Patrick Miller

Made in the USA
Lexington, KY
06 June 2017